PRAISE FOR

Kings County

"Can a person with a tattoo have a soul? To judge from a broad swath of contemporary fiction, the answer would seem to be no. . . . It's refreshing, then, that David Goodwillie's very good new novel, *Kings County*, depicts such people with genuine, unmitigated sympathy and good-fellowship, as if, in spite of their fashionable lifestyles, they are as fully human as anyone else. . . . After the first chapter or two, the pages of *Kings County* begin to turn quickly."

—**Adelle Waldman,** *The New York Times Book Review*

"Dazzling writing, propulsive storytelling, relevant and timeless characters—that's exactly what David Goodwillie has given us in *Kings County*. He's created a true urban tableau, at once gritty and hopeful."

—**Stephanie Danler, author of** *Sweetbitter*

"*Kings County* is a heart-wrenching love story, a character-driven suspense novel, and a lush thrill ride through the New York City aughts. For some of us who lived in Brooklyn at the turn of the century, it's a meticulous period piece that doesn't sacrifice immediacy for the nostalgia it provokes. For those who didn't, it's a scintillating glimpse into the zeitgeist that followed 9/11—the music, movements, and sense of impending upheaval that foretold our chaotic present."

—**Melissa Febos, author of** *Abandon Me*

"Goodwillie captures the rapturous soul of a bygone Brooklyn: the songs, the sex, the bars, the youth! And then the churn of relentless change, the broken hearts, the crushing realities. But it is the searing burn of discovery that makes *Kings County* a true and continual delight."

—**Joshua Ferris, author of** *Then We Came to the End*

"Goodwillie has the anthropology of New York down. He weaves suspense around a dark, page-turning mystery that stays palpable to the end, and his confident—and often comedic—narrative hand allows him to seamlessly fold in contemporary events and generate a necessary social document for this new age of unenlightenment."

—**Matthew Thomas, author of *We Are Not Ourselves***

"Goodwillie pins his characters to the page with a lepidopterist's merciless affection—and then, by some trick of resuscitation, lets them fly in a Brooklyn that's a kind of darkly miraculous forest populated by charismatic and errant fauna. *Kings County* is a thrilling and persuasive read."

—**Joseph O'Neill, author of *Netherland***

"With Tom Wolfean sociological precision, David Goodwillie casts an insider's eye on the Brooklyn creative class in a gripping novel as suspenseful as it is panoramic. *Kings County* is a grand, galloping ride."

—**Teddy Wayne, author of *Apartment***

"Goodwillie's setting is vivid and his characters rich, with flashbacks fleshing out their backstories. Those who like literary, character-driven fiction with a strong sense of place . . . will enjoy this coming-of-age story with elements of romance and mystery."

—***Booklist***

"Goodwillie guides his young, reckless, hard-working characters through the ins and outs of the early-2000s Brooklyn music scene . . . [and] paints his cityscapes with such vivid and knowing prose that the city grows around the reader like a warm glove, leading us to desperately, deeply miss New York as we tumble through these clever pages."

—***Interview***

"Goodwillie is back with an evocative exploration of New York in the early aughts. *Kings County* follows two fresh New York transplants as they try to make their own way in the big city. . . . But just how much struggling can they take in the name of art?"

—**Bustle.com**

David Goodwillie is the author of the novel *American Subversive*, a *New York Times* Notable Book of the Year, and the memoir *Seemed Like a Good Idea at the Time*. Goodwillie has written for the *New York Times*, *New York* magazine, and *Newsweek*, among other publications. He has also been drafted to play professional baseball, worked as a private investigator, and was an expert at Sotheby's auction house. A graduate of Kenyon College, he lives in Brooklyn.

Kings County

A novel

David Goodwillie

AVID READER PRESS
New York London Toronto Sydney New Delhi

Avid Reader Press
An Imprint of Simon & Schuster, Inc.
1230 Avenue of the Americas
New York, NY 10020

First Avid Reader Press trade paperback edition July 2021

AVID READER PRESS and colophon are trademarks of Simon & Schuster, Inc.

For information about special discounts for bulk purchases, please contact Simon & Schuster Special Sales at 1-866-506-1949 or business@simonandschuster.com.

The Simon & Schuster Speakers Bureau can bring authors to your live event. For more information or to book an event, contact the Simon & Schuster Speakers Bureau at 1-866-248-3049 or visit our website at www.simonspeakers.com.

Interior design by Kyle Kabel

Manufactured in the United States of America

1 3 5 7 9 10 8 6 4 2

Library of Congress Cataloging-in-Publication Data has been applied for.

ISBN 978-1-5011-9213-5
ISBN 978-1-5011-9214-2 (pbk)
ISBN 978-1-5011-9215-9 (ebook)

For the Woodstock boys

Yet, as only New Yorkers know, if you can get through the twilight, you'll live through the night.

—Dorothy Parker

Kings County

PART ONE

PART ONE

Chapter One

They came in hot, the band and Audrey Benton, a raucous cocoon of color and sweat. Security up front, cutting into the crowd, splitting it, radios squawking, someone saying, "Just stay close." But they couldn't be closer. They were the Stones entering Studio 54. They were the Beatles on the Shea Stadium infield. They were four nervous kids from the Catskills, sticking tight to the girl who'd gotten them there. The club thrummed and pulsed. The band kept moving. Heads down, hair down, don't let them really see you—just like Audrey had taught them.

Currents emanate outward, ripples become waves. In a room full of people looking for other people to look at, it was only natural to turn toward the commotion, the rock stars—for what else could they be, dressed like that? Audrey could hear the talking, people wondering who they were, who *she* was, all ink and tights and heels. Not model hot, so probably the real deal. They surged past the dance floor, past the DJ booth. Whistles and shouts, security throwing a shoulder, and then the crowd ebbed and they found themselves in a cordoned-off VIP area along a wall of floor-to-ceiling windows. The space was divided into three raised seating platforms, each surrounded by linked velvet ropes. They were led to the one in the middle, where a man sat, elevated and alone, typing into a phone. He stood up when he saw them, pocketing the device. His name was Lucas Duff and he was the band's new manager. This after-party had been his idea.

He greeted them in turn, Ben and Arthur, Easter and Gatesy. Audrey stepped up last and Lucas held his arms out wide. She submitted to the fleshy hug.

"Drinks!" Lucas declared. "They're sending someone over."

The four members of the Westfield Brothers peered around, a bit lost. If the theory behind roped-off seating areas was to promote privacy, it wasn't working. People were looking over, still trying to place them.

"Check out the view," Audrey said, pointing east across Manhattan, and for a moment everyone did. But their eyes were drawn to the lights beyond the lights, the city beyond the city, the borough where they lived.

"Looks small from up here," Arthur Westfield said to Ben.

"I know." The brothers collapsed onto a leather couch; Easter and Gatesy hovered behind them. Just like onstage, Audrey thought, eyeing a nearby chair.

"Come sit with us," Ben said, moving to make room for her. And so she did, flopping down between the two brothers. There was safety in numbers.

The problem was Lucas. He'd been jittery at the show but now was seriously high—a fact so evident no one bothered to acknowledge it. He sat down and took his phone back out. What was so important that it couldn't wait? It was almost one a.m.

The band members surveyed their new surroundings. It was the last place they wanted to be, this Manhattan club, fifteen years removed from the last time those two words, strung together, had held sway with the city's creative class. But there'd been no question of not coming. Lucas had said it was important—the image and exposure. The relevance of the right place. He was, and had been for years, Columbia Records' East Coast VP of A & R, and if he wanted to make a splash by having the after-party here, then Ben and Arthur weren't about to say no. Besides, the Westfield Brothers deserved it. They'd just played Terminal 5, a bellwether venue for a band on the rise, and the sold-out show had come off without a hitch. Even Audrey thought so. Especially Audrey. Because she understood what could have gone wrong.

Audrey Benton had been the Westfield Brothers' label rep—as well as their publicist, booker, manager, and greatest cheerleader—until two months prior, when Ben and Arthur had made the difficult decision to leave Whale Creek Records, the small, if influential, Brooklyn-based label where Audrey worked, for the (potentially) greener pastures of Columbia Records. The brothers had made the move with Audrey's blessing, if not quite her full-throated enthusiasm. She had discovered the four of them (or three of them: Gatesy had come later) years before, playing an open mic in Gowanus, and they'd been central to one another's lives ever since. So much so that after intense lobbying from Ben and Arthur, Audrey had promised to join them tonight—however bittersweet it might be. Even Lucas had approved. "I guess chicks never hurt at a club," he'd said after Ben and Arthur added her name to the guest list. It was his eloquent way of saying he understood. Everyone respected Audrey Benton—even the competition.

Now the brothers slumped, exhausted, into the cushions on either side of her. No one knew what would happen next. Lucas would put his phone down or a waitress would arrive. It didn't matter. Everything was a novelty, so nothing was. A Top 40 song came on and Ben wondered aloud who sang it.

"Katy Perry," Audrey said.

"How do you know that?"

"How do you *not*?"

Audrey enjoyed playing the generalist in a world of connoisseurs, but not being a snob was different from not knowing music, and her true tastes were redoubtable—the Westfield Brothers being Exhibit A. At least the other clubgoers had stopped staring. These were people for whom recognition was an ethic, and a careful study of the band had revealed no familiar faces. It was true that the Westfield Brothers had never had a radio hit. Certainly, most people in this room had never heard of them. But most people in this room weren't from Brooklyn, where the band was indie royalty—the kings of Kings County. Walking through South Williamsburg with Ben or Arthur (or Audrey, for that matter) was like walking through the Mojave with extra water; everyone was suddenly a friend. Except it was more genuine than that.

The noise was grating. Ben, the older, stockier Westfield, searched his pockets for the earplugs he'd worn onstage, while his whippet-thin brother stared quizzically at Lucas. "So where's Theo?" Ben asked Audrey.

"He really wanted to come, but his boss is in from LA and he has to prepare for their meeting tomorrow," Audrey said. "I left his name downstairs but I doubt he'll make it."

The brothers nodded. Though they'd played there twice now, Los Angeles remained a mystical place. They probed no further.

"It's too bad," she continued. "He'd have loved the show."

"Well, he'd hate it here," Arthur said, nodding at Lucas. "What the fuck is he—"

"Easy," Ben warned.

"No, seriously. This is bullshit. Hey, Lucas!"

"Hold on," the label man said, his thumbs jabbing at his phone. "Bit of a crisis. One of our employees has gone missing."

Arthur shook his head. Ben rubbed his. This was the music business. People went missing all the time. Audrey had warned them about Lucas. He was abrupt and abrasive and full of contradictions—he didn't, for instance, drink alcohol—but Audrey believed his bombast cloaked great talent and a large heart. She didn't know him well—they swam at different ends of the same pool—but she knew he'd earned his reputation. He'd survived as an A & R man for decades, had practically outlived the industry itself. Music was a young person's game, but it would be hard to claim, judging from the bands he'd broken, the songs he'd coaxed into existence, that anyone, even now, played it better than Lucas Duff. Yet the years were wearing on him. The wrinkled suit, too big, even for his oversized frame; the red splotches and peels of skin; and the hair, what was left of it, sprouting out like stubborn weeds. He looked awful enough to be important.

He must have sensed the band's uneasiness, because he repocketed his phone. He snorted like a horse and clapped his hands. "Still no waitress?" He looked around for someone who might fit that description, and then lost interest and launched into a monologue about licensing agreements, how they worked, how *he* would *make* them work—content and copyrights, splits and royalties. It was drug talk, ambling and unfocused, and it made Audrey nervous. How she wished Theo were here, and how glad she was that he wasn't. Because this place was everything they'd tailored their lives to avoid. Also, it was late now, and it was a long subway ride, and there'd be issues at the door, and . . . and . . . and . . .

And there he was! Standing in front of the platform, looking up at her. Such was Audrey's shock that her boyfriend appeared at first as an apparition, a manifestation of her reverie. The raw physicality. The blond hair and square shoulders. The half grin on his strong face. And then a second passed and she wasn't shocked at all. Her life with him was like this. Charmed. Fated. *Full*. That she experienced the same sensation—an avian lightness in her chest—as she had the very first time she saw him thrilled her immensely. She understood what it was. And never took it for granted.

She skipped down the platform steps, scissored the velvet rope, and, to the amusement of the band, all but leapt into his arms, where she remained, only pulling back when Theo finally did.

"I can't believe you. I told you to stay home. I mean, look at this place. No, wait, don't. Stay looking at me." She kissed him. "Did you get in okay? They have four different promoters working the door. Whatever, you made it. Come say hi."

The band was only too happy for the interruption. They greeted Theo one by one, standing up, clenching hands, leaning in—that ubiquitous male embrace. Ben introduced him to Gatesy, their latest drummer. Lucas remained seated. He looked annoyed.

"How was the show?" Theo asked. Of Audrey's many bands, the Westfield Brothers had always been his favorite.

"Amazing," she said. "The union guys finally had to turn up the lights."

"Just as well," Arthur said. "We'd run out of songs. Besides, it's a dead place acoustically. The soundboard's all fuzzy on the low end—"

"Artie," Ben interrupted, "he doesn't need the full recap. Here, Theo, come sit. We're playing Spot the Waitress."

"A band with no drinks," Gatesy said. "How's that for fucking rock and roll?"

"Let me go buy a round," Theo offered.

"Absolutely not," Audrey said. "Did you see the bar? It'll take forever. Plus, the label's paying and you just got here."

But it was too late. Theo had seen eyes light up in the wake of his offer, and before Audrey could stop him he was shrugging off his coat and taking orders.

"At least let me come with you," she said, but Theo wouldn't hear of it. He was stubborn in his kindness. He kissed her again and then ventured back down the shallow steps. Audrey's eyes trailed after him. So often he looked like the only man in a room full of boys. But it was more than his size. It was the way he moved, with sureness and deliberate grace—like there'd always be time.

Her mind drifted back, as it often did, to the morning after their first date, three years ago now, and the call she'd placed to her grandmother Connie in Cape Canaveral, to gush about her latest intrigue. Audrey wasn't a girl who fell for guys. She was a girl who tossed them (sometimes gently) aside. But now, out of nowhere, this big, shy, handsome, self-deprecating . . . She'd stopped and tried again but kept butchering the knotty language of enchantment until suddenly the word "dignified" tumbled out and abruptly Audrey stopped talking. Connie sighed through the phone. "'Dignified' is exactly how I used to describe your grandfather," she said. "It's the best thing a man can be."

And then it was her grandmother's turn. Hurricane season, trailer park politics, "medical" marijuana. As Audrey listened, she became acutely aware of how lonely she'd been. This was ludicrous. One night, and they hadn't even kissed. She thought of other nights, with other men—there were plenty to draw from—and the empty ways they'd so often ended, or hadn't. She muted the call to hide her sniffling.

She loved that woman.

And my God, she loved this man. She'd known it right away.

Theo was still visible from where Audrey stood. She could see the back of him, paused at the edge of the throng. He was wearing the jeans she'd bought him and an off-white button-down, dusted with flecks of paint. (Much of his wardrobe was blemished in this manner, Theo having begun painting their new loft before his clothes had found their way into drawers.) He had no fashion sense, per se, but living in Bushwick, the Edison Labs of emerging style, his functional austerity lent him an aura of relative sophistication. Add to this his more permanent features and it wasn't hard to imagine him an exile from some more reliable era. He wasn't preppy or bohemian or conservative or hip. He was just perfectly there, in space.

And then he was gone, sucked in.

The band had been watching him, too—or watching Audrey watch him—because when she turned back around, all four members were grinning.

"Look at you," Arthur said, "all loved up."

Audrey pretended to ignore him. She stepped over the corner of the table and fell back between the brothers onto the couch.

Lucas clapped his hands again. "Think this one's gonna last? Hah! Just kidding. I mean, come on, embrace the rep, right? A whole neighborhood of heartbreak in her wake."

"I'm right here," Audrey said. "You can address me directly."

"Hey, I said I was kidding. You don't need to get all . . ."

But the flimsy underpinning of this unlikely gathering was revealing itself. Everyone felt it and moved to control the fallout. A lot was at stake. The Westfield Brothers had spent almost a decade working their way up from basements to bars to concert halls, every step of the climb orchestrated by Audrey in her capacity as Whale Creek's Artist Liaison. Theirs was a rare bond. Bands existed in a world of grudges and slights (some real, most imagined), where fame forever beckoned beyond the edge of the stage. It would have been so easy for them to give up. And for Audrey, too, staving off the pressure to drop the Westfields after each unprofitable year, until the last two, when the major festivals had come calling and Whale Creek finally stopped losing money on them. Columbia Records had noticed immediately. But Ben and Arthur wouldn't switch labels without Audrey's permission, which she had begrudgingly given. How could she not? This was about the music, after all, about championing songs that got heard *outside* their world, *beyond* Brooklyn. Booking the band at Terminal 5 was about exactly that. Breaking them out. Taking that rare shot at . . . not the "mainstream"—they were too good for that—but some iteration of commercial success. Two words not in Audrey's vocabulary.

Of course she had mixed feelings. It wasn't the money. No, she was worried her boys would get lost out there. Indie acts rarely signed major record deals these days. Too much had to go right in a business where so little ever did. Tonight, for instance. Audrey had been against their playing the show (not that it was her call anymore). Terminal 5 was twice the size of most New York clubs. What if they *hadn't* filled it? Time was, the booker would have come backstage, slapped Ben or Arthur on the back, and said, "Don't worry, we'll get it right next year." Now the venues were owned by public corporations, and each night's gate was studied and archived. A few soft shows and you were playing bars again.

The Westfields had shared her concerns, but Lucas pushed back and the brothers had finally given in. Audrey had to admit, Columbia had certainly done its part. They'd wheat-pasted half of North Brooklyn, organized a webcast at NPR's offices, and landed the brothers interviews with *Pitchfork* and RollingStone.com. And the show had been stellar. Audrey could envision what would happen next—the new album date bumped up, the tour lengthened. Lucas had been right and she'd been wrong—wrong enough to wonder about other advice she'd given Ben and Arthur over the years. Sitting between them now, she thought about regret. Did the band have any, or did they take life as it came? Certainly, that was how Audrey had always lived. Planning her future, charting some kind of progression . . . these were things she'd never contemplated. People, not time or geography, delineated the chapters of her life. Bands and boyfriends, though her relationships with the former had always meant more, and lasted longer.

Until Theo.

She could apply those two words to every aspect of her life. Pre- and post-, before and after; it was almost biblical. Now, for the first time, the band was leaving and the boyfriend staying. She had other bands, of course, a healthy roster of them, playing their hearts out in makeshift East Williamsburg practice spaces, but she'd been with the Westfield Brothers longest. They'd become adults together.

"Hey, guys, sorry for the wait." Everyone turned at once. A miniskirted waitress had negotiated the velvet ropes and was now towering over them.

"Honey, where the fuck have you been all my life?" Lucas said, looking her up and up and up.

Of the many possible responses, the waitress chose flirtatious ignorance. Audrey, no stranger to the service industry, watched in admiration as the girl bent down to take Lucas's order: "Bottle of Grey Goose, bottle of Maker's, two bottles of champagne, all the bells and whistles."

"But Theo's getting us drinks," Ben said, an edge in his voice.

"Who?"

"Audrey's boyfriend. He's up at the bar."

"And he'll be up there all night. Anyone want anything else? Easter? Gatesy?"

"I'll wait for Theo," Easter said from behind the couch.

The other half of the rhythm section had wandered over to the ropes, where two iron-haired bottle blondes in wrap dresses stood, sipping cocktails through straws.

"Gatesy!" Lucas shouted, too loudly. "Drink?"

"Sure!"

*　　*　　*

The drummer wanted a mind eraser. Not bad, Theo thought, wondering if it might hold up later, in front of Audrey. They'd been trading potential opening lines since the night they met, inventing new beginnings, the first words of the fictional books of their lives. Audrey was better at it—she was funnier—but Theo had his moments, and he hoped this might be one. Also, it had the benefit of being true. The drummer *had* asked for a mind eraser. If only Theo could place the order.

He should have listened to Audrey. Theo Gorski was not small, and still it had taken him ten minutes and counting to get close to the three-sided bar anchoring the center of the club. Along the way he'd tripped over clandestine cube chairs and been stymied by human cul-de-sacs. Reedy night owls with unfocused eyes. Now he turned sideways, all six foot three, two hundred fifteen pounds of him, and sort of shimmied past a group of sharp-shouldered women, apologizing as he did so. He was twenty-two stories above Manhattan, at a nightclub on top of a hotel on top of a landfill. A city extended by refuse. Theo guessed he was the only one in the room who knew what lay beneath (and certainly the only one who appreciated the latent metaphor). He was full of such minutiae, and increasingly aware of its irrelevance.

Thank God he'd hit the cash machine earlier, still had seventy-five or eighty bucks. He ran through the order: mind eraser, Bulleit bourbon for Audrey, and beers for the rest. What was in a mind eraser anyway? Kahlúa, maybe, or Baileys; he couldn't remember, if he'd ever known. For the first time, it crossed his mind that their new drummer—*Gatsby*, Theo had heard the kid say through the din, but that couldn't be right—might have been messing with him. Not that it mattered. These were Audrey's people—*her boys*, she called them—and that was enough. He didn't mind being the genial plus-one. He'd grown used to balancing on the edges of couches, leaning in to hear snippets of talk, leaning out to digest it. There was no pressure to perform when he was with one of her bands. No one asked his opinion on anything that hadn't happened that night. Had he liked the show? The new T-shirts? As if he'd ever say he didn't. What a funny world Audrey's was, with all that posturing and beauty and talent. The trick to making it in music, Theo figured—because it was the trick to pretty much everything—was finding balance, some form of stability in the most unstable of environments. Audrey said the trick was to write great songs. The rest was just life. The two of them were different like that. Wonderfully so.

A hole opened up in front of him, and Theo, former football star, reacted quickly. Soon he found himself, if not quite *at* the bar, then near enough to call out an order. He watched the bartenders rush back and forth, shaking and pouring, shaking and pouring. All women, mostly skin. How that equation had changed. When he'd first moved to the city, it was all skin, mostly woman in this part of town. But he was dating himself.

Patience. Positioning. Incremental gains. God, this really was like football. Cash in hand might help. He fished out a twenty and waved it in the air. Like a dandy. Like a fraud. Surely, there was a more effective way to do this, but he didn't know it. Shaking and pouring, shaking and pouring, ice, ice, ice, and no one looking up. At least at him. It was the paradox at the center of Theo's life. For all his abundant physicality, he was decidedly modest and unassuming in temperament. He supposed he was *cerebral*, if a person could still be such a thing. "He not only has no ego, but, like, no mechanism for selfishness at all," he'd overheard Audrey tell her then–best friend, Sarah, one night early on, and while Theo knew that wasn't true, there was probably something to it in a relative sense.

The self he did have a mechanism for—an entire assembly line of machinery—was self-analysis. Not in a clinical way, but situationally: a kind of outsider's omniscience. He existed not in moments but near them; he didn't drive the narrative of his experiences so much as study their structures, the frameworks of his environment. For instance, while waiting at the bar, having adopted an overtly casual strategy of *not* looking at the bartenders, he began to take in his surroundings, beginning with the faux-crystal "chandelier" above him. It looked like the dripped-wax base of a candle turned upside down and magnified a thousand times for no discernible reason but poor taste. From there, he followed the ceiling to the wall of windows and the gunmetal skyline beyond—blurry lights in the black of October. He thought of people riding late-night subways. Protesters occupying Wall Street parks. Friday night crowds in clubs like this one. Theo peered around, stirred by the energy, the exuberance, the (im)pure stamina of the room, but no one caught his eye. These people didn't pause to ruminate; they paused for selfies, which, when taken with a flash, changed the windows to mirrors, endless reflection pools, and that seemed about right.

But he was projecting. For all he knew, half these revelers were first-timers like him. Just look at Audrey. Short shorts over red tights, with some kind of black leotard top. Plus heels. Plus a Slinky's worth of jangling bracelets up and down her arm. Plus—agghh, he had no idea what he was talking about, the names of these female things that other men learned through urban osmosis. The point was that Audrey had never been here either, and, further, actively hated places like this— exclusive clubs, posh rip-off dens, anywhere that catered to "society" kids or still offered bottle service at this thankfully late date in bottle-service history. But to see her you'd think she breezed through every night.

Someone fell into him, and Theo spun around to find a loose-legged prepster getting up off the floor. "Dude, I was pushed," the guy announced by way of apology. Then he took Theo's measure, held his arms up in a *no mas* gesture, and made himself scarce. This was ridiculous. It was way too crowded, way too loud. Theo turned back to the bar and this time raised his hand with some urgency. Several other hands were in the air, and Theo felt an odd surge of adrenaline. He fixed his gaze on the closest bartender, a willowy brunette whose hardness seemed more put on than permanent. He went again for eye contact, in hopes of ordering, yes, but also because the top she was wearing was low cut, and the glitter in her décolletage so potentially distracting that—

"Up here!"

Theo looked up, mortified. He'd only glanced down so as to actively *not* glance down, peeked so he'd know where *not* to peek. But how do you explain that? She started shaking a drink in front of him, the glass and shaker up by her head, as if to establish his allowable viewing frame. "I'm sorry," Theo said, "I wasn't—"

"What do you want?!"

He recited the order, face burning. She didn't flinch at the mind eraser, which was sounding increasingly enticing. In fact, she didn't acknowledge him at all. Somewhere above, a song ended and another began. Synthetic dance pop no one was dancing to. How long had he been gone?

The drinks appeared on the wet bar top in front of him, all four leaking down the sides. The mind eraser was two-toned.

"Eighty-seven!" the bartender shouted, leaning over.

Theo looked at the drinks. "But I only got these four!"

"I know what you got!"

Dazed, Theo reached for his wallet. His head swam with figures, none of which, when added together, reached the number she had named. Predictably, neither did the cash in his wallet. He handed over his debit card.

"Start a tab?"

*   *   *

"I'm going to visit the little boys' room," Lucas said to no one in particular. He stood up, patted his pockets instinctively, then walked past Gatesy and unhooked the rope. He stepped out. The two wrap-dress girls stepped in.

Gatesy ushered them up the steps. "This is my band," he said, "and this is Audrey. Be nice to her and she'll get you a record deal."

"*Really?* I can play ukulele," said one of the girls.

"Christ," Arthur muttered.

Audrey shook their hands and made small talk. She'd been on both sides of the female-with-band equation, seeker and sought, and understood the value of keeping everyone happy. She'd seen bands undone by blog posts, relationships implode from a single tweet. The wrap-dress girls asked about the cowboys-on-horseback tattoo on her left shoulder blade. It was the coolest one they'd ever seen, they said (or one of them did), and Audrey smiled obligingly. The brothers jumped in to save her and the conversation drifted like flotsam, every which way. Audrey listened to the banter, the reassuring constants of her inconstant world. She'd miss these boys.

How had they done it? Talent and ambition, sure, but these were New York words, and while they certainly applied to the Westfield Brothers, Audrey attributed their success to something less definable: a kind of urgency born of circumstance. Ben and Arthur Westfield were from Kripplebush, a Hudson Valley hamlet old enough to have traditions and secluded enough to keep them. Their parents were self-taught musicians who for years hosted ramshackle Sunday jamborees on their front porch, bringing old-timers down from the hills toting instruments from other epochs: dulcimers, lumberhorns, clackamores. They looked homemade but sounded otherworldly, and so did the accompanying voices, their mother's among them, above them, enveloping each song with careworn tenderness, the way a clean sheet fell on a bed. That's how Ben had once described it to Audrey. The parties—they called them *knockabouts*—would last all day: hymns, folk songs, mountain blues, half the town showing up most weeks, grilling food, drinking from unlabeled bottles, the aged and infirm propped up in lawn chairs, just watching and listening, the way you did in these rural outposts, for hours, for years.

And how could the two young brothers not become a part of it, not start fiddling and strumming and banging on things, not learn to play the songs they heard and then start writing some themselves, tough-luck stories and outlaw ballads, simple and derivative at first, but less so as time passed, teenage summers, the two becoming three when they added Easter Woods, their grade-school friend, a socially awkward musical prodigy from a meth-wrecked home, who slept over half the time, and then all the time, taking up residence among the instruments in the basement, their self-appointed curator and guardian. They started small: house parties and local festivals. High school became an annoyance, and then an afterthought, replaced by the kind of changeless small-town jobs that crushed a person without a sideline, an outlet, a mission. Ben became a bouncer. Arthur worked stints at the municipal dump, and in the warmer months reshingled roofs with Easter, until the latter, stoned, fell off an A-frame and fractured his skull. But he could still fiddle with a cracked head, and though the roofing concern went bust, the band gigs kept coming. They accepted every invitation, learning through trial and error the tricks of performing live, pedal loops and distortion, movement and stage presence, venturing forth to nearby towns, to neighboring counties, to the forlorn cities of industry still dotting the north-country landscape. Finally, they headed south to New York, once, and then again and again, metal to the magnet, until, like Easter in the basement, the temporary became permanent, and they found themselves subletting a bedbug-ridden, exposed-wire "work/live space" in the barren and not-yet-fashionable reaches of South Williamsburg, Brooklyn.

They arrived (as Audrey had not long before them) at the height of a specific cultural moment born of the jangly rhythms, retro stylings, and put-upon attitudes of a loose cluster of artistic-minded contrarians. These were the muscular years following 9/11, but the young denizens of their particular Brooklyn weren't political activists or aspiring intellectuals. They weren't unified in much at all beyond a loose belief in creative self-expression. But how to channel it? The art world was too insidery, photography too accessible, writing too antisocial and, in the end, too hard. What remained was music, and the sprawling canvas of indie rock. Part grunge, part Brit invasion, part disco and hip-hop, folk and electronic, fashion and spectacle, it could be stripped down or layered up, and, as such, was so fragmentarily derivative as to be thoroughly original. The barriers to entry were low, the odds of success—or at least stylish failure—enticingly high. And that was enough. By the first years of the new century, the immigrant neighborhoods of North Brooklyn had cracked open, and beautiful, bedraggled twentysomethings were pouring in. They arrived from that vast American other, dreamy theater majors and art school grads, suburban iconoclasts and Rust Belt misfits, some fully formed but most needing time among similar minds and sensibilities—other people doing weird shit, wearing weird shit, smoking weird shit, busloads of kids who understood firsthand the suffocating lassitude of cultural homogeneity, the illogical sameness of everywhere else. Of course, Williamsburg, the ground zero of this non-movement, had its own indigenous codes, and as it happened, just then, the prevalent look was exactly congruent to what

Ben, Arthur, and Easter already wore: Carhartt jackets and denim cut-offs, work shirts and wife-beaters. And while they understood that irony was involved (not everyone—in fact, almost no one—hailed from their type of manure-scented nowhere), they never did comprehend, or really care about, the complex sociological factors that produced that irony. In a world of layered artifice, they were wholly authentic. Not that they realized that either.

How they'd changed from those early days—grown up physically, acquired the tempered weariness of prolonged creative struggle. Arthur was now a genuine front man, handsome and charismatic, bending his skinny frame into the songs as if willing them to life. Ben, twice as large, was the sweat-drenched soul of the group, standing center stage, cradling his accordion like it was a baby in a sling. Tempos and moods, the entire spirit of the show, emanated from him. And then Easter and Gatesy, the two always lumped together, despite their evident dissimilarity. Easter Woods was shy and aging early but confident onstage as he moved between instruments—bass, fiddle, keyboards—while Gatesy, the drummer they'd found some months ago at a gig in New Paltz (after several others hadn't worked out), was a frenetic body of energy, perpetually surrounding himself with women he never brought home, his true interest, his real love, being the band itself—its members and music, its currency. In this most anonymous of cities, a band provided identity, community, and cover. Notoriety, if it came, only heightened the experience, the group becoming a separate life force its individual members were forever trying to comprehend and control. You made the band, and then the band made you.

Now, marooned on their VIP platform, Lucas nowhere to be seen, Audrey and the brothers watched as Gatesy, spurred on by the wrap-dress girls, began unhooking the velvet ropes in hopes of enticing more visitors. "Death to the social order!" he shouted, and the two girls squealed. Audrey could feel it coming, one of those harebrained incidents that so often occurred around band boys. They tried so hard to be mature, to be men, but they were still just kids with guitars, breaking what they touched, begging to be heard.

It didn't take long before the same security guard who'd ushered them in reappeared and methodically began rehooking the ropes to their stanchions. He asked Gatesy what the hell he thought he was doing, but the drummer just continued around the circle, until he was unhooking ropes the guard had just rehooked. For a while, they moved in synchronistic tandem, Gatesy taunting his apelike adversary, slowing down and speeding up, at one point even switching directions and confusing the guard into doing the same. Which is when the waitress arrived with a busboy in tow, carrying bottles, mixers, an ice bucket, and glasses. Naturally, Easter began lobbing ice cubes at Gatesy, who picked them up and threw them, harder, at the guard. The scene was teetering toward bedlam, security radioing for help, when Theo reappeared, staggering toward the platform like some long-lost explorer emerging from the jungle. Audrey caught sight of him just as Theo, in turn, glimpsed the bottles and glasses, the yet-untouched mind eraser. Theo was cradling one of those himself, along with three other drinks, his sleeves soaked, his expression pushing past exasperation to disbelief. Audrey stood up to both help and explain, but she lost sight of her boyfriend in the mess of people closing in from all directions. Here was Lucas, returning from the bathroom, only to be thrust aside by three newly arrived guards, and from the other direction, the club manager, his face betraying the antithetical requirements of his dual roles—peacekeeper and party host. It was a madhouse now, champagne popping, people pushing one another, one of the wrap-dress girls screaming as she slipped on an ice cube and fell to the floor—

"Lucas!" the manager called out, as if the label man could do something, as if the label man were even listening. Because he wasn't. Pale and sweating profusely, Lucas Duff was staring again at his phone. He was in some kind of trance, and it wasn't just the coke. Audrey and the Westfields saw it, too, and instinctively moved toward him, everyone converging near a downed section of rope—Lucas, Audrey, Ben, Arthur, Easter, and now Theo, who'd put down the drinks. Audrey slipped over to his side.

"What the hell's going on?" Ben asked.

Lucas looked up, glassy eyed. "A guy who was working for us scouting shows . . ." He wiped his nose on his sleeve. "I've been getting these texts all night. Apparently he . . . he *killed* himself. Jumped off the fucking Williamsburg Bridge."

"Jesus," Arthur said. "What was his name?" They were almost shouting above the noise.

"Fender. At least that's what everyone called him. Weird dude, but really knew his shit and had a great ear—"

But the brothers were no longer listening. They were looking at Audrey. Her lips had parted, her cheeks gone pale.

"Are you sure?" she said to Lucas. Her voice sounded unsteady, almost quivering.

"Sure about what? That he jumped? No, I'm not fucking sure. But the story's been going around the last few hours. That's why I've been distrac—wait, Audrey, what's wrong? Don't tell me you used to—"

"Hey!" It was Theo, stepping toward Lucas. Ben tried to get between them. Three big men standing toe to toe to toe, though all eyes were on the tallest.

"Easy, easy," Lucas said. He looked terrified. "Sorry, I wasn't . . ."

But Audrey's boyfriend stood his ground. It was the label man who moved, stepping meekly backward.

Everyone else huddled around Audrey. "You okay?" Theo asked, stooping slightly to meet her at eye level. "What just happened?"

"Nothing," she said, ridiculously. She felt claustrophobic, short of breath.

"It's probably not true," Ben said. "Lucas is all fucked up."

"I know." Audrey appeared dazed. "Look, we're gonna go, okay?"

"Are you sure?" Arthur asked. "Here, we'll walk you downstairs."

"No, don't," she said, grabbing her coat. "I'm fine. Let's catch up tomorrow."

No one believed her, but she didn't care. Her heart was racing. *Fender.* The name bore into her. She hugged the brothers, almost perfunctorily, and then took Theo's arm, which was there, waiting.

*   *   *

They walked across Ninth Avenue in silence, Audrey wobbly in her heels on the cobblestones. Theo put his jacket around hers as the wind off the river funneled past them down Fourteenth Street. At the corner of Eighth they descended underground, only to be flattened against a wall by a tide of bodies surging up. Manhattanites stumbling home from Brooklyn. For so long, this time of night, the crowds had gone the other way, but it was 2011 now; the scales of pleasure had tipped. Theo swiped his way through a turnstile, then passed his card back to Audrey, who did the same. The train sat in the station, hissing, belching; they hurried down the platform and stepped into the rearmost car. There were only four people inside: a homeless man slumped under blankets in a corner he'd cordoned off with yellow crime-scene tape; a European couple speaking in hushed voices as they studied a route map by the door; and a woman in a Con Ed jacket, eyes closed, lightly snoring.

Theo and Audrey sat as they'd walked, huddled close. What the hell had just happened? He'd never seen her react like that—to anything or anyone. Worse, she hadn't said a word about it since they'd left the club. As the train started moving, she buried her head in the crook of his shoulder, her hair obscuring her face. He pulled her tight to him. She'd talk when she was ready.

Sixth Avenue. Union Square. The car filling up. Theo scanned the ads running the length of the opposite wall: six panels dedicated to a new James Patterson book, four to an ESL school. Above the Con Ed woman's head was a new installment of the MTA's Poetry in Motion campaign: a stanza from Robert Frost's "Birches." An odd choice, considering the surroundings, but then, the whole series seemed unlikely—subversive, even. How had it ever been green-lit? Theo pictured an idealistic city employee navigating the endless bureaucratic hurdles. Things like that warmed his heart. A swinger of birches indeed.

Third Avenue. First. A kid with a stand-up bass flopped down across from Theo, the instrument remaining upright between them. Had Audrey known this Fender guy well (and what kind of name was that)?

Theo had never heard her mention him, which was strange. They'd told each other so much about their pasts. He knew all the major figures—her longtime friends, her significant lovers. He understood that things had happened to her, come at her, in ways unfamiliar to him, and if minor details hadn't been fully broached, well, he had learned to live with that fact, even admire it, at least as it contrasted with his own lackluster New York story. What mattered in the end was honesty: they trusted each other completely, and this, to Theo, meant everything.

What was happening? The train was easing to an unscheduled stop. The lights flickered off and on and off. Then the backups kicked in, as the train exhaled and went quiet. The kid in front of him brought the bass in against his body, allowing Theo a view of the car again. He scanned the riders' faces, some bathed in the glow of smartphones, others blank, lost in the non-time of here to there. Minutes passed. Theo listened for an explanation. He'd read an article once about the real meaning behind conductor announcements. A "sick passenger" actually meant a dead passenger; "police activity" meant a suicide. A jumper. A body on the tracks.

Audrey stirred. "What's going on?"

"We're stopped," Theo said.

She sat up quickly and looked around. "Under the river?"

"Yes, why?" Theo asked. As if he didn't know. As if the night hadn't already twisted in on itself. Could *this* have something to do with *that*? Of course not. They were in a tunnel, not on a bridge. This was just the city taking a breath before the ceaseless march resumed. Still, the coincidence gave him pause, being stuck under the river—the *moat*, as Audrey called it, which would make Brooklyn their fortress, their refuge—between lives old and new. The link never seemed quite severed.

Audrey hadn't answered, and he was about to ask again when the main power came back on, and soon they were moving, slowly, with effort, and he could feel the age of everything—the tracks, the system, the city. Five more stops.

Audrey was gazing at the homeless man, at the tape that marked his realm.

"Tell me something," she said.

"Like what?"

"Anything. I don't care."

Theo cleared his throat. "I thought of a good opening line."

She looked up at him expectantly.

"The drummer wanted a mind eraser."

She closed her eyes, buried her head again.

"God, so do I."

Chapter Two

Brunch people. They were everywhere and it was barely noon. Audrey checked her phone: three minutes past, to be exact. Sarah would be shocked at her punctuality, assuming Audrey could get through the throng of Burberry coats and Balenciaga bags clogging up the restaurant entranceway. She waded in, making it through the first set of double doors before encountering resistance, in the form of German tourists, or Dutch maybe, a half-dozen contemporary-art-world types who looked, in their improbable color combinations—blues on slightly bluer blues, etc.—like the visual equivalent of smelling salts. Balthazar, like most New York restaurants, suffered from a lack of space near the hostess stand, but Audrey had spent years moving through crowded eateries, and soon she'd negotiated the second set of doors and was peeling off toward the bar. She scanned the café tables, and then the bar area itself, but her old friend was nowhere in sight. She spied an empty bar stool by the service station and hurried over to claim it.

Brunch had been Audrey's idea. She'd texted Sarah just after eight a.m., and Sarah, no doubt sensing trouble, had responded immediately, asking if everything was okay. *Some wired shit happng*, Audrey had written. *Srry, WEIRD shit. Plus its bn forevr.* She knew Sarah would have plans on a sunny autumn Saturday but knew, too—no, she didn't *know*, not anymore, but she *hoped*—that her friend would cancel them. How long had "forevr" been? Eight months? Ten? For years, they'd been inseparable—best friends and roommates. Audrey Benton and Sarah Foster had met on a softball field in Williamsburg, not long after Audrey moved to New York, and from there had quickly spilled into each other's lives, like a sloppy chemistry experiment gone wonderfully right. The compound they formed bubbled with energy and glowed in the dark, *after* dark, and seldom had a night passed without the two joining forces to wreak havoc.

Back then, Sarah was waitressing at Indochine, on Lafayette Street, a former eighties hotspot turned downtown institution. Audrey preferred Brooklyn restaurants when it came to work but often trekked into Manhattan when their post-shift schedules aligned, to meet Sarah at Balthazar (a few blocks south of Indochine), where the food was good and the crowd intriguing. It was expensive, prohibitively so, but their drinks were usually comped by the bartenders or paid for by men at nearby tables. It was no accident that Audrey and Sarah preferred the front of the bar—two tall, stylish Brooklyn girls clad in tattoo-baring tops, their hair effortlessly unstyled, their laughs loud and confident. They were catnip (with cat eyes) to men with money, wild and exotic, but without the punk darkness or roller-derby kitsch. Grinning waiters approached with dirty martinis or champagne flutes, offerings from older patrons, and Audrey and Sarah would turn after a time to locate their latest admirers, both of them wearing coy expressions that might mean a half-dozen things, but most likely just one: that it wasn't going to happen. Unless, on the rare occasion, it might, at which point the well-coifed West Coast architect or French filmmaker or rich-kid painter and his tablemates slid giddily over to make room for the new arrivals. From there the night could expand in any direction, from the basement of the Mercer, to the roof of the Thompson, to a tiki dive on the Lower East Side. The girls had only one rule, and it usually held: they stayed together. Audrey and Sarah weren't interested in anything beyond a fun night. Anyway, the boys Audrey really liked were never trolling the bar at Balthazar; they were treading water back in Brooklyn—broke dreamers in frayed denim, just trying to stay afloat. But there was purity in that. And equilibrium. Still, Balthazar back then, Audrey thought, as she gazed around the restaurant . . .

Where was Sarah? And who were all these people? Balthazar had never been so packed, even in its heyday. Or was this still its heyday? She should have made a reservation, though the idea of calling ahead for *brunch* was too much. Audrey couldn't see the entrance anymore, which meant Sarah would never see *her*. She was about to venture back outside—they could go someplace else—when she felt a tap on her shoulder. Turning around, Audrey found herself face-to-face with a stunning mocha-skinned woman with an Afro so perfectly round she had to fight the urge to stare.

"If you'll come with me . . ."

"I don't think—" Audrey started to say, but then noticed the clipboard and the practiced smile and understood what was happening. She stood up and followed the hostess through the restaurant, the two tall women in lockstep, ignoring the eyes flicking their way. Sarah was sitting in one of the sought-after crescent banquettes along the far wall, applying lipstick with a compact. When she saw Audrey, she snapped it shut and wriggled along the vinyl-covered seat until she was free of the table. They embraced, almost tightly, and watched the hostess sashay away.

"Look at her," Sarah said. "We were never that fabulous. Or I wasn't. You had your moments."

Audrey was about to say something in mock protest, then realized her friend had used the past tense. She looked at the table instead.

"Impressive real estate."

"Judging from your text, I figured we might need some privacy." Sarah's phone vibrated beside her place setting. "Ugh, let me put this away." Instead, she picked it up and read the incoming message as she shimmied back into place. Audrey followed, balling her coat up onto the seat beside her. Then she saw Sarah's shearling-lined leather number hanging neatly from a nearby hook. Oh well.

"It's Chris," Sarah announced. "He says hi. He just finished running and has to go into work."

"But it's Saturday."

"Welcome to my world." She started thumbing a reply.

Christopher Van Vleck was Sarah's boyfriend, a title he'd held for six years and counting. They lived together on Eightieth and Lex, in a fantastically nondescript luxury doorman building with a private gym and garage—where, for $775 a month ($25 more than Audrey paid in rent), they parked their Audi A8. Chris was always insisting Audrey and Theo borrow it for a weekend, but the mere thought of the machine being in his charge sent Theo into a state of near-paralysis.

Chris worked as a wealth advisor for an old-line Wall Street firm specializing in money management, investment banking, and trading— not that anyone in Audrey's world got into such specifics. In this barely post-crisis era, finance was finance (i.e.: evil), and the conversation ended there. Which was fine with Chris. He accepted his status as a villain and for years had dutifully paid the nightly tabs for Sarah, Audrey, and their Brooklyn friends. At least, that used to be the case. These days, he and Sarah hung out with a more uptown, couple-y crowd—stroller pushers, museum members, *brunchers*—and rarely got out to Brooklyn anymore. Audrey believed this was Sarah's doing, for Chris, despite appearances, had always preferred edge to convention, recklessness to sensibility. In truth, Audrey was surprised he'd so willingly settled down. Not that he really had, at least in any official way.

Sarah, long removed from her Indochine days, now worked in client relations at Sotheby's, a job she'd secured fairly soon after moving in with Chris, whose parents happened to be major Sotheby's clients. As Sarah's career had evolved, so had her appearance, and Audrey used the texting time-out to absorb the latest changes. No more bangs, for one, which was probably for the best, as naturally blond as Sarah was, but there were plenty of accessories, including a gorgeous emerald necklace and a bold leather-banded watch. What really got Audrey's attention, though, was Sarah's dress, a half-sleeve khaki number that cinched at the waist but was otherwise billowy, almost flowing. Anthropologie, maybe, except she couldn't see Sarah shopping there anymore, if she ever had (too upmarket early on; too downmarket now). Not that the dress wasn't stylish; it just wasn't an outfit she'd have worn back . . .

when? When she wasn't trying to hide her tattoo, Audrey thought. She pictured the colorful flowers and thorns that adorned the entire upper half of Sarah's right arm. Audrey had been with her when she got it, over three long sessions at the now-defunct Kings County Ink & Leather, and still remembered the squeal Sarah had made when that needle first touched her skin.

Audrey rarely thought of her own tattoos anymore—at least when people weren't commenting on them. Now, though, feeling strangely defiant, she pulled her thin sweater off and tossed it onto her coat. She was wearing a halter top underneath, and as she tied her hair up in a knot, her principal tattoo, a western scene rendered in black ink, became visible on her left shoulder blade. It was a simple design—two cowboys on horses heading toward a distant mountain range—but impossible not to stare at. Audrey wished she had a backstory to go with it, like she did with her others (the word "Sucre" scripted on her abdomen and the poetic quote traversing the underside of her left forearm), but she was not from the West and had no particular affinity for cowboys or deserts. What she did love was the idea of the journey, of moving toward something majestic, however long it might take. Audrey, with the help of an artist friend, had worked on the sketch for weeks; Sarah, meanwhile, had picked hers from the parlor's "Popular Designs" sketch-book. Whatever—it ended up looking fine. And commitment-wise, it was hard to criticize a half sleeve, no matter how unoriginal.

Sarah was still texting when a waiter appeared. Audrey cleared her throat.

"Sorry," Sarah said. "Chris set a personal best and is feeling the need to relive every second of it. Six miles around the park. Now I feel fat."

"Blasphemy!" the waiter cried, swatting Sarah's words away. He was garrulous and campy and they loved him immediately. The three of them chatted awhile. Then Sarah ordered a prosecco. Audrey, coffee.

"Wow," Sarah said after he'd bid them farewell. She put her phone back beside her plate. "No alcohol? This *is* serious. Do tell."

Audrey took a deep breath, unsure of how to proceed. "I don't know much," she said. "I just heard about it last night, after a show."

"What band?"

"The Westfield Brothers."

"Ben and Arthur! They're still around? Oh, I miss them!"

"They signed with Columbia, believe it or not."

"If anyone deserves it. How did I not know about this? Auds, I'm so out of it these days. The only songs I hear anymore are the same ten eighties retreads they play at every single gallery opening. It's like music stopped after Joy Division. Too bad the art didn't. Thankfully, we've run out of wall space so Chris hasn't been buying."

Audrey reached over and fingered Sarah's necklace.

"*Paintings*, I mean."

"It's beautiful."

"Yes, well." The drinks came and they clinked, flute to cup. "You're stalling," Sarah said.

"I know, I know."

"Is it something with Theo?"

"God, no." Audrey paused. "It has to do with Fender."

Sarah produced an audible sigh and looked wearily up toward the ceiling. "What's he done?"

"Jumped off the Williamsburg Bridge. Apparently."

"*What?* How do you know?"

"The Westfields' new manager at Columbia told us—kind of off-hand. Fender had been scouting bands for them."

"Oh my God, Audrey. What else did he say?"

"Not much. It was a weird scene. I couldn't really keep it together, so I grabbed Theo and we split. I just . . . I don't know what to think."

"What do you mean?" Sarah stared at her. "You don't believe that . . ."

She didn't finish the thought, not out loud.

Audrey picked up a spoon and stirred her coffee, though she hadn't added anything to it. "I don't know. I searched online this morning, before Theo got up, but there was no mention of Fender or a bridge jumper—which is almost worse."

"What about Facebook or Twitter?"

"Fender's not on Twitter and he only has a Facebook *fan* page, which is absurd. He's got like five followers. It's never been updated."

"When's the last time you saw him?"

Audrey thought a moment. "About two years ago. Theo and I stopped into Zablozkis after a show at the Music Hall, and he was at the bar with a bunch of guys I'd never seen before. A hard-core crowd, kind of rough. He didn't see me, and I didn't go over. He looked pretty out of it, and anyway, so much time had passed."

"What did Theo say about last night? It's not like you to freak out."

"He asked what was wrong, and I told him it was nothing. But I can't stand lying to him."

"It's not a lie, exactly," Sarah said, furrowing her brow. "It's more a *withholding*. Spend some time with Chris and you learn the difference."

Audrey felt a surge of warmth for her old friend. The world she was navigating . . .

"Anyway," Sarah said quickly. "In terms of Fender, it's been, what, six years? If something was going to happen to him—to any of us—it already would have."

"But do you really believe he'd commit suicide?" Audrey asked.

Sarah considered the question. "Honestly, he never seemed like the type. He was crazy, not depressive. But what do I know. If you want, call Chris and get his take. He'll be in the office all afternoon. Apparently, he's behind on work because of all that Occupy nonsense. The park they took over is right outside his window, and he says the chanting is nonstop. Can you imagine, the poor guy? Anyway, speaking of work, tonight's the big fall Old Masters sale and they have me taking phone bids. I need to find a new dress."

Audrey reached across the table and touched Sarah's toned right arm, just above the elbow, where the red petal of a flower peeked out from under her sleeve. "I'm guessing something longer in the arms?"

Sarah rolled her eyes, only partly for effect.

And that was that. Twenty minutes of auction talk followed, Sarah expounding upon the vagaries of the art market as if it were critical to Audrey's future. Croissants were ordered and picked at, followed by the check, which sat noticeably unpicked at until Audrey offered to pay it. "Oh right," Sarah said. "Hold on." A lengthy search of her purse produced a single crisp ten, which she clipped to the bill. "Sorry, I've stopped carrying cash." *What about a card*, Audrey wondered, or was the check too small to warrant plastic? She reached into her pocket and made up the difference. Funny, she thought, Sarah had never been cheap when she had no money.

On went coats and sunglasses, and soon they were strolling down Mulberry Street as if this were any Saturday afternoon. Maybe it was and Audrey was just being paranoid. Sarah was right: years had passed. So much time, in fact, that Audrey no longer thought much about what she and Sarah (and Chris and Fender) had done. Hearing Fender's name had caught her off guard, that's all.

But that wasn't all.

And now Fender was gone.

She shuddered and tried to think of other things.

Sarah, meanwhile, was thinking of shoes. "Nolita in a nutshell," she said, peering through a storefront window. "Look at these prices. Five hundred and seventy-five dollars for ankle boots the Pied Piper wouldn't wear."

Audrey followed Sarah's gaze through the front window of a small boutique. There was something about it. She recognized the floor, a beautiful cracked-tile mosaic with red rosettes, and the faded-brick tenement walls, mostly obscured now by shelves of belts and handbags. And then she had it.

"This used to be the Ravenite Social Club," she said. "The Gambino crime family's headquarters. John Gotti ordered hits from right where that cash register is."

"How do you know that?" Sarah asked, mildly interested.

"How do you think?" Audrey tried to remember exactly what Theo had told her. Something about the FBI's bugging the place from an upstairs apartment. When the mobsters caught on they started taking walks around the block just to talk freely, but by then it was too late. Theo had imparted this knowledge on their third date, as they strolled the neighborhood hand in hand (a first for Audrey, the sustained hand-holding). He kept pointing at buildings and rattling off historical particulars—or starting to and then catching himself. But Audrey, every time, had asked him to keep talking, *begged* him to, this intoxicating man who got so lost in marginalia, in etymology, in process. Small worlds he could burrow into. How she had wanted to burrow in with him, and in so doing leave behind the intemperate life she'd perfected—the years of chasing everything lustrous, everything new. For a long time, Audrey had resolved to go it alone. Cohabitation. Codependence. Weren't these the opposite of independence? Then Theo came along and the only words that mattered were his.

"They should have let the mobsters stay," Sarah was saying. "Those purses are hideous. Let's head over to Elizabeth."

And so they did. Why was Audrey being so compliant? She didn't want to shop and couldn't afford to anyway. She had a thousand things to do, and also one: to find out about Fender. But something about being with Sarah, the comfortable rhythms of old friendship, strolling through Nolita on a Saturday afternoon . . . except they'd never done this back when they spent all their time together. The closest they'd come were half-hearted rummages through the flea market on Metropolitan. Why had Audrey really texted Sarah this morning? What answers did she think her friend might provide? None, she realized now. Chris was the one she should be talking to. And Lucas. Yet, she'd come to Sarah first. Was she using Fender as an excuse to rekindle their friendship? For a long time, Audrey had believed camaraderie was measured not by closeness but by complexity, adaption to circumstance, and in that way she saw Sarah's absence from her life as a phase that would reverse itself. Surely, her old friend felt this way, too, for a bond like theirs was so rare. How often did it happen in a life? Three or four times if you were lucky? But Audrey was just forcing things. Sarah was unnerved; it was obvious from the way she was acting. *Overacting.* Audrey had caught the disdain in Sarah's voice when she spoke of her Brooklyn years, like that entire phase of her life had been an unruly party she'd happened upon by accident (though she'd certainly enjoyed it at the time). Now here was Audrey, appearing all but unannounced on the grown-up side of the river, with all the chaos and uncertainty of that youthful past in tow. She should let her old friend be. But how to escape without being obvious?

Tory Burch solved the problem. Sarah gasped as they approached the massive orange doors of the garish boutique, and then, announcing she'd be right back, she hurried inside to greet two well-dressed women near a rack of tunic blouses. One of them squealed as Sarah hugged her, and then the doors swung shut and Audrey found herself alone on the sidewalk. She took her phone out and texted Lucas to ask where he was, then sent a longer message to Theo, wishing him luck at his lunch meeting with his boss. He'd been so nervous about it and she didn't understand why. She imagined Theo with her now, staring through the windows of Ms. Burch's varicolored empire, wearing that expression he sometimes got when he couldn't comprehend something the rest of the world took for granted. How *branded* everything was, how aspirationally thought out. When, Audrey wondered, had everyone started trying so hard to look like everyone else? Through the glass, she watched Sarah laugh at something one of the women was saying. She had such a great laugh, a contagious, throaty guffaw. Remove the context and she was still that cheerful, up-for-anything girl from small-town Illinois. In New York, though, context was everything. Where you lived, what you did, who you loved. A curious thought entered Audrey's mind: What if the problem wasn't Sarah at all? What if it was Audrey who'd drifted away by resisting the natural progression of events, by *not* changing? She was thirty-four years old and still reveled in her lack of convention. She had moved with Theo to the barren edges of Brooklyn because it was what they could afford, yes, but also to escape the incessant whirl of the city. *The natural progression.* Was there really such a thing? If Sarah no longer valued the unknown or unexpected, well, Audrey still believed they were the essence of life. But they scared her, too. Especially this news about Fender. Because if it was true, if he really was dead . . .

No. She refused to think that way.

Sarah was waving at her to come inside, but Audrey couldn't bring herself to step through the doors. She made a face and pointed at a watch she didn't have. Sarah gave her a brief, pouty look, then mouthed the words *Call me*. They blew each other kisses and that was that.

At the corner of Spring Street, Audrey's phone buzzed. Lucas, texting her back. *Heading into R&R building for recordng sess. Wts up? Wnt to aplogze for last nite?*

Sty there, Audrey typed. *cming to see u. and no. Asshole.*

Chapter Three

What the hell was that?

Theo shot straight up in bed. A loud bang—no, a clank, like a sledgehammer on a giant pipe. He turned, rubbing his eyes, toward Audrey, but she wasn't there. What *was* there was an Audrey-shaped impression—the mattress was old—and he stared at it as he found his bearings. Their bedroom was a small box with plywood walls, built (by Theo) into a windowed corner of the nominally-larger-but-still-basically-studio-sized space that could, theoretically or ironically, be considered a "loft" thanks to the height of the ceilings and its location in an area zoned for manufacturing. Theo listened intently but heard nothing through the bedroom door. He was covered in sweat. Weird, he thought, until he processed the temperature. It was subtropical, and his throat was dry—

CLANK!

The *radiator*. He exhaled audibly. So it began anew: another winter of climate warfare. With the exception of dividing walls and diminutive bathrooms, their building, a long-abandoned German brewery built in the 1880s, had gone largely unrenovated during its recent (and surely illegal) transition into "livable space." Nor was there a traditional super, though this fact didn't bother Theo. Performing his own repairs made him feel less urban, or at least less *urbane*. He understood, too, that the absence of rudimentary amenities—or, for that matter, a lease—contributed to the seriously-under-market rent they paid monthly, in cash, to a numbers runner named Miguel who kept office hours in the cleaning products section of Flushing Ave Finest Deli (which was, in fact, on Knickerbocker Avenue). But the radiator was a problem Theo hadn't yet solved. It functioned in one of two modes—completely *off*, or always, suffocatingly *on*—and the only way to survive the relentless five-month onslaught of steam heat produced by the latter was to open the windows to the elements. How absurd to wake up at three a.m. with a snowdrift forming on the comforter. And yet the alternative—the inability to breathe—was worse. To say nothing of the panging. Theo had tried everything. He'd shimmied the radiator toward the intake, but warping wasn't the problem. He'd attempted to bleed it but couldn't find a key that fit the ancient steam valve. A humidifier was the logical solution, but Theo, even at his most miserable, refused to buy one. He kept thinking of what his father would say (this was hypothetical, his father having never visited New York either before or after Theo moved there), or his brother, Carl, both of whom surely placed humidifiers in the same end-of-days category as Vespas and man-purses. It was Audrey who'd found the solution. Never a good sleeper, she'd been awakened one night by Theo's coughing; after watching him toss and turn, a Breathe Right strip affixed to his nose, she tiptoed out to the kitchen and returned a minute later with a large pot of hot water, which she placed on top of the radiator as if it were a stove. Soon, damp, humid, sinus-clearing steam began wafting through the room. Theo, awakened, had stared at it in disbelief—was it so simple?—and then, inhaling deeply, rolled over to kiss his girlfriend, who was already back under the covers, eyes squeezed tight.

The pot, refilled every few days, had worked well last winter, and Theo saw no reason not to stick with it (he'd grown up in a house where makeshift solutions lasted decades). Now only the panging remained as an ongoing concern. He stood up, stretched his tall, athletic frame, and opened the antiquated casement windows to the Brooklyn morning—

CLANK!

He jumped, startled. Could a radiator explode? Seven months of water pressure building up, a century-old system—

CLANK!

Christ. This last pang—the loudest yet—cleared Theo's head, and he immediately remembered he was meeting his boss, Win Groom, for lunch today. At the same time, he began recalling the events of the previous night—the club, the sudden exit, the long subway ride home. He opened the bedroom door. Audrey was nowhere to be seen, which was weird, though Roger, their cat, was not only in residence but pacing beside his litter box in a state of high dudgeon. Theo ambled over to scoop out whatever needed scooping, but the surface was unsullied. "What's wrong, little guy?" he asked, reaching out to pet him. But Roger raised a warning paw. Fine. Be like that.

Roger was gay. This sounded ridiculous, perhaps even impossible, but anyone who questioned the fact—and initially everyone did— needed only spend a few minutes with the cat to become an unequivocal believer. (The only exception to this had been Theo himself, who'd had suspicions but was nonetheless uncomfortable assigning a sexual pref- erence to a pet. It took a late-night visit from a gay friend of Audrey's to finally settle the issue. Staggering in through the front door for a last-stop drink, Bruce had spotted the newly acquired feline glaring at him from atop a nearby counter and, removing his earbuds, said, without prompting, "Holy shit, your cat's a queen.") Roger had arrived on the scene the previous fall. Audrey and Theo were walking home from a Cuban restaurant they'd begun frequenting when Audrey heard a series of soft but insistent meows coming from a weedy alley between two derelict storefronts. She stopped to investigate, and a moment later (a theatrical pause in the retelling) an angelic white cat, barely bigger than a kitten, stepped into the light. Audrey bent down, and the cat ran to her like a lost child to a parent. He figure-eighted through her legs, purred lovingly in her arms, and an hour later, having received a bath and some leftover "*pollo,*" nuzzled peacefully, perfectly, between Audrey and Theo in bed.

It was, in retrospect, the greatest con job Theo had ever seen. The minute Audrey arrived home from Petco the following morning, loaded down with $185 of supplies they couldn't afford, Roger (Audrey had named him right away) commenced a reign of terror that ranked right up there with Pol Pot's. He employed all the timeworn tools of dictatorship: bribery, intimidation, sudden violence. Finicky and vain, jealous and egotistical, the cat spent hours regarding himself in the vintage stand-up mirror, knocked over anything that might break, peed in open suitcases, and refused to make use of his litter box if it wasn't Zen-garden smooth.

First-time visitors elicited his particular ire, especially women, who always, despite repeated warnings, attempted to pet him. During extended visits, Roger would play the long con, lulling his mark into third-drink complacency, and then, without warning, leaping down to inflict skin-breaking damage. Those who dared return ignored the cat, or even shooed him away—treatment Roger, a submissive at heart, respected immensely.

Recently, and to Audrey's great amusement, Theo and Roger had brokered a loose détente, which Audrey had used as an opportunity to transfer to her boyfriend all cat-related responsibilities. This morning, though, Roger was acting like his rascally old self, not that Theo much cared. His mind was elsewhere. As was Audrey. Theo could count on one hand the number of times she had gotten up before him, let alone on a Saturday. But she'd made coffee before she left, and now Theo poured himself a cup. He took it mill-town black.

The cat meowed. The radiator clanked. Theo ignored both. He scanned the room for clues as to Audrey's whereabouts, but nothing appeared out of place. Reflexively, he wandered over to the desk—a sanded-down door on sawhorses—and sat at the computer. He tapped the space bar and was about to check his email when he noticed a hurriedly scrawled note beside the monitor. *"Hey hon, Grabbing lunch in the city w Sarah and wanted to let you sleep. Hope yr meeting goes well. Hollywood needs your help. Love, Love, A."* Theo read it again. Had Audrey mentioned having plans with Sarah? Probably, and he'd forgotten. He checked his phone. It was only ten thirty. Why'd she leave so early?

Theo had purchased their iMac desktop at a refurbished-computer store, and it showed. The screen flickered, the keys stuck, and the mouse had a mind of its own. Fearing a hard-drive meltdown, he'd spent several hours the previous week backing everything up to a flash drive, but he was hardly tech savvy, and it was unclear whether the drive had received/stored any of the data. They did have a laptop, Audrey's weathered Dell, but it was riddled with viruses from dubious song downloads, so the monolith on the desk did double duty—his and hers—often whirring to life with a dozen open tabs: Gmail and YouTube, music blogs and news sites, paused films and half-read manuscripts. Passwords on Post-its surrounded the screen, leading friends to marvel at how much Audrey and Theo trusted each other—what, after all, was more sacred than one's personal email account?—but transparency was a basic tenet of their relationship. It brought them close and kept them there. *Take a look if you want, I have nothing to hide from you.* Not that Theo had much to hide from *anyone*, a onetime point of pride he now saw as slightly pitiable. Had his life been so staid? It didn't feel like it, but listening to some of Audrey's stories, it was hard not to think he'd been in the right city at the right time and somehow missed all the fun. But he was who he was, and life had worked itself out. At least the love part.

The career part was less assured. Having survived his first three years in New York working odd jobs of a mostly physical variety, Theo, at age twenty-five, had landed an entry-level position at Prosaic Books and spent the next decade clawing his way up and into the publishing world. New job titles came every few years, bumps in salary less so. But he'd stuck with it, and eventually his work ethic, loyalty to Prosaic—one of publishing's few remaining literary stalwarts—and intense love of books advanced him to a level where he could acquire his own. It hadn't lasted long. The books he bought and edited were well reviewed but didn't sell, and when the economy went south, so did Theo's prospects. He survived the crisis itself, only to be downsized in 2009, when the recession refused to recede. But then, in one of those only-in-New York moments, he was quickly (re)hired by Wynne Groome (aka Dr. Win

Groom), his former boss at Prosaic, who himself had left the publisher after parlaying a bestselling self-help book he'd written into a flourishing new career as a screenwriter, documentarian, motivational speaker, and founding partner of the suddenly everywhere (but Malibu-based) production company Round Circle Films. It was here/there that Theo Gorski was currently employed as a literary scout.

That summarizing his employment history required such a jumble of syntax seemed undignified, but the larger issue was where that summation left off—that is, the wrong turn it had taken. For Theo was not a film person but a man of letters, of words read and considered. He had wanted to work with books since taking American Fiction his freshman year of college. Not just books but novels. Not just novels but great literature. He had dreamed of having a voice in that deepest of artistic conversations, and for a short time he *had*—or at least he'd been present while others had. Now that life had fallen away, and though his new "career" might appear more glamorous (it was not) and relevant to the moment (it very much was), Theo knew, deep down, that he was as mismatched as a man and a job could be.

Still, he was happy to be employed and extremely thankful to the man who signed his modest paycheck. Theo had always been something of a protégé to Wynne, or *Win* (Theo still couldn't get used to the new market-tested moniker and went with "W" in emails), though his hiring as Round Circle's literary scout had been, to the hiree at least, nothing less than shocking. Specifically, Theo's job entailed writing "coverage"—an assessment of a book's potential as a film—for upcoming fiction and nonfiction releases. This required getting early access to manuscripts, a task at which Theo excelled; editors liked him, and publishers liked Hollywood (even a whiff of a potential film adaptation could send them into a frenzy). But the second requirement, good judgment, had proven more elusive, for Theo's tastes were not Hollywood's tastes. He eschewed spies and bombs in favor of characters and complexity, and that explained why, after two years at Round Circle; after 215 manuscripts read, half as many "covered," and at least twenty wholeheartedly recommended; after six books had been optioned, four treatments written, and two screenplays completed; after all that time and effort, not one book that Theo Gorski had championed—fiction or non-, small press or large—had come close to being green-lit as a major, or even minor, motion picture.

When had the situation become worrying? Theo pondered this as he scanned his inbox. Win had remained steadfastly supportive as one Theo-recommended project after another faded into Hollywood oblivion. Don't worry, his boss had told him early on. Films were like Rube Goldberg machines when it came to getting them made, the failure of one part inevitably leading to the failure of all. And Theo had taken those words to heart, as year one became year two, as other scouts had other books green-lit, as Theo built bookshelves for his galleys-gone-nowhere. But over the last few months a noticeable shift had occurred in his communications with Win—unanswered emails, escalating minutes on hold, and finally, one day, a worrisome text: *T - gotta thnk mre comercialy - W!!* Theo had stared at these (almost) words for a long time. To think they'd been typed by a man who'd once edited Don DeLillo and Alice Munro. What did they mean, beyond what they meant? Also, what was up with the exclamation points?

That had been three weeks ago, and Theo hadn't heard from the West Coast again until Wednesday, when Win's assistant, Cecily, had emailed to say "Dr. Groom" was "coming through" New York and wanted to meet in person. Time (Saturday at two forty-five p.m.) and place (Café Loup) were given, but no agenda, and when Theo called back to see if he should prepare anything, he was told "the doctor" was "in a meeting." Was Win expecting some viable new film prospects? Of course he was.

thnk mre comercialy

(!!)

But Theo had no new prospects. A few upcoming books he'd found quite remarkable, but they ran along the same difficult-to-adapt lines as so many others he'd championed.

"I've got an idea," Audrey had said when Theo had mentioned his quandary the previous morning. They were in bed, sipping coffee as

Roger glared down from atop the bookshelf. "What do most of today's blockbuster movies have in common?"

"Superheroes."

"Yes! And where do those superheroes come from?"

"I don't know. Outer space? Atlantis? Industrial accidents?"

"Comic books."

"Well, sure."

"So go to a comic book store and find a new one."

"A new superhero?"

"Why not? I'm sure they're being created all the time."

Which was when Roger started peeing on Saul Bellow's *Herzog*.

Could it be so easy? Theo had been pondering it for the last twenty-four hours, and in that time Audrey's idea had evolved from "cute but naïve" into "elegant stroke of genius." Comics were the gateway drug of modern entertainment. Movies, graphic novels, video games, animation, porn . . . what *hadn't* evolved from them? Half of contemporary fiction was being written by comic book fanboys and -girls, so why had he always viewed them as a lesser art form? It occurred to Theo, not for the first time, that he might not *get* how stories worked. He came from a family oblivious to the arts, to imagination or creativity in any form, and though he'd tried mightily to shake that history, he knew it continued to haunt him. He had never been a writer and had failed as an editor, so it would only follow that his scouting antennae would be off as well. You could only blame cultural regression, other people's diminishing tastes, for so long before your own came into question. The lowest common denominator: maybe it was him.

So he had taken Audrey's advice. For hours the previous afternoon he'd browsed online comics stores and fan forums, but he may as well have been reading Etruscan. Hobby sites were no place for nonbelievers. He needed to flip through actual pages, speak with real aficionados. He needed *physical immersion*, and from what he could glean from the Internet, Forbidden Planet was the place to go. He'd walked past it many times—it was near the Strand, south of Union Square—but now, just to be sure, he decided to type the store's name into Google. He got no farther than the "F" before the "recent searches" box appeared. Theo stared at the list:

Fender

Fender suicide

Fender death

Fender bridge

Fender Williamsburg

Fender Columbia Records

Fender extortion

Fender felony

Fender murder

Theo felt a constriction in his lungs, like he'd been hit by a helmet square in the chest and wasn't sure yet what might be broken. The breastbone maybe, or the softer matter underneath. Audrey must have typed these earlier. What was she looking for? What had she found? He didn't want to know. Or he did, but from her, directly. He stared again at the words on the screen—not "Fender" (the name had already settled in, like a stalled weather front) but the descriptors that followed: "extortion," "felony," "murder." What had this guy been into?

CLANK!

He snapped out of it. He looked into the bedroom and then the other way, toward the kitchen. Roger had disappeared, but in his place, not a foot from the litter box, sat a large black turd. The coffee machine beeped twice and turned itself off.

He was out the door by noon—impressive, all things considered. Normally, he would take the stairs—they lived on the third floor—but the stairwell was currently impassable on account of a large, heavily stained couch wedged between the second- and third-floor landings. Impassable, and also impossible, if you saw it, to understand how the couch had arrived at such a place. The stairs were too narrow, the turns too tight, yet there it indisputably was, and had been, for weeks now—the fire hazard to end all fire hazards—leaving the building's dilapidated freight elevator as the only non-acrobatic means of egress. Theo would have reported the stairwell blockage, but to whom? Miguel, at the deli, either didn't speak English or didn't care to with him—both possibilities being equally unhelpful.

As it was, Theo enjoyed the freight elevator, its raw mechanics, its oak floor rutted by a century of weight—giant vats and barrel kegs from the days when Bushwick's brewers' row was thriving. Fourteen months ago, after Audrey and Theo had decided to move in together but before they'd agreed on a neighborhood, Audrey had attended a party in the very loft they lived in now. She had fallen hard for the vertically roomy space and, upon hearing it was becoming available, had begged her boyfriend to come check it out. Theo, if he'd had a choice—which, in truth, he had not—would have stayed in Manhattan, where he'd lived and worked for more than a decade. (After years spent in an Upper West Side crash pad with an ever-shifting roster of roommates, he had graduated to a tiny Tenth Avenue studio above the last of the Hell's Kitchen "Westie" bars.) Part of the problem was his ingrained aversion to novelty, be it geographic or cultural. But everyone feared change. Theo's specific issue involved a certain historical idealism he'd been clinging to since the day his fourteen-year-old self had stumbled upon the "New York" shelf in the Lawrence (Massachusetts) Public Library. He still remembered them so clearly, the yellowing biographies of poets and radicals and workaday heroes. He started signing books out, literary essays and lurid tell-alls, about fish markets, gambling parlors, downtown squats—the sensuous city in words—and at some point, during his condensed and fragmented youth, Theo began dreaming he'd one day live not just in New York, but on the island at its very center, the place where everything happened. By the time he arrived, of course, most everything was happening in the more affordable boroughs to the east, but he didn't care; he'd stay in Manhattan, survive at its fringes if he had to. Living in the city meant living in the city.

Yet here he was. He knew Audrey, who'd been priced out of North Williamsburg, would never move to Manhattan, so he braced himself for the Bushwick sales pitch: more space, cheaper rent, shorter commute (for her; he didn't have one). But in a stroke of brilliance, Audrey eschewed the gentrifying present for the long-forgotten past. Think about it, she told him, knowing he would. His European ancestors had built these buildings, *this* building, brick by brick, and soon thereafter introduced porter-drinking Americans to the wonders of German lager. She had researched the old breweries assiduously, and Theo listened as she recited dates and names—Piels and Rheingold and Schaefer—and who cared if her facts were slightly askew (or that the Gorskis were Polish, not German, though a grandmother on his mother's side had been Bavarian, so close enough). Certainly not Theo, who was amused, and in love, and soon found himself picturing his forebears, stolid men of hard routine and coarse pride, and while he understood he was being foolhardy, he did indeed feel a loose kinship, a keening appreciation, for their lives of labor, lives Theo's great-grandfather, and grandfather, and father, had lived—

He always did this, took that mental step too far, the one that turned him inward. It came from guilt, he knew, for he had left all of that behind—his degenerating family, his degenerating city. He could have stayed in Lawrence. Everyone else had: his brother, his childhood friends and high school teammates. Why had he pursued such a different path, a life of theory and thought, and so, too, its by-products, near-poverty and withering self-doubt? Certainly, his father hadn't approved. Leonard Gorski saw the educational assistance and financial aid his son had received, the scholarships and fellowships and internships, as nothing more than charity. The smothering liberalness of the nanny state. "And for what?" he'd often asked. "Where's the fucking paycheck?" That his father's entire career had been one of dependence on others—unseen corporate executives and crooked union bosses—was apparently beside the point. Not even beside it. On the other side of the planet from the point, which was . . . what? The point was that for a long time, in New York, as his failures accumulated, Theo retained a deep-seated fear that his father had somehow been right, that Gorski men simply weren't equipped to play the role Theo was auditioning for. It was Audrey who had convinced him otherwise, who had championed his dreams just as he was losing sight of them. Theo had been thinking of moving home. Instead, he'd moved in with her, into a wreck of a building that had once been a brewery, where immigrant men who had nothing to do with his ancestry had, for half a century, made watered-down, third-rate beer. No matter. The story, whatever the version, still sounded perfect to him.

He emerged into autumn sunlight and silence. This part of Bushwick (which was technically still Williamsburg but actually called Morgantown, courtesy of the closest L stop) was the latest of late-rising neighborhoods, and the early-afternoon streets were nearly deserted. All that bullheaded resistance, and he'd fallen in love with the place right away. This treeless carcass of post-industry, with its piled-high garbage and wastewater smell. Sometimes, in late afternoon, the sun bounced off the windows of the warehouses in such a way that Theo was reminded of his hometown, of the same sun hitting similar windows, thousands of them, along the sides of the Merrimack River textile mills that had once meant everything and now stood forlorn and abandoned. But the similarities ended there. Lawrence was stagnant, whereas Bushwick was searingly *alive*.

At least it would be later.

Audrey and Theo were not true pioneers. They'd arrived, instead, with the first swell of settlers, and had watched with timeworn gentrifiers' dismay as the swells became waves. Now every week or two brought a new designer-label consignment shop, or satellite art gallery, or "mixologist" cocktail bar. Black town cars had begun double-parking outside Roberta's, a high-end pizza joint turned culinary mecca that the *Times* had recently awarded two stars. Theo had heard that the chef raised chickens in a side yard and grew corn on the roof—or was it the other way around? He'd also heard—or overheard—a woman at the Archive coffee shop telling a friend, conspiratorially, about a secret second Roberta's under construction behind the first, twelve seats and twenty courses (or maybe Theo had that backward, too), a complete reinvention of what it meant to dine out. That this would—or might—exist amid rubble-strewn concrete lots and needle exchanges and raver lofts and bustling lumberyards and tagged-out slaughterhouses where blood ran across sidewalks like snowmelt down mountains signaled to Theo that, for the first time in his life, he actually *had* found the true center of something, Manhattan be damned. It had taken him a decade to gain his footing, but New York was funny that way. Occasionally, he thought he understood the city in a profound way. Most of the time he was confused about everything.

Who the hell was Fender?

Whoever he was, Theo had to forget about him for now. Today was about movies and superheroes.

He took the L under the river and got out at Union Square, a labyrinthine station where several subway lines crossed haphazardly. Ascending various ramps and staircases in an increasingly desperate state, he eventually emerged aboveground to find himself face-to-face with a heavyset Amish man—black hat, white beard, the whole deal—cradling a large flour-sprinkled sack of fresh bread. The man freed up a hand and tipped his hat, leaving fingerprints of flour on the brim. Theo froze in place. *Oh God*, he thought, *it's finally happened. I've stumbled into the middle of a live film set.* He'd had the dream—the nightmare—dozens of times since arriving in New York: the scene-in-progress, then the called-out "*Cut!*" followed by a furious dressing-down from some power-tripping PA. All around him, Amish extras in wool vests and suspendered high pants, pinned bonnets and white aprons, were walking, talking, *acting*, the man with the bread sack moving away now, hitting his mark, still in character. Theo, mortified, turned to hurry off in the opposite direction and . . . only then did he realize the extent of his own idiocy. He wasn't standing in the middle of a film set; he was standing in the middle of a farmer's market. Of course! It was Saturday. The Amish man was a real Amish man, and Theo had clambered up from the underground to find himself moored between a bread truck and a display counter, both the property of Pristwick Farms Bakery, Jasper, New York. How had that happened? He peered back at the station stairs, but no one else was climbing them. He must have missed a sign. Ha! Not a bad first line. He'd run it past Audrey later. Right now, he needed to get moving. Doling out "excuse me"s, he squeezed between two tables laden with baked goods. One of the Pristwicks pointed at Theo's pants. They were coated in flour.

He brushed himself off as best he could and started south through the busy market. A splinter group of Occupy Wall Streeters had commandeered the open plaza at the base of the square, and a crowd, including at least a dozen cops, was looking on with varying degrees of enthusiasm as the protesters held up signs and chanted slogans and teasingly taunted the officers. Theo paused to take in the scene. He was not politically active, but he was a watcher of the world, and the Occupy movement intrigued him—its momentum as much as its message (though who could argue against greater financial equality?). He kept meaning to trek down to Zuccotti Park and experience the phenomenon firsthand, but hadn't gotten around to it. Even Audrey was excited to go—"Who'd have guessed we'd get our generational shit together like this?" she'd said—and she hated politics more than he did. So what was the problem? Obviously, he was the problem. Spend your life turning pages and you forget to turn your head and look outside. Again, he thought of his father, bemoaning the books scattered across Theo's teenage bedroom. Not that the old man would have supported these dissident Occupiers either, flouting the rules and—okay, okay, not now. He was meeting Win in an hour and a half.

He skirted the assemblage—frothy with farmer's market rage—and hurried down Broadway, forgoing the Strand for the first time in his life. Across Twelfth, he came upon a window display featuring costumed mannequins squaring off in unlikely pairs: Batman and Princess Leia; the Green Hornet and the Lone Ranger; the Hulk and Iron Man. Here was Forbidden Planet. Here was his salvation. He walked inside and quickly found himself surrounded by a series of towering displays, waist-high action figures in elaborate packaging: GI Joes, Transformers, Doctor Whos. Beyond them stood a wall of T-shirts and toys, DVDs and video games. Theo retreated a few steps, confused by the garish commercialism of this strange alternative Disney. The place was so *mainstream.* Where were the misfit iconoclasts and trench-coated teens? He maneuvered past the shoppers up front and turned down an aisle marked COSPLAY. He'd seen the word before but didn't know what it meant; it looked Russian. Before him stood a corseted mannequin in a ruffled miniskirt, black knee-high boots, thick aviator goggles, and a feathered top hat: Amelia Earhart reborn as a Brontë sister in some industrial revolution of the future.

"We have more steampunk stuff in the back," said a voice to his right. Theo looked over, and then down, and discovered a round face peering up at him.

"Excuse me?"

"Steampunk." The girl—and she *was* a girl, surely no more than fifteen—looked Theo up and farther up. "Actually, forget it," she said. "Not sure what I was thinking."

She came up no higher than his chest, and again Theo found himself taking a step backward, this time not out of distaste but curiosity. She was small and exceedingly top-heavy, so that when he looked down he could see only cleavage and hair, the former being indecent, the latter long and dark and held together by a system of pins. At a slight distance, what there was of her outfit came into view: a zipper-front top and black thigh-high skirt covering the upper portion of her otherwise-bare legs (which, like her bare arms and bare midsection, were starkly pale). But these stylistic details were quickly shunted aside when Theo spotted, sticking up through strands of silky hair, the pointed ends of what appeared to be elf ears.

"Do you work here?" he asked.

"No, I'm following you around because you're totally my type. *Yes, I work here.*"

"Oh, good," Theo said, hearing himself as he spoke. He felt eighty years old. "I'm looking for comic books."

"Wow, bowl me over with specifics. At Trader Joe's do you tell them you're looking for food?"

Theo smiled for what felt like the first time in days. "Specifically, indie and small-press stuff. Do you carry that type of thing?"

"Like micro-comics and zines?"

"Exactly."

"Why?"

"What do you mean, 'Why?'"

"Are you an illustrator or something?"

"No."

"Then I don't get it. You don't look like an aficionado."

"*Aficion*ado?"

"A comic book dude."

Theo had never been interrogated by a salesperson before, but he was taking to it. He could handle being the butt of jokes when the person telling them was wearing elf ears. Not that she'd meant *aficionado* as a joke. Alas, if only she knew. He thought of Susan Sarandon's great line in *Bull Durham*, about the world being made for people not cursed with self-awareness. Or were kids these days the product of just the opposite? Too much knowing. He looked at her again, making sure, after the bartender fiasco the night before, to maintain eye contact. Plus, Christ, she really did look like a child.

"So who are you?" he asked.

"That's getting deep."

"The costume, I mean."

"I know what you meant. I'm Tifa Lockhart. Normally I would pause at this point, so you could be all, 'Oh yeah, of course, that's awesome,' but since you obviously don't know who Ms. Lockhart is, I shan't pause, and instead will just tell you she's Cloud Strife's hot childhood friend from *Final Fantasy Seven*."

Theo was biting his lip. "That's a video game? *Final Fantasy*?"

"Seven. Yes. Japanese. Who wants to be Lara Croft all the time?"

"And the ears?"

"They're permanent."

"Permanent?"

"I'm kidding! Ohmygodyoureembarrassing. Here, come on."

They set off, deeper into the store, the two of them like a side-show act.

"So tell me what steampunk is about," Theo said.

"No."

"But I'm a customer. It's your job."

"My job is to sell you the items you're looking for, which, as you've said, isn't anything steampunk related. What you haven't said is why you're in the market for crapola from the staple brigade. And don't tell me 'The Staple Brigade' sounds like a great band name, because a) it doesn't, and b) I'll go help someone else."

"You haven't helped me at all."

"I've got nothing to work with! Look at you," she said without turning around. "You're like my dad, except not. Also, you have powder on your pants."

Theo looked down. "It's flour."

"Congratulations."

"And I'm thirty-five. How old are you?"

"Don't be a creeper."

They turned a corner and the girl spun around. "Tada!" she said, holding her arms out and curtsying. Here they were, comics by the thousands, lining the rearmost aisles of the store. They were arranged in rows, like the albums—then cassettes, then CDs—in the music stores of Theo's youth. (Three eras of audio technology: Had he been young that long?) The salesgirl was lingering a few paces away. She'd taken her phone out (from where?) and was texting someone. Her parents probably, promising to be home by curfew.

Theo started browsing. Marvel, DC, Dark Horse. The comic books were thicker and glossier than he'd expected, and appeared, on the whole, as foreign to him as hot yoga or radical Islam. *The New Mutants. Northlanders.* A series called *Animal Man.* How strange, the variance of worlds, the things people came to love. *Batwoman. Daredevil. The Walking Dead.* Wasn't that an HBO show? Aha! He was onto something!

No, he wasn't. Someone else had been onto something, and Theo was years late to the game.

"Hey, Stan Lee, the indie section's over here. But I'm warning you: it's kind of a mess. People sneak their homemade shit in when no one's looking. 'Wrong-way stealing,' we call it, and if you ask me it's worse than the *right* way, because we can't tell until we scan the item and realize there's no barcode. You still haven't told me why you're interested in this stuff."

"I'm a film scout, which means that I look for story—"

"I know what it means. And what, you think you'll find some undiscovered gem back here?"

"That's the idea."

"Oh, *honey*." She tucked her phone into an unseen fold and watched Theo start thumbing through the cluttered stacks. Self-published graphic novels appeared beside flimsy photocopies barely four pages long. Titles and artwork jumped out, puns and mash-ups, breasts and UFOs. *Cleopatra in Space. Fuchsia Galactica. Breathers.* Theo studied this last one. Men in gas masks adorned the cover. *A world where the air is no longer safe to breathe.* An intriguing premise, though two hours of gas masks would be a tough sell. He moved on. *Xenoholics*: a support group for alien abductees. *Cerebus*: a misanthropic aardvark. *The Unwritten*: the wayward son of a famous novelist is kidnapped. Theo sighed. He thought of basements and bedrooms, awkward kids constructing make-believe worlds as stimulating as their real ones were lacking. He had been one of them—only no one had ever told him he could make believe. Instead, he'd been told to make do. To grin and bear it. No, even that was halfway hopeful. To *endure*. That was the ethic from which Theo Gorski had emerged, the droning backbeat of working-class life, as far from fantasy as a boy could get.

The world of comics was revealing itself now, the color and expression, the art. Delving in deeper, his eyes landed on a familiar name. *The Incredibly Fantastic Adventures of Maureen Dowd.* He pulled it out.

"Oh, that's a good one," Tifa said. Theo held the comic lower so she could read it. "She fucks George Clooney halfway through."

"*Maureen Dowd?*"

"No, Barbara Bush. *Yes*, Maureen Dowd."

He put the comic back where he'd found it. That this girl was familiar with Maureen Dowd—Theo would have had no idea at her age. She must be in college, he thought, though she truly didn't look it. The confidence, the precociousness, the ease with which she navigated her environment. She's the one who should be pitching films at Café Loup. She'd toss off a dozen ideas so quickly Win would have to slow her down to take notes. As for Theo . . . she was right; her comic book world couldn't save him. He was out of time.

He turned to his new friend. The smirk on her face said it all. He tried to think of a farewell that wouldn't sound condescending or just lame. "I should probably—"

"Don't," she said, and reached a finger up to his lips. "Don't ever say goodbye." With that, she wheeled around and marched off down the cosplay aisle, her ears sticking up through her hair. Theo watched her disappear. It was like watching the last lifeboat hit the water, from a severely listing deck.

Impermanence

The Space Coast, Florida
February 2000

"No cloud cover till three is what Houston says."

"Houston's in Houston."

"Well, I'm standing right here and saying the same thing. Christ, Sid, look at the sky."

"I'm worried about deviation values. Also, could be some wind."

"*Wind?* There's been no wind in weeks."

"Not down here. Upper atmosphere. Could mean a no-go."

"No-go, my ass. You firing-room boys are so damn pessimistic. Now help me lift this grill."

Audrey buried her head in the pillows. It had to be a dream; weather in these parts could permeate your psyche. But no, she was awake—she was pretty sure—because the talking continued. NASA jokes and acronyms. The men were only inches away, or what sounded like inches through the fiberglass trailer wall. Speaking of permeable.

"*Slow down, slow down,*" said one of them. Ed Beemis, it sounded like.

"Okay, but move your end around and—shit, watch out for the propane!"

Audrey opened her eyes. She felt like death. She'd shout at them to shut up but couldn't muster the energy. What were they doing in her front yard? Then it dawned on her. *Of course*. They were setting up for a party. There was a launch this afternoon.

She sat up in stages, assessing the damage. Throbbing head. Parched throat. Hair that smelled like halibut (last night's "Catch of the Day" at Dixie Crossroads). Also, her left hand hurt. She raised it in front of her face and saw dried blood through the Band-Aids. The fucking oysters. The kitchen had been in the weeds so she'd pitched in on her shift break and shucked several dozen sans glove ("bareback," the prep cooks called it). At one point the wait to be seated had been an hour; she kept catching glimpses of the line, snaking out the door and down the ramp past the fishpond. It was the usual launch-week assemblage: retired men in patch-covered bomber jackets; fractious families with high-strung kids; journalists and space geeks and doomsday weirdos. But she'd pocketed $192, which was pretty major. And that should have been the end of it—she'd worked a double and was exhausted—but the kitchen staff had insisted she join them at the Cold Spot on South Hopkins, and because she had a crush on one of the line guys, she'd relented.

The Spot was a biker bar, perpetually wavering between dicey and dangerous. Whiskey shots and beer chasers led to bathroom bumps and one-hitters, the latter courtesy of her friend and dealer Jasper Sash, who had a secret grow operation in the swamps west of Wedgefield. At some point before last call, Audrey had mentioned that her grandmother was running low (if she wasn't already out), and Jasper had promised to stop by later today to remedy the situation.

At least that's how she remembered it.

She reached down and pulled open the drawer built into the frame of her single bed. Her head felt heavier than her body. When had she gotten home? Three? Four? How hard was it to swallow two Advil and a glass of water before passing out? Impossible, it seemed. She felt around until she found an almost-appropriate T-shirt—"A-HA: The Hunting High & Low Tour"—and then slowly stood up and slipped it on, realizing too late that the blinds were open. She was wearing underwear, but still. She pulled on various strings until they were mostly lowered, entertained the thought of locating a bra, then decided it was too much work. Instead, she opened her bedroom door and, marshaling what remained of her strength and ambition, began a Hannibal-over-the-Alps-like journey to the bathroom at the far end of the trailer. Eight steps, give or take.

Her grandmother was nowhere to be seen.

She washed her hands and brushed her teeth (a shower, like a bra, would need to wait), then sauntered into the main room, having rounded out her look with the Daisy Dukes she'd found balled up on the bath mat. She called Connie's name. When there was no reply, she peered out the front window. The LeBaron was gone. Strange; her grandmother almost never drove anymore. Audrey looked around for clues. Their single-wide was comprised of two modest bedrooms separated by a central living/dining/kitchen area. Tight quarters, but Audrey had never felt claustrophobic—even when her grandfather was still alive. The place had plenty of natural light (thanks to sliding patio doors), but more important, Audrey had learned how to live small. The trick was to respect personal space. She and her grandmother wouldn't dream of entering each other's bedrooms without permission. Peeking, though, was a different story, and when Audrey cracked Connie's door, she frowned. The bed was disheveled and her grandmother's night-gown lay crumpled on the floor beside a pair of slippers. This from a woman who was famously neat. Audrey had no idea what it meant, but it couldn't be good.

She found cigarettes in her purse and lit one on the stove. No note on the counter or coffee in the pot. Flummoxed, Audrey opened the front door and stepped out into the Florida sun. The screen slammed behind her and the three men in her yard all looked up in unison. Ed Beemis, Sid Stevens, and Sid's son Kurt. Having moved the grill into place, they were now cleaning it. Kurt was holding a bucket, and when he saw Audrey he briefly lost his grip, causing soapy water to splash his shorts. The two older men chuckled.

"Mornin', darlin'," said Ed. "Sorry we're bangin' around." Ed Beemis was a retired astronaut who'd never been sent to space, his time having come and gone in the dark years following the Apollo program ("Like being a home-run hitter in the dead ball era," he liked to say). Still, this was Cape Canaveral, and being any kind of astronaut was like being any kind of king.

"I needed to get up anyway," Audrey said, taking a drag. She exhaled slowly, through her nose. "What time's the launch?"

"Twelve forty-three in the p.m.," said Sid Stevens. "First mission of the new century." Sid, like Ed, had a buzz cut and a handsome, sun-lined face, though it included a second chin, as he weighed substantially more. He was a retired NASA payload test conductor, and as such, provided the pedantic yang to Ed's blustery yin. Audrey liked both men a great deal. Sid's son, on the other hand, was a moron.

"Looks like we're a go," Ed said, peering up at the sky, which was a deep royal blue. "Though Sid here's worried it might be overcast up in orbit."

Audrey smiled. Space humor, like golf humor and army humor, was so unfunny it was kind of hilarious.

"Which shuttle?" she asked, because she knew men like Ed Beemis and Sid Stevens lived to answer such questions.

"*Endeavour*," Sid said. "Hasn't flown in a while, but she's still our best bird."

"Can I help with anything?" she asked.

"Absolutely not," said Ed. "Just promise to join us once you've had your coffee and gotten dressed. We'll have burgers and bratwursts and a keg on ice."

With that, Ed and Sid turned to assess the grill. Audrey assessed herself. She *was* dressed, she thought. Also assessing her—and far from subtly—was Kurt Stevens. He was in his midthirties, and gaunt, almost concave, with an affinity for baggy T-shirts and camo shorts, a look that worked if you were Eminem but didn't if you weren't. Everything about him seemed sunken: his cheeks, eyes, posture, prospects. Rumor was he'd once had his shit together—had dated cheerleaders and played varsity baseball at Titusville High—though this was hard to reconcile now. To Audrey's knowledge he was not employed. He lived in a single-wide a few lots down from his father, with a Winn-Dixie cashier named Donna and her two small children (the products of earlier unions). Not that Audrey thought much about any of this. She wouldn't have thought about Kurt at all if he weren't ogling her all the time. How was he his father's son? And how did he end up stuck here? Of course, Audrey could ask the same of herself. How was she her mother's daughter? And—no, she wasn't stuck here. Her grandmother needed her help.

Granted, Audrey wasn't known for sartorial modesty—she was already regretting the no-bra decision—but she was young, and this was Florida. Also, she was an actress, and if her professional commitments weren't exactly overwhelming her schedule, why not perfect her real-life role as American Trailer Park Queen—barefoot, bare legged, practically bare breasted (she was in a strategic T-shirt–cutting phase), her dirty brown hair hanging down past the cigarette in her mouth as she shot the shit with a washed-up astronaut.

"By the way, has anyone seen Connie?"

"She drove out of here a half hour ago," Sid said. "Didn't even say good morning. Tell her my feelings are hurt."

"Hope she's not buying anything for the party," Ed added. "She's not allowed."

"I'm sure she knows that," Audrey said, though just then she wasn't too sure of anything. She stubbed her cigarette out on the wooden railing, gave the three men—two, really—a little wave, and sashayed back inside.

The denizens of River Palms Mobile Park had been celebrating shuttle launches in Bill and Connie McAllister's front yard for over a decade now, and while most assumed the tradition was born of geographical circumstance—the yard offered an unobstructed view of Launchpad 39A, five miles north—there was far more to it than that. Connie had related enough of the story that Audrey could now piece together the entire chain of events.

Her grandfather Bill had purchased their lot in the mid-1970s, courtesy of an ad in *Popular Science*. DISCOVER THE EXPLOSIVE SPACE COAST, it proclaimed, above an illustration of sleek waterfront condos with rockets blasting off in the background. At the time, Bill and Connie were living in Benton Harbor, Michigan, a raw lakefront city known for endless winters and perpetual economic decline. No great stretch, then, to imagine her grandfather, a lover of science and an otherwise rational man (he was an engineer, a nuclear specialist), excitedly calling the printed number—1-800-SPACE-FL—and purchasing his future retirement home sight unseen. And then they did see it. He and Connie journeyed to Cape Canaveral a month later and were greeted not by a blue-green ocean and condos under construction, but a gray-brown river and twelve weedy acres zoned for mobile home use. (Bill framed the original ad and hung it above the trailer toilet, where, yellowed by time and humidity, it still resided.)

But River Palms had worked out wonderfully in the end. When Bill retired, a decade after that first visit, he transferred ownership of their Benton Harbor house, against his better judgment, to Audrey's mother, Sharon, and he and Connie headed south for good. They knew the mobile park had come to fruition but were still shocked by what greeted them: flower beds and full occupancy, every lot teeming with life. Bill gazed at their new vinyl-sided trailer and shook his head. How could a place change so completely? The answer was the burgeoning shuttle program, which had stimulated the region's economy (and the nation's morale). And it wasn't just the shuttle. Everything was shooting skyward from the launchpads on Merritt Island. Atlas rockets. Delta IIs. Delta IVs. A scarcity of housing had turned what little non-swampland there was into valuable property, including the area's trailer parks, which had been spruced up to attract the influx of NASA employees. Meteorologists. Maintenance men. Systems analysts. Even astronauts. Some had put down roots.

It was Ed Beemis who invited the McAllisters to witness their first shuttle launch, on a brisk January morning, from the VIP platform on the NASA Causeway. (Bill and Ed had become fast friends in the two months they'd been neighbors, having bonded over a mutual love of science and progress.) The launch had been scrubbed several times that week, and the crowd, bundled up on the grandstand, seemed, to Connie, surprisingly sedate. Ed, at least, was energized, talking a blue streak into Bill's ear, the two of them like kids at recess with only a few minutes to catch up. They passed a pair of binoculars back and forth as the countdown played through the speakers.

When the numbers reached zero, Connie stared out across the water and saw a mushroom of white smoke, followed by the speck of the shuttle itself, moving up and through it. A moment later—the speed of sound—the noise reached them and the ground shook, and as the craft cleared the pad, the collective feeling was not of celebration but relief. Smatterings of applause between exhalations. She watched, awestruck, as the shuttle rolled belly side up, like a pet craving attention, and angled east over the ocean. They always fly that way, Ed explained. He said something about gravitational pull. About the safety of those on the ground. It was a glorious thing to watch, the taming of all that technology. Through the speakers came the clipped argot of ground control, commands given and received. A minute passed and they heard the sonic boom. "That's the all-clear," said Ed Beemis, proudly, definitively. He clapped his hands together. Up in the sky, the shuttle had become a searing dot, the tiny tip of a billowing entrail—clear white amid piercing blue. They were painter's colors, Connie would later tell her granddaughter, and Audrey, having seen enough launches by then, knew exactly the shades.

People gathered what they'd come with. They talked traffic. Even Bill had returned his gaze to earth, having seen what he'd come to see. He looked around for the binoculars case. "Engines throttling up," said Ed Beemis, to no one in particular, and a moment later, over the speakers, those exact words were repeated. Bill grinned. He turned to Connie, but before he could speak Ed squeezed his arm, hard, then grabbed the lenses and sighted them skyward. Bill and Connie looked up and saw it, too, a sudden tumescence in the dissipating line of smoke—like a snake had swallowed a rat—followed by a series of separations, smaller entrails splitting off, twisting in on one another, starting down. "Too soon for the boosters," said a man behind them. "Oh Jesus," said Ed Beemis. The loudspeakers went silent for what seemed an eternity. In the sky, nothing was ascending. Connie found herself thinking not of fireworks raining down, though that's what it looked like, but of the music that often accompanied fireworks. The major chords, dramatic and overwhelming. For the briefest of moments, beauty and catastrophe existed as one, and then the scale tipped violently, and the speakers squawked to life: "Flight controllers looking very carefully at the situation. Obviously a major malfunction."

(Minutes earlier, at Sister Lakes Elementary School in Benton Harbor, Michigan, eighty-four children had placed their hands over their hearts and recited the Pledge of Allegiance. A color TV had been wheeled into the gym and they sat before it on the floor and stared at an image of a spacecraft on a launchpad. They were watching history, they'd been told: the first teacher traveling to space. It was that rare event that could hold even the most rambunctious third grader's attention, and as the countdown began, Audrey stopped bouncing on her heels and joined her classmates counting backward. They cheered when it lifted off, momentarily amazed, if not quite surprised, by the wonders of the world. The shuttle cleared the pad and entered a sky far more radiant than the one above their town. Then it angled onto its back, and Audrey decided the astronaut who was driving must be fiddling with the radio, the way her mom did when she drove through a stoplight. Otherwise, why not keep going straight up? Soon, the kids in the back—Audrey among them—started losing interest. A girl named Alicia pulled a set of cards from her pocket. The new Garbage Pail Kids. She showed them to Audrey, who immediately understood them to be a parody of the Cabbage Patch Kids so beloved by her prissier classmates. As they started flipping through the deck, a noise reached them from up front, a kind of collective gasp. Audrey squinted up at the TV and saw trails of smoke curving downward like ferns. It was really pretty. They must be going super fast, she thought, and turned back to her friends.)

At River Palms, the weeks that followed were marked by non-movement, nonlife. Like a nuclear winter, Bill said to Connie. He couldn't help but feel responsible (men of science being just as superstitious as men of God); his first launch and look what had happened. But what *had* happened? No one knew, not right away, and it was this widening mystery, and the need to discuss it, that brought people back together. Bill McAllister and Ed Beemis found that their friendship had deepened, and they vowed to see the shuttle soar again—only not from the NASA Causeway.

"Screw that bridge," Ed said. They were standing in Bill's front yard, having just returned from a hike along the Banana River Trail.

"Why don't we watch the next one from here?" Bill said. "View's pretty good. We can make it a community thing. Just need to check with Connie."

Fourteen years and many dozens of launch parties later, only one thing had changed. Now, as each countdown entered its final stage, Ed Beemis muted the broadcast, and the residents of River Palms held a moment of silence to honor the man who'd started the tradition. Then they raised a glass to Connie, and the volume went back up, and all eyes turned to the northern horizon.

But where was her grandmother now? Audrey ventured out to the back patio, a square of cracked concrete outfitted with a lattice-patterned table, three mismatched chairs, and an assortment of potted tropical plants. Beyond it lay a lush, dewy yard that gave way to a bank of high reeds leading down to the Banana River and the small dock where Audrey's grandfather had met with calamity. Connie ignored that part of the property, and Audrey couldn't blame her. But she also couldn't subscribe to her grandmother's see-no-evil policy. The river was one of the few constants in Audrey's life, and when Connie was gone she often wandered down the slope and onto the rotting wooden planks. She supposed she was tempting fate, though really, what were the chances it would happen again? (The last guy she'd dated seriously—i.e., five weeks—had told her it was her "coping mechanism," and maybe he'd been right, but she hated phrases like that, clinical explanations of people's habits and eccentricities, and when he'd started in on her "textbook intimacy issues" Audrey had broken up with him.) She found the river beautiful, with its manatees and pink herons. There were still alligators around, of course, but she always kept her eyes on the water and never dangled her legs off the dock. Repeating her grandfather's mistake: *that* would be tempting fate.

Maybe she should head down there now to clear her head, but one missing person was enough. Anyway, the patio was its own form of escape. If the front yard was practically public domain, the back was theirs alone. This was where Audrey and her grandmother spent their time together—eating, drinking, smoking, talking. Audrey lived for old stories about her grandparents, before marriage and work, before her mother, Sharon, was born, and Connie was happy to tell them.

They'd met in 1950, at a church social in Fort Smith, Arkansas, and fallen in love that very night. When Bill was sent to Korea three weeks later, Connie promised to wait. He was gone two years, but it could have been a decade; she wasn't going anywhere. Bill was alive in a way Connie had never known a man to be, and a month after he got home she defied her parents and set off with him through the Ozarks in a thirdhand Plymouth. The America they discovered was tight and provincial, rife with racism and unduly religious. But the country loosened as they traveled north, as industry replaced agriculture and silver cities rose from the flatlands. They danced in Detroit, heard jazz in Chicago, and swam in two Great Lakes. And that was enough. They settled down on the sandy shores of Lake Michigan.

It was funny, the things Audrey's grandmother remembered. Decades of marriage and family and friends, yet her favorite stories involved those early years of wanderlust. Not that Connie's free spirit had ever been tamed. Take her latest hobby: marijuana. Audrey thought it was hilarious, because really, what was the downside in your seventies? A lack of motivation? On the contrary, pot pepped her up. Connie loved everything about it, from the illicitness of procurement, to the rituals of preparation, to the smoking and all that came after. She'd even insist that Jasper Sash smoke with her before he left. "It's protocol," she'd gleefully exclaim (because she'd once heard Audrey say it) as she packed him an oversized bowl.

Audrey considered packing one now but then remembered Connie was almost dry. Probably for the best. She should be helping set up out front, or doing a quick load of laundry—she was working again tonight and had to de-fish her shirt—but both tasks seemed impossibly complicated. Instead, she slumped into a patio chair and, gazing wistfully at the pipe on the table, thought back to the night, three years ago, when she and her grandmother had first smoked weed together. It was a few weeks after Bill's accident and he was still in the hospital, his infection getting worse. Audrey was attending school in Orlando but making the hour-long drive back home most nights to keep Connie company—a straight shot east on Route 50 through swamps and cattle farms, miles of eerie black nothing. On the evening in question, she'd arrived to find the lights already out in her grandparents' bedroom. Good, she thought; Connie needed some sleep. Audrey tiptoed out back, lit a votive candle, and collapsed into the same chair she was collapsed in now. Then she relit the joint she'd been smoking in the car.

Audrey was twenty at the time, and halfway through her junior year as a theater major at the University of Central Florida's College of Arts & Humanities. It was nothing like she'd imagined. Most of her classmates were earnest Christian "thespians" who worked part-time as "performers" at Disney World while waxing poetic about one day "treading the boards" on Broadway. (She'd finally cooled it with the air quotes when Jasper Sash told her she looked evangelical herself, with her arms raised and fingers wiggling.) Audrey could tolerate almost anyone, but God-squadders tested her mettle. All that bright-toothed phoniness. She couldn't help thinking their "beliefs" had less to do with Lords and Saviors than with alleviating the burden of free thought that traditionally accompanied being human. Though what did she know?

Most of young Florida identified as Christian. She was the oddball, but she didn't care. She had the cape to escape to. And Connie needed her help. God, it seemed, had been slacking.

On the patio that fateful night, Audrey had, for the first time, thought about quitting school altogether. Her mounting student loans worried her, especially with her grandparents suddenly facing serious medical costs, but the bigger issue was "the theater" itself. Being in front of a camera was fine, even fun, but as hard as she tried, she couldn't fall in love with the stage. She didn't crave attention, she didn't like Shakespeare, and she sucked at memorizing lines. All of which explained why she forewent student auditions in favor of real ones—meaty roles like "Sexy Car Buyer #1," whose four-second scene involved a leggy emergence from behind the wheel of a brand-new 1998 Explorer SUV from Greenway Ford of Orlando. Audrey appreciated the transactional quality of commercial work. Stand here; say this; chest out; smile. She possessed a coltish all-Americanism that enticed people to buy (or so she'd been told). And what was wrong with that? Everything, to judge by her classmates' condescending attitudes. But she needed the money, and anyway, these were the same Hamlets and Juliets and (blackface) Othellos who went all frothy at the mouth when a Magic Kingdom scout showed up looking for new Goofys. Well, good for them; Audrey had plenty of drama in her real life. Fuck King Lear.

Had she accidentally said those last words out loud that night—she was quite stoned—or had Connie woken up on her own? Regardless, Audrey heard movement in the trailer and, moments later, saw the flickering figure of her grandmother through the candlelight. She was in her nightgown, standing just inside the sliding door. "Mind if I join you?" Connie asked.

"Of course," Audrey said, and motioned toward an empty chair.

"I meant with *that*." She nodded at the joint in Audrey's hand.

"Be my guest," Audrey said, intrigued. "But it's probably a lot stronger than what they had back in . . ." She had no idea when her grandmother had last smoked pot, or if she ever had. Connie sat down and Audrey handed the joint across the table. Her grandmother brought it to her lips and inhaled. She coughed once, and then leaned back and closed her eyes. When she opened them again, she turned and looked out across the yard. It was too dark to see far. Still, it was obvious what she was thinking about. Some memories were always well lit.

"I'll never go down there again," Connie murmured, as if to herself. But her granddaughter heard, and understood. It was Audrey, after all, who'd responded to the cries, and reached him first. It had been weeks, but she hadn't built up the courage to return to the scene either. No one had been back down to the dock—not since Ed Beemis hosed off all the blood.

Connie placed the joint on the side of the ashtray, then reached out and took Audrey's hand. "If something happens to your grandfather, I want you to know that this is your home. For as long as you want."

Audrey *did* know, though she'd never heard the words spoken out loud. They felt good, and she paused to absorb them—every last syllable. Until she realized what they also meant.

"He's not getting better, is he."

It wasn't a question. And it didn't receive an answer. Connie pulled her hand back and went quiet for a long time. Then, all at once, she shuddered, as if emerging from a trance. She picked up the joint and studied it with wide, flame-lit eyes. "Honey, this stuff is . . . I don't know. My limbs are starting to tingle." She giggled then, and so did Audrey, and soon their laughter was drifting off through the heavy air while tears streamed down their faces, from joy and sadness both. Audrey knew it then—that they'd somehow be okay, no matter what happened.

Bill McAllister died six weeks later, following a terrible drawn-out decline. Afterward, Connie entered a period of mourning, which led, in time, to a deeper depression. Audrey owed her so much, and here, she understood, was her chance to repay the debt. Or start to. But that meant growing up, changing her ways, transitioning from cared for to caregiver. Enough with the rebellious phases—grunge, goth, punk, straight-edge (this last one mercifully short). Even as she'd lived through them she'd been aware of their temporality, as if each were a necessary part of a canvas it would take a lifetime to complete—and understand. At Merritt Island High, she'd been a popular girl, known for being nonjudgmental in matters great and small. She was cool in an elemental way, DJing parties and organizing raves. Increasingly, there were boys, and drugs, though the former satiated any great urge for the latter. She liked being pursued, and she liked sex. As for friends, she gravitated toward kids with a look, an aesthetic, an *edge*. That she resided in a trailer park was occasionally mentioned, but the slight had no impact on her. Besides, this was the Space Coast. Everyone had a weird family background. Military. Scientific. Criminal. She lived in the strangest part of the strangest state in the country. The news was all sharks and sinkholes; evangelists and Scientologists; crackheads and lotto winners (often one and the same). No one paid taxes. No one walked anywhere. Audrey laughed when she heard NASA guys talk about Mars. Why try to go there when you already lived here?

But her high school days were long over, and then her college days were, too. The winter following her grandfather's death, she dropped out of UCF and began working full-time—more than full-time. Bill had been only marginally insured, thanks to a cash crunch after the Benton Harbor house "sale," and there were thousands of dollars of unpaid medical bills to deal with. Audrey found work in the classifieds, waitressing, catering, babysitting. She modeled seminude for retirement community painting classes, and fully nude for various "art" photographers—most of them harmless, a few less so. She did more TV ads, worked at a surf shop, put wristbands on kids at a beach club. Still, her focus was on helping Connie, a task she took to like a nun to the novitiate. And if this was the only part of Audrey's life that could be described in religious terms, it was also the part she most cherished. She had often been wanted but never needed. It took time, but eventually, through all the coming and goings, Audrey and her grandmother settled into a rhythm. A few nights a week, Connie would wait up—with weed and wine—and the two of them would talk on the patio for hours. At some point Connie asked her to stop calling her "Grandma," so Audrey called her by her name—like they were peers, best friends, coconspirators.

Out front, Sid Stevens was leading the early arrivals in a spirited, if tone-deaf, rendition of "America the Beautiful." Connie never missed a moment of these parties, which made her absence that much more worrisome. She must be stuck in launch-day traffic. Audrey thought about borrowing someone's car—but to do what? Drive around aimlessly? Get stuck as well? It was time to buy Connie (and herself) a cell phone. Most of Audrey's friends had them now, but phone plans were expensive, and reception on the Space Coast was notoriously spotty courtesy of the weird shit NASA was always up to. She peered in at the kitchen clock. Eleven fourteen a.m. Ugh.

She went inside, got her dirty clothes together, and made her way barefoot, through backyards, to the community building. The laundry room was empty, so she bought some Wisk from the Gemini-era vending machine and threw everything into the closest washer. (Audrey's shirts and shorts and bras and bikinis were very thin, and very small, and they all fit easily into one load.) Quarters next, and when the machine didn't start she hip-checked it into action. She was good at this part; far more challenging would be remembering to come back in an hour. Her record for number of days passed before switching clothes to the dryer was three, which, it turned out, was exactly the length of time it took for mold to develop. You could rewash your stuff a hundred times after that and never get the smell out. Whatever, she was working on life.

Audrey ambled back beside the unpaved main drive, stopping briefly to greet Mrs. Danforth, who was watering her window boxes. She and her husband were new arrivals from Omaha, Audrey remembered, glancing at the red Cornhusker license plate on their trailer to be sure. The plates were required by law (though most of these homes weren't going anywhere), and Audrey always took a moment to study them. So many states she'd never visited. Just now, she'd walked past Illinois, Montana, Nebraska, New York, Maine, California, New York, and New York. She felt a tinge of longing. And then a surge. She was twenty-three years old and lived with her grandmother in a Florida trailer park full of retirees. She could spin it any way she wanted, but these were the base facts of her life. And while she couldn't imagine leaving Connie alone, this couldn't be all there was. The dead-end jobs. The unfinished education. The half-assed attempt at acting. She thought of Kurt Stevens, stalled out at thirty-five. But that only made her feel worse.

The twang of a roadhouse country song reached her from her front yard—speakers had been set up—and when it ended she heard cheering. For a moment she thought Connie might be arriving home, but the carport, when it came into view, was still LeBaron-less. At least thirty people were milling about now, drinks in hand. Soon, they'd cut the music in favor of the NASA radio broadcast, but not just yet. Where the hell was her grandmother? She should talk to Ed, because even accounting for traffic, there was no way Connie should have been gone for so—

There she was! Turning in through the front gate. Audrey hurried over to the car as it crept up beside their trailer, marveling at the serendipity of Connie's appearing just as she was willing her to, only to realize she'd been willing her grandmother to appear from the minute she'd found her missing. The trunk popped open and Connie opened her door to get out. She looked up to find Audrey staring at her.

"Don't just stand there, darling, help me with these groceries."

"Where have you . . . you bought stuff for the party? Wait, are you okay?"

"Yes, yes, I'm fine," Connie said, peering around. "Oh, look at all the people."

But she wasn't fine. She seemed scattered and disoriented. Her normally pinned-down hair was wild, her blouse off by a button.

Audrey walked around to the trunk. Inside were a dozen bags filled with more food than they usually bought in a month. "Why don't you head inside," Audrey said. "I'll get everything. We can come back out in a little while."

She'd never spoken to her grandmother like this—like the woman was a child—but Connie complied. Audrey grabbed what she could and followed her in. She put the bags on the kitchen counter as her grandmother began manically fluffing couch pillows.

"I'm sorry," Connie said. "I should have left a note, but there was no time."

"What do you mean?"

"Here, let me put that food away. You don't know where anything goes." She hastened over to Audrey, practically elbowing her aside.

"*Hey.*" Audrey took hold of Connie's shoulders. "What's going on? You're acting crazy."

It took her grandmother a moment to focus, to return from wherever she'd been. "It's your mother," Connie said finally. "She's coming by."

Audrey pulled away. "*Here? Today?*"

"She called this morning, while you were asleep, and said she was 'in the area' and wanted to watch the launch with us."

"And you told her she could?"

"Honey, I didn't have much choice. She knows where we live!"

"That's news to me." Audrey patted her pockets for her cigarettes but came up empty. "What else did she say?"

"That it had been far too long."

"Only seven years."

"Actually, she sounded quite upbeat."

"Of course she did. She knows you'll write her a check."

"Audrey, that's enough."

"Maybe she can hit up some of the old guys out front as well."

"I said *enough*."

The two women stared at each other through narrow eyes, then Audrey looked away. When she turned back, her grandmother was trembling.

"It's okay," Audrey said, softening. She put her arms around her.

Connie shook her head into Audrey's shoulder. "I'm sorry, I just . . . I got off the phone and panicked, and the next thing I knew I was at the supermarket, buying everything in sight."

Audrey felt tears against her neck, and she reached for a dish towel. As she offered it to Connie there was a knock at the door. The dish towel fell to the floor.

"Oh God," Audrey said. "Already?"

"She told me she'd be cutting it close, which I figured meant twelve fifteen or twelve thirty."

Audrey looked at the kitchen clock. It was only 11:35. "Maybe it's Jasper Sash. He promised to stop by today—speaking of criminal visitations."

Whoever it was knocked again, more firmly. "I'm not getting it," Audrey said. She didn't care if she was being petulant. She wasn't ready for this.

"Fine." Connie wiped her eyes and took a breath large enough to move her shoulders. Then she walked across the room and, hesitating only briefly, pulled the front door open.

"Hello there, old girl, everything all right in here?"

Sid Stevens. Audrey wanted to run over and jump into his arms.

"Yes, of course," Connie said, through the screen. "Just running a bit behind."

"Well, we're almost inside of an hour, so hurry on up. I'll save you a hot dog. Oh, and you left your trunk open."

"I'll get it," Audrey said from the kitchen.

Connie headed for her room as Audrey went out and grabbed the rest of the groceries. As she closed the trunk, she heard Kurt Stevens call her name. She looked over and he raised his beer. Audrey attempted a smile in return but couldn't manage it.

Back inside, she started putting things away—soft cheeses, veggies and dips, bottled white instead of the box chardonnay they normally drank. Connie hadn't been kidding. Never shop in a panic was the lesson here. Also (while she was rolling with the aphorisms): if you work at a seafood restaurant, shower as soon as you wake up. Audrey could smell halibut and Connie hadn't purchased any. She finished in the kitchen and seized upon the open bathroom. She needed to compose herself. Her mother was coming. She turned the water on and stepped into the shower before it had warmed up. But she didn't care. She scrubbed her skin and shampooed her hair, once, twice, three times, until she realized she was digging her nails into her scalp. She didn't stop. She was angry. She was furious. She suddenly wanted to scream.

Audrey had lived in Michigan with her mother for the first fifteen years of her life but remembered the woman mostly as an absence, a human-shaped void. The sparsely furnished apartment in St. Joe's (Clint); the three-room bungalow in Saginaw (Warren); the extended-stay motel in South Haven (Barry). (Barry!) She recalled all these way stations, and all these men, but not her mother—in them, with them, with *her*. Then her grandparents relocated to Florida, and Sharon and ten-year-old Audrey moved into the family house, a cozy Colonial on the rapidly devolving east side of Benton Harbor. She had loved visiting the place when Bill and Connie lived there, but now it felt different. Tired and dated. Like a black-and-white movie in a Technicolor world. Or maybe the house was fine and she just missed her grandparents. Regardless, this was where Audrey lived, increasingly by herself, through her formative years.

Children never ask the right questions. Young Audrey McAllister wondered how airplanes could fly and parrots could talk but accepted her mother's constant absences and the problems they raised—rides needed, meals uncooked, utilities unpaid—without complaint. It was the only reality she knew. The reasons for Sharon's behavior during those years hadn't interested Audrey until recently, but the few times she'd brought the subject up, Connie would get shifty, even short, and so her wayward mother had remained a mystery, undiscussed and undiscovered. Now, though, with Sharon about to descend upon them like the tornado she'd always been, Audrey wished she and her grandmother *had* gone there, wherever *there* was, as much to build a unified front as to satisfy various curiosities. No, that was bullshit. Audrey wanted to know things.

She turned the shower off and stepped out through the steam. She could hear the revelers outside, smell the tang of barbecue through the bathroom window. She toweled off and dried her hair. Why was Connie so reluctant to talk about her daughter when she was so open about everything else? Did she blame herself? Audrey knew her grandmother believed in context and circumstance. A person didn't fall apart in a vacuum. But what had Connie done wrong? What had anyone done wrong? There lay the crux of the convoluted issue that was Sharon McAllister. Audrey, for her part, laid the blame squarely on her mother. In thrall to her addictions, Sharon had abandoned everyone in her life—everyone who knew her, everyone who could help. And so it was that in one woman's failures two others had come to grief. Luckily, her mother had been gone so long now that Audrey could almost forget about her. Almost.

For the first time, Audrey wondered what the woman might look like. Seven years had passed. Where did she live? (Somewhere in South Florida was all anyone really knew.) And what had she been through? Audrey thought about her own recent history. She'd *matured*, but she hadn't *changed*. She still said yes too much—to boys, bands, parties, trouble—and she was perpetually late. Surrounded by NASA men who told time to the second, Audrey rounded off to the hour. Well, she wouldn't be late for her mother.

In her bedroom, she waded through the remnants of her wardrobe until she spied a summer dress that wasn't too wrinkled or low cut. She slithered into it, spent three minutes on makeup and three more looking for shoes. How could she never find anything in a single-wide? For that matter, why was she trying so hard? Fuck it. She wouldn't. Sharon didn't deserve it. She yanked the dress back off and put on the same outfit she'd been wearing all morning (this time with a bra). Through the blinds, she could see old people dancing. Maybe things would be okay.

A crash came from the kitchen and Audrey ran out to find her grandmother picking up a fallen platter of chopped vegetables.

"Sorry, I'm a wreck," Connie said, shaking her head. In fact, she looked beautiful, and Audrey told her as much. She'd fixed her hair and changed into tan pants and a loose white blouse accented by an elegant shell necklace. A Billie Holiday record was playing, and a cheese board sat on the counter beside an open bottle of white wine.

"*T-minus thirty minutes!*" came a shout from the lawn, and everyone cheered.

The real-world clock read 12:03 p.m. It would be just like her mother to roll in dramatically, ten minutes before the launch. Or, more accurately, it would be just like Audrey's idea of her mother, actual evidence of the woman's movements being scant.

"Should we hit the party?" Audrey asked. "We *are* the hosts."

Connie grabbed the bottle. "I have a better idea. Get two glasses and follow me out back."

Audrey did as she was told. The winter sun was now directly overhead, and they positioned their patio chairs to soak up what they could. Connie poured the wine and for a moment they sat there listening to the countdown coverage emanating from the speakers out front.

"This must be what it's like backstage at one of those concerts you're always going to," Connie said. "Peace and quiet a few feet from a roaring crowd."

"There's like twelve people at the concerts I go to. And backstage is usually a bathroom."

They clinked glasses and fell quiet. Connie shifted in her chair. Audrey wondered what was bothering her grandmother more: Sharon's imminent arrival, or a lack of weed with which to temper its effects.

Just when the silence was becoming awkward, Connie leveled Audrey with an odd stare. "I know I've been reluctant to discuss your mother," she said. "But to be honest, I've never quite known what to say. I don't have an answer for how she ended up like she did. All those men and drugs and problems with the law. Bill and I tried everything. Camps and counseling. Money and support. She never lacked for love."

The hair on Audrey's arms was standing up, and she hugged herself to hide it. Among "all those men" was her own father. Who, exactly, he was, she'd never known, and probably never would. Of course, she'd asked when she was younger, a million times, and a million times her mother had lied or dodged the question, until the answer made itself obvious enough: Sharon had no idea either. What was Audrey to do then but make peace with her reality. Or try.

Connie must have sensed her granddaughter's unease. "After you came along, things got better for a while," she said. "She met that older man, Warren, who calmed her down, at which point we decided to move down here. Your mother asked for our house, all but demanded it, and we eventually gave in. What choice did we have? Bill sold it to her for a dollar and hoped for the best. At the signing, Sharon showed up quite literally penniless, and you, all of eight years old, had to give her four quarters that she then passed on to us. Otherwise it wouldn't be official."

Audrey dimly remembered that last part but recalled with far greater clarity her mother's tragic final act, six years later. Audrey was in ninth grade—this was 1991—and living by herself at the house (Sharon had all but disappeared by then). She was almost completely self-sufficient. She played third base on her softball team and skateboarded with punks; she dated a black boy, listened to techno from Detroit, and worked part-time at the local ice cream parlor. That is, she had made a life for herself. *By* herself. Her friends knew the situation, and even a few of her friends' parents, but no one had called child services or told anyone at school. In Benton Harbor everyone's family was messed up.

Then, one afternoon, Audrey arrived home to find her mother's dented Chevy Citation parked out front. The woman herself was talking on the kitchen phone with Grandpa Bill, in Florida, and barely registered her daughter's arrival. Why did she have to come home to make the call? Audrey wondered. And then it hit her: she had to pretend she still lived in the house! Audrey didn't need to hear both sides of the conversation to understand that Bill was refusing to send her money, because Sharon was yelling into the receiver. When that produced no results, she slammed the phone onto its cradle, ripped the cord from the wall, and threw it across the room. It hit the refrigerator and broke into pieces. Sharon ordered her daughter to pick up the mess, but Audrey didn't move. Up close, she could see how unhealthy her mother looked. Her hair, her skin, her *bones*. Once, she'd been a real stunner—Audrey had seen photos—and that's what she told her:

"Mom, you used to be so pretty."

How had young Audrey meant it? Certainly not in the way it was received, which was with shock, followed by indignation, followed by a slap, hard and without warning, across the side of Audrey's jaw. Her mother, enraged, wound up a second time, but Audrey was quicker. She hit back, a closed fist to her mother's sallow cheek, and watched her go down.

What followed was a fragile peace born of separation, Sharon disappearing again for weeks, before showing up at the house one Saturday morning in July to find her daughter entwined on the couch with her boyfriend, James. They were mostly clothed, but still. Audrey jumped up, ready for anything.

But Sharon was upbeat and appeared unbothered by her daughter's indiscretion. She sent James on his way, then told Audrey to run upstairs and pack because they were going on vacation. A weeklong mother-daughter road trip to see Bill and Connie down in Cape Canaveral. Wasn't that exciting? Sharon attempted to hug her daughter and Audrey attempted to let her. A *vacation*? She supposed stranger things had happened, though just then she couldn't think of any.

The drive took three days, with Sharon alternately sweet and manic, telling funny family stories and then, after a pit stop, getting back behind the wheel and denouncing for hours the many people who had wronged her. Audrey didn't listen. She'd never been out of the Midwest and couldn't wait to see Florida. Her grandparents, the launchpads, the beach—

"Maybe even Disney World," Sharon kept saying. But Audrey didn't care about Disney World. Didn't her mother know her at all?

It was 102 degrees on the morning they arrived at River Palms. Bill and Connie took them to lunch in Cocoa Beach, and afterward, Connie drove her exhilarated granddaughter to see the ocean for the first time—just the two of them. When they got back home, Audrey's grandfather was pacing the front lawn. There'd been an argument over money, Bill told Connie, and Sharon had peeled off in her car. She'd taken all her things and none of Audrey's. Still, Bill assumed she'd be back in an hour or two.

A day or two.

A week.

After that, they knew.

"It would be helpful if your friend Jasper got here before your mother," Connie said.

"I think we can call him *our* friend at this point. Also, it's Jasper *Sash*. You have to say both names. We've been doing it since high school."

"Why?"

"Just because. It doesn't make any sense."

"Tell me what does," Connie said ruefully.

Audrey spied her cigarettes on a side table and practically jumped up to grab them. She tapped one out and lit it, sucking in slow, blowing out slower.

"The way you smoke," her grandmother said. "It's the way women used to smoke when smoking was wonderful."

"It's wonderful right now."

"I'll bet," said Connie. "I smoked for years. Pall Malls. Bill made me stop in the midseventies, when the warnings showed up on the packs. Or anyway, he thought he did. I snuck them on and off for another decade. It sounds stupid now, but it wasn't even about the smoking itself. I just needed something that was mine alone."

"That doesn't sound stupid."

Connie leveled her eyes at her granddaughter. "Honey, you should never be afraid to keep a few secrets. Sometimes it's better that way."

Audrey bit her lip and considered this. Connie was the only person in her life who ever said anything profound.

"*T-minus twenty and holding*," someone cried, and then came the whiz and pop of a Roman candle. Somebody jumping the gun. NASA guys were like kids when it came to fireworks; they bought them in bulk up in South Carolina and spent whole weekends choreographing shows. There'd be one later tonight, though Audrey would be at work. She was always at work.

"How long's the twenty-minute hold?" Connie asked. "I always get confused."

"Ten minutes. Unless they find something wrong."

"So we've actually got a half hour?"

"Yup."

"Well, I daresay our dealer friend appears to be derelict in his duties."

"What does that make my mother?"

"She'll be here," Connie said. "She told me she'd never seen a launch before and that she wouldn't miss it for the world."

"How charming."

Audrey was restless. The idea of her mother controlling her actions even the slightest bit angered her more with each passing minute—or had, before time was put on hold. She drifted into a vague melancholia, her thoughts tinged with a sorrow she couldn't name. Actually, she could, and it was this: How does a mother abandon a child? How does someone cease to function as a feeling person? These were not new questions. They'd haunted her for years. Still, it hurt to relive it all. Audrey had come to believe the great depths of her mother's betrayal would be hers to navigate alone, but now she understood: her grandmother was hurting just as badly. Of course she was. Sharon was her *daughter*. Her only child. Audrey had misread her grandmother's stoicism as a lack of sentiment. All those years of pent-up anger, thinking no one would understand. But Connie would have. Connie did.

"You know what?" Audrey said. "If she shows up, she shows up. But let's at least go have some fun."

"You're absolutely right."

They stood up together and made their way around the trailer. What greeted them was happy chaos, forty-plus adults and at least a dozen children, running around with sugar-high abandon. Connie was accosted by Rose Beemis—"There you are!"—and led by the hand into the center of the fray. Audrey lingered on the outskirts until Mrs. Scanlon, whose daughter she babysat, sidled over to inquire about her upcoming schedule. Several times, Audrey glanced toward the main entrance of the park, until finally, annoyed at herself, she turned her back to it. They were at T-minus ten when Ed Beemis whistled once and brought the crowd to attention.

The tribute lasted a few minutes: a quick Bill McAllister anecdote, a moment of radio-muted silence, and then a glass raised to Connie. Audrey teared up; she always did. And then it was over, and the countdown was at T-minus six, and everyone was looking around for their loved ones like it was New Year's Eve.

Audrey wandered over to an empty part of the yard. She had witnessed upwards of forty launches now, and every one of them had stayed with her for days afterward.

"T-minus four minutes."

Her fucking mother. Of course she'd miss the launch.

"T-minus two."

The partygoers quieted down until it was just the radio—that dispassionate NASA voice. Audrey turned to the north, training her eyes on the tree line across the river.

Grand words filled her head. Majesty. Vastness. Impermanence. She felt her grandmother's hand on her shoulder and placed her own on top of it. At thirty seconds, the kids joined the countdown. At ten, everyone. And then there it was, the swell of smoke, followed by a shake of the earth and a breaking wave of sound as the shuttle appeared, rising slowly on the back of its rust-colored escort. Connie squeezed Audrey's shoulder. The elegance of physics. The miracle of a million moving pieces. *Endeavour* cleared the pad. Audrey looked back at the awestruck crowd in her yard, craning their necks, training their binoculars. Some of them had helped make the space shuttle fly. What a thought.

When she peered skyward again, the shuttle was doing its roll. "This part always makes me anxious," Connie said quietly. Audrey pulled her in close.

It had been the two of them for a long time now.

When the contrails began dissipating, they ambled back to the party. The mood was exuberant. Ed was explaining booster separation to a trio of fascinated teenagers. Sid had re-manned the grill. Connie joined a group of women she often played cards with, leaving Audrey to wander over to the keg. What the hell. She could toast her mother's continued absence from her life.

"*Hey.*" She turned around. Kurt Stevens was heading directly for her. "Let me get you a beer," he said, and cut in front of her. He wore a not-quite-gallant look on his face—like he'd laid his coat across a puddle but might snatch it up when she took the step. There were no cups left, so he found one on the grass and put it under the hose.

"Thanks," Audrey said dryly.

Kurt didn't bother tilting it, and when he handed it to her it was two-thirds foam. She would have thanked him again, but detecting sarcasm clearly wasn't his strong suit. Nothing was.

"Good launch," he said. "Guess they all are when they don't blow up, right?"

Audrey considered dumping the beer on his head, but the effort seemed too much.

"What are you hunting for?" he asked.

"Excuse me?"

"Your shirt. It says, 'Hunting High and Low.'" He pointed at her chest.

"Seriously? Kurt, I need to go get ready for work."

"Hold on," he said, reluctantly moving his eyes up to her face. "I've decided I want to take you to dinner. A real nice place."

"You're kidding." He wasn't kidding. "Kurt, I'm . . . seeing someone." She was actually seeing several someones, so it wasn't a lie, exactly. "Anyway, don't you live with your girlfriend?"

"We're done," he said. "Not that that's none of your business."

"It is if you're asking me out."

"Come on, I'll take you to Titusville. Dixie Crossroads."

"That's where I work."

"Perfect. You'll know what's good."

One part of her was relieved Kurt hadn't previously known her place of employment, and another was concerned that he now did. A third part—if she could be so complex—was amazed by his expectation that she'd say yes. Was her reputation catching up with her?

"Kurt, the timing's all wrong. Why don't we get some friends together and build a bonfire down by the river one of these nights?"

But his eyes had turned small. There was no reasonable way to say no to a man like this. "Surprised you want to go anywhere near that river," he said coolly.

"What did you say?"

"Nothin'. I'll see you around." With that, he turned and stalked off.

She wanted to chase him down, hit him in his bony face. But he wasn't worth it. She looked around one last time. The party would go on for a few more hours, but Audrey had had enough. She walked back inside and collapsed on the couch.

Her mother wasn't coming. Jasper Sash wasn't coming (not now, with all the traffic). And she had to be at work in two hours. How was she so exhausted already? Nothing had happened today. That wasn't true; men had been launched into space. What she meant was that *she* had done nothing. But that wasn't true either. She stared at the walls of the trailer and thought of young Bill and Connie driving through the Ozarks and finally admitted what she'd known for a while now. She was stuck. She'd misread her thirst for variety as a sign of forward progression. But only the names ever changed. Boys. Car dealerships. Space shuttles. Her life was as stagnant as the swamps west of the interstate. She needed to get out.

At some point, Connie bustled in carrying platters of half-eaten pasta and potato salad. "*There* you are," she said, deftly closing the front door with her foot. "Not in a party mood, I take it? Me either." Audrey watched her grandmother transfer the food into plastic containers with a mounting sense of guilt—this woman who had taken such care of her. How could Audrey return that favor and still live her own life?

It was closing in on two p.m., but Audrey didn't want to get ready yet. She began telling Connie about an upcoming audition—another tight-dress deal for a personal injury law firm—but was interrupted by a knock on the front door. Audrey couldn't believe it. She looked at her grandmother apprehensively. "Maybe it's Jasper," she half whispered.

"Say his last name, too," Connie whispered back. And that did it—broke the tension. Connie burst out laughing. "It's your turn," she said, and Audrey shrugged. Mother or dealer—she was ready for anything. She stood up, walked across the room, and, hesitating only slightly, pulled open the door.

"Audrey!" cried Ed Beemis.

"Thank God," Audrey exclaimed, and slumped against the door frame.

Ed looked at her quizzically as she stood aside to let him in. "I hope I'm not disturbing you, but I've barely seen—there you are!" Ed said, spying Connie. "How about one last drink before we call it a day."

"Oh, Ed, I'd love to, thank you."

Connie invited him out to the patio, and soon Rose Beemis joined them, followed by Sid and Grace Stevens and a few other stragglers—all of them red-faced and exuberant. Audrey brought the cheese plate outside, then put a Gershwin record on and turned the volume up. She watched them awhile longer. Connie, among her friends, looked like the happiest person on earth—and that's when Audrey knew. Her grandmother would be okay without her. These people loved her. They'd take care of her. As for her mother . . . Audrey recognized Sharon's traits in her own dissident nature, but that was all they shared. She owed the woman nothing. She thought about license plates. About cities she'd never seen. Becoming an adult didn't mean staying. It meant going—when you were ready, when it was time. And—*shit*—it meant switching your laundry over so you had something clean to wear to work.

Chapter Four

Café Loup was a handsome, low-ceilinged restaurant with dark wood fixtures, white brick walls, and a changeless, timeworn feel that served, paradoxically, to keep the place perpetually in vogue. Theo arrived at 2:35 p.m., ten minutes early for his appointment, but otherwise late for the lunch crowd, and the few remaining patrons sat lingering over coffee as a jazz trio tiptoed through a dusty classic. Win hadn't arrived yet, which was a relief. After the failed Forbidden Planet expedition, Theo needed time to formulate a Plan B. He sat down at a two-top below a photograph of Picasso smoking a pipe beside a wood-burning stove and looked for a waiter, but no one was around. Shit. Was the restaurant closing? It didn't seem possible. Nothing closed anymore. American Apparel sold hot pants at midnight. Art house cinemas had two a.m. showings. Four-star restaurants offered three-course breakfasts. Theo had been aware that mid–Saturday afternoon wasn't exactly prime time when it came to work meetings, but in the languid silence of the restaurant it hit home. In football, they called this garbage time. He imagined Win being driven back uptown after his real lunch at someplace like the Odeon, telling his driver to take a quick left on Thirteenth and double-park for a few minutes—he wouldn't be any longer than that.

Theo needed to relax. He let his mind drift as he peered around the subdued room. The history of the place. The city's vanishing worlds never vanished completely. In New York, there was always one last meat packer, one last seltzer truck, one last typewriter repair shop. Café Loup was the last literary haunt. Situated close to NYU, the New School, and the old-line publishers of the Flatiron District, Loup had for decades played host to an omnium-gatherum of book-world types attracted to the soft lighting, stiff drinks, and somewhat affordable food. But the real draw was the crowd. Legends sipped highballs in back corners (Theo had personally laid eyes on Gay Talese, Hilton Als, and Fran Lebowitz), while lesser names preened at lesser tables: agents and editors, biographers and theater producers, dandies and sophisticates, novelists turned professors, actresses turned retired. And, too, the necessary filler: the younger writers and older writers and wannabe writers, the couples on dates, the mothers with daughters, and at the bar, whiskey-drinking journalists, martini-drinking publicists, and, starting at ten p.m., the New School grad students, rolling in en masse after evening seminars, the introverted among them peeling off to read the *Paris Review* or *Granta*, alone but with cover aloft, in case somebody noticed. Theo recalled his own aspirational early visits and the sublime (to him) conversation always swirling in the air—talk not just of industry gossip but books themselves, the inner workings of words. In those days, he had known no one in publishing, but even years later, as a full-fledged editor armed with a company credit card, he'd arrive at Loup to meet a writer or agent for dinner and still, somehow, feel like an outsider. There was always a better table, deeper in.

A waiter swept past and Theo called out, too late. Had he not noticed him sitting there? Theo looked nervously at his watch, then pulled a notebook from his bag and read through what little it contained.

Plan B, such as it was, consisted of two book pitches. Both were obscure small-press novels that probably wouldn't be making the Hollywood rounds, but Theo had read them in that breathless, ineffable way that people who love books respond to those they love best. The first was an oddball story about two young friends, a straight Brazilian woman and a gay American man, trying to pull off a sham green card marriage. Common enough, especially in New York, but the twist comes when their government interviewer—a middle-aged loner from Queens—figures out they're faking it and tries to extort them. In the book he wants cash, but in the film, what if they changed it to sex? And what if she said yes? Maybe the two friends end up conning the con man, extorting the extorter. *gotta thnk mre comercialy!* Well, now Theo was. It had a gay angle, an immigrant angle, a sex angle, a crime angle . . . even a log line: *The Birdcage* meets *Indecent Proposal* meets *The Sting*. Because who wanted anything original anymore?

Which was exactly the problem with the second book: It was *completely* original, in that the plot that drove the narrative forward became a ruse that served only to illuminate the characters themselves. Their fears and foibles. Their quiet hopes. He didn't even know how to pitch this one, except to say that in an age of manufactured suspense, this was a story about people, relationships, humanity—

"Can I get you something?"

Theo looked up to find the waiter looming over him. So they *were* still serving. "Yes, sure, a drink please." But what? A cocktail sent the wrong message, though he could use one. And a beer, also tempting, seemed shoddy. A Diet Coke, maybe, though he didn't drink Diet Coke, which was too Hollywood anyway. "White wine would be great," Theo said. "Anything you've got open." The waiter nodded and walked off.

What had he just done? He hated white wine. But Win—even in absentia—had him flustered. It was his boss's great gift; he entered your mind and took up residence. He had always had a magnetic personality—too *smooth* for Theo's taste, but it was a charming, erudite smoothness. Win made eye contact, remembered names, and dished out compliments, so really, how could he be accused of phoniness in a time when people did none of those things anymore? In Theo's first years at Prosaic, Win (or Wynne, back then) had been the editor he'd most admired, for the man championed the *tough* books—the experimental novels and voice-driven memoirs that moved souls, if not copies. But while other Prosaic editors promoted their titles with deference and humility, Wynne marketed his by shouting from rooftops. This endeared him to his authors more than his colleagues, but the sad truth, Theo knew, was that literary fare needed as much buzz as possible, and if it took a gregarious editor prostrating himself on *Charlie Rose*, so be it. Wynne had the support of Bunny Beale, Prosaic's illustrious editor in chief, so what dissent there was remained muted, murmured—more or less unspoken.

Besides, change was afoot. Bookstores were closing, ebooks gaining traction, and no one had the slightest idea what it all meant. *Look what happened to the music business*, editors with no knowledge of the music business kept saying. Theo, still an assistant then, watched the progression of events with wide and fearful eyes. "We need to broaden our scope," ". . . be all things to all people," ". . . become a full-service publisher." These and other dictates were handed down by "management," a theretofore foreign word at the publisher that began surfacing regularly in meetings and all-staff emails. (Prosaic, once family owned, was now controlled by a complex nesting doll of corporations, the largest being a Norwegian holding company originally in the shipbuilding business.) Theo, like every mill-town kid, knew firsthand what "management" was capable of. The "all things to all people" strategy: it was always the last one. Teddy bears on bookstore shelves. Dollar oysters at the bar.

And sure enough, here they came: cookbooks, how-to, health and wellness, sci-fi, even romance, popping up in catalogs alongside the highbrow fiction for which Prosaic was known. One fed the other, went the argument, but the editorial-side purists weren't having it. Everyone, that is, except Wynne, who, seeing the proverbial writing on the wall, "broadened his scope" by adding to his list works of a somewhat less stringent intellectualism ("pseudo-" was the prefix often used behind his back). This coincided with his interest in Theo Gorski, Bunny Beale's earnest, hardworking assistant, who had done well line-editing some of her lesser titles. A deal was struck and Theo was transferred from her realm to his—a move Theo both welcomed (it was nominally a promotion) and worried over (Bunny ran things, after all). But Wynne made it easy. They were both New Englanders, and college athletes (even if Wynne's biography—Brookline, Brown, squash—differed in tone from his new protégé's: Lawrence, Colgate, football). And of course they shared a love of literature. Wynne, however, had other ideas for Theo—an entire genre of them.

No one ever settled on a category name—Pop Sociology? Pop Psychology? Pop Science?—so the books Wynne began buying were lumped into "Nonfiction," a decision that grew increasingly ironic over time. In-house, they were known as Wynne's One-Word Wonders (WOWWs), though the one-word titles were inevitably followed by long, unwieldy subtitles. Subject matter varied greatly, but taken together the books shared the goal, according to their editor, of "condensing mankind's complexities into digestible morsels." Wynne hadn't invented the genre, of course. *Cod* was the fish that changed the world, until *Salt* changed it more, followed by *Bananas*, and *Oil* (which actually *had* changed the world, Theo supposed), and on and on, until the concrete had given way to the conceptual, and suddenly the world was being changed not by fish or fuel but by trends and statistics, easy theories sprung from thin research and coincidence. People wanted fast answers, simple explanations, dinner party talking points, and Wynne was all too ready to provide them.

He signed up brainy celebrities, accessible academics, and futurists of every stripe—men and women in odd-shaped eyewear who championed words like "actualization," "counterintuity," and "solutionism," this last -ism moving to the fore as technology spun the culture like a centrifuge, ever faster, until no one cared about the past or present— only next year, next month, tomorrow, tonight. If Wynne's authors were the new vendors of ideas, he would control their frontier marketplace. Who cared if the reviewers called it "science by sound bite." Books were only the beginning. Think platforms, he said. Think brands. Think anything you want.

How appropriate, then, that the first WOWW Theo worked on was called *THUNK!: The Sound of Everything You Thought You Knew Suddenly Turning Out to Be Wrong*, an elongated *Wired* article penned by a Silicon Valley "disrupter" whose sole credential was a disjointed

TEDx talk delivered in a side room at a South by Southwest digital conference. The "book" was as inelegant as its title, 164 roomy pages of droll platitudes Theo couldn't believe Prosaic was publishing. Still, he dove in. Small edits led to large ones, and soon he was rewriting entire chapters, inserting details and footnotes, even adding a bibliography. And of course the book had bombed, been back-shelved, been pulped instead of paperbacked. Theo had ruined it by adding substance. His one souvenir from the episode was a Post-it note he found stuck to his computer the day the first sales figures came in. *T - Not everyone wants to be smart*, it read, in Wynne's unmistakable scrawl. Theo appreciated the message, even if it flew in the face of everything he'd ever believed, and he kept it on his monitor until the yellow corners curled and it fell, leaflike, to the floor.

Theo left Wynne's next title alone. *SPORTSWISE: Big Answers from Big Athletes* was uncomfortably similar to the pre-Theo *THUNK!*, in terms of both content and general incoherence. But it didn't matter. A month after publication *SPORTSWISE* appeared on the *Times* best-seller list, where it remained for seventeen inconceivable weeks. This kicked off a run of bestselling WOWWs, yet as the successes mounted, sightings of Wynne became more sporadic. His coworkers assumed he was busy—he still had his stable of reputable novelists, after all—but Theo suspected something else was afoot. He saw the expense reports— the flights to LA, the pricey hotels—but even he could never have guessed what would happen next. Everyone (including Bunny) found out at the same time, in the "Deal News" section of Publishers Lunch:

> *Source It!: How Asking One Simple Question Can Change the World*, which offers an easy solution to the many problems of modern life, by Prosaic executive editor Wynne Groome, to HarperCollins, in a major seven-figure deal.

"Well, what is it?" Bunny asked Theo, who'd immediately been summoned to her office (Wynne being nowhere to be found).

"What's what?"

"The fucking question!"

"I don't know," Theo answered, genuinely flummoxed, to say nothing of petrified, standing, as he was, before a highly agitated publishing legend. "It's like something from Beckett."

"Excuse me?"

"Well, not only do we not know the answer, but we don't know the—"

"Out!"

Nine months later, *Source It!* debuted at number one in the *Times*. By then, Wynne was living in Malibu, cowriting *Source It!: The Documentary* and raising venture money for Round Circle Films. Within a year, the documentary had been accepted to Sundance (where it would win the Audience Prize), a follow-up book was in the works (*Source It!: The Sequel*), Round Circle was on a content-buying spree, and its CEO now went by Dr. Win Groom—much to the bemusement of his former colleagues in New York. "He does have a doctorate," Theo pointed out once or twice, then dropped it. Why was he sticking up for Wynne (Win), who, in abandoning literature to chase—and apparently conquer—the zeitgeist, had become the personification of a cultural sellout? Because Theo was fascinated by what had occurred. Not just that Win *could* do what he'd done, but that he *had*. This man, who'd occupied the highest rung of literary life, giving it all up to go Hollywood on the coattails of a "book" you had to put quotes around.

But did you? *Source It!* posited a simple idea: that just by asking where something originated—be it coffee, a mortgage, or a religion—people could launch a consumer revolution that championed truth and transparency. *One question can change the world!* The logic was both sound and easy to apply. *Just be sure to tweet the results using the hashtag #SourceIt!* When the documentary—narrated by Tim Robbins and Tilda Swinton—was released, every do-gooder with a camera and a cause began knocking on Round Circle's rectangular door. And so it was that the great issues of the modern age—climate change, human trafficking, Wall Street malfeasance—were given a fresh, cross-pollinating life, and all because Dr. Win Groom had decided to stop editing challenging novels for a niche audience that would never notice he was gone.

Still, Theo felt a tremendous discomfort with the progression of events. It seemed the language he was trying to speak, the conversation he was attempting to have with the world, was of little interest to the other people in it. After Wynne became Win, Theo was promoted to associate editor. He inherited his former boss's authors and was given limited authority to sign others. In the two years that followed, he bought five novels, none of which earned out, but all of which Theo believed were works of genuine import. Bunny stood by him until, at age seventy, she took a forced buyout and retired. Literature had been her life, but so, too, had the daily lunches at Union Square Cafe—a luxury that, by 2009, had become impossible for "management" to ignore.

A month later, with his two biggest advocates gone, Theo, too, was asked to leave. *Told* to leave. He had no employment contract, so there was no buyout for him—just two weeks of severance and the opportunity to pay $483 a month for COBRA if he wanted health insurance. He did, but not at that price. Theo also refused to sign up for unemployment, believing it was meant for those in more dire straits. He was educated and able-bodied and could surely find another job. But he'd miscalculated his worth. The economy was in free fall, and the few publishing interviews he landed went nowhere. Weeks passed and his checking account approached zero. He was thirty-three by then, and the idea of changing careers (to what?) after eight years spent digging his way out of publishing servitude was too much to bear. But so was the thought of moving home. To live an American dream and end up where you started. He had never before considered the possibility.

Theo looked around Café Loup. The band was packing up. His watch read 3:20 p.m. The last time Win had been this late to meet him was two years ago, at Soho House in West Hollywood. Theo had been unemployed for three months when Win called out of the blue and offered to fly him out to LA. He'd heard about what "went down" at Prosaic and had a potential opportunity for him. Twenty-four hours later, Theo found himself checking into a large poolside room at the Standard, paid for by Round Circle ("We call it the Sub-Standard, but it'll do for your first visit"), and then cabbing it to Win's private rooftop club on Sunset, where he waited almost forty minutes for his host to appear. Before him lay Los Angeles in vivid twilight, the foothills and flats, the downtown towers. Later, Theo would wonder if the visual splendor of that night had swayed his decision—the lights that all but spelled his name. When Win finally did arrive, and Theo realized what was happening, he almost talked his way out of being hired, first admitting to a serious lack of movie knowledge and then reminding Win of his unfriendly-to-profit taste in books. But Win waved away these concerns as if casting aside the accumulated angst of literature itself. Round Circle was building on its early success, he said, and moving away from pop docs into features—smart films culled from smart books. "Don't be fooled by all this," he said, raising his arms to everything around them. "It's still about the story."

But West Coast Win was not East Coast Wynne. This Win was no longer married. This Win wore pressed jeans. And this Win carried himself with a silky new-age zeal that Theo initially thought was a put-on.

"Listen to me," he said, leaning forward, elbows on knees. "Stop with the authenticity bullshit. You've been unemployed for months. This is what's called a lifeline."

With that, Win quoted him a modest salary and Theo said yes.

Two years: it seemed like forever. He looked at his watch again. Win was now forty-three minutes late. And still, Theo sat there. *The spinning centrifuge*, he thought, no longer knowing what the metaphor meant. But it sounded good—good enough to be a WOWW if it weren't two words too long. At some point his phone buzzed. At least he's texted to apologize, Theo told himself, pulling it out of his pocket. But it wasn't Win; it was Win's assistant, Cecily, and she wasted no words. Something had "come up" and "Dr. Groom" couldn't make it.

Theo stared at the message. He could have had the decency to tell me himself, he thought pathetically. He needed some air. He turned to signal for the check, then realized the waiter had never brought him his drink.

Chapter Five

Audrey bounded down the steps, through the turnstile, and onto the platform just in time to see a northbound 6 pulling out of the Spring Street station. Of course. She leaned against the closest pillar, out of breath. A gym, she thought, or just a short run twice a week. A little meditation wouldn't kill her either.

When the next train appeared, thirteen minutes later, Audrey took one of the few available seats. She felt exhausted in a way she hadn't since the days when she rarely slept. Was she making a fool of herself, running around town chasing the vaguest of rumors? Probably, but the alternative—the not knowing—would be far worse.

She got out at Twenty-Eighth Street and started west, through a busy no-man's-land of small-time wholesalers, rug merchants, and import-export businesses. She rarely visited this part of the city and wasn't even sure what it was. Koreatown? The Flower District? The Garment Center? Halfway down the block between Broadway and Sixth, she noticed a small plaque on the sidewalk and stopped to read it:

TIN PAN ALLEY
28th Street between Fifth and Sixth Avenues was
the legendary Tin Pan Alley where the business

of the American popular song flourished during
the first decades of the 20th century.

She looked around, but the only music she could hear was the clamorous farrago of the city itself. This was the famed Tin Pan Alley? Funny, she'd never thought of it as a physical place. Her grandmother loved that music. Joplin, Mercer, Porter, Gershwin. Their names floated through Audrey's mind the way their songs had floated through their Cape Canaveral home. The music of her trailer park youth, a life both small and grand—confined by rectangles, bound by sky. She looked back on that time so fondly, even as it had faded in the decade since to a series of specific moments—all of which starred Connie.

In the last few years, her grandmother had become increasingly homebound, though she was still the life of the party at River Palms, constantly playing host to one neighbor or another. Connie's decreased mobility hadn't slowed her marijuana consumption either. On the contrary, she'd recently begun buying some "weight," according to Jasper Sash, who, as her longtime dealer, was in a position to know. On Jasper's most recent visit, Connie had asked to purchase an ounce. Being a man of capitalist inclinations, Jasper indulged her, only to suffer a crisis of conscience resulting in a late-night call to Audrey. She'd been asleep with her phone off, but she listened to the cryptic message the following morning. Unsure of whom to confront—dealer or grandmother—she had, as yet, called neither. She was confused. Why would Connie want an *ounce*? A few puffs always did her fine. Audrey made a mental note to get to the bottom of it.

She turned up Sixth Avenue, then walked west along Thirtieth Street until she reached a dreary early-century tower with stepped-back upper floors and a giant G-clef above the entranceway. The New York Recording & Rehearsal Arts Building. According to his text, Lucas was in here somewhere, barking orders through glass. Despite her general feelings about the man, Audrey couldn't help but be impressed he was working on a Saturday—especially after last night. The R & R building housed an eclectic mix of recording studios and practice spaces rentable by the hour, and music of every style and stripe could be heard in the corridors, from jazz to opera to hip-hop to good old rock and roll. Audrey walked past the unmanned security desk and squeezed into the elevator alongside three punkish postcollege boys and a buzz-cut girl, pale as primer, holding what looked like an oversized harp. Its case had wheels. They glanced in Audrey's direction, and she met their eyes with a half smile. These were her kind of people, dreamy and disheveled, cursed with the need to express themselves, announce themselves, perform. They could be anyone. It didn't matter. They were all the same in the end, trying to get somewhere from nowhere. Audrey couldn't imagine another way to live.

The girl with the harp was whistling to herself. She had a lip ring, which added a flutter to the notes. The others shuffled from foot to foot, fiddling with guitar cases, iPhones, carabinered keys. It was an Adderall world.

"Jess, can you stay the whole two hours?" asked one of the boys.

"I think so," said the girl. "My new boss doesn't care. She's totally into music."

"What does she do?"

"She teaches Reiki to pets over Skype."

"Cool."

The doors opened, and the band squeezed out. The doors closed, and Audrey was alone. The elevator sat motionless; she had no idea what floor to press. She took her phone out, but there was no signal—not in this building, not with these walls. Best, then, to take the Guggenheim approach: start at the top and work down. She pressed 16.

Studio after studio. Floor after floor. Gotham. Rebel Music. Ultra Sound. No one had seen an A & R man—not today, not for weeks. She peeked into practice rooms and opened unlocked doors. The building was seedier than she remembered, with graffiti lining the staircase walls and an omnipresent stench of weed. This was the minor leagues. The big bands had their own setups, or recorded at decked-out studios like Strange Weather or Electric Lady. Audrey was just beginning to lose faith when she arrived on the fifth floor and heard a familiar voice down the hall, fast and gruff and way too loud. She followed it to an unmarked door, then through a deserted reception area to a control room, where Lucas Duff stood, arms crossed, watching a band from behind a soundboard. Next to him sat a sound engineer, adjusting levels on a mixer. Both were wearing headsets. Audrey stood in the doorway for a minute before Lucas, sensing something, glanced in her direction. He flinched, startled.

"*Fuck*," he barked, and pushed his headset down. "You scared the hell out of me."

"Nice to see you, too," Audrey said. She walked in far enough to get a look at the band through the studio glass. The kids from the elevator, of course, playing their hearts out. The sound reached her, heavily muted. The girl with the harp was also the lead singer.

"She just whistled two notes at once," Lucas said.

"Must be the lip ring," Audrey replied.

"Yeah, well, not everyone's a Westfield." Lucas turned to the sound guy, who pushed his headphones down, too. He was thirtyish, had a white-man 'fro, and looked moderately stoned. But everyone looked stoned in music studios.

"This is Jason, my go-to engineer. He can make a car alarm sound like Joni Mitchell. And this, J-Man, is . . . how would you describe yourself, Audrey?"

"Hi, Jason," Audrey said, reaching over to shake his hand. She thought of saying she felt bad for him but stopped herself. She needed to keep things civil.

"Audrey works at Whale Creek," Lucas said. "Be nice to her. She knows *everyone*." Lucas looked pleased, having arrived at a phrase at once innocuous and open to tremendous interpretation.

Jason stared at Audrey a beat too long, and then, face reddening, turned back to the board.

Lucas nodded at an extra set of headphones on the console. "Want to listen?"

"Actually, can we talk a minute?" Audrey asked.

"If you can make it quick," Lucas said.

Jason shrugged. He unwired himself, grabbed his phone, and walked out. Lucas leaned into the mike just as the band was striking a final chord. He waited a moment, then pressed TALK.

"Let's take five, boys and girls. Smoke 'em if you got 'em."

"But we've only done two songs," said the singer.

"Don't worry, you sound great," Lucas said. "Just think about smoother transitions. You don't want to bury your hooks behind too much noise."

The singer considered this suggestion as she unplugged her instrument—it was electric—and leaned it carefully against a stack of amps. Then she shrugged and followed her bandmates out the door.

"How's the harp working out?" Audrey asked. She hopped onto the table beside the soundboard, her legs dangling just off the floor.

"How do you think it's working out? She hides behind the fucking thing. Can't sing without it."

"They're young. They've got that going for them."

"Everyone's young! It'd be better if they were fifty. Or Eskimo. Or polyamorous first cousins." Lucas sat down and swiveled his chair to face Audrey. "So what's got your knickers all bunched up?"

Audrey grimaced but let the comment go. She'd journeyed up here to gauge his reaction in person, but now it seemed like a mistake, like she was telegraphing the importance of the situation. Still, she pressed forward.

"I was wondering—"

"I know what you're wondering," Lucas cut in. "And the answer is yes."

"It is?"

"Don't thank me all at once."

"Okay, I won't."

"Well, you should," Lucas said. "It wasn't easy getting the approvals."

"For what?"

"For you to go on tour."

"I don't remember being in a band."

"With the Westfields."

"You want me to go on tour with the Westfield Brothers?"

"Isn't that what you came to ask me?"

"No! Why would I—they're *your* band now." Audrey felt the first pulse of a headache coming on. What the hell was wrong with everyone today?

"I'm talking about a short-term thing," Lucas said. "Renting you for a month. Look at me: I can't go out on the road anymore. But someone needs to. We're putting real money into this—twenty-two cities in thirty days—and we can't have them flying off the rails like they did last night. Gatesy disappeared with those two half-wit girls and missed a *Vice* photo shoot at ten thirty this morning."

"Who scheduled a shoot at that hour?"

"Exactly. That's why we need you. Come on, it's the perfect gig. They're brilliant, they're volatile, and they're your friends. You'll have a great time."

"Sorry, no."

"But this is what you do—coddle bands."

"I coddle my *own* bands. When they need it. The Westfields aren't twenty-two anymore. They're big boys, they'll be fine."

"We'll give Whale Creek signage visibility and work with you money-wise. I'll talk to your boss if that'll help."

"My boss already wants to kill you. And I don't need to work with you money-wise because I'm not doing it. I have a life here, and a job, and a boyfriend."

"The lovely gentleman who got in my face last night."

"He is lovely. And the answer's still no." Audrey hopped off the table and started for the door. Shit. How to transition now. She took a breath and turned around.

"Lucas . . . about last night, when you mentioned Fender—"

"I knew it! *That's* why you took off, isn't it?"

"Look, I didn't date him, but I did know him. So yes, I was upset. And I'm wondering where that news came from originally. That he killed himself."

Lucas peered at Audrey sideways. "I don't know. Someone at the office heard it."

"Who?"

She must have sounded more desperate than she'd meant to, because Lucas visibly softened. He leaned back and locked his hands behind his head. "I'm sorry," he said. "I didn't realize you two were close. I heard it from one of our A & R assistants, who said he'd heard it from someone else. It was all pretty vague. Hence all the texting back and forth. I was trying to get more information."

"Are you looking into it any deeper?"

"Audrey, he was barely even working for us anymore. The guy was a bum, a junkie. The last time I saw him he was selling loosies at two a.m. outside Death by Audio. He was so doped up he could barely stand."

The band was filing back into the studio. The drummer hopped up and down in mock anticipation, then shouted, "Hello, Cleveland!"

Lucas sighed. "Look, what do you want me to do? If he's still alive, he'll turn up somewhere. Probably on North Sixth, with a cup and a sign and a one-eyed pit bull. Jesus, if I knew you were gonna get weird on me—and *you* of all people—I wouldn't have even mentioned it last night. Now let me get back to the living, not that they sound much better."

"You really are an asshole," Audrey said, moving toward the door.

"Yeah, well, at least I'm consistent. Let me know when you change your mind about the tour. It starts in three weeks."

With that, Lucas put his headphones on and turned to face the band. Audrey headed for the elevator, passing Jason on the way. They nodded at each other. That music-world cool. Lucas was right; Audrey *had* gone weird on him. But at least he hadn't asked why. That's the good thing about the self-involved, she thought. They take what others say at face value, so they can get back to focusing on themselves.

The elevator arrived and Audrey stepped inside. The cab was mercifully empty. Six years had passed, and as far as she knew the other people involved—Sarah, Chris, and Fender—had never told another soul what they'd done. Occasionally, in the months afterward, she would hear a crazy rumor, third- or fourth-hand, but it was never that close to the truth. For the last several years she'd heard nothing. Still, Audrey had never quite believed it was over, because she came from a background where the choices people made always caught up with them—usually sooner, occasionally later. Was this, then, the beginning of that comeuppance? This mysterious death in the night? It seemed unlikely, but in Audrey's life, the improbable, again and again, had turned out to be true.

The elevator wasn't moving. She'd forgotten to press *L*. Now she did, and started down.

The Family Business

Lawrence, Massachusetts
November 1992

Common Application Essay Prompt #4: Choose a real person or character in fiction who has had a significant influence on you, and describe that influence in 500–750 words.

THE FAMILY BUSINESS
By Theo Gorski

Every man in my family, from my great-grandfather all the way up to my older brother, Carl, has been employed, at one time or another, at the Merrimack Valley Works in North Andover, Massachusetts. Today, people call it the AT&T plant, because that's who owns it now, but it's the same place. My father has worked there as an electrician for 24 years, and he's a "Proud Member of CWA Local 1365." It says so right on his truck! But this is an essay about my great-grandfather Stanley, who was the first Gorski to be born in America. He was also the first to live in my hometown of Lawrence, after moving east from Chicago. Most of what I know about him comes from family lore, but some of it comes from my own research. The interesting thing is that the two don't always match up. But let me start from the beginning.

Stanislov Gorski was born in 1905, in a poor Polish neighborhood called Back of the Yards on the South Side of Chicago. The name comes from the old Union Stockyards slaughterhouses, where many Eastern European immigrants worked. As a boy my great-grandfather helped his mother sell "worsted goods," which is basically yarn, door-to-door. But as a teenager he "fell in" with a local mob and began "running numbers" along his mother's route because her customers already knew him. (Running numbers is a type of illegal private lottery, or "racket.") Stanley was successful and soon he was given a larger territory. He was repeatedly threatened by the Irish mob in nearby Canaryville, but managed to keep the peace by "cutting them in" on his profits.

Stanley was 26 when Al Capone was convicted of tax evasion. He was 28 when Prohibition was repealed. These events had a tremendous effect on criminal "enterprise" in Chicago, and many mobsters ended up in jail or out of work. Around this time, which was the early 1930s, Stanley got married and then had a baby, who turned out to be my grandfather Arthur. (My brother says that it's more likely the baby came first, and then the marriage, but I don't know.)

With the rackets no longer lucrative and a young family to feed, Stanley decided to get "off the streets." The neighborhood bosses found him a floor job at AT&T's Western Electric plant in Cicero, where telephone parts and other things like electric fans were made. But this was just a cover. The real reason he was sent there was to organize a giant numbers game for the factory's 40,000 employees. Unfortunately for him, it didn't go well. For starters, the factory executives demanded a cut. Also, the Great Depression had started happening, and the workers, many of whom were newly arrived immigrants, needed to save their money. Lastly, unions were organizing for the first time, which made it difficult for Stanley to use his usual tactics, such as threats and coercion, to get paid.

This is where the story gets even more interesting, because up until this point the biography of my great-grandfather is basically undisputed by everyone in my family, partly, I think, because so much of what he did was illegal, and therefore went unrecorded. But that changed in the late 1930s, when Stanley "went straight." Business at Western Electric was booming and the rackets were no longer worth the trouble. But the factory's executives appreciated Stanley's strong work ethic, so they promoted him to the ranks of management.

In the 1940s, Stanley was sent east to help with Western Electric's expansion into New England. The company's first Massachusetts plant was in Haverhill, where they built electronic surveillance equipment for use in World War II. After the war, there was a "boom" in telephone communication, and soon Western Electric needed a much larger plant. In 1953, Stanley Gorski, now a major executive, helped break ground for the Merrimack Valley Works, just south of Lawrence. It opened in 1956 and soon employed more than 12,000 people, almost single-handedly keeping the area economy afloat after the collapse of the textile industry. Unfortunately, my great-grandfather wouldn't live to see the "fruits of his labor." He died of a heart attack in 1958, just days before he was to be promoted to senior plant manager, in charge of the entire "Works."

I have always wanted to find out more about Stanley Gorski, but no one in my family will talk about him, mostly because no one in my family will talk about anything. Then

I read this essay question and realized the opportunity it provided, so I visited the Immigrant City Archives at the Lawrence Public Library. ("The Immigrant City" is Lawrence's nickname.) There, I was able to find Lawrence's two daily newspapers from the 1950s on microfilm, as well as boxes of old Western Electric promotional and wire photos. Using these resources, I retraced the early history of the Merrimack Valley Works, starting with the plant's construction. I looked for the Gorski name in the articles but couldn't find it. Then I studied the wire photos. They showed men in fancy hats and suits, at ribbon cuttings for new buildings. They had names like Winslow and Harriman and Gardiner. But there were no Gorskis.

The last box I looked in contained images not of executives but of workmen, teams of laborers with saws and axes and smoke-spewing machines. In these photos, no one seemed to be aware of the camera, which made them far more interesting. And the names of these men: they were names out of my high school yearbook! Italians, Germans, Lebanese, Polish. I scanned the captions, one after another, and was down to the last stack, my eyes bleary, when I finally found it: his name, my name, listed among a half-dozen others below the words "Foundation Work: Digging Starts on Building 4C." The image depicted a group of ragged-looking men in overalls, working waist-deep in a hole. I had studied the few existing family photos of Stanley obsessively, so I knew which one he was: the large hulking man on the right, the one holding the shovel. Here, then, was the true story of my family in Lawrence. My great-grandfather was not a senior executive at Western Electric. He was a digger of ditches.

I wonder if my father knows the truth. Surely, my grandfather Arthur did, though he died when I was young. This version of history makes far more sense, considering the jobs held by other Gorskis. My grandfather and his brothers worked the assembly lines, my aunt (my father's sister) was a "quality control inspector" until she got laid off, and my father, as I mentioned earlier, is an electrician. In other words, as my chemistry teacher likes to say, my "findings support the facts." Still, I've decided to keep these findings to myself for now. Family dynamics are a strange thing, and I've learned that sometimes it's better to "let sleeping dogs lie." I, for one, enjoy knowing that my great-grandfather was a common laborer. Maybe he was run out of Chicago. Maybe he just wanted to start over. Either way, "going straight" couldn't have been easy. Stanislov Gorski may not have lived the American dream, but he lived a real American life. And I'll always be proud to be his great-grandson.

Theo leaned back and cracked his knuckles. Done. Finished. *Finally*. Except he was nowhere near done. With dread, he glanced at the word count in the lower corner of his word processor: 1,218. The guidelines clearly stated an uppermost limit of 750. On the positive side, Theo had, over the course of five previous drafts, chopped and sawed and otherwise edited his way down from a high of 3,239. Now he was absolutely sure that any further cutting would erode the foundation of the enterprise itself, that carefully calibrated mix of narrative suspense and academic rigor, personal history and *history* history. At the same time, he sensed he'd failed to reach the apex he'd been writing toward—that he hadn't quite said what he was trying to say. A flame of insight had flickered alive in certain moments of creative inspiration but just as quickly extinguished itself, half-formed, then fully forgotten. Perhaps some thoughts were too elusive for words. He put his head in his hands. He'd felt so good two minutes ago.

He saved this latest draft to a floppy disk and ejected it from the library's word processor. He was in the same archives room that appeared in the essay (writing at home having proved impossible), and

Mrs. Danzig had come by twice already to remind him the building was closing early, as it was the day after Thanksgiving. No matter. He had another appointment anyway. Also, the application wasn't due for another week. On his way out, he stopped by the circulation desk and asked if she might print the essay for him. She happily obliged, the two having formed a bond over their shared interest in Lawrence arcana (she'd even let him keep the photo of his great-grandfather, on the theory that no one else had examined the Western Electric boxes in her twenty-seven years as archivist, so a single missing image probably wouldn't tip the scales of history).

Outside, the stiff breeze of three hours earlier had become a cold whipping wind, funneling up the hill from the river. The streets were deserted. How could he be completely alone in the center of a city of eighty thousand? Certainly, the town planners had done the place no favors. Lawrence's few civic structures of note—city hall, the courthouse, the library, the high school—were architecturally unstimulating and surrounded the central common in such a way that the park felt more foreboding than bucolic. The buildings that told the true story of Lawrence, the massive redbricked textile mills lining the banks of the Merrimack, were not visible from where Theo stood. Yet he could feel their presence. Everyone could. They lorded over the town, over the entire region, in dilapidated silence, manifestations of the dying century itself. This was where Lawrence's economic future had been built and lost. Decades later, the city was still lost, its citizens, like the mills, pitted and hollow—just there. Except when they weren't.

He jogged down the steps, across Lawrence Street, and through the doors of the high school. The wide entrance hall was empty. Theo stood still, listening for life—a vacuuming janitor or practicing band—but heard nothing but cold silence. He climbed the central staircase to the fourth floor, taking the shallow steps three at a time, and headed for the administrative wing, where he'd been told Ms. Jansen's office was located. He'd never been to this part of the building and never seen Ms. Jansen in his life. When he got close, he took a slip of paper from his pocket, the note he'd found in his locker after classes on Monday:

> Dear Theodore,
>   Please come to my office at 3 p.m. this Friday, Nov. 27. The school is officially closed that day, but I'll be here. I'm in the Main Building, room 426. I'd appreciate you keeping this meeting between you and me.
>
>   Regards, Ms. Jansen
>   LHS College Counselor

Room 426 was just in front of him. The door was half open and a light was on. He stopped in his tracks. He was suddenly terrified.

Why was he being summoned like this? He was already going to college—Central Connecticut State, on a football scholarship. Coach Raab had informed him of the offer a week ago, and while Theo had been thrilled at the news, he'd also worried that his father wouldn't let him accept. But Coach had spoken to Leonard Gorski in person, and the old man had finally, grudgingly, given his assent by not actively *diss*enting. Now Theo just needed to send in the application and essay. Everything else, Coach had promised, would be taken care of.

But not by Ms. Jansen. In fact, Theo had been explicitly warned by Coach Raab to stay away from the college counselor's office, as she had, in Coach's words, a "history of meddling in processes she didn't understand." Finding her note, then, had been disconcerting. But Theo always did what was asked of him, so here he was. At least no one else was around. He walked the rest of the way to her door and knocked.

"Come on in!"

He pushed the door open to find a thin woman with long brown hair seated behind a metal desk. She stood up and shook his hand. "You must be Theodore. Thanks so much for coming. Here, make yourself comfortable."

"Thank you for having me," Theo said stiffly. He hadn't been called by his full name since he was a child, but he liked how it sounded. He shook his coat off, unstrapped his backpack, and took a seat in the only available chair. Ms. Jansen sat back down, too, and began sifting through a stack of papers. She was far younger and more striking than he'd imagined (or would have imagined, seeing as he hadn't thought about her looks until just then); it wasn't just her height and hair, which spilled down past her shoulders, but her clothes, too—blue jeans and a gray vest over a white blouse. How had he never seen her before? Maybe because the school had more than 2,500 students. Or because he spent all his non-classroom time on the football field. Or because he hadn't been aware, until recently, that Lawrence High even employed a college counselor.

To avoid staring at Ms. Jansen, Theo looked around the room. It was small and windowless, and the two of them seemed to take up half of it.

"I know," she said, as if reading his mind. "A school the size of a city block and the college counselor works out of a janitor's closet. If that doesn't tell you something about our place in the firmament . . ." She laughed dolefully and tucked her hair behind her ear. The word "our" danced through Theo's head—he so rarely heard it—and somehow it relaxed him. He made a note to look up "firmament" in the dictionary later.

"*Here* it is." She held up what she'd been searching for: a printout of Theo's transcript. "I was alerted to your classroom performance by more than one of your teachers," she said. "An A-minus average is rare enough. Then I find out you're also the captain of the football team."

"Co-captain," Theo said. "There are four of us: two on offense, two on defense." He wondered if he should elaborate, tell her he actually played both ways, but that would only complicate the offensive/defensive captain balance he'd just elucidated and require a further explanation involving his fellow co-captain Geo Rodriguez, who also played both sides of the ball and thus evened things back out. He stayed quiet.

"My point," she continued, "is that well-rounded students like you don't come along often. Now, I know Coach Raab has informed you of some college opportunities as they pertain to football—Central Connecticut State and a few others."

"Actually, just CCSU. He said they were offering me a scholarship and that I should take it."

"And?"

"I was kind of stunned, I guess. I told him my family didn't have money for that kind of thing, and that my dad probably wouldn't let me go anyway, but Coach said not to worry—that it was a full scholarship, all four years, and he'd talk to my dad for me."

"Do you know that Coach Raab's son is the head coach at Central Connecticut?"

Theo nodded eagerly. "That was a pretty major selling point. It makes it less scary."

Something clicked for the first time. Perhaps it was the expression on Ms. Jansen's face.

"Theo, I know we've just met, but I feel I should level with you. It's an exciting offer, and I'm sure you'd thrive there, on and off the field, but several other colleges have contacted us about you as well. Schools you haven't had the chance to consider because George Raab told them you weren't interested. For decades Lawrence High sent football players to places like Boston College and Syracuse and Penn State. But that doesn't happen anymore. Why do you think that is?"

"Our team isn't as good as it used to be," Theo said.

"But individual players are. Four in the last six years, and they've all ended up at Central Connecticut. Is that just a coincidence?"

Theo chose to let the question become rhetorical. He watched Ms. Jansen open a folder with his name on it and remove a small array of brochures.

"Take a look at these. They're excellent schools, and each of them would love to have you apply. There are others, too, and I'd be happy to give you their information if you'd like, but I think these four are the best fit in terms of football *and* academics."

She handed Theo the brochures. Cornell. Colgate. Bowdoin. Brown. He recognized the names from the box scores of newspapers. Schools that existed in some mythical world. He studied the handsome pages, aerial views of redbrick campuses and tiered stadiums, close-ups of students in lab coats and goggles, or seated in lecture halls, or sprawled in groups on fresh-mowed grass, every one of them toothy and whole-some and . . . Theo furrowed his brow.

"Are you sure these schools would want someone like me?"

"Of course! Don't sell yourself short." She explained that financial packages were available for applicants from all kinds of backgrounds, be it athletic scholarships or need-based aid or a combination of both.

Theo wasn't sure what she meant by this but guessed that his "background" qualified him. He looked at the brochures again, his mind working to frame a thought for which no one had provided the dimensions. "It's just that these students . . ." He pointed to a random image: an Asian girl, a Latino boy, and a black boy huddled around a microscope. It was like the setup for one of his father's jokes.

"What about them?" Ms. Jansen asked, her voice going flat.

Theo frowned. He didn't know how to explain it. He thought of his father. Was it possible the old man had been right? All those rants about "darkies" taking over the country. *His* country. "I'll pick a god-damn letter!" Leonard Gorski liked to shout at Pat Sajak from his couch-shaped living room throne. "How about an S! SpicksSpades-SlantsSpooksSambosSandniggers . . ." He could go on and on, any letter you wanted. As children, Theo and Carl had heard their father use these slurs mostly with drinking buddies, but these days they peppered his every exchange. His accountant was a "sheeny," his boss a "Nip," his doctor a "wog." Theo recalled his father arriving home from his last checkup. "You should have seen that bastard trying to bend me over," he said as he walked in the door. "The fuck if I'm dropping my pants for a goddamn coolie!"

His father was intensely bigoted and half insane, but as Theo gazed at the faces of America's best and brightest, he had to admit . . . there was nary a white one among them. And while that was fine in itself—half of Theo's friends were Hispanic—it surely wasn't fine for his chances of being admitted to one of these colleges. But how to impart this concern out loud? He crossed his legs, attempting an air of seriousness, but his chair, like so many chairs he encountered, wobbled worryingly beneath him.

"It's just that I'm *white*," Theo finally blurted out, "and most of these students . . ." He held up a brochure, resignedly, like it was a surrender flag.

The expression on Ms. Jansen's face went from concern to bemusement. And then she started laughing. What could possibly be so funny? It came to him, all at once—like a math equation you puzzle over for hours, then solve a week later in the shower. And it wasn't just the puzzle of race politics, of marketing and political correctness, that revealed itself. It was everything. The larger truth of his circumstances. Of course he should go to college—the best one that would take him. He'd worked so hard for the opportunity, and this woman seated before him, she could make it happen. He listened, his head growing lighter, as she told him about each school, its academics and athletics, culture and reputation. She knew what classes Theo was taking—that he was acing AP history and Spanish but having trouble with calculus and, weirdly, English (he'd been told to "present his written thoughts more concisely"). She opened a drawer and removed a Common Application form.

"All four schools accept this," she said, "so you'll only have to write one essay."

"I've already written one. For Central Connecticut. Would you like to see it?"

"I'd love to."

Theo dug into his bag and produced the four newly printed-out pages, which he handed over with some majesty. Ms. Jansen tucked more hair behind her ear and began to read. Theo sat there in front of her and took stock of his life.

Had Coach really lied to him? Withheld information so he'd go to Central Connecticut? The warning he was given, to stay away from Ms. Jansen: it made sense now. All this scheming, and the funny thing was, Theo didn't even like football that much. He cringed at being defined by his actions on the field, even as he understood the importance of being defined by *something*. People got lost in a town like Lawrence. Disappeared in plain sight.

Not that Theo was very often overlooked. He'd begun to grow in seventh grade and by freshman year found himself inhabiting a six-foot-three, two-hundred-ten-pound frame of mostly muscle. Growing up, he'd played whatever sport his brother, Carl, three years older, was into. Whatever sport didn't cost money. Baseball, basketball, street hockey. Then, inevitably, football. He enjoyed the team part more than the competitive part, but when kids started hitting, he hit back harder. By sophomore year, humble Theo Gorski was flattening running backs with a simple lowering of his shoulder, and the crushing contact, pad on pad, turned heads on far-flung fields. What these heads would then witness was Theo helping his victims up, or trying to, if they could get up at all. He played tight end on offense and linebacker on defense (in an age of specialization, Coach Raab still believed his best players should be out there all game), and was, his junior year, named All-Conference at both positions, a first in the football-rich history of Lawrence High School. His stats were even better this year.

So yes, football had come to define him. It gave him status. Seats at tables and glances from girls. Still, shyness had kept—or saved—him from overt popularity. Plus, he enjoyed studying, which befuddled the arbiters of cool. Theo didn't care. He liked classrooms and he liked books. But no Gorski had ever made it past high school—his father and brother hadn't even made it that far—and money for "further education" didn't exist. Pondering college was like pondering a meteor strike: it was theoretically possible, and would certainly be exciting, but his time would be better spent on more terrestrial matters. Like apprenticing for a trade. His father knew people.

But as his senior season had gotten under way this past fall, Theo had started hearing talk. A college recruiter witnessed his two interceptions against Acton-Boxborough. Another was present for his 135 receiving yards versus Lowell. But no postgame introductions were made, so Theo didn't give the rumors much credence. The season ended, and with it, Theo thought, the football chapter of his life. Again, he was accorded All-Conference honors, but Lawrence missed the playoffs—a common occurrence in these waning years of the Raab era—and that failure stifled the joy Theo should have felt in his individual achievements. Then, two weeks ago, he'd been summoned to Coach Raab's office after classes. He navigated the endless cubicle maze of sports administrators and assistants, and found Coach installed like an effigy of himself in his bunkerlike lair. He was on the phone, so Theo waited in the doorway.

There wasn't much to look at—the office was windowless, the yellow cement walls barren—so Theo took up a surreptitious study of the great man himself. Coach Raab was seventy-three years old and had been stalking the sidelines of LHS football games for more than three decades. His nickname was the "Walking Institution," an increasingly misleading moniker considering Coach now moved in a wincing shuffle, as if he hadn't just witnessed a lifetime of hits but absorbed them all himself. In a sense, he had: football meant that much to him. Along the way, he'd become a local legend, a paradigm of hard work and perseverance in a community that championed these traits above all. But change had come to the game, and Coach Raab was unable— or unwilling—to adjust. High schools now played like colleges, with shotgun passing formations and blitz-heavy defensive alignments, fake punts and onside kicks and razzle-dazzle option plays that left the LHS coaching staff staring at their clipboards in hapless confusion. Eight seasons had passed without a winning record, and the inevitable whispers had begun. Theo felt bad for his coach. They'd gotten along well, inasmuch as anyone could get along with a man who spoke in grunts and scowls. Coach Raab patronized Marco's, the same union dive favored by Leonard Gorski, and this fact seemed to have softened the great man to his star player's circumstances. Theo imagined his father acting as boorishly there as he did at home, though he knew that couldn't be the case. The Marco's crowd would never put up with it. They were a species that had largely died out, men for whom minor incidents loomed large and major ones were repressed or ignored. (Tony Conigliaro, a promising Red Sox outfielder derailed in 1965 by a fastball to the eye, still enjoyed their cultlike devotion, while Bill Buckner, chief architect of New England's unshakable malaise, went strenuously unmentioned.) They held stubbornly to a way of life that served to compound their misery. If only a town could have an epitaph.

When Coach Raab hung up the phone that day, he spoke without preamble: "I want you to go to college. Central Connecticut State." He delivered these words not to Theo himself, but to the lone framed photograph (of the 1977 state championship squad) on his desk. Theo, stunned, didn't know what to say. He was overwhelmed by the moment, the incongruity of it, so he said what he was thinking, what he was always thinking.

"What about my father?"

"Your father," Coach repeated, finally meeting Theo's gaze.

"I think he'd have a problem with me going away."

"But it's free. And we're not talking Texas. The school's less than an hour from here."

Theo realized he wasn't showing any enthusiasm. "Coach," he said, "I appreciate the offer, but I don't think he'll let me go. It's not the money or distance. It's the idea itself."

Coach Raab leaned back in his chair. They were tiptoeing around something more potent than common sense. And then the moment passed. Coach sat upright, back to business.

"It's simple," he said. "Do you want to go to college or not?"

Theo nodded, said yes.

"Good. Then it's settled. My secretary will give you the forms and application. Fill everything out and write the essay. I'll handle your father."

"I shouldn't say anything?"

"Let me talk to him first."

Ms. Jansen's office was a lot like Coach Raab's. Every room in Lawrence looked and felt the same—dim and disconsolate, as predictable as the people. No one Theo knew was interested in the unfamiliar. At the same time, no one liked the world that was. What a strange dichotomy, that working-class narrowness of scope. Four generations in America and the Gorskis still kept their heads down, as if ignorance were not just a refuge but a point of pride. His father had never left the country. And his mother, a distant woman who tiptoed through rooms, was incapable of anything but minor pleasantries and rote conversation. (Once, when she was twenty, she'd driven to Montreal with a boy she was dating. They went to restaurants and a jazz club, but what she really remembered was sitting on a bench by a river, watching other couples stroll past. She only mentioned the trip by accident, when Theo asked if she'd ever gone on a vacation, and immediately afterward she'd covered her mouth in disbelief and made him swear to keep her confession a secret. He always had. Still, he wondered how often his mother had relived that long-ago weekend in all the ugly years since.)

Ms. Jansen was frowning at his essay, pen in hand. At least she was taking it seriously. When should he tell her about his father and how all of this was a fool's errand? It was one thing for Coach Raab to twist arms down at Marco's. But selling the old man on an elite college would be impossible. Education was the subversive underground of Leonard Gorski's totalitarian state, tolerated only as a delivery mechanism for team sports. And yet they barely spoke at Theo's games. Weird, considering Leonard not only attended them (home *and* away), but spent those two hours every autumn Friday night receiving friends at his fifty-yard-line seats with all the ceremony of a pasha accepting tributes from the hinterlands. Breathing hard between plays, Theo would glance up and wonder why the hugs and back slaps he spotted in the stands never found their way home. Did Leonard's drinking buddies ever notice the man's absence of filial interaction? Probably not. Lawrence was full of such relationships. Invisible walls, erected from spite.

Ms. Jansen put her pen down but kept staring at the pages, *through* the pages, as if thinking of something else. Finally she swiveled in Theo's direction. The essay was heavily marked up.

"It's too long," Theo said, his heart sinking. "I realize that."

"It is," she agreed. "But it's also . . . Theo, it's *remarkable*. You should see the plagiarized drivel that passes for a college essay these days. But this—can we talk a bit about your writing?"

Theo's eyes were like moons, white all the way around. He nodded eagerly. He'd been waiting for that question half his life.

"I've suggested cuts in a few places," Ms. Jansen continued, "including a lot of the clichés, most of which you've already put quotes around. It's like you instinctively knew they shouldn't be in there. You need to trust yourself, and the reader."

This sounded like very good advice.

"But I'm most interested in your ending. You uncover this fascinating historical fact about your great-grandfather, but instead of sharing it with your family, you decide to"—she flipped to the last page—"'let sleeping dogs lie.'"

"Cliché!" Theo said. "I'll take it out."

"Yes, but why *not* share what you've found? I get the impression history means a lot to your family. To your father."

Theo considered this. "I think my dad is afraid of anything he can't control. Layoffs. Immigration. Growing old. And so the things he *can* control, like his family, and his family history . . ." Theo paused, trying to shape his thoughts. "He kind of revels in misery. That's why he never leaves Lawrence. That's why he loves the Red Sox. Like, he *really* loves the Red Sox. I was named after Ted Williams, and my brother for Carl Yastrzemski. 'The only great Polack in American history.' See? Defeatist. Anyway, as it applies to my great-grandfather, I think the story of him being this big important man whose descendants squandered their fortunes and luck fits nicely into my father's worldview. If you believe the American dream is a sham, and that everyone's out to get you, then it's easy to accept your circumstances. To never *strive*, I guess, to change them." He was speaking in platitudes, he knew, but platitudes were the oral currency of a place like Lawrence—surface words, safe ideas. He tried to move beyond them. "But if the opposite is true, if the Gorskis started at the *bottom*—quite literally in a ditch—and then worked their way up, then we've actually been heading in the right direction, generationally speaking. And that means there's no impediment to doing even better, or at least trying. Except we're not. *He's* not. Which means he's failed."

He had never spoken of his father in this way. As a man afraid to face the world. In fact, Theo had spent his life respecting, if not quite revering, him. So many of his friends' and teammates' families had fallen apart. He knew the stories, most involving alcohol or money problems or violence, and differing only in degrees. Leonard Gorski shared these vices, but not to a disabling degree. He'd always kept a roof over his family's collective head. So why Theo's change of heart? Because now, for the first time ever, someone appeared to believe in him.

"What was your father's reaction when he heard about the scholarship offer?"

"He came home from Marco's last Saturday night and I could tell from his expression that Coach had talked to him. I was watching hockey with my brother, and instead of joining us, he just stood there and said, 'You think you're better than everyone, then?' And I said, 'No, of course not.' And that was it. He turned and walked upstairs. We haven't spoken since—including the entirety of Thanksgiving dinner."

"So how do you think he'd handle this?" She motioned toward the brochures.

"I think he'd throw me out of the house. Central Connecticut is one thing. But *these* schools? He'd see it as a betrayal. I don't know. It's hard to explain if you're not from here."

"I am from here. Or nearby, at least. Lowell."

"You don't look like you're from Lowell."

"Because I left."

"And moved to *Lawrence*?"

"Other places first. California. New York."

"Why did you ever come back?"

"To take care of my parents. But also to help other people get out there and experience the world. Because it makes you a different person. A fuller person. And yes, that's a cliché." Ms. Jansen laughed. "But the thing is, they're mostly true. You just have to say them in your own voice. You have to think for yourself."

The Gorskis lived on Maple Street, three blocks north of the high school, in the heart of the old Eastern European quarter bordering the Spicket River tributary. Hundreds of Polish and Lithuanian families had once populated the fire-trap tenements lining these narrow thoroughfares, but only a handful still remained. The exodus began when the mills started closing and gained momentum in the sixties and seventies, when Hispanics moved to Lawrence in great numbers. Now salsa and merengue blasted from beat-up cars with thousand-dollar subwoofers, and Dominican boys lounged on corners whistling at one another's sisters. Of the original Polish, only the stubborn and infirm remained. Theo's parents were among the former.

He walked into the wind, pitched slightly forward. In his jacket pocket were the brochures, folded neatly in half, like a love letter. Cornell. Colgate. Bowdoin. Brown. It occurred to him that Ms. Jansen had been plotting this for some time. Maybe she'd already spoken with the powers that be at each of these schools, sent them his transcripts, his football stats. She'd told him to spend the next few days editing the essay and choosing a school—or two or three. She also suggested they keep things a secret from Coach Raab, as Coach Raab Jr. might rescind the scholarship offer if he found out, and they needed Central Connecticut as a backup. "But you do need to tell your father," Ms. Jansen had implored. "Try to make him feel like he's part of the process." Theo had balked at this idea but finally relented. He knew she was right.

Now, though, as he turned onto his dilapidated block, facing his father seemed an impossible task. To steel himself for it, he drifted over to the patchy expanse of weeds across the street from his house. It was the size of a small park, but the city hadn't bothered making it one. No playground, no trees, no benches: just empty space. He didn't *have* to tell his father. He could submit the applications and wait to learn his fate without the old man's ever finding out. Except he couldn't. He'd need family income information for the financial aid forms. Now, there was a conversation that wouldn't go well. Not that many others did.

He gazed at the house he'd grown up in, a simple two-family duplex with side-by-side front doors. The Gorskis lived on the right side; the left stood empty, the Polish couple who had formerly leased it from Leonard having decamped for South Boston in the mideighties. For a while, Theo's father had advertised it for rent. Several Hispanic families expressed interest, but no whites, so his father had let it sit vacant, for months, and then years, until the place became uninhabitable—rotted through and rat infested. All of this, with his own family barely scraping by. The obstinacy boggled the mind.

Theo knew it was wrong, but something inside him equated leaving this place with failure, with disloyalty and abandonment. Once, he'd thought Lawrence the center of the world, his house the house of all houses, but it looked so tragic now, the gray paint peeling, the roof missing shingles. An air conditioner balanced crookedly in his parents' bedroom window, an extension cord running down the *outside* of the house and back through the window below. That his father, a man who lit entire factory floors, refused to repair the circuits in his own home . . .

Theo watched his breath dissipate in the air. Then he crossed the street, opened the gate to the chain-link fence his father had erected years earlier (in an effort to keep out all the people who hadn't been trying to get in), and climbed the steps to the front door. He could paint the scene inside, right down to the coaster that would be next to, but not under, his father's sweating beer bottle. And sure enough, there it all was—Leonard on the couch, white haired and wiry, and Carl in the nearby lounger. Both were watching college football on the RCA, with its jerry-rigged antenna bending toward the window as if it, like everything else, were trying to escape. Theo guessed the two hadn't spoken for the better part of whatever game it was—Iowa-Nebraska, it looked like—but now Carl nodded ever so slightly, his eyes never leaving the television. The Gorski version of *How's it going? Please come join us!*

Poor Carl. Working odd jobs at the plant and still living at home. How would he deal with Theo's leaving? Would he take it as a challenge to examine his own life, to commence living it? Theo hoped so. But Carl had so much of their father in him—and their mother. Stubborn loyalty. Muted fear. *Weakness.* The word arrived out of nowhere, and Theo rallied around it, reaching into his pocket for the brochures. His father hadn't yet acknowledged his presence.

"Dad, if you could take a look at these when you get a chance," he said, tossing them onto the coffee table beside the sports section of the *Lawrence Eagle-Tribune*. "It's something I've been thinking about—besides Connecticut." He left it at that. The game had cut to commercials but his father still refused to look over, so Theo started up the stairs. He tried to guess how far he'd make it—the first landing?—before the outburst, but he came up three steps short. Except it wasn't an outburst. It was an *explosion*, an *eruption*, a deluge of profanity followed by Theo's name. Theo turned around and walked back down the stairs. He'd made his choice.

Leonard Gorski was standing now. Carl was as well, his eyes flickering between his father and brother. Carl knew anything was possible. He'd grown up in Lawrence, too.

"*What the hell are these?*" Leonard shouted, launching the brochures back at Theo.

"Better schools," Theo replied. "And they offer financial aid just like—"

"*Fuck* better schools!"

"Dad," Carl said.

"First I'm accosted by George Raab in front of everyone at Marco's, telling me my son has 'earned the right' to go to college. Like I have no say in what my family does. But at least George is one of us. This shit"—he motioned toward the brochures scattered across the carpet—"you don't know the first thing about what's out there."

"And you do?" Theo said.

Leonard tensed up. His cheeks came alive. "*What the fuck did you just say?*" He took a step toward his youngest son. Carl maneuvered between them.

"Don't, Dad," Carl said, and put his hands on his father's shoulders.

"Get out of my way!" Leonard pushed Carl back into Theo, who caught and righted him. The two brothers looked stunned.

"Let me tell you something," their father continued, spit flying from his mouth. "You go to one of these places, you don't come back. Understand?"

"Dad, listen to yourself," Carl said.

"*You listen to yourself!*" Leonard roared nonsensically. "You want out of here, too? Just say the word."

"Stop it," Theo said quietly.

"I'll take either of you!" Leonard shouted, not backing down.

"Me then," Theo said, and cut in front of his brother.

"Fine. Good." Leonard raised his hands in a fighting stance. He looked like a street brawler in an early-century publicity still. His son towered over him.

"Theo," Carl said.

"Come on," Leonard beckoned. He pushed Theo's chest, but unlike Carl, Theo didn't give. He just stood there, fists balled. And then *he* took a step forward.

"Don't do it," Carl pleaded.

Their mother appeared on the stairs in her nightgown.

"What kind of father doesn't want his son to go to college?" Theo said, and took a second step forward. There was no more space between them.

"Theo, you'll kill him!" Carl shouted, and grabbed at his brother. Theo shook him off and . . . and then he stopped. He stood there a moment, holding his breath, then unclenched his fists, exhaled, and slowly backed away. For Carl's sake. For his mother's. When he left the room, his father started shouting after him—insults and threats. The man sounded insane. Theo climbed the stairs again. He embraced his teary mother, but she made no move to hug him back, so he dropped his arms and continued on to his room. He heard the front door slam shut and then his father's truck screeching out of the driveway. By the time Carl appeared in his doorway, Theo had located his football equipment bag and was filling it with what clothes and books he had. He was shaking.

"Where are you going?" Carl asked.

"I don't know. Next door, I guess. For now."

"It'll be cold."

"I know."

Carl nodded solemnly. "The back window should be unlocked. I'll come over later, bring you a sleeping bag and some blankets, help you clean out a room."

"Sure," Theo said, biting his trembling lip. "That'd be great."

Chapter Six

She perched at the foot of the bed, one leg dangling off, the other tucked seductively under the first, wearing the same red dress as always: spaghetti strapped, tight through the torso, too short for anything legitimate. Chris looked past her, searching the room for clues. A teddy bear propped on the pillows. A nightstand radio playing trashy Europop. Everything bland and impersonal except the girl herself. Her stare entranced him.

Do you like toys? he asked innocuously.

The girl shifted what little weight she carried and the dress rode higher.

Yes, of course, she responded. *Who doesn't?*

Chris could think of someone but preferred not to. The girl seemed impossibly bored. He tried to come up with a more original question but couldn't.

What kind of stuff are you into? he asked.

He didn't care if he sounded like an idiot. Because she didn't care either. She leaned forward and the strap fell off her right shoulder. Slowly, she pulled it back up. Chris was infatuated. He could see the tiny sparkles in her makeup.

To think she was half a world away.

Cameltoe close up dancing dildo fingering live orgasm oil striptease vibrator zoom shaved tattoo stockings. No feet please.

It was a canned response, a keyboard shortcut, and it pierced his quivering heart. How much did these cam girls make anyway? Chris leaned back in his ergonomic chair and closed his eyes. Through his office window came the chants of Occupy protesters in the park across the street, and in the background, the din of their drum circle (renamed the "Seventh Circle" by the traders upstairs). The beat had started one morning two weeks ago and had yet to let up.

The girl on the screen—her handle was "NatashaXXXNextDoor18"— moved toward the camera and again her dress fell, farther this time, and the swell of her right breast became visible. Chris had been "visiting" young Natasha, mostly at lunchtime, for several days now, but was always careful to use his personal laptop and the "Ponder&Co-Visitor" Wi-Fi network. His goal was simple: convince her to get completely naked without "going private"—that is, without paying $4.99 a minute for the privilege. Why Natasha? Because almost all the other cam girls were naked from the get-go, and Chris liked the challenge. Plus, he could watch her for hours—though watching was all he could do. The wall that separated his office from the hallway was frosted glass; "getting comfortable" was out of the question.

Besides, "NatashaXXXNextDoor18" was just a mood-enhancing stand-in for the real target of his current workplace affections, a free-lancer named Kinsey, who not only existed in three dimensions but was, at that very moment, sitting in a conference room just down the hall. Alas, there was no progress to report on this latter front, so Chris focused his energies on his laptop screen, where he *was* making head-way. He had discovered, for instance, that Natasha was indeed her real name, and that the "18" referred not just to her stated age (though she looked older) but the historic district of Budapest where she plied her leg-dangling trade. Occasionally, he asked (typed) other questions, the usual fare—did her friends know what she did? Had she ever met an "admirer" IRL?—but they'd been either skillfully deflected or completely ignored.

He was about to inquire about the god-awful music she was playing when Natasha muted the sound and started speaking to someone off camera.

Who's there? Chris typed, genuinely curious. He watched his question float up and out of the chat box, lost among the comments and come-ons of Natasha's other devoted followers. The perverted masses. Which would make him . . . what? He'd been at his desk for an hour and had yet to log on to his Bloomberg terminal. Not that he had much real work. Client portfolio reviews wouldn't begin until after earnings season wound down next week.

He picked up his cell phone. He had no new messages, so he reread the text Sarah had sent two hours ago: *Jst finishd lunch w Audrey @ Balthazar - fnding somthing for work tonite - u shld come to the action . . . xx.* Chris hadn't responded yet, as the missive didn't contain a question that needed answering and could therefore be temporarily ignored. Also, it had annoyed him. The innocent-sounding "fnding somthing" surely meant a dress, which surely meant $1,000. Why a woman needed a new outfit for every party, wedding, or, in this case, "action" was a mystery for the ages. ("Inaction" would be more accurate, considering the auction in question was of old masters and the average bidder would be pushing eighty.) He understood that working at Sotheby's necessitated an extensive wardrobe, and further realized that Sarah, coming as she had from Williamsburg's more *dynamic* fashion scene, had needed to play catch-up. His problem was the tireless zeal with which she'd taken up the challenge. Occasionally, in their shared walk-in closet, he caught sight of a romper or crop top from those earlier days and marveled at how Sarah had moved so *thoroughly* from that world to this one. He had been her facilitator and encourager, and yet—and this was completely unfair, he knew—he had come to miss the woman she *had* been, back in Brooklyn, charging hand in hand with Audrey through all those endless, indelible nights—the blistering bands and squalid basements and black tar rooftops. The countless poor decisions. Chris had watched, bemused, and then saddened, as Sarah had drifted away from Audrey. No, it had been more purposeful: a willful separation. All that weight and drama, that creative intensity, left behind across the river. So why were they suddenly having lunch together? It was the type of thing Sarah would have told him about were it planned ahead of time. And hell, he would have asked to come along. But enough. On this day of carnal infatuation, the last person he needed to get stuck on was Audrey Benton.

He studied his laptop screen. NatashaXXXNextDoor18 was splayed across her bed, pecking at the keyboard in front of her. There was no sign of her mysterious visitor.

Your name is ambiguous, Chris wrote. *The girl next door part and the XXX part. Which are you?*

Again he watched his words—his handle was "Carson Johnson," which happened to be the name of Sarah's recently born-again high school boyfriend—float up and out of the chat box. Natasha was ignoring him. As well she should have. "Ambiguous." He was an idiot. He tried again:

Who were you talking to? Is there someone there with you?

I tell you in private, she typed.

The "Go Private" button was right there. He'd clicked on it many times with other cam girls, watched them writhe and rub, slow-playing for time. Almost always, their performances were staid, choreographed affairs—even the hard-core types, the toyers and squirters—and Chris would watch with mounting disinterest until, exasperated, he'd end the session without so much as a "thanks" or "goodbye." Just close the window midmoan. Happy masturbators are all alike; unhappy masturbators are unhappy in—

Cameltoe close up dancing dildo fingering live orgasm oil striptease vibrator zoom shaved tattoo stockings. No feet please.

Chris sighed. Kinsey was only three doors away. He'd casually strolled past the conference room earlier and spied her—or her outline anyway—through the frosted glass. He wanted to walk down there again but couldn't think of a good excuse. The bathroom, copier, and coffee machine were all in the other direction. What was she even doing here after all the trouble she'd caused? Not that the company could fire her at this point.

"ALL DAY, ALL WEEK, OCCUPY WALL STREET. ALL DAY, ALL WEEK, OCCUPY WALL STREET. ALL DAY, ALL WEEK, OCCUPY . . ."

Chris got up and stepped over to his window. Zuccotti Park was swarming with humanity, and the noise had become impossible to ignore. It didn't help that he was on a low floor, or that his venerable neo-gothic building, which ran along the park's south side, had single-pane windows (welded shut for reasons Chris preferred not to dwell upon). Unlike the great majority of his colleagues, he supported the Occupy movement—at least in principle. He wasn't wild about the finger pointing, or the sweeping condemnation of a sector that almost single-handedly propped up the city's economy. But he'd absorbed the lessons of the financial crisis: banks *were* too big, financial "instruments" too complex, lobbyists too powerful. In other words, the game *was* rigged, and the people who made money the focal point of their lives would always be corrupted by it. The protesters—the real ones, not the gutter punks and neo-Deadheads increasingly occupying the occupation—had some valid arguments, and he was curious to see where their efforts might lead.

Certainly, they were off to a rousing start. Hell, they were more organized than half the banks they were railing against. Chris thought back to the early days of the takeover, weeks ago now, when Occupy was just a lunchtime distraction. The first tables and tents, a few signs targeting the tourist buses on Broadway. Chris had assumed the cops would shut things down after a night or two, but the park was private property, which complicated any intervention. Meanwhile, the protesters got smart, quickly adopting rules—no amplified voices, no drugs or drinking, no needless confrontation—that made them difficult to arrest as rabble-rousers. The mayor had thought the spark would burn out; instead, it had caught and spread—to other cities, other countries. For all Chris knew, he was witnessing the beginnings of a worldwide movement.

Still, the whole thing was a major pain in the ass. The chants and speeches, the fucking drums. On conference calls, Chris employed the mute button until it was his turn to weigh in, which he did with what sounded like a palace coup occurring in the background. Again and again, he assured clients in Dallas and Charlotte and Kansas City that he wasn't under siege. At the same time, coworkers from other parts of the building had started roaming the north-side halls, sneaking peeks from any office with a decent view of the park. One managing director had even taken to carrying binoculars. "Those radical babes are no joke," he said. A prophetic statement, considering what had happened next.

Four days had passed since "Signgate," but Chris could still recall every sordid detail. The previous Tuesday morning, at seven forty-five a.m., he'd emerged from the 4 train at Wall Street, juggling the *Post*, his iPhone, and a shoulder bag. Wall was one stop farther than Fulton, the normal terminus of his commute, but the extra station meant not having to walk past the protest. Not that he'd been hassled, exactly; it was more a strange sensation of being . . . left out. Chris Van Vleck was accustomed to belonging, but Occupy was someone else's party. And while the guest list was theoretically open to all, it was not open to him. He had never been on the wrong side of the cultural divide, and he found it unnerving. "No one likes being reminded of their asshole-ness" was how one of the brokers upstairs had summed it up—almost eloquently, Chris thought.

He'd trudged up Broadway and was about to turn into his lobby when he saw a mob of protesters gathered along the southern edge of Zuccotti. They were linking arms and chanting as they pointed up at the side of a building. *His* building.

"THE WHOLE WORLD IS WATCHING. THE WHOLE WORLD IS WATCHING. THE WHOLE WORLD IS WATCHING. THE WHOLE WORLD IS—"

What the hell was happening? Chris ducked past a line of news trucks, then turned around and looked up. He saw them immediately, two crudely drawn signs—black words on giant sheets of white poster board—taped across the inside of several windows. *On his floor.*

THE 1% IS BUSY WORKING. WE ENCOURAGE YOU TO TRY IT!

Then, farther over:

THE PEOPLE UNITED ARE DELUDED AND SHORTSIGHTED
YOUR CONCEPT OF REBELLING IS RIOTS RAPES AND YELLING.

For a panicked moment, Chris thought this second sign was actually hanging in his office, but he counted windows and realized, to his great, if fleeting, relief, that it was in the conference room a few doors down. "Motherfuckers," said someone behind him, and Chris couldn't disagree. Who could possibly be so stupid? He hurried back to Broadway, crossed Cedar Street, and ducked into his lobby. He felt hunted.

Upstairs, all was quiet—wealth managers being late arrivers—so he slunk past his office and down to the conference room. The act felt illicit. It looked darker than usual inside, but also empty, so he cracked the door open—slowly. It took a moment to put things together. Of course it was dark; the signs were blocking the light. He stared at their blank backs. Such an uproar they were causing outside—hell, across the world, judging by the news trucks—and here he was, utterly alone with them. Markers and masking tape lay strewn across the long table, but he saw no clues as to the perpetrator. Obviously, he needed to tear the signs down.

He'd been replaying what happened next—or didn't—for the last four days. Chris remembered the thought of repercussions entering his mind, what would happen if—when—he removed them. His bosses wouldn't say anything, not publicly, but his coworkers would rib him for months, even those few who would have done the same. He'd made it this far by avoiding office politics, to say nothing of *politics* politics. He worked in a glorified frat house, and the slightest chink in someone's I-don't-give-a-fuck armor would be immediately exploited. And what about the TV cameras trained on the windows at that very moment? Surely, they'd pick up his image through the glass, and, well, this wasn't the best time in the history of finance to be attracting attention to oneself. Still, if he crouched down low, maybe—

He heard her before he saw her, the angry *shush-shush*ing of a woman on a mission, and when she appeared in the doorway he froze. Like a burglar in a movie when the lights come on. And then they did come on, and she was throwing her bag down and surging past him toward the windows—dyed black hair, tucked-in blouse, short pencil skirt, and white headphones around her neck.

"You dickheads can't be this fucking stupid," she shouted as she ripped the oversized sheets down, one by one. The room grew lighter with every liberated window, and when she was finished—it didn't take long—she glared at Chris. He had picked her bag up off the floor and now held it out tentatively. She snatched it away and several items spilled out—lipstick, loose change, cigarettes, two tampons, a MetroCard—

They both bent down.

"Get away from me!" she hissed.

"Easy," Chris said, standing back up. "I didn't do it. Actually, I was about to take them down when you—"

"Shut up. I know you didn't do it. You don't have the balls."

She had a knee on the ground, collecting the last fragments of her personal life, when Chris noticed them—the stocking-line tattoos running up the back of her legs. The seam in her actual tights had shifted in the chaos, revealing their more permanent twins, and Chris glanced at where the four parallel lines disappeared beneath her skirt. Then she stood up, made a slight adjustment, and the ink lines were gone. She was gone. Stomping off down the hall. Had she said something else? Chris wasn't sure. *Stocking lines under her stocking lines.* His mind reeled with possibilities. Who the hell was she?

"Signgate" led off the local news that night and, predictably, made the cover of Wednesday's *Post* (headline: THE EMPIRE STRIKES BACK). Later that morning, Ponder & Co.'s CEO, Henry Ponder III, apologized to a pseudo-aggrieved Jim Cramer live on CNBC (the two were actually close, Cramer having started his career as a broker under Ponder at Goldman). He swore the perpetrators would be found and punished in short order, and an hour later an all-company email was sent out, announcing an investigation and a $5,000 reward. That'll do it, Chris thought, but even he was surprised by the speed of the betrayal. The culprits were unmasked before the markets even closed, two muni-desk morons with a sizable wager on which sign would garner more press attention. Both were suspended without pay until further notice (surely less than a week, considering the money municipal bonds were bringing in).

But the real story, at least in-house, was the alluring sign destroyer, who was soon revealed to be a freelance photo editor, hired to organize and enhance various images—executive headshots, growth charts, multiracial stock photos—for the company's redesigned website. Rumor had it she, too, had received an apology from Ponder, along with a temporary office and a bump in her hourly fee. That the space they provided was the very conference room she'd freed from tyranny was, Chris understood, a not-so-subtle indication of the company's true feelings. Let her stew in her own mess.

Chris, of course, had been thrilled by the assignation and spent the second half of the week "strolling" past the conference room at increasingly frequent intervals, but she seemed to have vanished. At the same time, an entire underground of "tattooed temp" gossip began springing up around the office, and at P. J. Clarke's on Friday after work, Chris had learned that her name was—incredibly—Kinsey ("like the sex dude"); that she'd been spotted by Sid Eichlinger sitting cross-legged at an Occupy "Planning Circle" Wednesday afternoon; and lastly, that she was now working off-hours, so as to have as little contact as possible with people like him. Chris digested all of this with increasing annoyance, his private crush having clearly gone prime time. When had everyone gotten into the alt-girl look?

He'd left Clarke's a few minutes after a linebacker-sized trader with armpit stains pronounced Kinsey a "strong buy" and spent the cab ride uptown wondering why she'd ever want to work at a place like Ponder. Even as a freelancer. He decided to ask her himself. Maybe "off-hours" meant Saturdays. Surely Chris could find *something* to do in the office.

His hunch had been right. Here he was and there she was, but now what? Should he happen past the conference room a second time? No, it'd be too obvious. He'd have to wait. He retreated from the window to his desk and tapped the space bar to wake his laptop back up. How long had he been gazing down on the protes—holy shit, Natasha was topless! *Finally*. And Chris wasn't the only one who'd noticed. Her chat box was blowing up, and he felt a pathetic tinge of jealousy as he joined in:

I thought you didn't get naughty on this side of the paywall.

He waited for a witty response as a flood of other comments rolled past. From "FarTooBig" and "MarseillesMister" and "SqueezeThemHarder." From "JewBoy69" and "OctopussyMan" and "ChelseaMorning."

Cameltoe close up dancing dildo fingering live orgasm oil striptease vibrator zoom shaved tattoo stockings. No feet please.

That's all she had to say? Chris was disheartened. He had wanted to bend her to his will, make her do what she said she wouldn't but now had, now *was*, right then.

He heard a noise in the hall and looked up. White headphones! On what looked like an apparition, shape-shifting through the frosted glass.

"Hey," he called out. "Hey, wait!"

He saw her slow, and then stop and . . . backtrack to his door. He swallowed, dryly.

"What," she said, her eyes darting around his office. There wasn't much to see.

"I just wanted . . . after the other day . . . to introduce myself, like officially. I'm Chris Van Vleck." He thought of walking over to shake her hand—she was all of four steps away—but she didn't look particularly receptive. "Also," he said, "I wanted to apologize."

Kinsey didn't react. She was leaning against the door frame in a smocklike gray dress with black tights. She looked past Chris, out the window, so he stepped back over to it, inserting himself into her visual frame. He wasn't used to apologizing, or even pretending to apologize, and he assumed she would ask why, or for what, but she remained silent.

"What I mean is that I should have ripped those signs down as soon as I got out of the elevator. They pissed me off, too. Not that I'm totally on board with everything going on out there"—he gestured vaguely behind him—"I mean"—what was his coworker's line?—"who wants to be called an asshole, right? Even if it's true!" He chuckled; she didn't. "Anyway, I was just about to tear them down, but then the cavalry arrived and—"

"What are you working on?" she asked, still gazing out the window.

Chris exhaled. "I'm studying revenue projections for a social media start-up called LifeScape, a kind of an Ancestry.com-meets-Facebook play, but with a pretty strong branding side. I manage"—he hated to say it, so he tried to sound ironic—"*high-net-worth* portfolios, which are pretty conservative by nature, investment-wise, but I like to mix a few long shots in. Keeps things exciting. And when one of them hits . . ."

But none of them had ever hit, because little of what he was saying was true. While he did help manage money for several wealthy families and individuals (much of his own family's wealth was managed by the bank—though not by him—and Chris knew all too well that his employment there was no coincidence), it wasn't major money, and he was extremely restricted in terms of what he could invest in. Early-round start-up financing was certainly out of the question.

"Anyway," he continued, "Saturdays are a good time to get a jump on—"

"You're a terrible liar."

He tried to hide his shock. "What are you talking about?"

"You're not studying revenue whatevers, you're watching porn. Probably because you're married and aren't getting it at home."

Chris felt his face go flush, from both embarrassment and exhilaration.

"First of all, I'm not married," he said. "And second of all, what are you talking about, watching porn?"

"You're not?"

"No!"

"You're a fucking idiot. I can see your laptop screen in the window reflection. She looks pretty hot; you should get back to her."

Chris wheeled around. Sure enough, there was the lovely Natasha, like a hologram on the glass, not only still topless but now touching herself. (What the fuck?) He turned back to his sparring partner. She was still there, which Chris took as a positive sign.

"Her name's Natasha," he said. "Nice girl."

"I'm sure. But she's getting ripped off on that site. BlueTubes is better. They take forty percent, not fifty. But why am I telling you? *You're* the revenue expert."

Escalation. Chris could play that game, too.

"You may as well just come out and say you like me."

She unfolded her arms and slid her right hand down the side of her dress, as if searching for a pocket. But the dress had no pockets, so she awkwardly picked at her stocking before shifting her weight and refolding her arms.

"So you cheat on your wife?"

"My girlfriend. And no."

"Bullshit. That's like your fifth lie, and I've only been here two minutes."

The chanting had reached a crescendo:

"ALL DAY ALL WEEK OCCUPY WALL STREET, ALL DAY ALL WEEK OCCUPY WALL STREET, ALL DAY ALL WEEK OCCUPY WALL STREET . . ."

Without asking to come in, she walked over and joined Chris at the window. Down below, people were sitting in circles, listening to speakers, waiting for food.

"I was there the whole first week," she said. "Slept right where that green tent is now. And it was *wild*. We kept waiting to get hauled off but nothing happened. I was in charge of laying out the *Occupy Wall Street Journal*, and I guess I still am, though we've only published one issue."

"You still haven't told me your name," Chris said.

"You've been sitting in here waiting for me to walk by. You already know it."

Chris suppressed a grin. "Well, it's not often we get political activists in these parts."

"Believe me, this isn't my typical gig. But I saw the listing on the Freelancers Union website, and when I found out the job was near

Zuccotti, I took it. Organizing photos for a bunch of suits. How bad could it be, right?" She laughed ruefully.

"I'm sure your fellow revolutionaries love you working for the enemy."

"I'm sure your wife loves you lusting after Russian cam girls."

"She's Hungarian."

"Your wife?"

"Ha ha."

"See, you are married."

"No, you've just worn me down."

There was heat between them; Chris could tell she felt it, too. Why else would she still be here? She moved to his desk and leaned over to study the screen.

"It's a set," she said. "No twenty-year-old's bedroom looks that anti-septic. Probably a pimp in a warehouse running half a dozen girls at a time. Do you ever see one of them start talking to someone just off camera? That's her being checked up on." She studied Natasha. "I must say, you have good taste."

"You should take her private."

Kinsey ignored him. Here was the chess game of the sexes that Chris so badly missed. He was dying to ask how she knew so much about cam girls, and she knew it, which meant he couldn't give her the satisfaction.

"Nice stocking tattoos, by the way. Quite a commitment."

"God, you really are a cliché. Your wife must be straight as fuck."

"My *girlfriend*, and for your information she's hooked up with a few women."

"I meant *preppy* straight. As in, look at you with your little Suicide Girl fetish, so clearly rooted in the frustrations of your vanilla life. Is she from Connecticut? On Saturdays does she drag you to Ralph Lauren after brunch at JG Melon?"

"Where have you been all my life?"

Natasha produced a large dildo from her bedside drawer and began licking it.

"Gross," Kinsey said, and stepped back over to the window.

"I read in the *Post* that Kanye's visiting Occupy," Chris said. "I'm sure he'll offer everyone some keen insights into the failures of Sarbanes-Oxley."

"Kanye's cool."

"He's a jackass."

"Dude. You're wearing khakis."

This was, unfortunately, true, and while he could remind her that jeans (of which he had several hip and well-worn pairs) were forbidden in the office, he ceded the point. But Kanye had always been one of Chris's cultural weak spots. Time and again, he'd heard people whose taste he respected speak of the guy in reverential tones, and he just didn't understand why. Leaving aside the whole "George Bush doesn't care about black people" episode, which *had* been pretty epic, everything the rapper did was so completely opportunistic as to be absurd. Chris couldn't help but recall those long nights in Brooklyn with Sarah and her friends, and all the cocaine talk about exactly this, the real and the other, and what the difference was, and who had come from where, and why that mattered, everyone weighing in post–whatever show, four conversations at once, about which bands would make it and who would get them there, Rick Rubin and T Bone Burnett, the names behind the names, everything making sense in the moment but the next day half-forgotten, when, back at his desk, his head throbbing, his voice gravelly—

His phone was vibrating. He pulled it out and was about to press Ignore when he saw the caller's name and panicked. "Audrey B." As if there were another.

"What's the problem?" Kinsey asked, intrigued by Chris's indecision. "I'm guessing this isn't your wife either?"

"A friend," he said, realizing how ridiculous that sounded under the circumstances. Audrey never called him. Maybe something had happened at lunch. "Can you hold on a second?"

"Of course," Kinsey said, and smiled.

Chris answered the phone. Audrey's voice was garbled, like she was walking in the wind. Still, he could hear anxiety in her tone and was about to ask if she was okay when Kinsey turned for the door. "I'll be in the park later," she whispered as she moved past, and before he could object, she was gone. Then Chris heard a moan. And another. He turned to his desk, cell phone still to his ear, as the moans got louder and more lustful. Fuck! Kinsey had turned the sound all the way up. Chris dove for the laptop just as NatashaXXXNextDoor18 was reaching the "climax" of her performance. "Yes! Yes! Yes!" she screamed, before Chris managed to mute her.

"That doesn't sound like Sarah," said Audrey, coolly, into his ear.

*   *   *

In a devilish nod toward Audrey's newfound literary life, Chris suggested meeting at Ulysses on Pearl Street. That she'd found love with a man who preferred words to sound was a source of both amusement and jealousy to Chris: amusement because he'd never seen Audrey with a book before Theo came along; jealousy because he'd never managed to sleep with her back when everyone was single. This second fact was the great black mark on Chris's otherwise impressive carnal résumé. Passions had been so capricious in that Brooklyn scene, the main goal being to keep emotion at a safe distance, heartbreak being both time-consuming and déclassé. Chris, who had always blanched at the predictable tropes of the banker crowd (even as he displayed so many himself, from his love of black fleece vests to his gallery-hopping Thursday nights), had found in libertine Williamsburg a group of twentysomethings untethered to family or societal obligation, and thus free to explore themselves in ways his repressed uptown friends would never dare. What was often said of the indie crowd—they had hidden trust funds; they were faux-contrarians—could not be said of Audrey and Sarah's circle, most of whom balanced multiple jobs and artistic pursuits with a deft sleight of hand. (And anyway, so what if someone came from money but wore white bucks or striped jumpsuits or bangs down past her eyes? Why did limo liberals get such a bad rap when the alternative was the tedious redundancy of limo conservatism?)

Chris's Brooklyn friends were intoxicating—especially Audrey, with her cavalier approach to life. But she'd scared him, too, because it was no act. For a few weeks after they met, Chris had thought it would happen, that *they* would happen. He could feel the tension building, the two of them the last ones left at every Grand Street bar, on every rooftop at dawn. But each of the moments had passed, and somewhere in that frenzied accumulation, the larger moment had as well. Audrey started up with someone else, a session player with a topknot (of all things). Chris was both disheartened and relieved, and convinced himself that their near miss had been a mutual, if unspoken, decision, based on the realization that getting together—and then, presumably, coming apart—would have destroyed both their fast-evolving friendship and the fabric of the larger group. In truth, he knew he was out of his depth. Long strings pulled at him, attached at the far end to his parents, his caste, his world. It was hard to join society if you weren't born of it, but harder still was escaping it if you were. Though he liked to believe his spirit was free, he was not a true free spirit. He needed stability and routine to counter excess and uncertainty, and as he began to understand this, he found himself gravitating toward Audrey's blond-haired best friend—also beautiful—whose autonomy, he discovered, contained certain loopholes. Plus, she would fuck him.

Walking south toward the bar, Chris became increasingly curious about the purpose of this surprise get-together. Audrey had said only that it was urgent. He pictured her, waiting impatiently—he was running late—and wondered what she'd be wearing. It had been ages since they'd been alone together, absent the safety of significant others. She had never fully understood, or perhaps forgiven, Sarah's metamorphosis, just as Chris had never quite gotten over Theo's arrival on the scene. He supposed it made a perverse kind of sense that after so many years driven by style and impulse, Audrey would fall for a man of substance and consideration. Or substance and deliberation. But definitely substance.

Theo Gorski. Chris had never been more wrong about a person. He'd thought the guy was dead weight when Audrey first brought him around. Quiet, oafish, socially inept. Yet there she was, the rock-and-roll prom queen of the Northside, burrowing into him as they walked down Driggs like she might otherwise freeze to death. Of course it had taken all of one conversation with him for Chris to change his mind, and soon he found himself preemptively asking if Theo would be coming to whatever concert or party they were going to that night. Sarah said he had a man crush, and Chris didn't disagree. Theo's patience and thoughtfulness belonged to some other time than theirs, and Chris watched in fascination as those qualities rubbed off on Audrey. She started slowing down, paying attention, even discussing current events. Once or twice, Chris spied a *New Yorker* peeking out from her purse.

He and Sarah, three years ahead of Audrey and Theo in couples time, had just decided to move in together when Theo came thumping along, and Chris had assumed the girls would remain close. Instead they'd lost touch in that way so common to big-city friendships. Partly it was geography, but the larger problem lay with Sarah, who wanted a clean break from the cheap drugs, chipped nail polish, and tawdry romances of her Williamsburg years. She was done with the grind of creative poverty. Occasionally Chris would suggest inviting Audrey and Theo over for dinner (Sarah had spent God-knew-what redoing their kitchen), or better yet, L-training it out to the Burg for old times' sake, but Sarah would obfuscate and say something that sounded enough like yes that she couldn't be accused of saying no. Her reasons were many, Chris knew, but only one held weight, and discussing it was off-limits. What had happened still scared her that much.

He arrived at Ulysses ten minutes late but still paused to regard himself in the glass façade of the building next door before striding inside. Halfway around the large oval bar, he spotted her—or the side of her—at the rearmost table. Her halter top revealed just enough of the tattoo on her left shoulder blade to make a person ask to see more. That's what Chris had done the first night he met her, at a bar called Black Betty, and he still recalled the thrill of watching her pull her bra and dress straps down with none of the histrionics that so often accompanied such revealings—no drawn-out sighs or comments about being tired of having to show it to everyone. Audrey was pretty in an off-kilter way, with wavy golden-brown hair and exaggerated features that Chris believed accentuated her allure. Her oversized mouth turned her smile radiant. Her set-apart eyes emanated a dispassionate cool. Her too-broad shoulders highlighted the litheness of the figure they framed. And her throaty voice, while the bane of what she jokingly claimed could have been a great singing career, suggested a life more fully lived than most. It occurred to Chris that these particulars made Audrey intensely American, though how, exactly, he wasn't sure. Seeing her now, though—he'd become rooted in place—the answer came to him. Makeup! She wore almost none. Obviously, he'd been around too many Sotheby's girls lately, and the contrast had allowed him to finally—

"Hey, Patrick Bateman, stop being creepy."

Chris snapped out of his reverie. Audrey was frowning at him. "Sorry," he said, recovering quickly. "It's just that you look so old and haggard."

"It's the pregnancy weight."

"The *what*?"

"Shut up and get over here." She stood up and they hugged across the table, Audrey holding the sides of his head afterward, like a mother with a child just back from summer camp. Chris found it endearing, though he found most everything Audrey did endearing. She had ordered two frosted mugs of beer, and as he took a seat she skidded one over to him. "Sorry, it's just a Budweiser. I know you hedge fund guys are into all that craft shit."

She'd been calling him a hedge fund guy for years now, though she was perfectly aware of what he actually did. Chris didn't care; he knew Audrey never fell back on easy stereotypes. She possessed a complete lack of propensity toward judgment, a trait as refreshing as it was naïve.

They caught up quickly. Chris asked about her lunch at Balthazar and winced when Audrey said she'd left Sarah shopping in Nolita. He braced for a question about the moaning on the phone, but it didn't come. Instead, Audrey got to the point.

Which was Fender.

Chris repeated the name slowly. What had he expected? An engagement announcement? A (real) pregnancy? Not really. Not yet. But *Fender*? As open as he was to intervals of dissoluteness, Chris ultimately believed in files and boxes and all things having a place. Only one episode in his life remained stubbornly uncategorized, and Fender resided at the heart of it.

He listened as Audrey recounted the previous evening's events, followed by her so-far-futile attempts to make sense of them. As he absorbed her words and their possible implications he began to feel an old rush of adrenaline. How had his life become so dull?

"Let me guess," Chris said, gleaning where she was heading. "You don't think he killed himself."

"I don't know what to think," Audrey admitted. "It just doesn't seem like something he'd do. Jumping off a bridge, and with no witnesses?"

"He always did like an audience."

"And there's nothing online. I searched for an hour this morning."

"Do you want to go to the police? Maybe they have some information."

"I don't think that's a good idea," Audrey said, shaking her head. "What if they've found his . . . his *body*, and are digging through his past for clues? Then I show up, not even a close friend, and begin asking questions. They could get suspicious."

Chris frowned. Audrey had always been so sure of herself, but now she seemed scared. "Don't tell me you think this has something to do with . . ." He didn't finish the sentence. He didn't have to. He understood then—though perhaps he'd always known—that they could never fully move past the events of that not-quite-long-ago summer. What had happened was too momentous, how they'd left it too open-ended.

"The thought crossed my mind," Audrey said finally. "Do you think I'm crazy?"

No, Chris didn't think she was crazy. Audrey was, in her way, one of the sanest people he knew. If *she* was worried, then *he* should be worried.

"But it's been six years," Chris said. "Why now?"

"I don't know. According to Lucas, Fender was destitute and shooting dope. I mean, he's a loose cannon *without* a smack habit. Imagine him as an addict. Anything could have happened."

Chris's exhilaration was turning to anxiety. What they were talking about, or around, was almost unthinkable. An old friend dead because of something they'd done.

"Did you bring this up with Sarah?" Chris asked.

"Yes, but she didn't want to talk about it."

"Sounds about right. And Theo?"

Audrey looked down at her beer.

"Don't tell me you haven't told him."

Her eyes searched the table, the coarse grains of stained wood. Then she slowly shook her head. "The four of us promised each other we'd never tell anyone."

"Sure, but—"

"But *what*?" Audrey's green eyes flicked up at him and Chris knew to probe no further. Still, he was stunned. He'd assumed, given the significance of the events, that she'd unburdened herself ages ago, had told Theo, if not quite everything, then at least the more salient details. The two of them were so open about their lives. Chris remembered physically recoiling when he learned they trusted each other with their email accounts. Who the hell did that?

"So what do we do?" Audrey asked.

Chris smiled ruefully. "We wait to get picked off, one by one. Maybe we should all go spend a weekend in the woods together, make it easier."

Audrey closed her eyes and rubbed her temples.

"Okay, okay." Chris reached for his beer. "I don't think there's much we *can* do but wait to see if Fender—"

"Don't say it."

"*Surfaces*?"

"You're the fucking worst."

But it had worked. She visibly lightened up, and Chris took the opportunity to change the subject. He asked about the Westfields, and Audrey recapped the show the previous night.

"How did I not know about it?" he said, genuinely perturbed.

"Sarah asked the same thing. I guess they don't wild-post on the Upper East Side."

"What's wild posting?"

"You're seriously hopeless."

They finished their beers, Audrey downing the rest of hers in two gulps. She stood up and stretched her legs, stretched everything. Chris got up, too.

"You know," he said tentatively, "it's okay to tell Theo. If I were him, I'd want to know. Or at least have been told. I can't imagine a more trustworthy guy."

Audrey smirked. "Now, there's a subject you can speak to with authority."

"I'm just saying."

They put their coats on and walked the length of the bar. When they got outside, they hugged.

"Don't worry," she said, "I won't ask about the girl in your office."

"I was wondering if you heard that." Chris attempted to laugh in a genuine way. "It was the computer. A little Saturday afternoon entertainment."

That this statement was actually true was not comforting. Audrey was well aware of Chris's weakness for women and accepted it in the same way she accepted all human foibles: they were basically none of her business (even when they arguably were). But that hardly meant she approved. As far as Chris knew, she had never said anything to Sarah, but he also knew there was, conceivably, a line that could be crossed. He thought again of Audrey's tattoo. The cowboys and distant mountains. Why couldn't Sarah have gotten one like that?

They parted, promising to stay in touch. Audrey was taking the subway back to Brooklyn. He should head home as well, though he supposed a quick stop at the protests couldn't hurt. He was always intrigued by new scenes. To say nothing of new tour guides.

The Two Best Players

Williamsburg, Brooklyn
May 2002

The Turkey's Nest was empty when Audrey walked in, save for Gavin, who had the sports section of the *Daily News* open on the bar.

"ESPN's not enough?" she asked, nodding up at the TV playing highlights in the corner.

"I'm a Mets fan," Gavin said. "They don't get much national coverage."

Audrey filed this away. She hadn't yet chosen her New York teams—she was still new to the city—but the Mets sounded promising. She liked underdogs. She chose a bar stool near the front window and dug the latest *Backstage* out of her bag. Gavin was already pouring her a draft.

She paged through to "Auditions & Casting Calls." These were her parameters:

- No unpaid gigs (she was too broke)
- No SAG jobs (she wasn't a union member)
- No singing or dancing (not her forte)
- Nothing involving travel (no car)

- No reality TV auditions (her actual life was close enough)
- No modeling (negotiable, depending on $$ and situation)

This left . . . not much. A low-budget horror film shooting on Staten Island. A pharmaceutical company voice-over. Two listings for female "atmosphere." Audrey circled each and then cross-referenced their call times with her work schedules. She'd been in Brooklyn for three months and had landed exactly that many auditions. Of those, two had gone poorly. The third, an online training industrial for Citibank, had appeared promising (two callbacks!) until the HR woman running the casting asked Audrey where she, *personally*, banked. Thinking it was small talk, Audrey informed her, practically laughing, that she *personally* banked at the Payomatic check-cashing center on Bedford and North Fourth. At which point the woman pinned her lips together in a kind of antismile and slowly edged away. Audrey was not called back again.

She drank her beer and looked out the front window. It was four thirty on a beautiful spring afternoon and she'd just worked the dreaded Saturday brunch shift at Enid's. Seven hours of ketchup bottles and 10 percent tips. Now she was experiencing that familiar sensation of simultaneous exhaustion and invigoration. Wiped out and worked up. After a dinner shift, you could take it one way or the other, double down on the high or go home and crash, but lunches were more challenging, with all those open hours afterward. You could almost have a normal night, if there were ever one to be had.

"Find anything?" Gavin asked. He was an actor, too, when he wasn't bartending or writing plays or working at a UPS Store in midtown. In Florida, Audrey had been the only one of her friends who worked part-time full-time. Here, everyone did.

"'Atmosphere,'" Audrey said.

"Atmosphere's important." Gavin peered around. "Maybe not in *here*, but . . ."

"Look at this: a listing for aspiring Knicks City Dancers." Audrey circled it facetiously. "And to think I moved here to get away from cheerleaders."

Gavin took her pint glass and refilled it. "It's on me," he said.

"That's quite a buyback policy."

"You're my only customer. I have to keep you happy." He picked up the *Backstage*. "You should check their website on Thursdays when the listings go live. By now half of this stuff's already been cast."

Audrey thanked him, pretending she hadn't heard this advice before. The problem was that she didn't have a computer—or most other benchmarks of a conventional existence. A bicycle, for instance. Or a TV. Or a cell phone. Or friends.

Somehow two years had passed between Audrey's deciding to move to New York and her actually doing it. Partly she'd needed to save up money. But there'd been other problems, too. A boyfriend. A health scare (Connie's). And then a five-month delay courtesy of 9/11. When she finally arrived it was the dead of winter and Brooklyn lay buried under sheets of black ice and gray slush and brown roadside snow. Everything that should have been white but was not. Despite growing up in Michigan, she was ill-prepared for the cold, a decade in Florida having dulled her to the vagaries of seasons. She had no clothes for raw weather and no extra cash to remedy the problem. In truth, she'd been so busy tying up the loose ends of her life in Cape Canaveral that she hadn't planned the next stage of it beyond buying a Greyhound ticket and printing out (on the Merritt Island Public Library's one Internet-connected computer) a New York City transit system map.

But Audrey was resourceful, and it had taken her less than an hour to get from the Port Authority to the Bedford Avenue stop on the L. Why Williamsburg? Because every decent band that barnstormed through her lackluster part of mid-Florida spoke of the place the way Ed Beemis spoke of the moon. Yet, on that first day she emerged from the subway to find nothing resembling the hothouse of artistic freedom and experimentation she'd envisioned. In fact, she found little that wasn't sleet or snow, until she found the Verb, on North Fourth, a no-frills café where she sipped her first New York coffee and, twenty minutes later, landed her first New York job. After a sleepless night at an economy hotel overhanging the BQE, she returned to the Verb for her first day of work and was offered a just-vacated room—for $630 a month—in a barista named Jodi's barebones apartment on North Ninth. Two days after that, she found a second job, at Enid's in nearby Greenpoint. With her first modest paycheck, she bought a used winter coat.

February and March: how brutal those months had been. Running, so often literally, from job to job, shift to shift, just trying to get by. She'd arrived with $970. If that had looked like a princely sum stacked in small bills on her bed in Cape Canaveral, it looked like her entire future when she handed it over to Jodi, along with the promise of more to come (there was a security deposit, too). Audrey was as good as her word but completely broke afterward. Less-than-twenty-dollars broke. Less than ten. What a shameful feeling that was, to wake up in the morning and have to game out how she'd eat that day. The Verb had free coffee and Enid's provided staff meals (and ground beef and chicken stock she could sneak home from the kitchen freezer), but restaurant shifts were irregular in those first months, and there were times when she went to bed hungry.

Twice, in mid-March, she called Greyhound to inquire about tickets home. She missed Florida—the weather and water—but mostly she missed her grandmother. Audrey had done all she could before leaving, setting up visiting schedules with Ed Beemis, Sid Stevens, Jasper Sash, and others—not that anyone had to be convinced. Connie was doing well; she had just enough money (from Bill's pension and life insurance), and her social calendar was always full. But in the depths of a New York winter, guilt came all too easily. The sense that she'd abandoned the woman. Sculpting latte foam into misshapen hearts, Audrey imagined terrible accidents. At night she dreamed of funerals. And why not? It had already happened once. So what if Connie had insisted that her granddaughter move to New York? That didn't mean Audrey should have.

But she didn't return home. She waited out the winter, and then one Saturday in April, as if a whistle had blown, everyone poured onto the streets at once. Smoking, drinking, flirting, scheming. Audrey, accustomed to the apathy of her Florida friends, was at first overwhelmed by the sheer energy of her new surroundings, the ardor and buoyancy of youth in the wild. At the same time, she could tell these were her people and Brooklyn her town. But her life was small. She was lonely, or at least aware of being constantly alone. Her two roommates didn't speak to each other, or, very often, to her. Jodi, the barista, was a vegan animal rights activist who taped Polaroids of abused animals all over the apartment, including, for reasons Audrey couldn't fathom, the refrigerator. Pouring a middle-of-the-night glass of water, or making eggs at noon, she would find herself face-to-face with wretched images of furless cats or three-legged puppies, their eyes wide and haunted, their names (just to cement the personal connection) written in black marker across the bottom. Audrey couldn't take them down; she was only a subletter.

As was Randall, the third roommate, and a full-time dumpster diver with the gaunt frame to prove it. If the animal Polaroids hadn't soured Audrey on using the fridge, the "finds" Randall kept inside it—blackened fruits and browned greens—would have done the job. He and Jodi had gone to the School of Visual Arts together, though they were no longer close (if they ever had been). Audrey sensed she'd landed in the middle of some silent war for radical/anarchist street cred, with the poor refrigerator bearing the brunt of the artillery.

They lived on the first floor of a detached row house built to lodge the immigrant stevedores of centuries past. Drab vinyl siding now covered the original brick façade, but the building still contained classic flourishes, wavelike moldings and dark, wood-paneled walls that resembled the exterior of a vintage Bonneville station wagon. Audrey's tiny bedroom was tucked away in the back. To counteract the issue of space, a Murphy bed had been installed by a previous tenant, and for a while, Audrey dutifully stored it in the wall every morning. But the task quickly became annoying, and then Herculean, and within a month she'd succumbed to the fate of seasoned Murphy bed owners the world over and just left it down, thus removing both her aggravation and any hint of floor. Quickly, the bed became the focal point of her domestic life. She slept on it, ate on it, stored clothes on it, and listened to music on it. Occasionally, she fucked on it.

Her window, like her bed, held the possibility of opening up the room, but instead only added to its claustrophobia. It was barred, due to neighborhood break-ins that still occurred with some frequency, but the bigger problem was the view it offered, which was not of a quaint yard but an identical window attached to an identical house four feet away. To look outside was to look back inside the peeling-wallpaper kitchen of an octogenarian Italian couple, though Audrey only ever saw the wife, a stout woman who cooked in a stained white apron tied over an ankle-length dress. Breakfast. Lunch. Dinner. The woman lived in front of countertops—though Audrey was hardly one to talk, there being plenty of countertops in her own life. Still, her neighbor depressed her, and she vowed to get blinds when she could afford them. But Audrey could never afford them, and after a while, she stopped wanting them anyway. It wasn't that she was voyeuristic, exactly, for the woman went through the same monotonous routine every day. Rather, it was the knowledge that that routine was taking place, that Audrey could peek over and know she'd be chopping onions or stringing pasta, that in this still-foreign world she could count on one person being consistently there. As for the woman spying on Audrey, that never happened. And why should it? She'd no doubt lived here for decades, witnessed countless young people come and go. Transients, opportunists, layabouts. Audrey had seen her on the street a few times, her stockinged calves like water balloons, tying up garbage or pushing a fold-up shopping cart. She always tried to make eye contact, but the woman kept her head down. Maybe it was a territorial thing. This was *her* neighborhood, or had been. But surely she'd come from somewhere else once, too. Why did old people always forget that?

Audrey's commute to and from Enid's took her through McCarren Park, a blocks-long expanse that in the frigid heart of February had seemed as seedy and unwelcoming as any place she'd yet encountered. But then the weather changed and the park came to life like a classic film being colorized. Wool-sweatered twentysomethings fussed with cigarettes under lampposts. Couples walked their dogs unleashed. Next came coolers and soccer balls, Frisbees and guitars. The color of the grass marked the passage of time. Homeless men assembled. Running groups ran past. By early May blankets were being spread out in line with the fortifying sun. On them sat pale-skinned bodies, their robustness suggesting gymless winters, their artful tattoos communicating irreverence, or politics, or maybe just the age. Here is Brooklyn, Audrey thought. About time.

She was settling in now, meeting people. Almost everyone at the Verb played in a band, or wrote about bands, or anyway loved music. Her favorite coworker, a dreadlocked art school dropout named Gerard, spent his nights busking on the L-train platform with a classical guitar. Audrey didn't take the subway much—she'd been back to Manhattan only twice—but was so intrigued by his sound that she started paying the fare (or, if she'd been drinking, hopping the turnstile at the Driggs Avenue entrance) just to hear him. Recently, he'd begun playing with a group of guys—more a collective than a band—and they'd named themselves TV on the Radio. Kyp, another Verb barista, with a serious Afro and a devoted following of female customers, was talking about joining them, too. "But what would happen if we went on tour?" Gerard asked him, one morning, as the two men made cappuccinos and Audrey worked the register. "There'll be no black dudes left in Williamsburg."

Gerard had a point. For a place—or a scene within a place—comprised of kids escaping the stifling similitude of Texas or Ohio or even uptown Manhattan, Williamsburg sure did have a prevailing aesthetic. The outfits and motifs, the haircuts and body art, the curated design. That's what a "scene" was, she supposed: like minds doing like things. Still, Audrey missed the incongruities of home, where, for instance, the rigid aesthetic of NASA could coexist in harmony with the yard sale disarray of the larger Space Coast. America unvarnished. The closest approximation in her new neighborhood was the Turkey's

Nest, a no-frills dive with a warped pool table, cheap drinks, permanent holiday lights, and a friendly actor-turned-bartender named Gavin.

She watched him pour drinks. The *Backstage* was still open on the bar, but wet now, from spillage. There was, of course, a finite amount of time that a woman like her could sit alone in such a place without being hit on, and Audrey sensed the end of that time approaching. The Nest was filling up. To her immediate right stood two guys waiting to order. Audrey kept her eyes forward, assuming one of them would speak to her, but they were busy talking to each other. Something about a softball game. Curious, she glanced their way. They were decked out in sweats and caps, their Rawlings mitts stacked on the bar in front of them. Audrey had a sudden yearning for her own softball days on the swampy fields of Merritt Island High School. She'd had a fluid lefty swing and a strong enough arm for third base.

"Do you play?"

Audrey looked up. She realized she'd been staring at their gloves. "I used to back home," she said. "I just moved here."

The answer appeared to be the right one. They introduced themselves—Jake and Jake—then paused, momentarily embarrassed. They looked like each other, too. The closer Jake was wearing a blue Twins jersey with "Hrbek 14" across the back, the other a too-tight "1985 Little Falls Mets Penn League Champs" T-shirt. Their identical mesh caps had interlaced "TN" logos.

The Jakes explained that they were the captains of the bar's coed softball team.

"And guess what we need," said Jake One.

"Girls," Audrey said.

They nodded and asked if they could buy her a beer. She put the *Backstage* away.

Audrey had never been much of a joiner. Her Florida friends were artists and self-styled rebels who bristled in group settings and vanished at the first sign of conflict. But that was then. Her new life required a new strategy, and here was a chance to mold one. Plus, she liked these guys: their ironic jerseys and unironic exuberance. She submitted herself to a few mostly softball-related questions and was soon being introduced to more players congregating around the bar. They'd all just come from practice, across the street in McCarren Park.

It was a jocular assemblage that quickly grew to include girlfriends and other non–team members. A few recognized Audrey from the Verb. Another had been to Cape Canaveral. Beers became margaritas and then shots, and at some point, a few hours later, it became clear that Audrey was not just the newest member of the Turkey's Nest Gobblers but would in fact be playing in the season opener the following morning against a bar called Pete's Candy Store. "Don't take them lightly just because of the name," someone said, and Audrey promised she wouldn't. Around midnight, she stumbled home to look for her glove. She was pretty sure she'd brought it north.

*　　*　　*

Despite alarm clock issues, a sizable hangover, and a frantic second search for the glove she'd unearthed the night before (she refound it, disturbingly, in the kitchen beside an empty pint of Häagen-Dazs), Audrey arrived at the park with five minutes to spare, only to find both softball fields empty. Weird. She was sure the Jakes had said the game started at eleven a.m. Maybe it had been canceled? Too bad; she'd been excited to play. She sat down and unlaced her cleats, which she'd discovered in the closet with her glove. In fact, she'd put together quite an outfit, highlighted by a vintage Kennedy Space Center T-shirt and knee-high softball socks. She'd even gotten her shift later at Enid's covered, in case there were postgame activities—this being a bar league and all.

She was about to head over to the Turkey's Nest to ask around when she looked up and saw them, trudging through the distant outfield like a battle-worn army, a dozen bodies lugging bats and equipment bags. The Jakes were leading the way. They looked like they hadn't slept.

When they reached Audrey they apologized, before explaining that the team always met at the bar beforehand to shake out the cobwebs. A period of greetings and introductions ensued. As a former resident of Florida, Audrey was used to very little occurring over a large expanse of time, but for the next fifteen minutes almost nothing happened at all. Game time came and went with no game threatening to break out. Eventually, the other squad arrived, looking just as haggard as the Gobblers, and Jake One took it as a cue to gather his team near first base. A few players started stretching, but the main point of the huddle was to share two freshly rolled joints—the Williamsburg version of a team-building exercise. They were enormous, and when the first one reached Audrey she took a modest hit. It didn't matter. Her brain caught fire. The stuff was potent, at least compared to Jasper Sash's swamp grass. The thought—her last of any coherence—soothed her. At least Connie was smoking the light stuff.

Her teammates paired off to throw. The nerves that connected Audrey's mind to her body were a twisted mess, but she managed to nod when Jake Two asked to play catch. She jogged onto the field and held her glove up in an exploratory fashion. The ball came toward it.

Like a rocket launch, a good high progressed through a series of stages, each connected to the one before and after but also specific to itself and prone to deep analysis. In this way, throwing a softball back and forth, and chasing the softball when it sailed past her, and then chasing the Labrador who reached the ball before she did, and then finally catching the dog and wrestling the ball out of its fangs . . . each of these activities took place outside of time, so that when Audrey finally turned around she was surprised to see Jake Two still standing there, waiting patiently. It felt like half a day had passed.

At some point, the Gobblers reconvened to go over ground rules, but the meeting quickly degenerated into a maelstrom of opinions regarding concrete walking paths and overhanging trees and the complex geography of two facing diamonds sharing a single outfield. Also, an empanada man had set up shop down the left-field line and refused to move. Audrey looked from face to face and was overcome by a hot flash of emotion. How readily her new teammates had accepted her. It was what she'd always liked about sports, the easy intimacy of shared experience. There was only one other female present (the rules required two in every lineup), a stolid girl with a blue bandana tied around her short black hair. She caught Audrey staring and flashed a quick smile.

The batting order was being read. Audrey heard her name, followed by the words "first base." She'd never played first base, but before she could lodge a protest her teammates were leaning in for a cheer— "*Gobble gobble!*"—and then running out to their positions. Audrey remained where she was. Jake One started jogging out to the mound but saw her and stopped.

"You okay?"

"I'm too stoned to play first base," she said.

He laughed. "You'll be fine. You caught everything I threw you in warm-ups."

Audrey not only distinctly remembered *not* catching everything—as evidenced by her wrestling match with the dog—but she could have sworn she'd been playing catch with Jake *Two*. They did look alike, and both were now wearing Turkey's Nest T-shirts, but they were hardly twins. Or even brothers. Or were they? No, of course they weren't. They had the same name!

This was her tenuous mind-set as she arrived at her position. But instinct took over. Rituals long forgotten. She stepped a few feet off the line as the opposing lead-off hitter dug in. She'd failed to watch how fast Jake (One or Two) was throwing during his warm-ups, and when the first pitch of the game left his hand she was relieved to see it had arc on it. The batter took it and the umpire . . . Oh my God, the umpire! How had she not noticed him? He was a shaggy-haired thirtysomething punk in paint-flecked jeans, a white dress shirt with ruffles up the front, and, on his head, what appeared to be a leather football helmet dating back to the formative years of the sport. "Strike one," he called out, with a cigarette hanging from his mouth, before promptly overruling himself. "Sorry, I meant 'ball one.' " Then he gave a safe sign, which made no sense at all. The Gobblers' catcher—the bandana girl—threw the ball back to the mound. No one seemed the least bit fazed.

Audrey was good at venturing through life without all the pertinent information, but this was next level. She punched her glove and tried to focus, but her mind refused to cooperate. She watched the Pete's leadoff hitter fly out softly to center for the first out, and then, sensing a presence, wheeled around to find a guy standing directly behind her—as if a game weren't being played. Except he was wearing a glove. Confused, she wondered if he'd been sent over to back her up as some kind of short fielder, but then looked past him and figured it out: he was the left fielder from the game on the other diamond. He started talking to her a few pitches later, and by the time the count in *her* game was full he'd asked for her number. Why not? He wasn't bad looking. And she wasn't exactly lighting it up on the love front. But she couldn't remember her apartment landline. "I'll give you mine," he said, and began to carve it into the infield dirt with his cleats. His heel was dragging out the last number when the Pete's batter grounded sharply back to the mound. Audrey watched Jake stab it before remembering she needed to cover first base. She hustled over, caught the throw, and stepped on the bag. Her teammates started toward the dugout. There were three outs? Shit, she'd missed one somewhere. She ran back to the bench, wondering how long the digits in the dirt would last.

She had no idea where she was hitting in the order, but it obviously wasn't toward the top, because bandana girl was digging into the batter's box and Jakes One *and* Two were swinging bats near the backstop. She sat next to a cooler of beer and tried not to zone out. Someone's boom box was playing Missy Elliott's "Hot Boyz."

Audrey's gender-mate hit a soft line drive over short and raced down to first. She took a wide turn, clapped her hands like Rickey Henderson, and retreated to the bag. One of the Jakes stepped up to the plate. Audrey was handed another joint, and as she inhaled (more modestly now) he smacked a hard ground ball up the middle for a clean base hit. Audrey began to look away, but a movement in her peripheral vision sent her eyes back to the field just in time to see the ball being smothered, incredibly, by the glove of the opposing shortstop, who—and how had Audrey not noticed this before?—was a *girl*. She spun to throw the lead runner out, only to realize, at the last possible moment, that the second baseman wasn't covering the bag (he'd become a spectator like everyone else), so she pulled her arm back, like a quarterback spying a better receiver, and, still spinning, fired the ball across the diamond to first. The throw, a perfect strike, beat the Jake in question by half a step. A moment of audible silence ensued, before the umpire, who had ventured out in front of home plate, said, "Great play, Sarah. I think he's definitely out."

Then came the deluge: claps and whistles and a chorus of "holy shit"s and "she's so good"s, and Jake One or Two was getting razzed as he came back to the bench, and everyone on both teams was grinning widely and reaching for their beers. Out at shortstop, Sarah whoever-she-was raised her index finger toward the outfielders. One down.

Audrey stared dumbfounded through the dugout fence. It wasn't just Sarah's talent but her look, a perfect balance of athletic (cleats, knee-high stirrups, smudged eye black) and flirtatious (come-hither shorts, a snug Pete's Candy jersey, and a side-worn ponytail with dislodged wisps of blond hair). When three outs were recorded and Audrey trotted back out to first, Sarah stepped up to the plate and roped the first pitch she saw down the line for what would have been at least a double if the Gobbler third baseman's glove weren't in the way. The hardest-hit ball of the game, and she was out before leaving the box. That was baseball. Or softball. Or, anyway, life. Sarah shrugged and ran the short distance back to her dugout, the way college players did on TV.

Audrey was about to take a seat to watch the bottom of the third when one of the Jakes called her name. She was leading off. Of course she was. Everyone else had already hit. She picked up a bat and swung it experimentally.

"Play ball!" the umpire cried.

Audrey walked up to the plate and took her stance in the left-handed batter's box.

"Just so you know," said the umpire, "I don't have my contacts in. I can't see shit."

"So who's calling balls and strikes?" Audrey asked.

"The catchers," said the Pete's catcher—also female—from behind her mask. "Though he can overrule us."

"Which, as a feminist, I would never do."

In came the first pitch. It hung in the air a long time, and Audrey, overeager, swung too early and missed.

"Strike," said the umpire. "Obviously."

Like Audrey, the catcher had also missed the ball. She retrieved it from the backstop and jogged it out to the pitcher.

"She's got a cannon for an arm," said the umpire. "She just doesn't like to use it."

Audrey was too mad at herself to laugh. How had she swung through a ball that was barely moving? She dug back in determinedly, but the next pitch floated wide.

"Outside," said the catcher quietly.

"Outside!" the umpire called. Audrey glanced back at him. "What do you want, I'm a volunteer. I'd do soup kitchens but the hours are no good."

Now Audrey smiled. The guy's leather helmet was ridiculous. Everything about him was ridiculous, but he seemed beloved. Characters in Brooklyn weren't the wackos they were in Florida. Up here, they ran the joint.

The catcher jogged the ball back to the pitcher again. "Haven't seen you before," the umpire said to Audrey.

"Not that you can see, of course."

"Women, I can see. Balls and strikes are less inspiring. I'm Fender, by the way."

Audrey introduced herself and told him it was her first game.

"Well, a little advice from a seasoned veteran. Don't grip the bat so tight."

The pitcher toed the rubber and the fielders readied themselves. Audrey relaxed her grip as the ball was released, slow and high, its arc a geographical equation, a thing she could solve. As she followed its path she thought of Sarah out at shortstop and was suddenly determined to impress her, to make some kind of statement of arrival, at which point she swung—a bit too early, but it felt like solid contact—and watched the ball launch up and over the first baseman's head. She sprinted to first, rounded the bag just as the right fielder got to the ball, and then . . . kept going, past the Pete's first baseman, over the half-erased phone number, and on toward second. Here it was: their inevitable collision. Three months of labor and loneliness, passing strangers in stairwells, on sidewalks, waiting for New York to open up to her. She slid feet first, and felt the bag and tag at the same time, and then Sarah was falling on top of her, and rolling off, and the two of them were lying there in a cloud of dust, turning to each other, already laughing—

"Safe!" Fender cried, running toward them. "Absolutely safe! I think."

They trekked over to Pete's, on Lorimer Street, the two teams dirt caked and buoyant. The Gobblers had lost 8–3, but no one cared. Audrey followed her teammates through the barroom and down a narrow hallway to the backyard, where festivities were already under way. Jake One or Two handed Audrey a PBR and made more introductions. It was an easy crowd to fall in with. Most were still in uniform, though the girls had made subtle changes—shed layers, bared shoulders, let their hair down. Sarah had unbuttoned her jersey to reveal a tank top underneath. When she saw Audrey she mouthed the words, *There you are*, and walked right over. The air was heavy with cigarettes and barbecue, and they claimed a table upwind from the smoke. For a while, they spoke of the game, but then moved beyond it, to the places they'd learned to play. Sarah was from Mattoon, Illinois, and she sighed, a bit sadly, as she described the place. Its confines, its limits. No one famous had ever come from Mattoon, she said, marveling at the odds. It was an old train town, and once a week the *City of New Orleans* still came whistling through, but under cover of night, as if to spare its passengers the view. Sarah had gone to the state university, in Springfield, where art history classes and varsity softball had comingled with just enough sorority sordidness that she'd graduated late. Audrey could envision it: the good-girl athlete becoming, semester by semester, boy by boy, increasingly adventurous. No wonder she'd ended up here. Sarah had been in Brooklyn for almost two years already, and while she'd clearly settled in, she'd hardly settled down. As for money, she lived as Audrey did, in small denominations—waitressing in Manhattan and working at a frame shop. Art was her thing, though she saw herself as a facilitator more than a creator. "Vital support staff for the genius of others" was how she put it.

Soon, Audrey was telling her things, too. About acting and Enid's, Connie and Cape Canaveral, the years in Benton Harbor.

"Isn't your last name Benton? Are you from the first family of the town or something?"

Audrey laughed. "More like the last. Really it's McAllister, but I was on the Greyhound coming up here and, I don't know, *Audrey McAllister* doesn't exactly roll off the tongue, especially in the acting world, so I decided to go with more of an homage. I thought about changing 'Audrey,' too, since it sounds like something a delusional mother with stars in her eyes would come up with—which is exactly what it is."

Audrey spotted Fender, still wearing his helmet. "What's his deal?" she asked.

Sarah chuckled. "I think he'd be borough president if the borough of Brooklyn consisted solely of Williamsburg. He's a walking piece of performance art."

"And his name is really Fender?"

"I have no idea. I mean, it can't be, obviously, but that's what everyone calls him."

Audrey hesitated before asking the next question, as it was a delicate one in these parts. "What does he *do*?"

"Besides umpire blind?" Sarah laughed. "He's in a few bands and does some scouting for labels, I think. He's one of those people you can hang with all night and somehow you know less about him than you did in the beginning. He runs in a lot of different circles. Some of his friends are pretty hard-core."

"Music-wise?"

"Drug-wise."

Audrey eyed him across the concrete yard. He certainly didn't look sinister. He had a regal nose and a shag haircut. From a distance he looked like a British stage actor who'd raided the wardrobe department at the beginning of a bender he was still on.

". . . a big penis."

Audrey snapped her head back in Sarah's direction. "What?"

"I've heard he has a big penis," Sarah repeated. "Though I can happily say I can't confirm it."

"Small victories," Audrey said.

"And right on cue . . ."

Sarah stood up as Fender approached.

"Here they are," he said. "The two best players. I knew you'd find each other." He and Sarah hugged. Audrey waved from the far side of the table.

"There's a party later on Roebling," he said, "some band friends. Should be a cool scene."

Audrey had been thinking about music more and more, and acting less and less. If Fender had said it was a gathering of theater people, she'd have said thanks but no thanks. But a music crowd? She looked at Sarah, who shrugged.

"I'm down," Audrey said to Fender. "But first you have to tell us—is it true you've got a big dick?"

"Oh good." Fender laughed. "You'll fit right in."

Chapter Seven

The numbers flickered like phosphorous, ever upward, thousands and tens of thousands and sometimes hundreds of thousands of dollars and euros, pounds and krones, yen and yuan. Where were yuan even from? Sarah wondered, suppressing a grin. Say that ten times fast. Still, she should know the answer.

She hadn't expected to be this bored. She'd been assigned a VIP client and was prepared, phone on ear, paddle in hand, to do his bidding. But half the auction had gone by—entire schools of painting—with nothing but silence from the other end of the line. Once, believing she'd been disconnected, Sarah had whispered an urgent, "Still there, Mr. Gable?" to which her client had responded, "Yes, don't worry," in an accent so smooth she imagined he must be stateless. *Mr. Gable.* Also registered to bid were Mr. Bogart, Mr. Cooper, Mr. Tracy, and Mr. Peck—all of them clients who wished to remain anonymous. The difference was that Mr. Gable was actually in attendance, or so Sarah had been told by Piper Wentworth, the head of Client Services, in a hurriedly scrawled note at the top of her reserve sheet (*S, your bidder is here tonight so look sharp! P*). But where? Cell phone talk was prohibited in the seated area of the auction room, so he must be luxuriating in a skybox or packed in among the standing-room crowd in back. Except the standers, like the currency numbers, were fleeting in nature, most of them journalists or art advisors forever ducking in and out. Which left the six private perches, shrouded in curtains and glass, high above the sales floor. Three were visible opposite the phone bank, but she dared not peek up.

Another weird thing: she had no idea what lots he was interested in. This was a major auction—the fall old masters sale—and most phone bidders communicated their desires (both painting- and price-wise) beforehand to ensure their proxies would be ready. But Sarah and Mr. Gable had had no such conversation, so she sat and waited, her left ear sweating into the receiver. She was trying hard to forget her lunch earlier with Audrey Benton. Why was her former best friend drudging up all that ancient history? That *awful* history. Audrey had seemed distraught, nearly paranoid, and Sarah had almost told her as much, but what was the point? People make their choices; they end up where they end up. She and Audrey had come together in a specific time and place, and if those years had been exhilarating, they'd also been hard. It wasn't fun being poor, even when "fun" was your raison d'être. That Audrey had found permanence in a world meant for passing through was unfortunate, but it was also no longer Sarah's business. Maybe she shouldn't have been surprised about Audrey's crazy Fender talk. Conspiracy theories were the province of those who'd gotten stuck along the way. Sarah's mistake had been to suggest Audrey call Chris. He'd no doubt be thrilled to revisit their sordid back catalog.

Her eyes darted toward the elevator bank. Where was her boyfriend anyway? Chris never missed an evening auction if Sarah was working. Old masters weren't his thing, but good theater was. Stories to tell. And what could be better than immoderate millions bid by implacable souls? Sarah had texted him before the sale, but then the lights dimmed and she'd had to put her phone away. She'd check it at a pause in the action. If "action" was the right word.

She looked out across the hushed sales floor. Before her sat some of the wealthiest people in the world. This wasn't the newfangled art crowd, in their checkered Vans and Comme des Garçons capes, bidding vast sums on the still living. No, this was the fading aristocracy, patient and discriminating, affluent elders with archaic concepts of beauty: moody canvases in elaborate frames, frescoes of food and portraits of slaughter. They'd make for a good portrait themselves, Sarah thought: *Gentility at Work*. She watched men do math in catalog margins, women fan themselves with addendum sheets, currency numbers flicker ever upward.

What she should have been watching, considering her educational background, were the paintings themselves—which appeared, one after another, on a revolving carousel to the auctioneer's right—for they illuminated the great history of the Western world (or a certain version of it), from the Middle Ages through the Renaissance to the burgeoning centuries beyond. The Dutch and Flemish. The English and French. Tons of Italians. Even the odd Russian. Sarah had loved studying the old masters back in college—she'd majored in art history—appreciating then, as now, their concreteness of thought and attention to detail. The curl of a lip. The dull silver of armor. Flakes of powder in a royal wig. What you saw was what you got, and how much of art, of *anything*, could you say that about?

Of course, the old masters were old news these days, for the New York she lived in was the most contemporary of towns. Chris, the scion of Park Avenue collectors, had pushed her toward a gallery job in Chelsea—it would have taken only a phone call—but Sarah had stubbornly resisted. If she saw her own middle-American past as increasingly uninteresting, more worldly histories remained an obsession. And so a different phone call had been made, and she was offered a job at Sotheby's. She'd hoped to work as a cataloger in one of the marquee painting departments, but if the "Van" in Chris's last name had gotten her in the door, it could get her no further. So she'd landed in Client Services, the nebulous female catchall. Sarah looked down the phone bank: Of the ten employees taking bids, eight were women and seven were unmarried. All eight were taller and thinner than Sarah—quite a feat considering she stood five foot seven and wore a size 4. The joke was that Client Services should be renamed Full Services, the funny part being that it wasn't a joke at all. In the last year, three coworkers had been whisked away by clients they were "advising." The whole cycle was terribly sexist, but no one seemed to care. In fact, most everyone—employees and clients alike—played their role happily and with great panache, as if they'd been rehearsing their entire lives. Art, beauty, wealth: all of it was for sale in the wood-paneled auction rooms on the corner of Seventy-Second and York.

So what was Sarah after? The question had been shadowing her since she first moved to New York. It wasn't money anymore; in fact, she no longer had to work. She and Chris had been together five years, cohabiting for three. So much of that time had been wonderful. So much still was. Yet she'd begun to lose track of things. Her old friends in Brooklyn. Bands she'd once loved. But these were concrete problems and still repairable. Harder to measure were the ephemeral concerns, like expectation and a sense of progress. How had she managed to escape the suffocating lassitude of the heartland only to find, a decade on, some purer form of it on the Upper East Side? What was normal and what was not? What should she be wanting? Five years was a long time. Too long, her married friends had started telling her. Things that should be happening were not. And things that shouldn't be were. Like Chris disappearing on nights such as this one. He could still be at work. Probably, he was. But she was far too prideful to text him and ask. The paths such a query could lead down. And anyway, she had no evidence of wrongdoing. Except his absence. Which was its own type of proof. Its own type of future.

Eight months ago, Chris had come home from a meeting with his family's accountant and told her that because of his new tax bracket (he'd gotten a raise), he'd actually be saving money if she quit her job when they got married, a statement she found at once insulting, confusing, and reassuring. *When they got married.* It was the first—and last—time he'd mentioned that word. What did it mean? She had labored a great deal of her young life. The skin on her hands was permanently dry from restaurant work. Still, she was not ready to sit at home. She enjoyed the auction house, its high glamour and assumption

of belonging, even if—and yes, it was time to admit it—she was falling out of love with the art itself, a development she attributed to the
marketplace surrounding it. The sale today, for instance: painting after
painting depicting the wretchedness of humankind. *Faust Selling His
Soul*; *The Rape of Proserpina*; *The Temptation of St. Anthony*; *The Fall of
Man*. What a muddle of gloom these canvases were, to say nothing of
the muddle of their authorship. *School of . . . Studio of . . . Attributed to . . .*
Why did people spend so much money on depressing pictures with
shaky provenances? Sure, the works were old. Sure, they had "that look."
But the answer, she knew, was far simpler: *because they could*. Perhaps
this was the real reason she'd chosen Sotheby's, and, if she had to take
it further, her boyfriend, her (his) neighborhood, her (his) world. She
wanted the life that New York had always dangled in front of people
like her, fresh-faced arrivals from the star-spangled ether. She believed
in trajectories, advancement, upward mobility. Just look at the crowd
tonight: for every five who'd grown up on Fifth or Park, surely one
had grown up on a cracked-blacktop street like hers, on the west side
of Mattoon, Illinois. Or maybe the ratio was worse, but the point was
that these ranks could be broken into, or at least married into, if you
had the right wardrobe, said the right things, and had survived intact
your more youthful travails in lesser quarters of the city.

But she was being unfair to herself, for she was very much in love
with Chris, and would still be with him no matter who he was, or
where—

". . . in a few more lots."

Her mind had wandered so far away that the words didn't register.
Then she realized they'd been spoken and quickly moved the receiver
that had migrated down her neck back to her ear and said, "Excuse
me, sir?"

"Let's be ready in a few more lots," her client said. Or repeated.

"Yes, of course," Sarah answered, paging quickly through the catalog
to catch up. Where were they? She squinted up at the projection screen in
the front of the room. Lot 102: Sir Thomas Lawrence's *Portrait of a Busty
Lady*. What? She peered across at the painting itself, newly arrived on

the carousel, but it featured no breasts, busty or otherwise—just the head of a woman with unruly hair. Sarah was confused. How could a painting from the early 1800s have a title like that? She consulted the catalog.

Oh, God. She was such a moron. It was called *Portrait Bust of a Lady*. She stifled a laugh.

"What's so funny?"

Sarah went rigid in her chair. He was *watching* her.

"Oh, nothing. I was just—sorry. I'm ready when you are."

"No, please, do tell."

His voice purred through the phone. She was dying to scan the skyboxes but again forced herself not to. Instead, she turned her panicked attentions to the auctioneer, who was signaling like a symphony conductor, coaxing out bids in his best faux king's English.

"It's the painting," Sarah said, cupping her hand to the receiver. "I"—what was she doing?—"I misread its title. I thought it said *Portrait of a Busty Lady*."

Gable chuckled. "Certainly that would help the price. Has it even reached the reserve?"

The reserve was the number below which a lot would "buy in" and be returned to the consignor. It was usually arrived at via negotiation— the owner demanding a high reserve, Sotheby's angling for a low one—and was always kept private. The *Busty Lady* was estimated at $40,000–$60,000, but the bidding was still mired in the low thirties. Sarah looked at the confidential reserve sheet in front of her.

"You know I can't tell you that," she said.

"But it never hurts to ask."

Sarah was blushing. How long had he been eyeing her? And why had she told him the thing about the name? Self-consciously, she glanced down at her own breasts. Her black dress was work-appropriate but inarguably snug. Still, the room was dim, and how many times had Chris asked her not to wear black because it hides a woman's curves? He could be such a child, with his cleavage this and side-boob that, and God forbid she not wear a padded bra (the last thing she needed) when they went out with his male friends.

Where was that jerk, anyway?

Also, where was Mr. Gable? The *Busty Lady* had sold for just over its low estimate, and the auctioneer had moved on to an unexceptional painting of a double-chinned woman holding a lute. Sarah checked the catalog. *Portrait of Alice, Countess of Shipbrook* by Francis Cotes. She'd never heard of Cotes. From either side came the murmurs of her coworkers, inciting their bidders to battle. It sounded like the world's most civilized telethon, and Sarah knew she should be doing the same. But Gable didn't strike her as a man who could be talked into much, so she stayed quiet. A minute later, the gavel came down—the countess had sold for $40,000—and another Cotes appeared on the carousel: a craven-looking sea captain pointing toward parts unknown.

"Not very inspiring, are they?" Mr. Gable said into her ear.

"The paintings?"

"The bidders."

"I don't know," said Sarah. "They're better than the contemporary crowd."

"Ah, yes. The philistines at the hedgerow."

"I like that," she said, feeling emboldened. "Very perceptive."

"It's the title of a book."

"Oh. Of course. I thought it sounded familiar." *You're such an idiot*, she practically mouthed to herself.

"Might I say, if I could be so bold, that you look quite lovely this evening. So many auction house women are—I don't mean this in the wrong way—of a type."

Now it was Sarah who fell speechless. She'd been expecting a condescending remark about her lack of literary knowledge. Instead, well, it was very bold indeed—way over the line, in fact—but in this environment, from that voice, it sounded like the most daring of compliments. Nervously, she switched the phone to her other ear.

"Thank you," she said. "I'm sure you're quite dashing yourself."

They began talking, in low voices, of trivial things. The flamboyance of the auctioneer. The horrid lighting. She laughed. He laughed. She said she imagined he was wearing a tuxedo. He told her he had been, at a benefit the previous night, after which he'd caught some jazz at the bar at the Mark. She liked jazz, she responded; she'd have to check it out sometime. She was just doing her job, she told herself. Then Gable said, "Okay, this one," and suddenly she really was.

The auctioneer announced the lot: *Still Life with Peaches, Pears and Grapes* by Luis Melendez. Melendez, Sarah knew. He was the greatest Spanish painter of the eighteenth century, and *Still Life*, estimated at $200,000–$300,000, was one of the most valuable lots of the sale. She gave the spotter a discreet nod, letting him know she might be a player. And then she delivered her standard recitation.

"I'm sure you know all of this, Mr. *Gable*"—why not—"but I have to tell you anyway. The bidding may move rapidly, so be ready. Also, the increments could change based on the number of people involved. Just say 'bid' and I'll put my hand up. Your paddle number is fifty-three."

"Fifty-three," he repeated, and thanked her.

The painting—a close-up study of fruit spilling from a bowl—rounded into view, and like so many others, it was at first glance unremarkable. Then details emerged, pits and bruises, depth and color—vivid oranges and yellow-greens that complemented each other in florid harmony. If it wasn't a masterwork, it was close. But why, amid this brushstroke cacophony of gods and kings, would a man like Gable be interested in a bowl of fruit? He must be acting on behalf of another party. A museum, perhaps. Which would make them both proxies.

The early action was sporadic, two bidders on the floor, one on the phone—no one expressing overt enthusiasm. Sarah checked the reserve. It was set at the low estimate—the highest it could possibly be. Strange, she thought, and then read the provenance and understood why. The painting had failed to sell at an auction five years ago, with an estimate of $750,000–$950,000. To make sure history wouldn't repeat itself, the specialists had beaten the consignor up on the estimate—and hence the reserve—this time around.

The bidding crawled higher. "One fifty to my right . . . one fifty . . . one sixty on the near side, thank you, sir . . . one sixty . . . one sixty . . . may I have one seventy-five . . . asking one seventy-five . . . yes! . . . one seventy-five it is on the phone with Elise. . . . Elise, dear, your paddle number . . . ah yes, lucky number sixty-nine . . . now, where were we . . . one seventy-five with number sixty-nine and the next bid will be two hundred thousand . . . a show of hands at two hundred . . . any hands . . . it's a beautiful bowl of fruit, albeit spilled . . ."

"Tell me what you think of it," Mr. Gable said.

"It's a steal if it sells within the estimate," Sarah said with conviction.

"Why?"

She thought a moment. "It's different. The artist is showing you these blemishes and flaws, and his honesty makes the painting more powerful in its totality."

"I see," Gable said. "Then we won't let it get away from us."

"Should I bid?" *Shall I!* She was supposed to say "shall I." She felt intoxicated.

"You haven't told me your name," he said.

She couldn't help herself. She peeked up at the three skyboxes but could see only curtains, shadows. *She* should ask *his* name, his *real* one, though that was against the rules.

"It's Sarah."

"Well, Sarah, we seem to be getting along well. Let's stir the pot. Jump the bid to four hundred and fifty thousand dollars, please."

Had she heard him correctly? She checked the board. The current bid was $250,000. "Are you sure? You'll be raising it two hundred thousand."

"Yes, I'm aware of that."

Bid jumping was a rare and risky strategy, the idea being to intimidate others into dropping out earlier than they otherwise might. In Sarah's experience it backfired as often as it worked. But she wasn't here to debate tactics.

She stood up. "Four fifty!" she called out, holding her paddle up defiantly. The room went silent. Every head turned her way.

"Four hundred and fifty thousand with Sarah on the phone," said the auctioneer with genuine surprise. "With that, we've separated the wheat from the chaff." He raised his nose and looked around the room. "May I have four seventy-five for this delectable assortment of fruit?"

It took several seconds for those seated to recover. People were whispering, revisiting their catalogs. "Tell me," Gable said idly, "are you an artist yourself?"

"More of an appreciator." She could feel her heart. "I majored in art history."

An arm climbed slowly upward. An elderly man in a tweed suit, near the front. He had a sun-splotched face and a shrunken neck. The auctioneer registered the bid with blithe geniality.

"Go," Gable said before she'd even asked. Sarah raised her paddle.

The auctioneer leveled his arm, like a game show presenter, in her direction. "That brings us to five hundred," he said jauntily, and turned back to the man seated near the front. "A nice round number, but let's press on, shall we? How does five twenty-five sound?"

"Expensive," the old man croaked, and the room tittered knowingly. It was down to the two of them, or three, for Sarah felt a part of the proceedings, too. She wanted to ask Gable questions, even now, especially now, in the heightened theater of the moment. He would like that.

"Five ten," the man mumbled. Bidding smaller increments was a sign of weakness, but the auctioneer obliged. Gable sighed through the phone, as if he'd expected more of a fight.

"Put your hand up and keep it up," he said, and Sarah, feeling thrillingly submissive, did so. Sure enough, that was the end of it. Asked to bid $530,000, the old man crooked his neck in Sarah's direction and, seeing her cold determination, conceded with the slightest shake of his head. The auctioneer performed a perfunctory "Going once . . . twice . . . ," and then hammered down the sale, which, including the buyer's premium, came out to $614,500. The room applauded enthusiastically. It was the highest price of the evening.

"Congratulations," Sarah said, her voice rich with feeling.

"Come now, we did it together. I find beauty impossible to pass up."

She didn't know what to say. She'd become a character in a classic film, where no one cares that the dialogue is stilted because true romance is, by its nature, sentimental. Sarah made a show of immersing herself in the catalog. There were still a dozen paintings to go.

"That's enough," Gable said, clearly still watching her. "We got the best one."

"Okay, we'll quit while we're ahead."

"Or we could continue elsewhere. How about a late dinner at Daniel? A little celebration."

So this was how it worked. Sarah had refrained from overt flirtation—hadn't she?—but the tension had mounted all the same. She could feel it: the static electricity through the clearest of phone lines. And still she knew nothing—of his appearance, his identity, his life. And if that was, in the end, too deep a chasm to cross, it was also not the reason she politely, and after some deliberation, declined. She said no because she lived with a man she loved, and if that love was indeed bruised and pockmarked and spilling out messily in every direction, it was also, she believed, too rare a thing to be bought or sold in high-ceilinged rooms of commerce.

Mr. Gable accepted her decision gracefully. "Perhaps we'll cross paths again," he said, and Sarah, quite professionally, she told herself, responded that she very much hoped so. Then they hung up and that was the end of it. Which was not to say that Sarah's behavior had been beyond reproach. For she realized, as she tidied up her area, that she'd removed the silver band Chris had bought her—a "warmer-upper," he'd called it at the time—from her ring finger, where she'd taken to wearing it to ward off potential suitors. When, exactly, she couldn't remember, but now she quickly slipped it back on, and as subtly as possible—for the auction was proceeding apace—checked her cell phone under the table.

Still no messages.

The Weight of the World

New York, New York
July 2004

"Hey Atlas, you coming?"

"Two minutes!" Theo shouted. He was scrambling. Usually he was the first one up and ready, but this morning he'd shuffled out to the bathroom, bleary eyed and semiconscious, only to find his four roommates milling around, fully dressed. Dan had looked at his watch and told him to hurry if he wanted to leave with them, and Theo, astonished, had said he'd be right there.

Their apartment on West Ninety-Fifth Street was a five-bedroom maze of walls shoddily constructed within the former parlor room of a once-respectable hotel. Bones of bygone elegance—light sconces and marble floors—still existed high up on walls and underneath stained carpeting, but the building's post-hotel stint as a flophouse had exhausted most of its original luster long before it was sold and (sort of) renovated. When Theo first moved in, five years ago now, he'd become enamored with the neighborhood's fluctuating historical fortunes and, in his spare time, traversed the surrounding blocks, studying the prewar architecture in an effort to place himself contextually within the city's firmament. He liked the idea of being one among millions, anonymous and untethered. He was a stranger even to his roommates, having taken his room sight unseen, courtesy of a listing on the Colgate alumni online message board: "$595/mth for charming rm in giant apt on tree-lined UWS St." He had yet to learn that "charming" was a synonym for "tiny," or that the street might contain trees elsewhere but that his view would be of the garbage cans located mere feet from his pillow (several times a week he was awakened by bottle collectors riffling through the bins). But the price was right, the location was decent, and that was all that mattered.

Five years later the price was still right, though Theo's original roommates were long gone, as was the second wave, and most of the third (he had no idea whose name appeared on the original lease; he was just glad it wasn't his). With each roommate's departure came a yearning to move along himself, settle somewhere more dignified, more adult. But at age twenty-eight, he still couldn't afford a place of his own, or even a two-bedroom with a roommate—not in Manhattan. And he hadn't moved to the city to live in an outer borough. He wasn't adventurous like that.

As long as he'd resided there, the apartment had been an assemblage of strangers, grunting greetings in hallways, waiting impatiently for the lone bathroom. But the current roster was showing glimmers of cohesion, even camaraderie. They came from different backgrounds and worked in different fields, but all four were social, even fun-loving, and they treated Theo like a benign older brother who'd earned both their respect (for his physical and intellectual heft) and affectionate ribbing (for his monastic self-seriousness).

Now he was making them wait. He turned off the stand-up fan (he had no AC), grabbed the half-read manuscript on his bedside, and entered the living room to mock cheers. Here they were: John, Dan, Trevor, and Stuart—a digital marketer, an apprentice builder, a grant writer, and a phone store sales clerk—all of them moving toward the front door. It was hot, and Theo swallowed a quick glass of water. "Atlas chugged!" Dan exclaimed, adding a new twist to the latest apartment joke. The nickname had arrived courtesy of the manuscript-laden hiker's backpack Theo lugged daily to and from work. (The oversized pack had become a sixth roommate of sorts, with its own chair in the foyer near the brick wall that Dan had deemed structurally unnecessary and recently started taking apart so as to "open up the space.") As he did every day—though usually without an audience—Theo walked over and stuffed the manuscripts he'd taken to bed with him in among the others, after which he bungee-corded the pack together (the zipper was broken), bent his knees like a power lifter, and, to the delight of the others, heaved the thing onto his back in a single powerful motion. "Okay, good to go," he said, double-strapping it to even out the weight. They marched out the door one by one into a scorching summer morning.

Aware of the pleasure his roommates derived from his daily backpack exertions, Theo attempted an air of nonchalance as the group started east on Ninety-Fifth, but the pack this morning felt heavier than usual, and it was all he could do to keep up. Fragments of conversation filtered back to him, the week's more salacious headlines—Martha Stewart's prison sentencing; Governor McGreevey's coming-out speech; the ongoing Barry Bonds saga—but Theo was too winded to contribute. He rested against a light pole on West End, but then the WALK sign lit up and everyone was moving again. Already he was sweating through his shirt. Maybe this was the beginning of his physical decline, or, worse, the onset of a more specific malady. A heart attack! They slow you before they stop you, no? No. His heart was fine. Or not *fine*, just medically undamaged. But his love life was another story. It was no story at all.

He caught them again on the corner of Broadway, but the fivesome was splitting up here, Theo heading to the 1-2-3 a block north, the others continuing east to the A train. They slapped hands and nodded heads and went their separate ways. Again, Theo wondered why everyone was so buoyant at such an early hour, but his curiosity dissipated as he clambered down the station stairs and through the turnstiles. The platform heat intensified the under-city smell. It had been a while since the last train, and the crowd was three deep. He couldn't wade in, not with his backpack on, so he stood stoically on the outskirts of the throng until the 1 train finally came hurtling into view. The doors opened and a few brave souls emerged, pushing through the crowd that now surged past them into the vacated space. Theo shuffled forward, like a prisoner in leg irons, sensing the annoyance of those around him. He was only a step away—he could feel the icy inside air—when the chime sounded and the doors closed, with Theo right up against them, staring in at a gray-haired woman staring out. His shoulders sagged and the pack seemed to gain weight. All at once, the heat came at him, and the odors, and he was about to back up, find some room to breathe again, when—and this never happened for him—the doors *opened* again, and half of humanity pushed into him from behind. He stepped forward in an attempt to keep his balance, to remain upright, and in the process somehow crossed the threshold between platform and train as the doors closed again—behind him, behind his backpack. He couldn't believe his luck.

"Asshole," someone said.

The train lurched forward. Theo stood as if in a cylinder, arms pressed to his sides, sweat trickling unimpeded down his face. He felt conspicuous, surrounded as he was by shorter people, but the cold air at altitude was revitalizing, practically life altering, and when the conductor announced that due to signal problems in the Bronx the train would run express to Columbus Circle, Theo sensed that mystical city karma taking up residence on his side of the ledger.

They picked up speed. The backpack's aluminum frame was digging into him. This was getting ridiculous. He had to do something about these manuscripts—like not bring so many home. But he couldn't help himself. The slush pile was so tall, and making it shorter satisfied him greatly. Worse, he was a completist (or, fine, slightly OCD). He couldn't imagine getting fifty pages into something good and then having to stop because he hadn't brought the other 250 home. But nothing was ever good. He often started half a dozen manuscripts in a single night, only to cast them glumly aside upon coming to terms with the obvious. So how about convincing his bosses to accept electronic submissions? Imagine the freedom of commuting back and forth with only an "e-reader"—whatever, exactly, that was. Like everyone else in publishing, Theo kept hearing they were the future of his industry, but he couldn't imagine their catching on. Manuscripts were one thing, but who would want to read the finished product on a screen—portable or otherwise? Art should come in ancient forms. A book between covers. Ink on white pages.

It was a different primeval custom—Prosaic's open submission policy—that had first attracted Theo to the famed press. Of the major New York publishers, only his still accepted unsolicited manuscripts, though no one could remember one ever becoming a book. No matter. Theo believed the concept alone was powerful: that anyone could submit his or her work to a legendary publishing house directly, without an agent, and know it would be considered for publication. Theo, as it happened, was the employee tasked with the considering, for the slush pile was his domain, and he lorded over it with great purpose and sincerity.

He had known, upon arriving in New York, that breaking into publishing would be difficult, especially for someone with no connections or experience. But he was determined. It took him three years of manual labor—furniture moving, art handling, the occasional nonunion construction gig—to save up the $7,500 cost of a six-week publishing course at Columbia. It was an unspoken prerequisite for aspiring editors but hardly a guarantee of employment, as evidenced by Theo's months-long job search. He applied for the lowest positions at the best imprints but again and again lost out to recent graduates of Yale and Brown, Oberlin and Bard, colleges so liberal they made Colgate seem like a technical institute.

Then, miracle of miracles, he'd been offered his current job at Prosaic. His title was editorial assistant, but for almost a year the closest he got to editing was the proofing of catalog copy. It was this accumulating frustration that led Theo to inquire, of an executive editor he admired named Wynne Groome, about possibly reading some slush. The request was received with amusement—slush had always been the province of interns—but within hours the pile was his. The following night, the interns invited Theo out for happy hour. The poor kids worked for free, and still they insisted on buying his drinks.

Hundreds of manuscripts later, Theo was still searching for some-thing, *anything*, remotely promising. He knew the odds were against him. He understood that the system in place basically worked. An author smart enough to write a good book was smart enough to find a good agent (who, in turn, was smart enough to find a good publisher). But it was hardly foolproof. Theo could rattle off dozens of classics that had initially been rejected. *Gone with the Wind. Animal Farm. Little Women. Lord of the Flies. Catch-22. Harry Potter.* Even the gods of literature had met with early indifference. Joyce's *Dubliners* was turned down eighteen times, *Moby-Dick* even more. Mistakes were made, greatness was over-looked; such was the subjective nature of art. Theo was the end of the line: the last reader at the last publisher that still offered a chance at glory. He felt the weight of responsibility with every step he took.

He felt it standing still, as well. Several more commuters had squeezed onto the train at Columbus Circle, and now he couldn't move at all. The air-conditioning was blasting and his clothes were sticking to him. He was either too hot or too cold—he couldn't tell which. When the doors mercifully opened at Times Square, he shuffled out and spent a torturous ten minutes winding through corridors before emerging onto another platform and—again the good fortune—straight onto a waiting N train. Now Theo could stand, and even turn around, without worrying his backpack might decapitate someone. They were halfway to Thirty-Fourth Street, his mind drifting into the fruitless realm of last night's submissions, when he peered down the length of the car and saw a woman who looked exactly like his college girlfriend Eleanor Thorpe.

It *was* Eleanor Thorpe.

Immediately, he turned away, which was stupid, because it wasn't like she'd miss him if she looked up. But she was engrossed in a book, which gave him time to consider his options. There were only two: say hello or don't. Why, aside from his sweat-soaked appearance, shouldn't he? They'd dated for an entire school year—his junior, her senior—and parted ways on good enough terms that her promise to stay in touch had, to Theo's ear, carried open-ended possibilities. The main issue, he'd believed, was geographic. She was moving to New York; he had one more year at Colgate. He assumed she would visit (or that he would), but after a few increasingly spaced-out emails she'd stopped writing. Theo's last missives had gone unanswered.

It had taken him longer than anticipated to get over her. He'd stayed single, if not quite celibate, most of his senior year, and when he, too, moved to New York upon graduating, he got her number from a mutual friend and taped it to his bedroom mirror. But he never called, for reasons—as he sneaked another look in her direction—that eluded him now. Obviously, he'd been scared—of rejection, yes, but also of having to admit that his "literary life," so carefully mapped out by the two of them across those frozen upstate nights, had yet to begin. As for Eleanor, he just knew she'd be doing something fantastic, and when he opened his *Colgate Scene* alumni bulletin early that first New York spring, he learned how right he was:

> We've chased Eleanor Thorpe ('97) down in Bangkok, Thailand (of course!), where she reports the following: "Busy working with Project HOPE to strengthen international child trafficking laws and establish a T visas program for victims who assist in the prosecution of their captors. The days are long but incredibly rewarding. If you find yourself in this part of the world, please get in touch. Always looking for a good excuse to head for the beaches, they're just gorgeous! Speaking of gorgeous, I made it back to NYC for Molly Preston's ('97) wedding at the boathouse, and caught up with Georgina Kaplan ('96), Megan Winslow ('97), Reese Braverman ('95), and so many others. Miss everyone!"

At which point he'd placed her number in a drawer. Out of country, out of mind. Except that Theo found himself rereading her alumni update often in the weeks that followed. He was both proud of her and ashamed of himself. But what really bothered him was the wedding. She'd come back to New York and never gotten in touch?

What was he doing? Just walk over and say hi. She was the only girl—or woman now: they'd all become women, while the men remained boys—that he'd ever been in love with, or *almost* in love with (he wasn't exactly sure), and now here she was, not only in New York, but in his train car. Alas, he remained in place. It was her turn to come to him. To make it easier, he positioned himself directly in her field of sight. He ran his hand through his sweat-matted hair and peered out the window at the blackness moving by. What a prideful fool he was.

That they'd met in the library had always seemed fitting, considering each had a genuine interest in the academic portion of the college experience. If Theo's presence at Colgate was a minor miracle (thank you, Ms. Jansen), Eleanor's was more an act of subversion against a family tree bowed heavy with Ivy Leaguers. Yet there they were, seated at the same table. Eleanor was surrounded by books on women's suffrage, including—Theo couldn't believe it—*Bread and Roses*, a detailed account of the 1912 woman-led mill strike in Lawrence, Massachusetts. Theo had read it more than once, the strike being his hometown's only legitimate contribution to US history. It said something about his priorities that he would peek at a girl's books rather than the girl herself. And it said something about his lack of experience that when he did finally glance up, he was immediately stupefied by her fine-spun beauty. He was also immediately busted.

They laughed about it for months, the serendipity of that first encounter. He'd never seen her before, which wasn't unusual considering the time he spent in the weight room and the field house and Kerr Stadium. For football still defined him. If he was no longer the star he'd been in high school, he was still a starting linebacker on a Division I team. He had stature, and size, and an easygoing way that people mistook for self-assurance. Girls liked that he was "different," and they displayed their interest in various non-subtle ways. Theo kept a polite distance. He didn't mean to be aloof; he was just shy. His football-oriented popularity felt disingenuous, almost condescending, which, in turn, made him self-conscious. He became overly aware of his physical presence, his relationship to the space around him. He supposed he had the wrong mind for his body type. Then Eleanor came along, and for the first time, his incongruities fell into something like alignment.

The Thorpes had made their fortune (in paper, of all things) long enough ago that the subject of money was never discussed by Eleanor or anyone in her family. It wasn't a question of manners so much as boredom, money being less a goal unto itself than an idle reality. Her world was so far removed from Theo's that he'd quickly learned not to dwell on the vastness of the intervening space. The Thorpes had several homes, including a horse farm in Quechee, Vermont, and a private island near Bar Harbor, Maine ("But that's two summer places," Theo had said, idiotically), though Eleanor rarely visited any of them, preferring instead to fill her breaks from school with a complex array of intern- and externships Theo could never keep straight. Her grievance was not with specific members of her family—she was close with both parents—but with the blue-blooded world the family inhabited. Given the financial freedom to do anything, America's elite did little but conspire to protect that freedom, she once told Theo, who, lacking evidence to the contrary, accepted such wisdom as gospel. That Eleanor could wage class warfare so sincerely was a testament to her self-assuredness (itself a consequence of the upbringing she so readily dismissed, but Theo didn't like to nitpick), and as the months passed Theo found his own scattered ideas about how to live solidifying into a kind of ethic. With Eleanor, *through* Eleanor, he began to believe the vague goals he'd set for himself—moving to New York, working with books—might truly be attainable. And why not? There he was at Colgate, of all places. And there he was with her.

Now, seven years later, here he was with her again.

The train arrived at Herald Square and the chaotic dance resumed. Theo, being jostled from behind, was forced a few steps closer to Eleanor. He glanced at her again. She was wearing a white button-down shirt tucked into a brown calf-length skirt, with a matching jacket laid neatly across her lap. Her strawberry-blond hair was still long and framed the face he knew so well—the thin lips and straight jaw and oft-furrowed brow that betrayed her inherent skepticism. He could see, too, what she was reading: David Mitchell's *Cloud Atlas*. Theo hadn't realized it was out yet. How was it possible she'd gotten a copy—

"Theo Gorski, what on earth are you doing?"

He looked up from her lap. "Eleanor," he said, immediately flustered. "Wow. I was just—"

"Oh, honestly!" She stood up, took two strides, and threw her arms around him. "That's quite a backpack."

The train shuddered, as if clearing its throat. They both grabbed for the closest rail, the synchronicity suggesting some greater harmony. Theo, his face reddening, searched for something to say. His eyes landed on her book. "How's *Cloud Atlas*?"

Eleanor laughed. "I'm glad some things never change. I haven't seen you in years and the first thing you ask about is the book I'm reading. Come on, I want to hear everything. I've got three stops."

"I've only got two." Quickly, nervously, he filled her in on his life—where he lived and what he did (which sort of explained the backpack)—thinking the whole time about how foolish it all sounded. How small.

"I'd rather hear about you," he said finally, very much meaning it. "Last I knew, you were in Bangkok."

"Oh God, it's been that long?"

Longer, Theo thought. He braced himself for a dose of understated heroism.

"I'm working at Dewey Ballantine," she said.

"That sounds like a law firm."

"Are you joking?" She squinted at him. "No, you're not. Honestly, Theo. Yes, it's a law firm. One of the biggest in the world. I'm a second-year associate working in project finance. Energy, infrastructure—whatever scraps the partners feed us. Though it's actually pretty fascinating. I'm on my way to Union Square to meet some Brazilian investors about a mag-lev train project in São Paulo."

Theo grinned dumbly. "I didn't know you went to law school."

"Yup. Columbia. I had a place on Ninety-Third and Broadway. I wish I'd known you were . . ."

She continued talking, and he continued listening, but some important wire connecting her speech to his hearing had come loose. *Two blocks away for three years.*

The train was pulling into Twenty-Third Street. "This is my stop," he heard himself say, and he heard her say, "Oh no, already?" Then he said something about working at a publishing house in the Flatiron Building, and she was guessing that he wasn't on Friendster or MySpace, and he was saying she was right, he was not, and then asking if *she* was—though why did that matter if he wasn't?—and the whole time he wanted badly to switch back to the present from whatever distant tense had overtaken him, but the doors were opening and people were moving and Eleanor was hugging him again and placing something in his hand, and before he could even look down to see what it was he was following his fellow commuters out onto the platform. Only when he turned around and waved goodbye did he realize he was holding her business card. He ran his fingers over the embossed lettering. Printed in the lower left corner were her email, phone, and fax.

Had she sensed his surprise? His astonishment? His disappointment?

He climbed the station stairs, his thighs aching like they used to after football workouts, those endless reps and sets and seasons—that whole chapter of his life so inane now. That people had made such a big deal of it. He emerged into the searing world at the corner of Twenty-Third and Fifth, and staggered the blessedly short distance to the revolving doors of the Flatiron. Inside, he stopped to acclimate, the way divers did at depth, then spotted an open elevator and made a run for it, or a sort of run, and for the second time that morning, hurriedly squeezed through two closing doors.

Theo had always enjoyed elevators, those small boxes of human proximity, because they were the last place in the city where nothing happened. Even his most caffeinated coworkers rode them in egalitarian silence. But his brusque arrival had upset all of that, throwing into disarray the calibrations of the packed cab. He heard the irritated sighs, which were bad enough, but he could see everyone, too, because he was *facing* them. There was simply no room to turn around, not with his backpack on, so he just stood there amid a small army of business-casual troopers. Humiliating but survivable, he told himself, until he realized, in a single horrific moment, that the commanding officer of that army was directly in front of him. Bunny Beale: Prosaic's editor in chief, and a woman as misnamed as any in the history of nomenclature. A bead of sweat fell from Theo's brow onto his shoe. "Excuse me," he mumbled, mortified.

Another thing about elevators: people could see without looking. Everyone in the cab was immediately aware of Theo's situation. Bunny was the publishing world's very own Anna Wintour, and being in her presence rattled even the most seasoned executives. She was tall and bony, almost Theo's height in heels, and as he set his gaze just above her head, he found himself wondering what could possibly be in the $35 salads that she had delivered to her office every day from Union Square Cafe. The elevator seemed not to be moving, though surely it was, and had been, for several seconds. Theo was only going to the fourth floor, Prosaic's lowest (it housed the mailroom and several rows of cubicles), so at least he'd be getting off first—assuming someone had pressed the button. He definitely couldn't reach it; he could barely blink. He tried to focus on something external to his current situation, and, of course, his mind landed with a thud on Eleanor. He should have checked her finger for a wedding ring. She was twenty-nine now. Not that she struck him as the early-marrying type. Though she hadn't struck him as a corporate lawyer either. Not even close. He just couldn't believe—

"What *on earth* is in your backpack?" It was Bunny, from just below him. Her breath was minty and not unpleasant. Theo looked down at her. He was trembling.

"Manuscripts," he said. "Sorry."

"From where?"

"The slush pile."

"The *slush pile*?"

Theo nodded.

He hadn't believed physical movement possible, but he was wrong. People were retreating from him, inch by precious inch. The elevator slowed. Theo decided to get off whether it was his floor or not. When the doors opened he backed straight out, like an SUV from a narrow garage, and as he did so, he saw the "4" on the wall. Thank God. The doors closed and he breathed a sigh of relief, understanding for the first time what that term truly meant. And then, without warning, the doors opened again. There was Bunny, staring at him.

"You're Theodore," she said.

"Yes."

"My office in ten minutes."

A dozen pairs of eyebrows rose in unison as the doors closed again, this time for good. At least she knows my name, he told himself, suddenly wishing she didn't.

He trudged toward his cubicle. The last lap. The final mile. In the annals of astounding commutes, surely this one warranted some ink. He almost didn't care what would happen next—his demotion (to what?) or firing—because he deserved it. He was tired of not "getting it," of people not "getting him." But what was there *to* get? What was he offering the world? How could such a big person cast such a small shadow?

He arrived haggard, almost ruined. Bending awkwardly at the knees, he rested the backpack on his desk and twisted himself out of its straps. Blood rushed to his head, and he grabbed for the cubicle wall. Eight years of saying no to smelling salts and now he'd give anything for some. He sat down quickly and, hoping no one would walk past, put his head between his legs and pushed against his ears—an old football trick from before the concussion craze. When he felt human again, he headed for the bathroom to do something about his appearance. It was worse than he'd even imagined.

He made it to Bunny's office with a minute to spare. Her door was half open but she was on the phone. Chellis, her assistant, was nowhere to be seen, so Theo sat in a hallway chair to wait. How could he explain himself? All those nights of reading and he'd discovered no one remotely publishable. He was an ambassador for the talentless. A doorman for the disturbed. He should put that on his résumé.

Inside, Bunny was tossing out six-figure numbers. Barely nine thirty a.m., and already a negotiation in progress. Should he let her know he was there or risk being accused of lateness? He settled on the former and slowly edged into her line of sight. Without a glance in his direction, Bunny waved him in.

Her office was more modern than he would have guessed. The art was abstract, and the furniture had a decidedly Design Within Reach vibe. Within reach for an editor in chief, maybe. He lowered himself tentatively into a chair. Books covered the walls, and Theo actively scanned their bindings, so as not to appear to be listening in. But how could he not? From what he could gather she was making a $500,000 bid on a debut novel. At least I got to witness this, he thought, or began to think, because a moment later the phone receiver came crashing down. He all but jumped in his seat.

"Agents," Bunny muttered. She typed something into her computer and then looked up at Theo for the first time. "You've been here two years," she said.

"Almost three, actually, yes."

"Doing what?"

"A bit of everything," Theo said. "Proofreading, logging and traffic, event planning, pre-pub marketing, messenger work—"

"Coordinating the messengers?"

"Being one."

"You're riding a bicycle around the city?"

"I take the subway or walk."

"And who's sending you on these errands?"

Theo had her full attention now. The answer was Wynne Groome, who'd taken a liking to him. But Theo wasn't about to rat out an executive editor.

"I'm not sure I should say."

"I see." Bunny leaned back in her chair and studied him. "And the slush? How did that fall to you?"

"I volunteered. But I bring the manuscripts home, so as not to take away from my work."

"Have you found anything worthwhile?"

"Not yet, but there've been a few . . ." Theo didn't finish. He felt his cheeks begin to burn.

Bunny sat forward again, put her elbows on her desk. "We haven't published an unsolicited manuscript since nineteen eighty-six. Give the pile back to the interns. I don't want you carrying that crap around anymore."

Gleaning from her words the possibility of continued employment, Theo peeked over at the door as if looking for a witness, but someone had closed it. He was sitting all alone with the most powerful woman in publishing.

"I really don't mind," he said. "There's always a chance something's fallen through the cracks. I mean, the system, such as it is—"

"The *system*? We barely have a business! The slush pile is a time-consuming vanity project that stopped making sense decades ago. We don't have enough editors to read the *agented* submissions." She held a button down on her phone. "Chellis, how many manuscripts came in for me yesterday?"

"Um . . . hold on," Chellis said through the speaker.

Chellis, Bunny mouthed, shaking her head.

"Okay, twelve yesterday, and four so far this morning," said Chellis's voice. "Also, Martin Amis just called. He has a meeting in midtown and wants to know if you're free for lunch at Le Bernardin. Which you're not because you're having lunch with Ms. Urban at Gramercy Tavern."

Bunny rolled her eyes for Theo's benefit. He did his best to share her annoyance.

"Call Martin back and tell him lunch at Le Bernardin would cost more than his last book made. Actually"—she picked up the phone, taking Chellis off speaker—"I'll call him myself. What I want *you* to do is talk to one of your little Sarah Lawrence friends over at Viking and *discreetly* find out what they're bidding on that"—she consulted her notes—"*Marisha Pessl* novel." She pinched the top of her nose between her eyes. "What do you mean you don't know anyone at Viking? What do you kids do at all those parties . . ."

Theo sat there dumbfounded—that this world of letters still existed, if only in a few offices, in a few cities. That was enough. He watched Bunny sigh and then hang up. "Useless," she said, shaking her head. "Though I doubt we'll get the book anyway. A shame because it's quite good." She leaned back in her chair and considered Theo for a few terrifying seconds. "Chellis is leaving," she said, lowering her voice.

"Oh, I hadn't heard."

"Neither has she." Bunny began to smile but caught herself. "Anyway, I want you to replace her. Starting Monday. Familiarize yourself with all of our authors, including the backlist, and for God's sake, get to know some people at other imprints."

"Yes, of course. Thank you."

"Calm down, it's just answering phones."

But it wasn't just answering phones and Theo knew it. It was, at age twenty-eight, the start of a career. The beginning of a life. Bunny picked up the phone again, which he took as a sign to back out of the room and close the door. Chellis was eating an egg sandwich. She gave him a half wave with her mouth full. Theo waved back, his mouth bone-dry, and hurried down the stairs.

Bunny Beale. It wasn't possible. He had no pedigree, no connections, no experience. Oh, stop it! For once, just enjoy the moment. Why him? Why *not* him? Who on earth cared more?

The backpack was still sitting on his desk. He un-bungeed it and began pulling out the wedged-in manuscripts. He noticed a few red flecks on the pages—eraser rubber, it looked like—which was weird because he hadn't used a pencil on any of this batch. He pulled more out, and with it more flecks—like space dust now, getting on everything— and that's when he saw them, the four bricks, stacked two and two, at the bottom of the pack. He pulled a folded sheet of paper out from between them. *HEY ATLAS*, it read, *LIGHTEN UP A LITTLE*.

Chapter Eight

They strolled arm in arm down Flushing Avenue, just another (not entirely) young couple heading out for dinner on a Saturday night in Brooklyn. The flat autumn light had receded and Theo felt a slight chill attach itself to the breeze. Or maybe it was his mood. His life. He was reeling. He seemed to have lost his job, for starters. But that was understandable, if one valued performance over loyalty (which Win Groom certainly did). What was bothering him far more, at that moment, was Audrey's behavior—or, more precisely, her lack of it. The Fender situation—whatever that might be—was consuming her, yet she refused to acknowledge as much. Now here they were, walking to a restaurant when all Theo wanted to do was stay home and talk. Communication had always been their strongest asset, but suddenly neither seemed capable of even a rudimentary discussion. To fill the awkward silences, Theo began pointing out various urban landmarks and geographical oddities. He knew this wasn't the time, but he couldn't help himself. He clung to the familiar like an infant.

"Wow Car Wash," he said as they passed Wow Car Wash. "Vanessa's Video" . . . "Chico's Laundromat" . . . "Iglesia Pentecostal." He noticed a brick façade tagged with the word READ and said, "Look at that," and then another with a cartoon-lettered CALL YOUR MOTHER, which he almost acknowledged as well but managed not to. Theo had been drawing Audrey's attention to New York's visual peculiarities since their first days together, though back then he would catch himself and quickly apologize, embarrassed by his naked wonder, his need to be heard. No, that wasn't it. It was more his need to share, his *desire* to share. He recalled the first time Audrey took him to her office at Whale Creek. He'd never been to Greenpoint before and was immediately drawn to Manhattan Avenue's farraginous spectacle of cultures—Polish meat shops and Puerto Rican barbers and Yemeni newsstands. Occasionally, he'd catch a glimpse of the street's namesake island across the river, but they may as well have been glimpses of London or Sydney or Seoul—any far-off city, any world away. Again and again, he found himself excitedly pointing out some small irony or obscure sight, until Audrey finally stopped in front of the gothic spire of St. Anthony's and fixed him with a cockeyed stare. He braced for bad news.

"You know, I've walked this street hundreds of times and never noticed half the things you just pointed out," she said. Then she kissed him on the mouth as two Polish women scurried up the church steps, hissing.

Now, three years into their relationship, Theo's urban play-by-play had become an essential part of their lives together. Audrey had learned to have her phone at the ready, to look up answers to questions Theo might otherwise mull for hours afterward. The age of an ancient tobacco sign. The official boundary of a borough. Mostly, though, his interests ran toward subtle quirks of language and humanity—the cryptic beauty of the commonplace. He imagined the city as a song you had to open your eyes to hear.

South of Flushing, the spartan streets of East Williamsburg gave way to the Latin diaspora of Bushwick proper. This was prime narrative territory, rife with microcultures and butchered language, but Theo was feeling self-conscious. He glanced at Audrey but saw only hair. Usually, she emanated outward, making eyes with stroller-bound toddlers, smirking good-naturedly at leering stoop sitters, but now she burrowed into him, arm around his waist, head against his shoulder. It felt to Theo less like a show of affection than an attempt to evanesce. They walked down Wilson Avenue in silence.

Colon was wedged into a century-old tenement storefront on Troutman Street. They'd discovered the restaurant by chance, a few weeks after moving in together, and had quickly become regulars—that is, until *New York* magazine ran its fawning review early in the summer. They hadn't been back since, and the reason was plainly evident on the sidewalk out front, where a dozen people stood huddled in the semidarkness, texting and smoking as they waited for tables. How different the scene had been on that first visit, almost two years ago, when, trudging down the then-desolate block on their way home from a birthday party, Audrey heard muffled salsa music and stopped to investigate. "Look," she'd said, pointing to some chipped gold letters stenciled onto a fogged-up window. "I'm surprised some tagger hasn't added an 'oscopy.'" They couldn't see inside, and there was no posted menu or health department grade— nothing to suggest the place might be open to the public. But the music was unmistakable now, and the scraping of plates, and that was enough. Before Theo could protest, Audrey was leading him through the door.

They were greeted by a small, mustachioed man in a burgundy shirt, who performed a half bow and introduced himself as Victor, the proprietor. He led them to a wooden table against the back wall and tried to light a candle with matches. After several attempts, Colon's only waitress appeared with a lighter and solved the problem. Victor regarded the flame with satisfaction, then stepped back, clapped his hands, and announced that there were no menus tonight.

"You mean, no specials," Theo said.

"I mean no menus." He pointed at the table, where there were indeed no menus. "You eat in my hands please." Then he bowed again and disappeared. Audrey burst out laughing.

They looked around. The restaurant was a cluttered palimpsest of stylings, with mismatched mosaic floor tiles and purple sponge-painted walls, adorned, in turn, with decidedly amateur oil paintings of toiling farmers and field hands, modern-day nautical instruments and lifesaving equipment, and replica posters from classic French and Italian films.

On the ceiling, near the bathroom door, hung a partially torn Soviet flag, and above the bar, the Stars and Stripes. As for the crowd . . . there wasn't much of one. Of the ten or so tables, only two were occupied, and exclusively by heavy-lidded old men speaking in Spanish.

"There's a cat sitting on the service station," Audrey said.

Indeed, there was. Also, the lighting was too bright. And the glasses were spotty. And the salsa music was canned and playing on repeat. But in spite of it all, and because of it all, Colon was perfect. They ate ravenously that first night, and drank rioja by the carafe. When they were finished, Victor appeared with a bottle of Madeira and pulled up a chair. He was anywhere from fifty to seventy years old and of uncertain marital status. As for Colon, it was the name of his hometown in Cuba—"a bastion," he called it proudly, though of what he never said (sugar plantations, Google would later inform Theo, though from the available images "bastion" seemed a strong word). At some point Victor was called away, and Audrey and Theo let the restaurant settle in around them, this perfect little cantina in a Puerto Rican barrio, with its Cuban owner and communist/capitalist/seafaring sympathies. And then they were gazing at one another, and at exactly the same time they half stood, over the table, and kissed each other softly, intoxicated less by alcohol than the distance they'd traveled—from the sidewalk, from their loft, from everything before. When they disentangled, there was clapping from the men up front and Audrey, grinning broadly, blew them a kiss of their own. The bill came to $38.

So much had changed since then. Now, as Theo and Audrey edged through the front door, they were quickly swallowed up by a bottleneck surrounding the small hostess stand. Taller than those around him, and stuck in place, Theo cataloged Colon's metamorphosis: the new wood-plank floor, the lowered lights, the raised prices (a chalkboard menu hung on a nearby wall), and look at that: a live three-piece bluegrass band playing in the corner. Not that he could hear them. He couldn't hear anything but noise.

When they reached the (noticeably non-Hispanic) hostess, she made a big deal of studying her list of uncrossed-out names. "Two people is an hour and a half," she said finally, her deadpan tone suggesting this was a perfectly reasonable amount of time to wait for a table at a downmarket restaurant on a side street in Bushwick. For many years, Theo would have accepted this news with the kind of fatalism known to all city dwellers stuck in some spiraling absurdity. Now, though, he paused in anticipation of Audrey's stepping forward to take charge—because she always did. Time and again, Theo had watched her pull the hostess or shop clerk or bouncer aside and quietly impart whatever snippet of information was necessary to bring the moment to a positive conclusion. Often, she'd be recognized before she even opened her mouth. She knew that many people, traversed that many scenes. Tonight, though, she remained rooted in place behind him, and if Victor hadn't appeared just then, his arms spread like he'd been expecting them for hours, Theo would have no doubt reverted to form and retreated with Audrey into the night.

But the universe had righted itself, and after apologies, handshakes, and—for Audrey—a lingering double-cheeked kiss, the proprietor herded them through the throng of crowded tables. Theo was reminded of the night before and the insanity of that overcrowded club. His life was becoming a never-ending attempt to get from one side of a room to another. When they arrived at the other side of Colon, Victor said something to two older men seated at the front of the bar, and they immediately stood and presented their stools to Theo and Audrey. Theo recognized them as members of Colon's original posse and began to protest—where would they sit now?—but Victor headed him off with a dismissive wave. They thanked the men and sat down, Theo contorting his body onto the stool only to find that the bar wasn't deep enough for his legs. Maybe he should stand, he thought, but that would be an insult to the newly evicted. So he wedged himself in diagonally, with his knees facing Audrey.

"What a mess," she said when Victor was gone. "Saturday night. I should have known."

Theo felt an elbow hit his left arm. He turned to find a man with a lumberjack beard attempting to cut his food. "Sorry, dude, tight quarters," the guy said.

"My fault," Theo responded. "I'd move down if I could." But he couldn't, and anyway, for the first time in his life, he thought he and Audrey could do with a little space between them.

Following his non-meeting at Café Loup earlier in the afternoon, Theo had taken a long, soul-searching walk around the West Village before L-training it back to Brooklyn. He arrived home to find Audrey staring at their computer monitor. She didn't hear him at first, but when he shut the door she wheeled around. "Jesus, Theo," she exclaimed, and put her hand to her heart. With her other, Theo noticed, she swiftly tapped a key to minimize the open desktop window. "Tell me everything," she said, hurrying over to hug him and then leading him to the couch. He fell into the cushions and exhaled. She sat beside him and tucked her legs up under herself.

He tried to sound upbeat as he recounted his farcical experience at Forbidden Planet, but he was no actor, and by the time he got to the Café Loup part, Audrey was massaging his shoulders.

"What exactly did Win's assistant say in her text?" she asked.

"She said that something had come up and he couldn't make it." Theo considered reaching into his pocket to show Audrey the actual exchange but couldn't bear to look at it again. "Not even something *important.* Just . . . something. So I texted her back to see about rescheduling, but she didn't respond. Which is when I understood just how inconsequential I've become to them."

Theo removed Audrey's hand from his neck. He felt ashamed.

"You should have seen me," he continued, "shuffling down Seventh Avenue, checking my phone every two minutes like some teenager. Of course, I ended up texting Cecily again, and when she *still* didn't respond, I knew I was in trouble, considering the sole purpose of her job is to be attached to her phone at all times. If she was surfing in Malibu she'd have it clipped to her wet suit in a waterproof case. So obviously she had her marching orders. Still, I *know* Cecily—not personally but we've talked on the phone. So I decided to call instead. And guess what."

"She *was* surfing."

"Close! She was at the beach."

"So what. It's Saturday."

"Well, she answered the phone in what sounded like a wind tunnel, and then gave me the runaround until I said I was going to call Win directly, at which point the wind miraculously disappeared and she told me, very sternly, not to do that. I asked her why, and she said, 'off the record,' that Win was restructuring Round Circle's Content Discovery Department—which isn't even a thing, by the way—and that my employment had been 'transferred to freelance status.' *Freelance*: what a word. So seemingly benign, so manifestly lethal."

"So you weren't *fired*."

"Yes, I was. 'Freelance' just means I can keep sending them ideas, and *if* something comes of one of them, *then* I'll be compensated. Of course, as we know, nothing comes of anything I send them."

"Are they canceling your health insurance?"

Theo nodded. "I can get COBRA, though I've been through that before."

"I'll get you on my plan somehow," Audrey said. "Oh, baby, I'm so sorry." She put her hand on his cheek and kissed him tenderly. Soon they found themselves entwined among the cushions and pillows, but their clothes stayed on. Being on the receiving end of sympathy was, to Theo, the opposite of an aphrodisiac. He knew he was old-fashioned in this regard—sympathy being a leading currency in this touchy-feely world—but he was old-fashioned in all kinds of regards, and clear-eyed stoicism in the face of life's setbacks was hardly an original sin. At the same time, he needed look no further than his own parents' repressed relationship to understand that vulnerability, a certain give-without-take, lay at the heart of genuine human relations.

Audrey, he knew, was engaged in a similar battle, the two of them stumbling but determined to counter their natural autonomy, their hard-won self-reliance. Both were private people—Theo more obviously, Audrey, perhaps, more deeply. Something thick and immovable lay behind her inviting façade. Theo liked to think it was the source of her strength (that she was who she was, coming from where she'd been, was intoxicating to him), but on the couch just then, it had seemed more like a torment. Because something wasn't right; she had retreated inside of herself. It was hard to detect, for outwardly she appeared just the opposite: doting and overly supportive. But Theo detected a certain hollowness to her behavior. She was doing and saying all the things she normally would, but rotely, almost mechanically. She was, Theo realized, acting.

"How about a drink?" she said, and stood up, brushing cat hair off her shirt.

Roger himself was sitting on the kitchen counter, but he jumped off as Audrey approached. They moved past each other warily, and the cat continued over to the couch. He hopped up and settled into the spot Audrey had just vacated.

She made cocktails—a vodka tonic for Theo, something whiskey-based for herself—and then brought them over and arranged herself on the far side of the cat. At which point Roger jumped down and darted away. Audrey put her drink on the coffee table. "I need to get out of the house. Let's go get dinner." Theo readily agreed.

While Audrey ducked into the bathroom for a quick shower, he wandered over to the multipaned windows and gazed out at the twilight. The view was stunning if industrial bleakness was your thing—slate-gray warehouse rooftops and high, heavy fences and vivid graffiti tributes. He saw the lights come on at the Boar's Head warehouse on Rock Street, and then, seconds later, a field of halogens at the HVAC repair center a few blocks farther on. Sparks were flying at the granite-cutting yard, and looking up, he watched the outline of a plane on approach to LaGuardia, an entire string of them, like a constellation on the run.

He sipped his drink. It was a big city; he'd figure something out. He craned his neck toward Manhattan—though the island was barely visible from the windows—and when he turned back his eyes were drawn to a glint of rippling darkness between buildings. English Kills, the old maps called it, the sludge-filled denouement of Newtown Creek. Until the BP oil spill in the gulf, it had been the most polluted body of water in America; perhaps it now was again. He supposed he should find solace in its beauty at dusk, but Theo could think only of surfaces, appearances, artifice. He was doomed, he realized, to a life of teasing out metaphors, comparing one thing, however poorly, to a seeming other, the whole practice a subtle, never-ending rebuke of the reality that lay before him. But this *was* a city of artifice. Why couldn't Theo apply a layer of sheen, or a level of irony, to his own life? Why couldn't he play dress-up once in a while?

Audrey was singing in the shower. So not everything was turned on its head. Maybe nothing was, and he was only imagining the tension. He peered around the room, as if to make sure the air was visibly free of friction. Roger was staring at him from the couch, so he looked away, toward the kitchen, the bathroom, the desk. Their computer was asleep, or at least laying low. What had she been doing when he first walked in? It must have something to do with Fender, he thought, which meant that this wasn't going away. So why wasn't she talking to him about it? He'd just conducted a full autopsy of his professional life and she couldn't open up about a troubled former friend? Should he bring it up at dinner? As far as he knew, Audrey had never kept anything from him. There had to be a good reason, but just then, he couldn't imagine what it might be.

Mojitos arrived, followed by a series of delicious small plates, courtesy of Victor, who, despite their continuing insistence otherwise, believed Audrey and Theo were the pioneering spirits behind the current onslaught of Caucasian business. They ate with their elbows in, cocooned amid the clamor: pork empanadas and sweet fried *platanos maduros* and jalapeño chilis stuffed with garlic cream cheese. Soon, Theo was sweating through his shirt and it occurred to him that aside from the food, the restaurant's most authentic nod to Cuba might be its lack of climate control.

"They need fans in here," Audrey said as if reading Theo's mind. That they were on the same page, however briefly, buoyed his spirits. Audrey performed a highly gymnastic maneuver to remove her shawl-like outer layer of clothing, wriggling free to reveal a thin blue tank top. Theo felt the energy around them change. He didn't have to look to know half the eyes at the bar were on her, men and women both. Her shirt was tight but not low cut. Her broad, freckled shoulders—and the western landscape tattoo on the left one—were what drew interest; her evident ease and self-possession were what turned the looks into stares. But if she consistently attracted attention, she never acknowledged it, and Theo couldn't remember a time when he'd felt jealous in her presence.

What was he doing? He needed to ask about Fender.

But she was eating now, and drinking, and appeared content. A surge of warmth spread through him, an ecstatic pain he'd long ago recognized as love. He hadn't known you could physically feel it, that love existed as a sensation beyond other emotions—joy and despair and desire—until Audrey entered his life. (The feeling had never been so urgent, so vividly real, with Eleanor.) And of course it scared him. And it scared her, too, in exactly the same way. She'd admitted as much.

"Try this," Audrey said, and hovered half an empanada in front of his mouth. He ate it. "Say what you will about the crowd, but the food has definitely improved."

"Audrey."

"It's because Victor finally kicked himself out of the kitchen."

"Stop," Theo said. He rubbed his temple.

"Stop what?"

"Whatever it is you're doing."

She retreated to her own airspace. "I'm talking."

"Yes, about superflu—about nothing."

"I know the word, Theo, thanks."

"Sorry, I didn't mean . . . it's loud in here."

He smiled weakly, as if to defuse what might have been lit. They were almost shouting to be heard. Still, he pressed on.

"Are you okay?" he asked. "After last night?"

"I'm fine," she said. "I overreacted." She looked down at her plate and stabbed at a jalapeño. "It was a name I hadn't heard in a while, and I was caught off guard. Fender and I weren't close anymore, if we ever were, but . . ."

"Jumping off a bridge," Theo said, and saw the man to his left glance over.

"Exactly." Audrey shrugged. "I guess it rattled me. But anyway." She squeezed his hand like she'd just had a great idea for a Halloween costume. "How about another mojito?"

They walked home in near silence. They'd barely argued, but it felt like they'd fought all night. Theo was tired. Tired of thinking, of analyzing. Just let things be, he told himself. Maybe the hour (and the alcohol) was getting the better of him. The sheer number of people on these haunted streets at night. He felt almost violated. He and Audrey had moved out here to leave the city behind—its crowds and prices and worse. Left unspoken, but very much understood, was what else they were escaping: their pasts. Theo's inglorious New York life. And Audrey's, too glorious by half. The plan had been to reinvent themselves together, two as one, in this tattered junkyard Eden that had seemed theirs alone. But the masses had found them, the great swarm descended, and it wasn't difficult, after several drinks, to connect this claustrophobic strain in their union with their increasingly encroached-upon paradise.

Arriving at their building, Theo peered up at their apartment windows and was surprised to see lights on. He was fastidious about turning them off, energy efficiency having been drilled into him by his otherwise fascist electrician father. He unlocked the iron door and held it open for his girlfriend. The couch was in the stairwell, so they took the rumbling elevator up three flights and started down the wide hallway, Audrey's heels clomping along the cement. Theo decided he would try again, in the calm of their home, to tease out what was bothering her. He'd open two beers and—

"*Theo*," Audrey hissed, snapping him to attention. She was frozen in place. Theo froze, too, and then saw what she saw—their apartment door, half open. Instinctively, he moved in front of her. He squeezed her arm, telling her to stay put, then took a step, and another, until he could see a sliver of the inside—their small dining table and the back of the couch. He listened for the slightest sound but heard nothing. Not even the cat.

For the first time all night, his thoughts organized themselves sequentially. He had locked the door when they left (and even if he hadn't, it would never swing open by itself). He glanced at the door handle. No scratches or dents, and the lock was still in place. They must have used a credit card. He'd used one himself a few times, with little resistance. He scanned the length of the hall and, seeing no one, began edging closer. Audrey tugged on his shirt.

"It's okay," he whispered, "just taking a look. Move back to the stairwell. If you hear something, run."

She didn't fight him, but she also didn't retreat. Theo gathered himself and slowly pushed the door farther open. He knew it wouldn't squeak. And he knew no one could hide behind it because a coatrack was there. In other words, he'd see them coming. He'd have a chance.

What did not occur to him was to tiptoe back down the stairs and call the cops. This was his home, *their* home, and he would stand and fight for it. The door was open enough now for him to stick his head inside. He listened for a moment—again silence—and then peered, slow as he could, into their loft. What he saw first was the desktop computer, toppled onto the floor. And then everything else: drawers open in the living room, the kitchen, their filing cabinet. Lamps were overturned, papers scattered, and the door to their only closet stood wide open. The entire main room was visible now, and no one was in it. That left only the bedroom, its door closed, the lights off. He felt Audrey behind him, her hand on his back. "Is someone—?"

"I don't know," Theo whispered.

And that did it. He was through with not knowing. In a single motion, he stepped around the door and broke an arm off the coatrack. Clothing dropped to the floor, jackets and scarves and hats. He moved across the room, taking long strides, the makeshift weapon clenched in his hand. "Hey!" he shouted. "Hey, come on out!" But he wasn't waiting for a response. He kicked the bedroom door open and reached for the light, and when it came on he had the wooden arm over his head, ready to strike . . . but no one was there. He stood in the doorway and surveyed the damage. The dresser flung open. Books everywhere. He took a deep breath, or started to, then heard a scrambling sound under the bed, and again raised his club, only to see Roger's white head peek out. Looking sheepish. Looking petrified.

"Fuck," Theo said, and exhaled. He retreated to the main room. Audrey was standing in front of the desk, a hand over her mouth. She was staring at something.

"What is it?" He dropped his weapon and hurried to her side.

She pointed at a single sheet of paper lying where the computer had been. Running down the center were four names, neatly typed:

AUDREY BENTON
CHRIS VAN VLECK
SARAH FOSTER
FENDER ✓

Theo picked it up and turned it over, but the other side was blank. "I don't understand," he said. "What's this from?"

She didn't answer. Theo eyed the surrounding mess, the papers and folders and files littering the floor.

"You didn't write it?" he asked.

Audrey shook her head slowly.

"Are you sure? There are years of stuff scattered every—"

"*Yes, I'm sure,*" she said, her voice both urgent and lifeless. Theo turned to her. She was shaking. He put his arm around her shoulder, but she didn't lean into him or accept the embrace. She just stood there. Stiff. Staring. Theo followed her eyes back to the paper.

"What does the check mark mean?"

Roommates

Williamsburg, Brooklyn
July 2005

Poetry is a Northern man's dream of the South. "Nice," Everett said. He traced the words across the inside of Audrey's right forearm. They were two days old and her skin was still red and tender to the touch. Everett had tattoos, too—all the band boys did—so Audrey was spared the questions asked by other men, older men. How long it had taken. If it had hurt. What it meant. (It had taken three hours. It had hurt a bit, in a stinging, itchy way. And, no, it didn't mean anything beyond the phrase itself—a melodic ode to a southland she wasn't really from.) They were lyrics to a song by a friend and occasional lover named Cary Winslow, whom Everett probably knew, since everyone knew, or had heard of, or had played with, everyone else in the Brooklyn scene. But enough about Cary. It was five a.m. and Everett was the boy she'd brought home.

She closed her eyes and pictured him, hours earlier, prancing across the stage at Warsaw, his guitar slung low, indifferent to the fitful attentions of the half-full hall. Everett was a beautiful kid, if not quite handsome, with a thatch of dark hair on his head but only wisps on his chest. She could tell he was younger than her by the way he kissed, aggressively, not lingering, and that was fine. She sat on her bed and unbuttoned her shirt while he tried to remove her jeans. No small task. They were tight, and so fitted at the ankles that Audrey, on particularly punishing nights, could go several rounds before managing to wrestle them off. But Everett was showing admirable determination. Off came one pant leg, and then, in a sharp tug that almost took her real leg with it, the other. He stood and faced her, a silhouette in the predawn light. Audrey fell back on her elbows. She was drunker than she wanted to be.

"Now you," she said.

Ever the performer, Everett went slow. Audrey liked his confidence. When he was down to his Calvins, she motioned toward the turntable atop a plastic crate in the corner, and he stepped over and turned it on. Tenderly, he lowered the needle onto the vinyl and nodded as Big Star's "September Gurls" began to play. Then he stripped down the rest of the way and climbed on top of her, already semihard. A good sign, considering all the lines and weed and whiskey. She rolled him over so she was on top and let him pull her thong down. Just her bra now, but the cleavage-obsessed boys in New York never removed them right away. She reached down between her legs and began to touch herself. Everett watched, and then he took her wrist and brought her wet fingers to his mouth. He sucked on them, slowly. *So he knows what he's doing.* She ran her hand down his chest and stomach and onto his cock. It wasn't small, and she told him as much as she worked it slowly up and down, experiencing the always-genuine thrill of it swelling in her fingers. "Good boy," she all but purred. When he was fully hard, she replaced her hand with his—this wasn't the time to learn what he liked—and watched him masturbate, increasingly intrigued, increasingly turned on. Every man did it so differently. "Take my bra off," she said, and he did as he was told, with a smooth twist of the back clasp between thumb and forefinger. Her breasts separated but hardly fell (thank God), and she unshouldered the straps and tossed it aside. She spit on her hand and reached down between his legs, all the way underneath. The space between: it was the key that unlocked a man. Everett whimpered like a child after a crying fit and went at himself harder and faster until Audrey bent over and, removing his hand, proceeded to lick his cock in slow motion. Then she took it in her mouth. She was good at this—sometimes too good—so proceeded with caution. Everett propped himself up to watch. Soon she felt his hand on the back of her head, pushing it down, tentatively at first, and when she didn't resist, more forcefully. He had more than she could take and her eyes began to water. She thought of her makeup, what was left of it, and then—the fucker—he squeezed her nose. She gagged, feeling him against the back of her throat, and wondered what it said about her that she didn't stop until she finally had to come up for air. Jesus Christ. She pushed him back onto the pillows and after catching her breath, blew him without interference, using her mouth and hand in tandem, pausing every time he built up. She wanted him to last. When her lips became numb, she straddled him again. Everett fumbled around, trying to touch her, but she stopped him. That could come later. She took his forearms and held them down on either side of his head, and then lowered herself, not *onto* him—not yet—but against him. She was wet and she moved back and forth, slowly, and it felt like she could come right away if she wasn't careful, so she reached back and began to guide him into—

"Fuck!"

Everett threw her off, roughly, and reached for the sheets. A light had come on, and Audrey, disoriented, looked up at the overhead. "No, *there!*" he exclaimed, and pointed across the room. Audrey flipped around, wondering if someone had walked in, but then witnessed the problem, in the leaden form of Mrs. Graziano staring at them bleary-eyed through her kitchen window. Audrey, uncovered, stared back. The old woman rubbed her eyes, then shook her head and turned away. "Close the fucking curtains," Everett cried from deep beneath the covers.

Audrey stood up. She didn't have curtains. She had an extra bed-sheet, which she now pulled across the window. "It's okay," she said. "She's used to it."

"That's comforting."

"To seeing *me*, I mean!"

But Mrs. Graziano was used to seeing men, too. Not that she made a habit of spying, but still. Why had the old woman never gotten curtains herself? Maybe she enjoyed the view, or the company. Audrey liked to think something existed between them, a silent female understanding—about desire or need—that spanned the generations. Or at least the four feet between windows. But they'd still never spoken. On the street, the woman refused to make eye contact.

"You can come out now," Audrey said.

"That *face*," Everett gasped, refusing to show his own. Audrey dipped under the sheets and found his mouth. They kissed in the blackness, hands roaming, trying to regain momentum, but it suddenly felt as late as it was. Everett began touching her, and for a while she let him, but he lacked rhythm and she lacked patience. She coaxed him along, guiding his fingers to the right spot, but it didn't help. He paused, restarted, paused again. Finally, she moved his hand away, and he didn't move it back. She whispered his name. Nothing. Seriously? He'd been chasing her for months—emailing, calling, inviting her to gigs—and now he was . . . asleep? She emerged from under the covers and swallowed a Xanax from the pillbox in her bedside drawer, hoping it would offset the coke, which had offset the weed, which had offset the Adderall, which she'd taken the previous morning because she'd been hungover. From what? She tried to remember what she and Sarah had done the night before, but amnesia—perhaps willful—got the better of her. Finally, around seven a.m., sleep did, too.

"Where's the bathroom?" A hand was shaking her shoulder. She brushed it off. "Seriously, wake up. I gotta go bad."

A name. Audrey kept her eyes closed, stalling. Dinner . . . concert . . . after-party . . . *Everett*! She raised her arm in the general direction of her bedroom door. "Other side of the living room," she rasped.

"What about your roommates? Are they home?"

She buried her head under the pillow. How would *she* know? Anyway, that's part of the deal, buddy. She remained silent. The pain in her head was pervasive. When Everett slipped out, she checked the alarm clock. 1:33 p.m. Fuck. What had happened? Drugs. Whiskey. Ten thousand cigarettes. No sex. She listened through the wall for sounds from Sarah's room but heard nothing. She must be at Chris's place, she thought, and began drifting off, only to be awakened again by Everett's return. She opened a single eye. He was standing inside the door, completely naked.

"I couldn't find my boxers."

"Ever heard of a towel?"

"I don't know where you keep them."

Audrey looked at the towel hanging on the door beside his head but didn't bother.

"I thought your roommates were gone," he said.

"I never said that."

"Because one of them's definitely here. I just met her."

"Sarah?"

Everett shook his head. "The other one. Small, pixie hair, pale as fuck."

"Iris."

"I guess. She didn't exactly introduce herself. She just raised her eyebrows and walked past me into her room."

"Sounds about right," Audrey said.

"You're not mad, are you?"

"No, I'm hungover."

"Well, here." Everett took her hand and placed it on his penis, as if that might solve the problem. It might, actually, Audrey thought, feeling it harden. He asked if she was on the pill. She was. She didn't mention condoms and neither did he. (She knew this was stupid, but good luck had made her careless.) Everett maneuvered above her. She spread her legs and told him to go slow. And he did, for a little while. Then he sped up, and she bit her lip and braced herself against the wall. He pulled her left leg over his shoulder and pushed in deeper. *My God*, she thought. Or did she say it out loud? She grabbed his hair, he grabbed her neck, and they fucked, hard. The Murphy bed was squeaking, but Audrey didn't care. She was about to orgasm but prolonged the moment, savored it, dwelled in it, until—no!—he beat her to it, pulling out without warning and, predictably, coming all over her tits, which she thoughtfully pushed together for him. Whatever. Still better than higher up. They lay there in silence. Then she pointed at the towel.

She kind of liked him, certainly enough to be with him again. She thought about taking care of herself, of making *him* take care of her, but Everett was already getting dressed, so she slipped her underwear on and grabbed a white oxford from the nearest pile of clothes. Through the thin wall, she heard the front door open and shut, then keys thrown on the counter, and a minute later, Sarah in the kitchen, singing "Hollaback Girl."

"Which roommate is that?" Everett asked.

"The other one," Audrey said.

Everett eyed the window like it might be an escape route.

"It's okay, she's my best friend. She doesn't bite—that hard."

Audrey stood up, a bit unsteadily, and opened the bedroom door. Sarah was making coffee.

"Oh shit," she said, "I hope I didn't wake you up." She peered past Audrey, grinning. "Though it is the middle of the afternoon."

"This is Everett," Audrey said. "We saw his band play a few weeks ago at Mercury Lounge, remember?"

Sarah nodded. "The Silver somethings."

"Doves," Everett said, looking around the apartment. His eyes landed on Iris's closed bedroom door. "I should get going," he said. "I have work."

"Where?" Audrey asked, realizing she had no idea what he did offstage.

"Tribeca. Guitar for Rich Kids 101. Glam, I know."

"It's okay, we're all about the hustle," Sarah said.

Audrey bit her tongue and led Everett out to the hallway. He turned to her at the top of the stairs. "I meant to ask you. I talked to my bandmates last night and we were wondering—"

"No."

"You don't know what I'm about to say."

"You're going to ask if I'll work with you."

"Well, yeah." Everett frowned. "I mean, you like our sound, right?"

"Of course, but I just fucked you. It's a conflict of interest."

"It's a *convergence* of interest."

"Sorry," Audrey said. "Strict policy."

"Right. Because you're so clearly into rules and regulations around here."

"You can find a label with more juice than Whale Creek."

"But we want *you*. Will you think about it? Please?"

"Fine. But I'm just saying that so you'll leave." She smiled and they kissed. Then he turned and clomped down the stairs. The air in his wake smelled of sex and smoke and leather. The smell of her twenties.

"He's quite the dish," Sarah said when Audrey walked back in. "How'd it go?"

"Better this morning than last night."

"Brooklyn boys."

"Surprised you remember."

"Ha ha."

The kitchen wasn't large enough to accommodate two bodies, so Sarah poured Audrey coffee and they moved to the couch. Sarah picked up the latest *Vanity Fair* on the table in front of her—"Iris *subscribes*," she whispered—and began leafing through it.

"Where's Chris?" Audrey asked.

"A tech conference in San Fran."

The effort she put into making this sound effortless struck Audrey as disingenuous. The problem wasn't Chris Van Vleck, per se, or where he lived (Upper East Side), or what he did (financial something); the problem was that he wasn't an isolated case. Audrey and Sarah had been known to dip their toes in the giant wave pool that was Manhattan— meeting up at Balthazar or Barbuto or Pastis to see friends and flirt with strangers—but they'd always ended up back in Brooklyn with the boys they dated for real, the prancing rough-around-the-edgers, creative but self-centered, sweet but self-destructive. Until recently, Williamsburg had defined Audrey and Sarah to the point of caricature, the two of them like encyclopedia illustrations of the word itself. They believed in its cultural import. They understood its layers and contradictions, because they were walking contradictions themselves, honest hustlers, hardworking layabouts, changing outfits in public bathrooms, applying makeup at Sephora, and while they were always close to broke, it was a stylish and—at least nowadays—amusing type of poverty. They lived in small rooms with no AC but laughed off the sweat, the uneven floors, the bad water pressure. They knew how to get by. They knew this phase was temporary.

But *temporary*, Audrey was coming to understand, could mean different things.

Audrey's definition was linear. She had found her scene, and her goal was to rise within it. Success, she believed, would come with experience, which she was busy amassing. She was hardly a planner—she lived by instinct and guile—but she could be practical. Take her acting career, for example. Three years of auditions and casting calls; of résumé mailings and monologue recitations; of "drinks meetings" with small-time agents, assistant directors, friends of friends of friends . . . all of this, all the time, and the only legitimate credit she could point to was a New York Lottery commercial in which she'd played a convenience store clerk with a name tag (Summer!), a winning smile, and three perky lines. She'd landed it (thank you, *Backstage—finally*) during a searing heat wave a year earlier, having beaten out dozens of cleft-chinned girls fanning themselves with their own headshots in a saunalike talent agency hallway, all of them with better haircuts and stronger acting credits. Call it serendipity, or simply her time. A week after it aired, in regional markets statewide, she'd signed with a manager and joined AFTRA. Then . . . nothing happened. Or, more accurately, more auditions happened but nothing came of them. And then the auditions dried up as well. Of course, there was ancillary stuff, short films and no-budget music videos, but even these projects had winnowed as more nonacting jobs came along. Bartending shifts. Catering gigs. Fit modeling for designer friends. And, most recently, "band outreach" at Whale Creek Records. It was this latest job—still part-time—that increasingly took up her days.

Sarah's definition was more literal. If Audrey's station seemed increasingly temporary, Sarah's entire Brooklyn *life* seemed so—like a stopover, a fling. Or maybe Audrey was just hurt. Sarah had been her trusted companion since that first softball game in McCarren Park. They'd become close in a way that Audrey, tomboy that she was, had not previously believed possible between women, and they'd vowed to live together at the first opportunity. It had come the previous summer, when Audrey's roommate Randall departed for the greener pastures of a vegan squat. Sarah replaced him, and soon thereafter, her banker fixation began. She was still working weeknights at Indochine in the city, so becoming entangled with a suit or two was to be expected. But Chris was the third banker in a row. "It's officially a trend," Audrey had said, mostly teasingly, the following morning. "It's officially a progression," Sarah had answered, mostly defensively.

Except Chris had come back for more. And more. And after that, he was just around. Audrey quite liked him, despite his hedge fundness (he was actually in *wealth management*, he had tried to explain, before realizing that sounded even worse). In fact, Audrey had introduced them. As a lifelong Manhattanite, Chris approached Brooklyn like an adventure tourist, but he was boisterous and inclusive and enjoyed live music. Plus, he always paid for everything. What, then, was Audrey's problem? It wasn't jealousy, or a sense of abandonment (she still saw plenty of Sarah), but something less quantifiable and harder to explain. It felt like a bond of common purpose was being broken. The two of them had started on a journey together, and now Sarah was . . . drifting. Except her actions were more calculated than that. What was that awful expression? *Upward mobility*. Sarah was leaving her behind.

Audrey looked around the living room for a pack of cigarettes, to no avail. "Clap Your Hands is playing at Union Pool tonight," she said. "Wanna go?"

Sarah looked up from the magazine. "Have I seen them before?"

"I don't think so. They're new but tight. And peppy. You'll like them."

"Preppy?"

"*Peppy!*"

"And they're called Clap Your Hands?"

"Clap Your Hands Say Yeah, if you want to get technical." Audrey shrugged. "It's the state of things."

"Why not," Sarah said. She tossed the *Vanity Fair* on the table and embarked on a few half-hearted yoga poses on the living room rug. "I'm thinking of going running."

"I'm thinking of robbing a bank," Audrey responded.

"Busy around here," said a voice behind them. The two girls wheeled around to find Iris standing in her bedroom doorway, wearing jeans and a vintage "Buckingham Nicks" T-shirt. Sarah, halfway into a standing bow pose, righted herself.

"Bit of a slow start," Audrey said as Iris crossed to the kitchen and put a kettle on the stove. She drank a lot of tea.

"I'm going running," Sarah said again, and this time appeared to mean it. She slipped into her room and shut the door. Sarah didn't dislike Iris as much as feel uneasy around her—mostly, she'd admitted, because she couldn't figure the girl out. Audrey couldn't either, but she was more accustomed to weirdness and thus approached their third roommate as a puzzle to be solved (though there were clearly pieces missing).

Iris was a Craigslist find who'd moved in two months earlier, after Jodi—Audrey's other former roommate—absconded to a loft in Gowanus with a PETA activist. Iris was a small, curveless girl with short Jean Seberg hair and a flat face that imparted an air of perverse toughness. Audrey sensed that things had happened to her, though what those things might be she didn't know. Iris was furtive and quiet. She gave half answers to whole questions—a habit that drove Sarah to distraction—and could be jarringly abrupt in the course of the most banal apartment encounters. The details of Iris's day-to-day life were equally opaque. What *was* known: She was originally from Kansas City but had moved to New York to attend Pratt and had been bouncing around various creative and academic scenes ever since. These days, she was pursuing a graduate degree in philosophy at the New School, while working on a writing project that kept her busy most mornings at her bedroom desk, surrounded by quote-filled Post-it notes and leaning towers of heavily underlined books. At least that's how Audrey imagined Iris's room, as she and Sarah had caught only glimpses of it, a fact that widened the ongoing speculation about what Iris was really up to. Still, Audrey believed a kindred spirit might lie beneath Iris's gruff exterior and, a few times, had invited her out at night. But Iris usually had her own evening plans, and swank ones at that, judging from the heels and strapless dresses and black cars double-parked out front. "Banker boyfriend," Sarah had speculated one night, peeking out the window at the idling sedan. "Has to be." *Well, you would know*, Audrey managed not to say.

The kettle whistled as Iris rummaged through the fridge, the front of which was still adorned—in honor of Jodi—with a photo of a toothless pit bull.

"I like the new ink," Iris said, examining the expiration date on a carton of milk.

"Thanks," Audrey replied, looking down at her forearm. When had Iris noticed it?

Sarah emerged from her bedroom looking like a second wife, in a skin-hugging running outfit with Nike swooshes everywhere. She fiddled with her iPod and stretched her right hamstring for about four seconds. "I need to get one of those Minis you can strap to your arm," she announced, and then walked out the door.

"Do you have any others?" Iris asked.

"Friends?"

"Tattoos. Besides your shoulder, obviously."

"One. Down here." She pointed at her pelvis. "The word 'Sucre.' I was nineteen and lost a bet with a chef at a French restaurant I was working at in Florida."

"Were you fucking him?"

"Ish."

Iris sipped her tea with both hands. Audrey waited for more—she was enjoying her roommate's bluntness—but nothing came.

"We're heading out to see a band later if you're not doing anything," Audrey said.

"I know. I heard you guys. Clap Your Hands."

"You know them?"

"Of course." Iris started back toward her room. "I have a drinks thing in the city, but I'll try to swing by after." She stepped inside and closed her door.

Audrey spent what was left of the afternoon listening to demos and visiting band pages on MySpace. That she was being paid, however little, to do this both thrilled her and softened the blows of other failures—the monologue-memorizing in restaurant storage rooms, the bottom-shelf shopping at off-brand drugstores, the postdawn walks of shame. She was good at her label "job" and the roles it required—fan and facilitator, marketer and muse.

"But you're not a muse," Sarah had told her a few weeks back. "Muses are unattainable."

Fair enough, but the rest applied. Musicians just wanted her around. All those boys and girls with instruments and nerve. Was it her discerning taste? Her calming presence? Certainly, unflappability was a valuable trait among the impressionable and confused. How many music conversations had morphed into therapy sessions? A few friends and then a whole band. A few bands and then half of Bedford Avenue. She'd become a link between parties, at parties, bringing musicians together. Stellastar. The Fiery Furnaces. Grizzly Bear. She drank with them, dropped by recording sessions, and went to shows when she wasn't waiting tables or tending bar.

In that way, people assumed Audrey Benton had been working in music long before she officially was. Life details were scarce among her crowd. Brooklyn was a borough of scheming night owls, pretending they knew one another's names. But so many *did* know hers. Rumors swirled around Audrey, entering rooms before her and persisting in her wake. Most weren't true (she'd never dated Conor Oberst or slept with Julian Casablancas); some were almost true (she hadn't introduced the members of TV on the Radio to each other but she'd been around them at the time); and several—always the most interesting—were absolutely true (she'd grown up around astronauts, her grandfather had died from an alligator bite, and there was a good chance she could get your band a record deal).

Calvin Blank was the man who changed her life. He'd approached Audrey the previous October, between sets at Arlene's Grocery, to ask if she might be interested in working at his label, Whale Creek Records. She said she hadn't heard of it. That was because it didn't exist yet, he told her. Audrey followed him from the concert space to the barroom, where Cal bought her a drink and explained things.

He was a fiftyish ex-hippie, voluminous in size and deep of voice, with curly gray hair and glasses that kept sliding down his nose—like a young Santa Claus. Cal told her he lived mostly in Vermont, having retired to a "gentleman's farm" after a brief but productive career as a coder. But music had always been his first love, so he'd started a small label in Burlington a decade back. Up-and-coming jam bands, he said, and Audrey tried not to physically recoil. Cal's goal had been to find the next Phish or Widespread Panic, but his timing was off. The Dead was dead, grunge was king, and jam bands were fading into bootlegged oblivion. Anyway, the point—and thank God he was getting to one— was that he'd enjoyed owning that first label, despite its ultimate failure, and was thinking of trying again. He'd learned his lesson in terms of genre, and what intrigued him now were the bands emerging from Brooklyn—"this whole *indie* scene," he said, as if the word was still foreign. This time, though, he'd be strictly absentee, behind the scenes, and was hoping to find someone to run things day-to-day. He'd been asking around and Audrey Benton's name kept coming back. Audrey blushed at this, not quite believing what she was hearing. Then things became surreal. "I want you to be my first employee," he said. "You find and nurture the talent, and I'll do the rest." They'd start small, sign an unknown band or two, and take it from there. He'd pay her by the hour but couldn't do much more than minimum wage until they sold some records. He also couldn't provide benefits in the beginning. No problem, Audrey thought. She'd never had health insurance, so why start now? When she asked if she'd really have autonomy over who they signed, Cal laughed. "My taste is so bad they shouldn't even let me into places like this. I'll just be along for the ride."

Words to live by, Audrey thought.

They shook on it, and Whale Creek Records was born. Cal had taken the name from a melodic-sounding—but thoroughly toxic—estuary near his office in a former glassworks factory at the northern tip of Greenpoint. He still lived in Vermont and only came down once or twice a month, so she'd have the run of the place—if that was cool with her. It was. Everything was. The next day, they met at world headquarters. The office wasn't small, exactly, though Cal had been renting the space for years and half of it was taken up with the inner workings of old computers. She played him some CDs and MP3s, and he said he liked what he heard, especially the rawer stuff, the analog sounds. So did she. That same night, she took him to Cakeshop on Ludlow Street to catch a rough-and-tumble family act called the Westfield Brothers. The show was a train wreck and there was an argument onstage. Afterward, Audrey apologized. They're too young, she admitted. But you're right, they've got something, Cal said. Sign them up if you want. Let's see if they can make a record.

And so she did. And so they were. Or at least they were trying.

In truth, Cal could have been starting a bossa nova label and she would have signed on. For Audrey had been slipping—into habits, cycles, more debt. Her life had come to resemble tragicomic performance art. Even the simplest of activities—like her and Sarah deciding to see a movie, then spending an entire week failing to get to the theater six minutes away—often proved too taxing to carry out. To say nothing of housekeeping and grocery shopping, routine tasks that could induce paralysis, hours spent prone on beds and couches, until darkness—that addictive drug made up of actual drugs and endless temptation—finally, fortuitously, arrived. And now Sarah had started up with the bankers, leaving Audrey to venture forth unchecked. Pulled in different directions, she chose them all, the nights becoming mornings, the mornings afternoons.

Whale Creek had saved her from all that—or some of it, anyway—and given her a reason to wake up, beyond whatever body might be passed out beside her.

Audrey left the apartment at seven p.m. Still happy hour most places. She hit Sweetwater for a beet salad and two half-priced cocktails, stopped by the Music Hall for a quick talk with their booker, then headed to Iona for a drink with Poe Mansfield, a lesbian guitar player of minor renown who'd been ousted from two all-girl bands in less than a month and was now weighing her options. Audrey suggested she write some songs of her own.

She arrived at Union Pool right on time. The openers had just finished and the faux-vaudeville stage was a chaotic mess of mikes and wires and two bands' worth of musicians trying to sort it all out. She backtracked into the courtyard and looked around for Sarah. It was a cloudless summer night, hot but bearable, and a sensation of blithe contentment came over her. She wandered around a stone fountain and past the Union Pool taco truck, imagining the layout of the place in its original incarnation as a swimming pool supply store. Visible above the exterior wall was the elevated BQE, surrounded by the kind of grimy wasteland that always bordered urban highways—grated storefronts and barren lots lined with dumpsters. What a perfect place to play rock and roll.

She gazed back at the gathered crowd, the youthful beauty amid decay, wobbly in heels, decked out in denim, layer upon flimsy layer, sheared and sheen, everyone smoking, half in hats and caked in eyeliner, the detritus of her generation waiting patiently for three-dollar tacos. She joined the line behind two WASPy-looking dudes in tucked-in shirts. She was seeing more and more of them around, and knew what it meant, what was coming. Lacrosse sticks in McCarren Park. Pet boutiques on Driggs. She'd recently heard about the high-end towers being planned along the waterfront. Rumor had it the development was called the Edge, though Audrey didn't think anyone, even real estate mopes, could be that tacky.

Someone pinched her ass and she wheeled around to find her best friend grinning at her.

"Pretty firm," Sarah said, "considering your exercise regime." They hugged.

"I need to find a gym," Audrey said. "My hangovers last days. It's a sign of aging."

"It's a sign of drinking."

Sarah rummaged through her purse and excavated a pack of cigarettes. She tapped two out and found a Zippo in her face before she could get one to her lips. Its owner had gone heavy on the cologne and even heavier on the tribal tattoos. They indulged him for just long enough to get their tacos paid for, then Sarah faked a female emergency and dragged Audrey off by the hand.

They ate on a bench, shielded by oversized ferns, then grabbed drinks and threaded their way into the concert space. The house lights were down, the room packed shoulder to bony shoulder. Audrey led Sarah up the near side and then cut in toward the center as the band took the stage—five boys, untucked and unkempt. They cozied up to their instruments, and a spotlight came on just as the keyboardist began to play a familiar—to Audrey, at least—progression. Then the drums kicked in, and the guitar, and before the singer even opened his mouth, Audrey knew she was listening to the song of the fall, or the winter, or whenever it was that lightning would strike these kids. Because it *would* strike. They had all the necessary elements, including a singer who couldn't sing. Instead, he wailed, mournfully, in a quivering tenor that rendered the lyrics indecipherable. It didn't matter. The effect was singular, if not without influence.

"He sounds like Thom Yorke," Audrey shouted into Sarah's ear.

"He sounds like Benicio del Toro in *The Usual Suspects*," Sarah shouted back. "I can't understand a word!"

Clap Your Hands launched into another song and Sarah bopped up and down to the driving drums. She wasn't *into* music; she just liked what she liked. Audrey watched the band closely. They had confidence. But did they have a full album of songs? She'd heard they were avoiding major labels, but every band said that until major labels came calling. Audrey had spied the Wichita crew when she walked in, and if anyone had the inside track it might be them. But her friend Fender was lurking back there, too, and he'd recently been scouting for Columbia.

Oh, stop and enjoy the show. Audrey downed the rest of her beer and closed her eyes. She let the synthesizers surround her, drown her in noise and heat, and soon the strangest of thoughts came into her head. She thought it was good to be young. Toward the end of the set, Sarah set off for the bar, and not a minute later, Audrey felt a hand on her left shoulder. She looked over, and there was Iris, standing beside her in black jeans and a loose striped T-shirt. She looked like a skate rat. They hugged, awkwardly, and turned back to the stage.

When the song ended, Iris leaned over. "I want to invite you to something. I couldn't back in the apartment, it was too crowded." Audrey remembered them being alone in the kitchen, whereas now they were surrounded by 150 people. But whatever. "Here," she said, and slid a business card into Audrey's hand like it was a dime bag. "It's on Monday night, we can go together. I'll give you the details tomorrow. And please, keep it between us."

Before Audrey could respond, Iris was slipping away through the crowd. The next song began. Sarah returned with two more beers.

"Did I just see Iris walking out of here?" she asked.

Audrey nodded. "She stopped by to say hi."

"She's so weird. Who shows up for one song?"

One song, it turned out, was all the band had left, too. When the set was over, the lights came partway up and the crowd began its rhythmic clapping. Clap Your Hands indeed. Sarah joined in, and it was only then that Audrey realized Iris's timing hadn't been a coincidence. She must have been watching the two of them, waiting for a separation. Why? There was light enough now, so Audrey took the card out and, using her cup as a shield, glanced down at it. She frowned. The clapping turned to cheers as the band came back onstage. The keyboards again. The drums. The room getting smaller. Audrey turned the card over.

"Oh my God," she said, but no one could hear her.

Chapter Nine

Audrey chained her ten-speed to a NO PARKING sign directly across Union Avenue from the colorless bunker that housed the Ninetieth Precinct. What an unsightly structure, to say nothing of the surrounding neighborhood. She was still in Williamsburg, though it felt as far from Bedford Avenue as Benton Harbor. Everything around her seemed made of concrete, from the high-rise housing projects to the dark blocks of Hasidic apartment buildings, their cagelike balconies a too-obvious metaphor for the hermetic beliefs of those who lived inside. The bridge was somewhere nearby, and the Navy Yard, and the infamous Marcy Houses, but all Audrey could see was urban gloom, stretching off in every direction.

She waited to cross alongside an Orthodox family with too many children to count. But the light was long, so Audrey did count them, or started to, until the mother took a step forward to shield her brood from whatever crime of indecency Audrey might be considering.

Screw the light. At the first gap in traffic, she hurried across the avenue, and then up a wheelchair ramp and through a set of double doors. The reception area was claustrophobic, its walls lined with out-of-date Police Tips posters and framed headshots of various men in charge—of the precinct, the department, the city, the world. Several uniformed officers milled around, hats in hand, and Audrey, who had spent enough nights with small packets in small pockets to be instinctively wary of those who enforced the law, averted her eyes as she strode up to the Plexiglass window against the rear wall. At the desk beyond sat a round woman wearing purple eye shadow. She was engrossed in a romance novel. Audrey waited. The phone in front of her rang incessantly—several lines blinking at once—but the woman ignored it.

After what seemed a particularly inconsiderate amount of time, Audrey cleared her throat. "Excuse me, I'd like to speak with someone about a possible missing person."

The receptionist looked up with only her eyes. "Boyfriend or husband?"

"Sorry?"

"Someone like you, it's one or the other."

"Is there an officer I can speak with?"

"It's Sunday, miss. And we're short-staffed courtesy of those Occupy people on the Brooklyn Bridge. Why they can't stay in their park I don't know, so unless it's an emergency—"

"It is," Audrey said quickly.

The receptionist considered her through the glass. Then, with the forbearance of a patient submitting to a rubber-gloved exam, she picked up the phone and pressed a button. Audrey couldn't hear the conversation, but she caught the receptionist's wry smile at the end of it. "You can talk to Detective Renzo," she said. "Wait by that door over there. When you hear the buzzer, open it and take a seat in the first room to your right. Interview One."

Audrey did as she was told. She pulled the door when it buzzed but was too late. The door buzzed a second time, and again she missed it. She understood she was being fucked with, so when it buzzed once more she yanked it open hard, and heard snickers behind her as she entered the inner sanctum. The interview room was a few paces down the hall. She stepped inside and the door slammed behind her.

The room was barren, just a table, two chairs, and four white cinderblock walls. Audrey saw no visible cameras or two-way mirrors. The good cop/bad cop stuff must happen elsewhere. Interview Two, maybe. She took a long deep breath, trying to center herself. What was she doing here? She'd told Theo she was biking over to Whale Creek for a few hours, which he must have thought strange, not because she rarely went to work on Sundays, but because her life—*their* lives—still lay scattered and broken across the warped wood floor of their loft. In the immediate aftermath, Theo had wanted to call the cops, but Audrey had convinced him not to, citing the apparently true fact that nothing had been stolen (Audrey's only valuable jewelry—two rings and a small diamond necklace Connie had given her—was still in the top drawer of the bureau). Also, Audrey reminded him, they were living with no lease in a commercial-use building that wasn't up to code, so the fewer cops nosing around, the better. Theo, more focused on their immediate safety, hadn't pressed the matter. It was late and they'd been drinking. The would-be burglar, he theorized, must have been a junkie or homeless guy someone had buzzed in by accident. Certainly, there were enough of them around. Audrey had quickly agreed, though she was already sure Theo was wrong.

The names. Until she saw them, her concern about Fender's whereabouts had only been a theory—and a loose one at that. Now it was much more. How else could that page have gotten there? Was it possible she'd typed the list long ago and then stuck it in a drawer, only to have it unearthed in the ransacking? She supposed it was (suddenly, *anything* was). But the names had been positioned so neatly on the desk, while the rest of their papers had been dumped across the floor. And what about the check mark beside Fender's name? And the timing? And the fact that nothing they owned had been taken? Theo assumed it meant the break-in must have been random; Audrey believed it meant the opposite. That someone was sending her a message. Well, she'd received it.

Of course she hadn't slept. Hadn't even tried. As Theo dozed fitfully beside her, Audrey lay awake, her anxiety crystallizing in the darkness, becoming fear, sweat soaked and pulsing, her thoughts moving in a thousand directions, and then only one, backward through time, to scenes she'd spent years attempting to bury, trying to erase. Now they came flooding back, the awful nightmare dormant no longer.

At some point she must have left the bed, for she was curled up on the couch when Theo emerged just after sunrise. She'd been staring out the window, or at the window, or maybe at nothing. Her mind was numb, her synapses exhausted. Still, she attempted an air of normalcy for Theo's sake. He asked if she was okay, and she said yes—just a bit scared. She saw his wariness, sensed his circumspection. But she didn't know where to start, so she didn't, and instead got up and made coffee while Theo tried to piece together their broken computer.

She showered and slowly dressed, laboring under the weight of her new reality. She needed to find out what had really happened to Fender, and there was only one place she could think of to go. So she told Theo the lie about having to work, then kissed him and said she'd be back in a few hours. When she got outside she pulled her phone out and, straddling her bike, dialed 311. An operator answered and Audrey asked what police precinct the Williamsburg Bridge fell under. The woman wasn't sure, bridges being jurisdictionally complicated, but her best guess was the Ninetieth. She gave Audrey the address.

Fifteen minutes passed before the door to Interview One opened and a large man in a boxy black suit walked in. He introduced himself as Detective Renzo and extended a hand across the table. Audrey stood up and shook it. She told him her name.

"Missing persons, is that correct?" he asked, consulting a notepad with those two words scribbled on it.

"Just one."

"One what?"

"Person. Missing. Maybe not even. It's kind of a weird situation."

"When is it not?" said the detective ruefully. "What are we talking about?" He looked at her left hand. "Not a husband, I guess."

"We're talking about a friend," Audrey said. "And I don't know if he's missing, exactly. He might have committed suicide. Jumped off the Williamsburg Bridge."

"And you know this how?"

"A rumor I heard."

"A *rumor*. And when might this have taken place?"

"Within the last few days, I think."

"What's your friend's name?"

"Fender. Or that's what he goes by. I don't know if it's his real name. I doubt it."

"Close friend, is he?"

"He was," Audrey said tightly.

"Physical description?"

She did the best she could, considering Fender's various looks and guises had fluctuated over the years. As she spoke, the detective eyed her somewhat less than professionally, so she returned the favor and observed him, too—the blood vessels in his doughy cheeks, the dandruff on his shoulders, the gel in his short spiked hair. She had a feeling this wouldn't go well.

When she stopped speaking, Renzo again consulted his notepad, to which he'd added nothing. "Why don't we go upstairs," he said, "see what's in the system."

They walked the length of the hallway and climbed a staircase to the second floor. Detective Renzo paused at the top to catch his breath and then led Audrey through a frosted-glass door marked SQUAD. Were it not for the odd can of Red Bull, the room could have been a film set from the golden age of cop shows, the desks covered with files and coffee cups, typewriters atop cabinets, a few early-generation computers. Men in suits identical to Renzo's sat hunched over paperwork, or perched on desks conversing with the hunchers. When Audrey appeared the room fell suspiciously quiet. Renzo walked to his desk and gestured with faux grandiosity to a metal folding chair on one side of it. She sat down. The detective woke his computer with a cautious tap of the space bar and then landed in his own chair with a heavy grunt. The screen came alive and asked for a password. Renzo consulted a set of letters taped to the monitor and carefully typed them in with a single index finger. He pressed Enter. Nothing happened. "Goddamn it," he said, and started over.

"Think he'd know uppercase from lowercase, seeing as solving cases is his job," said a gravel-voiced detective across the room. Laughter ensued. Audrey suppressed a smile.

Detective Renzo squinted at the monitor in frustration. It was difficult to watch him, but there was nowhere else to look. The only windows were up near the ceiling, a narrow strip of small glass squares that proffered the idea of light more than light itself, that task having been ceded to buzzing overheads that reminded Audrey of her elementary school.

"Aha!" said Renzo, his face lighting up with the screen. "It's an I, not an L. Look at that. Now, where were we?"

Audrey wasn't sure. "My friend Fender," she said tentatively.

"Right. Our supposed jumper. So who is he and what's your connection to him?"

Audrey was ready for this question and proceeded to recite a heavily condensed version of the following: Fender was the original Williamsburg character, an affable musician/philosopher/night owl/umpire who had for a long time lived in the old girdle factory on North Fifth, before the building was developed and he became an itinerant couch surfer, a creature of whim and circumstance, broke and increasingly troubled. He and Audrey had been quite close—though he'd been close with so many—before he'd succumbed to drugs and the ceaseless scheming of addiction. He wasn't active on social media, his old phone number no longer worked, and she had no idea where he was living these days. Indeed, she'd seen him only once or twice over the last few years, and always randomly, at shows or bars, looking ragged, even dazed. For a period of time, she, like everyone else, had been concerned, but then Fender had sunk beneath even the stratum of worry, and after a while no one spoke of him at all. He became a cautionary tale, a negative statistic—now, perhaps, quite literally. Not that such stories were uncommon in her world. It was just that Fender had been so ubiquitous for so long, the crowd-pleasing jester of the early Northside scene— sidled up most nights at Trash Bar or Clem's—before the neighborhood evolved, became something more temperate, or anyway, less injurious.

She'd always assumed he'd pull out of it. So when Audrey had heard he'd committed suicide, jumped off a bridge of all things, she'd found the news difficult to believe. He just wasn't the type, no matter how far he'd fallen.

"But what I don't get," said the detective, "is why *you're* here. It sounds like you barely knew him anymore. An acquaintance doesn't usually go to the cops. Not before a loved one."

The obvious response was that Fender was probably short on loved ones these days, but Audrey had been caught off guard. "I don't know what to tell you," she said. "I heard this rumor and asked around. Sure enough, no one's seen him in a long time."

"Where'd you hear it?"

"From someone I work with in the music business, who heard it from someone he works with. I realize it's like fifth-hand. That's why I came to you. I figured you guys would have a record of . . ."

"Jumpers."

Audrey nodded.

"When it comes to swan songs, the vast majority prefer the GW. And that's the Port Authority."

"But the Williamsburg is you guys, right?"

"Depends on where the body's found. An East River jumper could wash up anywhere. We've found them on Staten Island, in Red Hook . . ."

"There was the homeless guy at Hunters Point," said a nearby detective.

"And the one last month on Wards Island," said another.

"And Randall's Island."

"Same island."

"But different bodies, dumbass."

Now the voices came from all corners.

"Remember the one on Roosevelt?"

"And the Mexican kid in the Navy Yard?"

"He wasn't Mexican, he was black. Mexicans don't jump from bridges. They make it this far north, they're thrilled to be alive."

"Hey," said the only Hispanic cop in the room.

"All right, all right," said Renzo. "My point, Ms. . . ."

"Benton."

"He doesn't have a point," said the gravel-voiced cop. "Because even if we did find a body that matched the description of your friend we couldn't tell you until we notified his next of kin. Department policy."

Audrey turned to Renzo for clarification.

"It's true," he said, shrugging.

"Can you at least check your records and tell me if you *don't* have someone matching his description?"

Renzo winced. "Afraid not, because as we just explained, bodies can wash up anywhere, and another precinct may have something we haven't heard about yet. Then I'd be telling you an untruth."

"So why'd you just spend ten minutes turning your computer on?"

Snickers emanated from the peanut gallery.

"For that matter, why'd you even bring me up here?" Audrey sat back, exasperated.

"You asked to see someone," said the detective.

Someone with a fucking brain, Audrey wanted to tell him. Though, of course, Renzo had a brain. He knew what he was doing. He'd been poking her, testing her, hoping she might slip up—even if he didn't know what he was looking for. Funny, she thought as she stood and put her coat on. His instinct had been right: she *was* hiding something. She'd been hiding it for years now. She who so valued honesty, lying not just to Theo, but to a roomful of detectives. Or was "lying" too strong a word, when hers were sins of omission rather than deceit? No, they were one and the same.

A robbery and a suicide. Except the former hadn't been a robbery at all. If they were connected, it would make sense that Fender's death wasn't what it seemed either. She'd been trying to push the thought from her mind all weekend, but now, standing in the middle of the Ninetieth Precinct squad room, she could no longer ignore the word. "Murder." There it was. A possibility. Which would mean *her* life was in danger, too. For Fender and Audrey had been in it together. All four of them had been. The names on the list. The page was in her pocket—like she could ever forget what was on it. She had to get back to Theo. She had to tell him the truth. Why on earth had she hidden it so long?

Because he would have left. Theo Gorski was too good for someone like her, and always had been.

Detective Renzo took her contact information, gave her his card, and followed her out to the stairs. He stood there and watched her descend them. The receptionist was still reading. The cops still clustered around. She stepped outside and looked across the street. Her bike was gone.

Unions

New York, New York
April 2008

"Wanna know the worst thing?"
　　"Not really."
"He got arrested two weeks ago."
"Dad? For what?"
"Threatening a reporter."
"You're kidding."
Theo's brother shook his head. "Remember Bernie Shultz?"
"From the *Eagle-Trib*? Sure. He used to cover my games."
"Well, he's on the baseball beat now. Writes a column about the Sox."
"So what happened?" Theo asked.
"Apparently Dad drove down to the newsroom and got in his face. He's had a hard-on for Bernie for a while now. Says his coverage is 'chinky.'"
"'Chinky'?"
"Slanted."
"Christ."

"He started writing letters to the editor last summer, taking issue with just about everything Bernie had to say. Even got a few published before he crossed the line and got banned."

"But the Sox won the Series last year," Theo said. "What'd Dad have to complain about?"

"I guess he thought Bernie was too deep in the bag down the stretch. The Sox were playing wicked good ball, but old Len Gorski on his Barcalounger kept calling Bernie a fraud for drinking the Kool-Aid. You shoulda heard him when he opened the paper every morning. Beckett pitches lights out, or Papi or Youk goes deep, but he doesn't give a shit because he's so angry with the article itself. The celebratory . . . tone."

The word threw Theo momentarily. That Carl would say something so astute. He took a sip from his Miller High Life. He was on his third, Carl his fourth.

"How'd he get arrested?" Theo asked.

Carl shook his head, almost admiringly. "So, the Sox swept the Series—which was amazing, by the way—and that shut Dad up for a few months. But then February rolled around and we were back to square one, with Bernie making bold predictions and Dad throwing fits. This, mind you, while the team was still in Fort Myers for fuck's sake. Anyway, he must have started contacting Bernie directly, because a letter came in the mail—one of those 'cease and desist' deals from a lawyer—and the next thing I knew the boys in blue were payin' me a 'courtesy call' to say they got Dad in the hoosegow. Not the bullshit jail on the common; the real one, down off 495. Turns out he drove over to the *Eagle-Trib* and confronted Bernie in person while the paper had a restraining order against him. The fuckin' pisser."

Theo tried to visualize the scene, poor Bernie Shultz looking up from his computer to find Leonard Gorski towering over him in a fury. Theo couldn't help it: he started laughing. Carl glared at him, annoyed, surely, at his insouciance, his chosen distance from it all. But then a wary smile crept across Carl's face, too. They sat there and sipped their beers, and for the first time all night, the brothers began to relax.

It wasn't that they didn't get along. On the contrary, they were as close-knit as they were dissimilar. But being close to someone wasn't the same as being in someone's life, and fifteen years of increasingly sporadic reunions had taken a toll on fraternal relations. Theo rarely went back to Lawrence, and Carl had never been to New York—before now. It was hard to pick up where they'd left off when so much time passed between the leavings.

Certainly, Theo had been looking forward to Carl's visit, even if the true catalyst for it was not brotherly bonding but a trade show that Carl's girlfriend, Carly, was working at the Javits Center. Carl and Carly had been together for three years, though Theo had met her only once, the last time he went home. Carly Castorelli was an amateur bodybuilder who traveled from gym to gym, competing in unsanctioned competitions and selling non-government-approved growth supplements out of the trunk of her car. At age twenty-nine, she'd been engaged twice and married once, to a Buick salesman from Dracut who'd failed to return from a test drive one afternoon, leaving Carly with twin girls and an emptied-out bank account. That she *remained* married—from an overabundance of Catholicism or an even further-fetched belief that Mr. Buick might after four years return—didn't seem to bother Carl, though Theo saw it as a slap in his brother's face. Theo also noted, albeit to himself, that if the issue *was* Catholicism, then Carly's adherence to doctrine was sporadic at best, for Carl now lived with Carly, Carly's kids, and Carly's mother in the Castorelli house in Methuen. If the couple wasn't living in sin, they were certainly living close by.

Carl examined with barely masked disdain the extensive selection of animal-head microbrew taps directly in front of him. He was clad in a navy blue Adidas tracksuit, the top of which was unzipped just enough to reveal a white Fruit of the Loom T-shirt and a tarnished silver chain he'd been wearing for years now. Carl was as scrawny and dark haired as Theo was well built and fair, and he couldn't have looked more like a Masshole if he were an extra in a Ben Affleck film; at the same time, he was doing a decent impression of a certain virulent strain of the current Williamsburg aesthetic, and Theo realized, to his own amusement, that his brother might look right at home at the concert they were about to attend.

They were sitting in a sterile and mostly empty East Village sports bar that Theo had chosen for its proximity to Webster Hall, where a band called the Westfield Brothers would be playing at some point later in the evening. It was the brothers' second stop, the first being an abortive meet-up at St. Mark's Bookshop, two blocks south, where Theo had hoped he might find a hot-off-the-presses copy of *The Duchess of Des Moines*, the most recent—i.e., second—novel he'd acquired and edited at Prosaic. It was about living a dignified life in a dying city, and he'd planned to buy a copy for Carl. Except, there had been no copies. And also no Carl. Eventually, Theo stepped back outside, where he found his brother pacing the sidewalk, the idea of venturing inside the store having proved too great a shock to Carl's book-free ecosystem. "Why the fuck did you want to meet here?" he asked by way of greeting. What could Theo say? They'd walked to the bar.

Theo had never heard of the Westfield Brothers, but in a panicked rush to find a cultural event to take his own brother to, he'd scoured the critic's picks on TimeOut.com and found the band's Webster Hall concert listed prominently. He listened to a few songs online and was impressed enough to buy tickets. Thankfully, they weren't too expensive. Then, three clicks later, they were. Service fees. Delivery fees. Convenience fees. Convenient for whom? Certainly not Theo. Alas, taking Carl anywhere touristy was out of the question, as were decent restaurants. He looked again at his computer screen. What the hell was wrong with him? Could there be a smaller decision to be made anywhere in the world? And yet. His eyes settled upon the name of the venue. Could this be the same Webster Hall that had featured so prominently in the arcane histories of his hometown—the venue Margaret Sanger, that towering figure of American activism, had filled with the starving children of Lawrence's striking millworkers back in 1912? He turned to Google, and soon an entire lunch hour had passed. But he'd been right! This Webster Hall was that Webster Hall. They'd arrived by train, 119 malnourished sons and daughters of Lawrence, only to be marched downtown and paraded in front of the New York City press. Yet the stunt was a success. The public sided with the workers. Theo took it as a sign and bought the tickets, fees be damned.

He glanced at his watch. Seven forty-two p.m. He wasn't sure what time the headliners went on, but they should probably make their way over. Carl's focus had shifted from the beer taps to a basketball game on a TV above the bar, a no-doubt-thrilling replay featuring Western Illinois and South Dakota. Theo wanted desperately to cut through the bullshit and find out how his brother was really doing. He'd tried to get together with him each of the last two nights, but both times Carl had claimed exhaustion, done in, apparently, by all those long, vigorous hours spent manning the XXX-Treme Power Performance Vitamin Boost booth at the Stronger World Health & Fitness Expo. Whatever. Carl was here now. Maybe they could stay out after the show.

Theo sipped his beer. He supposed he should feel bad for his brother. Thirty-six years old, and the biggest move he'd ever made was from his parents' basement to his mother-in-law's attic. Not even. Someone else's mother-in-law. Before signing on as his girlfriend's unpaid sales assistant, Carl had spent sixteen years working at the same AT&T/Lucent plant as their father, dodging round after round of layoffs, until the plant finally closed, a year ago, and both father and son found themselves unemployed. At that point their union, IBEW Local 2222, should have stepped up and found them both work—Leonard had been an active member for decades, Carl for several years—but that hadn't happened. Theo figured their father was somehow to blame, and sensing an opportunity to get at Carl's issues by way of Leonard's, he asked, as casually as he could, what had gone down.

Carl kept his eyes on the TV. "You don't want to know," he said.

"Humor me."

"There's nothing funny about it."

"It's an expression."

Carl glanced at his phone on the bar, but he had no messages.

"What happened is that Dad's an asshole," he said. "I mean, the plant closed, which sucks, but it wasn't the end of the world. The local would have fed us contract work until something full-time came up. Dad was always loyal. Hell, he helped rig the no-show rolls for years. Plus he's still got his master's license, and there aren't many of those around."

Theo asked if his brother had one.

"Fuck no! I'm still a journeyman because Dad never got me enough hours. He was always teaching other guys all this complex shit while he sent me to fix dimmer switches in the break room. So finally I got myself transferred to assembly. Not that it mattered. We all got canned anyway." Carl gripped his beer with both hands. "Somehow Dad got it in his head that it was the union's fault. That they'd abandoned their members and just accepted defeat. He didn't see the bigger picture—that manufacturing was shrinking, to say nothing of telecom. You know what he's like: what he can't fix, he fights. So he decided to open his own business, said it would just be me and him, and when I told him that sounded good, that 'Gorski and Son' had a nice ring to it, he said, 'No, it doesn't, "Gorski Electric" does.' So that was a great start."

Theo sighed sympathetically.

"Oh, it gets better. Because then he decided to make Gorski Electric an open shop."

"Why?"

"That's exactly what I asked, and he gave me all this shit about the mentality of the modern union man. How everything revolved around what you could get away with *not* doing. 'Forget quality! Forget fraternity!' He had a point, obviously, but still. You should have seen him scraping the Local 2222 sticker off his truck. Can you imagine? He'd had that thing on there since, like, Reagan."

The truck was only eight years old, but the larger sentiment was true.

"So, of course, the Local brass heard about it and Gorski Electric was cut out of all the decent jobs—even when we were the low bid. All we got were Yellow Pages calls. Garage doors and fuse boxes. Pretty soon, Dad became impossible to be around, so I moved in with Carly, and two weeks later I quit. He's still not speaking to me."

"I'm sorry."

Carl took a long sip. "It just wasn't what you'd call a viable situation, but neither was sitting on my ass at Carly's. It must have been December by then, because we were getting all these early-season snowstorms, and I got it in my head to start a plowing company. Why not, right? All you need's a truck. So I found an old Chevy for eight hundred bucks, a real beater but it ran okay, and I bought a plow off Craigslist, and by New Year's I was good to go. Then guess what."

"No more storms."

"No more fucking storms. So now I've got a pickup and a plow sitting at Carly's place and I'm selling her supplement bullshit. Or trying to."

"Does the stuff work?" Theo asked.

Carl slapped his hand on the bar. "Of course it doesn't work! Look at me." Theo kept his eyes on his beer. "Also," Carl added, "I think she's banging an MMA dude. Now tell me what this band's all about."

*　　*　　*

Audrey was scrambling. Everyone was scrambling. From the side of the stage, she watched big Ben Westfield untangle amp cords while Easter Woods set up his pedals. Around them swarmed stagehands, a sound guy, and various members of the opening band, all of them rushing to assemble or tear down, plug in or load out. Things were running forty-three minutes behind, and for once it wasn't the Westfield Brothers' fault. They'd been scheduled to play on Webster Hall's studio stage while a West Coast band-of-the-moment called Fleet Foxes performed upstairs in the grand ballroom. But the Foxes had canceled their show midafternoon—either their bus had broken down or their guitarist was in a Philly jail, depending on who you asked—and the venue had bumped the Brothers up to the newly vacant big stage in hopes of moving a few hundred last-minute tickets at the door. At eight p.m., Silver Doves, the Westfields' supporting act, had strummed their first chords and been greeted by silence—not the audience's but their own. Somehow, amplification had not made the journey from the

studio stage (where the bands had done sound check) to the ballroom—
the two stages having different mikes and boxes and backlines—and
now the scene had turned chaotic as Ben and Arthur, told that the
problem had been only partially resolved, attempted to electrify their
instruments and not themselves. Audrey wished she could help, but
she knew very little about the technical side of music—the wires and
laptops and soundboards, those complex tools of noise. Besides, she
had a million other things to do. She checked her phone. Her texts
were all exclamation points; her voice messages were men shouting
over music. Everything was always an emergency. The trick was to
prioritize. So first: the van. It was about to get towed. She slipped down
the fire stairs to the foyer of the club. Malcolm Z, Webster Hall's
longtime head of security, was blocking a large portion of the entranceway, but he turned sideways to let her pass. "Just in time," he said, and
Audrey thanked him for texting her a heads-up. To Malcom's left stood
a line of pasty goth kids waiting for the decidedly unhip nightclub half
of Webster Hall to open. To his right was Audrey's crowd, the Westfield
fans, getting wristbands or casually smoking behind the ropes. She
probably knew half of them and would have ventured over to say hel-
los were the front axle of the Westfields' decrepit camper van not at
that moment being lifted off the street by the grinding winch of an
NYPD tow truck. She stepped around to the driver's side and hopped
up onto the running board. The operator lowered his window and
Audrey started talking. The negotiation took thirty seconds; the man
asked for a kiss and Audrey offered him a hug and two tickets to the
show. He didn't want the tickets, he said, jumping down from the cab
and opening his arms wide. He really made it last, too, the bastard, but
a minute later the van was earthbound. She watched the front tires hit
the pavement, dodged a second embrace, and hurried back inside to
check on their merch vendor, the indefatigable Mariah (no one knew
her last name). Mariah had been given the job because she was sleeping
with Arthur Westfield; as such, the position could be seen as a reward
or exile, depending on one's point of view. Mariah had gone with reward,
until two nights ago, at Maxwell's in Hoboken, when she'd been

informed by friends that while she was selling T-shirts at a merch table in the bar other girls, fresher to the fold, were rolling cigarettes and adjusting tube tops in the back of the Westfields' van. She'd learned this just as the show was letting out, and she immediately left her station to confront them. Only the quick thinking of the bouncer out front saved the band from a scene. What the Westfield Brothers were not saved from, however, was $1,375 of suddenly unattended-to merchandise exiting with their fans. Audrey blamed herself. She should have seen it coming. Mariah was the same girl who had volunteered to work the door at a warehouse show a few months back, only to lose the list of advance ticket buyers. Her solution was to split the line of 150 impatiently waiting concertgoers in two, telling those who'd already paid to move to the left and those who hadn't yet to move to the right. Only five people moved to the right, and the band lost $850. Yet here she was, still on the ride. At least the girl had moxie, Audrey thought, climbing the staircase into the back of the ballroom. The house lights were still up and the crowd was growing restless. Approaching the table, Audrey braced herself for disaster but found instead an orderly intermission crowd surveying the various wares. She watched, relieved, as Mariah handed a T-shirt across the table and took a twenty in return, and continued watching as—*fuck*—Mariah pocketed the bill instead of placing it in the cash box. Audrey sighed. Outright theft was too much. After the show she'd pull Mariah aside and make her empty her pockets. If more than two or three twenties appeared she'd fire her on the spot. Audrey turned to assess the room. The stage was still littered with musicians. She weaved her way expertly through the buzzing crowd and then glided past Michael, the guard, and through the backstage door. She thanked him without breaking stride and, turning back around, ran smack into the thick torso of Ben Westfield. "*Ow!*" she cried. "Shit," Ben said, and then saw who it was. He apologized, mumbled something about the monitors, and disappeared around a corner. Audrey rubbed her forehead. People were moving past her, rushing past her, with tuners and amps and guitars. Trying to get out of the way, she ducked down the short hallway and into the Westfield

Brothers' dressing room. Arthur had left the stage and was now sitting cross-legged on a small rug toward the back of the crowded enclave. A half-finished set list lay on the floor in front of him. "What's the drummer situation?" Audrey asked. "I don't know," Arthur said. "I think Jackson's on strike." "But you have to go on in like five minutes." "Yeah, I was hoping you might talk to him." The Drummer Situation may as well have been the name of the band, because there always was one. They'd gone through four in as many years, and Jackson Starke, their latest, was on the outs. It had been a bad match from the start, the brothers being as freewheeling as Jackson, a Julliard-trained jazz enthusiast, was exacting. No one could figure out why he'd been so keen on joining the band in the first place, but he had been, and since he was technically gifted, and Ben and Arthur had been in a pinch (Rex, their regular drummer, had broken his foot when a keg fell on it, and he still couldn't hit the kick pedal with any authority), they'd brought Jackson on board. Big mistake. Dude couldn't hang. And in Westfield world, anything could be overlooked but that. As with Mariah, things had come to a head in Hoboken, when, in the heated apogee of "Knife Fight in C," Arthur jumped onto the drum set, a signature move requiring a modicum of finesse that wasn't always present so late in the show, as it was not at Maxwell's, the result being the collapse of the floor tom, hi-hat, and ride cymbal, which, fine, was about half the kit, but—and here lay the crux of the conflict—it was still playable! Three drums and one cymbal remained standing, and the rest of the band, sans Arthur, who was sprawled out with two drums on top of him, was still carrying on with abandon, except for Jackson, who had not only stopped playing but had jumped out of his seat to corral the breakaway components of the set, leaving the band rhythmically naked. The postshow frost had grown thicker in the two days since, to the point where Jackson, upon arriving at Webster Hall, had refused to use the same dressing room as his bandmates, opting for the only marginally less combative climes next door. (Silver Doves were, after all, invitees of the Westfields and came down firmly on the side of their patrons.) Regardless, Jackson was needed tonight, and it fell to Audrey, as always, to talk him down from the ledge, or up from the depths, or anyway convince him to play. If she hurried she might miss running into Everett Mack, Silver Doves' lead singer, who was still breaking things down onstage, and whose years-long infatuation with Audrey refused to subside. She'd slept with him once—as in one time—and because she'd refused to again, he now acted like some cornered animal whenever she was around, stewing, pacing, occasionally lashing out. Well, too bad. The Westfields needed their drummer, so she hurried next door. Jackson Starke was frowning at his phone in a back corner. Without a word, she grabbed him by the arm and led him physically from the room. He didn't resist; he must have known someone would come get him. Still, he hadn't been expecting the lecture Audrey now delivered as she pulled him down the hall, the unminced themes of which were commitment and loyalty and "fucking stepping up." What was wrong with her? Why was she suddenly so annoyed, so angry, so anti-man? Because she was tired—of their antics, their immaturity, their refusal to face up to what needed facing up to. Which meant that she was tired of herself. "Just get out there and play," she said, and all but shoved Jackson onto the stage. He approached the drum set and, resignedly, began tightening and tuning. It was now fifty minutes past showtime. She should check on Mariah again. She should—"Heads up!" someone cried, and Audrey ducked. "Hah! Got you!" Ben Westfield said with a laugh, and she felt his big paws envelop her. She all but fell into them. The stage was emptying and the lights went down. Easter gave her a high five as he walked past them down the hall. Next came Everett (no high five), and finally Jackson (also no high five). "How'd you get him out of his funk?" Ben asked, watching the drummer retreat. "I'm persuasive," Audrey said, and Ben grinned. The crowd started clapping. "Think I'll head for the cheap seats," she continued. "The farther away, the better," Ben said. He hugged her again and loped off toward the dressing room. Audrey knew what would happen next. Ben would bring the band together, tune them into the task at hand. She pushed through the stage door and slinked to the back of the room. She liked being anonymous, watching with the crowd. A minute later the Westfield

Brothers ambled out onstage. They looked united. They looked like a band. Appearances, Audrey thought. Arthur strummed a heavy G chord and the rest of her boys joined in. She closed her eyes.

*   *   *

Timing. Some people just didn't have it. Theo Gorski didn't have it. All his calculations and they'd still arrived an hour and a half early. Carl had stuck it out through the not-bad opening act, followed by an interminable intermission (was every show so disorganized?), but when Carly's texts had turned all caps, his brother's brio had vanished. Slump-shouldered, he mumbled something about getting a beer tomorrow and then slipped away. Too bad, because the Westfield Brothers were alive in a way Theo hadn't known music could be, harmonizing, switching instruments, caterwauling around the stage. He tried to enjoy himself, to experience the music as those around him were—simply, exuberantly—but the notion of brothers lay thick in the concert haze.

What Theo felt was not pity, or sadness, or self-serving relief. No, he felt—and how was this possible?—envy. That Carl had someone in his life, however irrational or emotionally abusive she might be—that he had, in fact, a sort of family—served to highlight Theo's abiding loneliness. What was he doing wrong? He was thirty-two years old. Even in a city where age was amorphous, he could no longer be considered young. Certainly, he didn't *feel* young. He needed to get out there, to engage, but shyness paralyzed him, and his job only made it worse. For books, and the solitary hours they required, were the delivery mechanism of his introversion.

A blast of horns and a plaintive wail from the lead Westfield brought him back to the moment. The singer was standing wobbly-legged on the drum set, while the accordion player, who was not a small man, had dropped to his knees, as if felled by the song itself. And the horns were clarions, and the drums a call to action, and here came an electric fiddle, screeching from the shoulder of the keyboardist, his bow string fraying from the friction, the whole symphonic creation awesome to hear and contemplate. Theo stood there openmouthed, like he'd just seen a car crash or witnessed resplendence.

And then it was over, all at once, and seconds of silence gave way to minutes of raucous applause. An encore was inevitable, Theo knew that much, and he watched as the crowd pressed toward the stage. Most were couples, or groups of look-alike friends, but slightly in front and to the right of him he noticed a tall woman with broad shoulders and light brown, almost golden, hair. She appeared to be alone, and was, at that moment, looking down at her phone (its illuminated screen was what had caught his eye). He immediately looked away, or tried to, but as he followed the tunnel of cellular light back into his own business, he glimpsed a line of scripted ink on the underside of her right forearm. He couldn't help himself; he scanned it, once, and then again, the phrase ringing a distant bell of remembrance, the opening line of a college-read poem, perhaps, or dialogue from a classic film. *Poetry is a Northern man's dream of the South.* He glanced up at its owner, but just then her phone went dark and she was pitched into blackness.

That should have been the end of it. Not even. Nothing had happened. He'd glimpsed a tattoo at an indie concert in downtown Manhattan. Stop the presses. Except Theo was experiencing the strangest of highs, a fluttering mania that spread through his chest like adrenaline. Maybe it *was* adrenaline. And then he remembered it, the origin of the phrase, and through some combination of oxygen deprivation and know-it-all pride he must have accidentally said it out loud, because the woman turned toward him. He could see the outline of her face, if not its features.

"Sorry," he said, attempting to speak while simultaneously experiencing heart failure. "That tattoo on your forearm. It's from Fitzgerald. It caught my eye."

She peered down at it and then back up. Was she frowning or smiling?

"I wish," she said. "They're lyrics by a songwriter friend of mine. Maybe you've heard the song."

Her voice was raspy and knowing, and Theo was about to agree, just on principle, but he was suddenly quite sure of himself. He'd come across the phrase a few years back, during a winter of panic following his promotion to assistant editor. Having decided he was woefully unversed in the lesser works of certain American greats, he'd taken it upon himself to play catch-up, and for months on end had become a shut-in, reading away his weekends, despite attempts by roommates, friends, and even one or two temporarily interested women to rouse him to action, to get him some air. And what had come of all those pages? Nothing—lesser works being lesser works, and classics being immaterial to modern life—until now.

They were facing each other, but it was still dark, and loud, and Theo was doing that thing where he looked at a person but didn't see them, not out of rudeness, but the opposite—deference, embarrassment, tact. He'd already invaded her privacy once. Still, he couldn't help himself.

"I'm pretty sure it's from a short story called 'The Last of the Belles,'" he said, trying to sound casual. "Maybe your friend got it from there. I mean, it's a great line."

"What's the story about?"

An obvious question, but Theo stumbled, for as she asked it the house lights flickered, confirming both the imminent reappearance of the Westfield Brothers and the heretofore-only-guessed-at beauty of the woman before him. It was a generous, big-mouthed beauty, stunning in its way, and if Theo had been aware of it before then he'd have never spoken to her. As it was, he was having plenty of trouble.

"It's about a pretty Southern girl who turns down all the local suitors in her town and falls instead for a strange, uncouth Northerner." He realized, as he was saying the words, their theoretical real-world applicability, and was relieved to have detected no trace of a Southern accent in the woman's sultry voice. "But she ends up rejecting him, too, and lives out her days haunted by chances never taken. At least that's how I think it ends."

He felt the weight of her stare, and a corresponding weightlessness inside himself. "I'm so stupid," she said. "How could I not have known that? It's literally burned into my skin!"

"The story's really obscure," Theo said.

"It can't be that obscure if we're talking about it."

He watched a frown cross her face. Had he managed to transfer his own perpetual state of confusion to someone else? If so, he should take it back; it suited him far better. It was his turn to say something but he couldn't think of what it should be, so he said, "I'm Theo," but the delivery of the words coincided precisely with a loud roar announcing the band's return. She hadn't heard him, thank God. She'd already turned back to the stage, where the Westfields were launching into a song that everyone but Theo appeared to know. He exhaled. So that was that. A single minute in a lifetime of minutes. Which was to say, this would pass. Was already passing. Soon, her boyfriend would return from the bathroom, or she'd slip up closer to the stage or maybe downstairs to the coat check line. Just enjoy the rest of the show, Theo told himself, and afterward, get back to your normally scheduled life. It's not so bad.

And it's not so great.

And she's still here.

If anything, she'd moved closer to him. He was almost sure of it, though he dared not glance her way again. Another wave of anxiety passed through him, this one far deeper than the last. He thought he might throw up. All those beers on an empty stomach. Except he'd eaten pizza before meeting Carl, which meant this was a different malady entirely. Medically untraceable. The band was still playing, louder now than ever, but he heard them only as an afterthought, like distant traffic. Was this a panic attack? He'd never had one, or even quite believed in them. Well, he should be more open-minded. Out of the corner of his eye, he saw her rub her forehead. Maybe she was feeling queasy, too. In any event, it was a good time to leave. Cut his losses. He started backing away, almost tiptoeing, which was ridiculous, he knew, but—

"Where are you going?"

The room was spinning. "Want to beat the crowd," Theo said.

"You don't like the band?"

"No! I love them. Or it. Really well."

He thought she might be biting her lip, stifling a laugh. And then it seemed like the room had gone silent, which wasn't a good sign, until he realized it actually had. The lead singer had grabbed an acoustic guitar and was fingerpicking the beginnings of a ballad under a spotlight. The rest of the band fell away.

He felt a hand grip his right forearm, lightly and for only a moment, and as he looked down at where it had just been, she said, low voiced, almost whispering, "Theo, you should stay."

PART TWO

WHALE CREEK RECORDS

99 Commercial Street
Brooklyn, NY 11222

November 1, 2011

Dear Theo,

This is probably a huge mistake, writing a letter instead of talking to you face-to-face. But I just can't bear to watch your reaction. It would break my heart. I love you so much, Theodore. Every trait and complexity and contradiction. Throw them all together and they add up to something even greater. A kind of ethic, I guess you could call it. You're the only man I've ever known who actually thinks about how he should live in the world. It's why I'm with you. And why I can't imagine being with anyone else. Still, for a girl used to getting by on wits alone, your intrinsic goodness can be daunting to live alongside. And live up to. That's one of the reasons I never told you about any of this. I always thought you'd leave me. I still do.

I'm ashamed, not of the specific events from my past, but of the long lie that has followed. A lie I'm only revealing now because I have no choice. You've asked several times if this Fender thing is the reason I've been acting so distant this past week. Well, the answer is Yes. Not only that, I think the break-in and the list of names we found on the desk are tied to Fender too. And that's what's finally forced my hand. I'm scared, Theo, not just for our relationship, but for our physical well-being. Because I think we're in real danger.

What am I talking about? Let me start from the beginning and have the chips fall where they may. I know, I know: cliché. But shit, writing to someone who swears by the written word is intimidating. We swore by a word once. Do you remember? It was Trust. And we always had it, from the moment we met. I keep thinking of those nights, early on, when we'd stumble out of Rosemary's and down the hill to the old refinery piers off Kent. We'd sneak onto those rotting docks and sit there for hours, telling each other the stories of our lives. We were trying so hard to be grown-ups, all serious and self-aware, and soon we were attaching clinical diagnoses to our various tics and behaviors. My mother left me, so I must have abandonment issues. Your father was abusive, thus your aversion to conflict. Whatever it was, we always ended up laughing about it, because we knew we had no idea what we were talking about. But we also understood, even in those early months, that we now had each other, and that made our pasts seem suddenly manageable. I remember I used to sit on those same piers by myself back when I first moved to the city, and when I'd look across at Manhattan at night I'd feel like an imposter. Like I was in a Fifth Avenue dressing room, trying on clothes I could never afford. But being with you, I could sense that person disappearing, at least the scared and neurotic parts of her. We both could. I stopped defining myself through the eyes of men. You opened yourself up to new experiences. And just like that, we became devoted to each other. What was our trick? Total transparency. We promised to share everything, from our hopes to our histories. You kept up your side of the bargain. I thought I could too. I tried so fucking hard. But I never quite got there.

For two days now, I've been sitting here, alone in my office, trying and failing to start this letter. This confession, I guess you could call it. Two days of tears and torment, followed by sleepless nights beside you in bed, as you ask again and again what's wrong. Well, I am what's wrong.

This is what's wrong.

It started six years ago, in the summer of 2005, when I was living on North Ninth with Sarah and that weird girl Iris who I've told you about. I'd just started at Whale Creek but was still working at Enid's, and trying to act, and doing ten other part-time things to cover rent and pay the interest on my stupid student loans. I mention this not as an excuse for my decisions but to provide some context. I was flat-out broke.

KINGS COUNTY

One night Iris slipped me a business card during a concert at Union Pool. It was an invitation to a party the following week at the Gramercy Park Hotel. "A Sybaritic Gathering," I remember it said. I didn't know what "sybaritic" meant, and it wasn't until I read Iris's scribbled note on the back, saying they'd pay me $1,000 just to show up and look pretty, that I understood what it might be. I put the card in my pocket.

Iris and I spoke in the apartment the following day. The parties were roving affairs, she explained, organized by two club promoters named Eric and Gordon. Discreet girls, discreet men, discreet locations. The clients were mostly older and from out of town. The scene was always fun and low-key, she assured me, ten or fifteen people max, depending on the week. Sometimes, smaller groups split off for drinks in the lobby bar or dinner at a restaurant. Occasionally, a poker game broke out. But that was rare. It was mostly about the girls.

And that was the extent of it? I asked Iris. A thousand dollars for a few hours of champagne and small talk? It was if I wanted it to be, she answered. And a thousand was just for starters. Regulars made even more. Fifteen hundred, even two grand.

If it had sounded slightly preposterous before, it now sounded preposterous in an entirely different way. A can't-say-no way. Of course, I wanted to ask Iris if she ever took things further, because she'd kind of just implied as much, but I didn't know her like that. Anyway, why not see for myself? Were these parties any different from the shit Sarah and I used to pull at Balthazar? All those flirtatious free meals with rich Europeans. But cash up front wasn't quite the same as someone picking up a dinner tab. Cash implied something. Or maybe it didn't. I didn't really care. Morality didn't much interest me. Adventure did. People did. Money did. That's the headspace I was in.

Theo, I feel so incredibly self-conscious. So twisted up inside. I want to be completely honest, but I don't want to hurt you more than I already have. Or am. So let me just say this. I went to some parties. Six or seven, I think. They weren't particularly memorable. The men were exactly as advertised. Older. Married. Sad. Some were comfortable with the trans-actional nature of the proceedings. Others were awkward and seemed embarrassed to be there. I almost felt bad for them.

The girls intrigued me far more. They were pretty, but they were also smart. At least half were students and approached the situation with wry detachment. At the same time, they took their roles seriously. The hotels changed, but the routine remained the same. Each of us met with Eric beforehand, to get paid and okayed. Outfits. Appearance. Soberness. No drugs were allowed, though it wasn't that type of scene anyway. The men were drinkers, cigar smokers. Most weren't after anything more than cleavage and conversation. But there were exceptions, men who zeroed in on a certain girl, and when that happened, and both parties were willing, Eric stepped in and made arrangements. Maybe a dinner date. Maybe more. I heard numbers. $3,000 for a night. $8,000 for a weekend getaway. But always, it was made clear, we were being paid only to be there. Anything more was our own decision.

I fell in deeper. I went to group dinners at Gotham, the Strip House, and yes, Balthazar. We sat in back corners or private rooms. I was hit on but never openly propositioned. Other girls were better read, better looking, better dressed. More willing. But Eric kept inviting me out, to the point where Iris got annoyed and stopped talking to me. She was on the outs by then anyway. Apparently, she'd been taking notes for some kind of memoir. She'd told a few of the girls about it, and one of them had gone to Eric.

One night, he asked if I knew anything about it, since I lived with her. I said I didn't, which was mostly true. I'd never even been in Iris's room. Eric and I were having a late drink at the Rose Bar after a party upstairs had wound down, and things were getting a bit flirtatious. He was obviously a player, but he was also witty and self-assured. Again, I'll spare you the details, but at some point we went back upstairs, and whatever happened happened, and I fell asleep. When I woke up hours later it was light outside. Eric was gone, but there was an envelope on the bureau with my name on it. Inside were fifteen hundred-dollar bills and a two-word note: "Cab money."

So this was the other side. I had now been paid for sex. Did it matter that it was a misunderstanding? That I'd thought we were just hooking up? I considered returning the cash but decided I was being ridiculous. My entire life was a series of compromising acts performed for money. Was sex so different from waitressing? It didn't feel like it. In fact, it felt pretty honest. A black-and-white exchange in a world devoid of such clarity. Still, I didn't tell Sarah, or even Iris. There was power in my secret, and allure. When Eric texted me about the next party, I told him I'd be there.

I was treated differently now. Eric walked me around, introduced me to specific people. Occasionally, he'd ask if I was interested in someone, and my answer was usually no. Usually, but not always. Twice I slept with a party attendee, and I was paid each time. They were both in their late forties and nervous. The sex was unremarkable and I never spent the night.

It didn't bother me like it should have. And in less than two months I'd made eight or nine thousand dollars. Sometimes I wished I had someone to confide in. Iris was the obvious choice, but she was still ignoring me. I think she thought I was the one who'd snitched on her.

The rules loosened, the nights splintered, and as men came and went, it became difficult to know the actual clients from the hangers-on. One night, after a dinner at Bond Street, I found myself among a small group in a dark corner of Temple Bar. The dinner had been thrown for an out-of-town real estate investor and included several of his friends, mostly dreary men in dark suits. So when Eric asked if I might want to "spend time" with someone, my hopes weren't exactly high. Then he nodded toward a trim, middle-aged man standing at the bar. I'd met him fifteen minutes earlier but couldn't remember what we'd talked about. Which variation of nothing. I told Eric I was a bit too drunk and wanted to call it a night. Then he whispered a dollar amount in my ear, and I changed my mind. Eric went to finalize the transaction and returned with instructions. I listened carefully. They weren't the normal kind.

The client wanted to role-play, have me dress as a nurse or maid or stripper. Eric asked if I was cool with that, and I said sure, why not. It sounded more interesting than straight sex, and anyway, I was purportedly an actress. We couldn't be seen leaving together, so I was told to wait fifteen minutes and then take a cab to the Crosby Street Hotel. Eric gave me a cell number.

When I texted the client, I asked if he had a specific scenario in mind. No, he said. I could choose. I thought about it. I was wearing a loose, see-through blouse over a black bra and a knee-length pencil skirt with a zipper up the back. *How about waitress?* I texted, and he said fine. He gave me his room number.

I don't know how to write what happened next. I've tried so hard not to revisit that night. To pretend I'm not still affected when I so obviously am. I suppose I deserve this reckoning. This comeuppance. To finally write it all down, not as some private therapeutic exercise, like I once thought I might, but instead, in a desperate letter to you. I feel so pathetic, so small. Like the weight of all this might finally be too much to bear. But what choice do I have? I should have faced this a long time ago.

Here's a not-funny joke. What does a hooker feel like when she's walking through a hotel? A hooker. It felt like everyone was watching me, like everyone knew. The front desk staff. The camera in the elevator. The hidden eyes behind peepholes. His suite was on the top floor. I knocked. He opened the door and I don't know why but I shook his hand. Then I laughed at the awkwardness of the moment, but he just retreated into the room and arranged himself on a couch. It was dark. Beyond the couch was a dining table, and beside it, a room service tray on wheels. He'd just ordered food, he told me, to make the scene more realistic.

We talked for a minute, though I don't remember what was said. He was one of those men who looked older than he was. His hair was peppered with gray and he had an unsightly mole on his forehead. He took off his suit jacket and loosened his tie. I told him I'd go to the bathroom, and when I came out we could start. He nodded.

Lipstick. Hair up. Shirt in a knot. When I emerged, he was still sitting there, legs crossed, reading a newspaper. He didn't look up. I'd been ready for almost anything except complete disregard, and right away it put me on edge.

I wasn't sure what to do, so I asked him to follow me to the table, and to my surprise he stood and came across the room. I pulled out a chair, and he sat down. Then I hurried over to the stereo and turned it on. Something dramatic started playing. Beethoven, I think, but I don't know classical music.

It probably says something about my acting talents that I forewent a gum-chewing diner waitress or sultry nightclub server in favor of a more sexualized version of my real-life self. I even pretended we were at Enid's and recited their menu while I set his place. I served him water, then a beer, then the sandwich he'd ordered from room service. And that's when things got weird.

He told me to move his fork an inch, so I did. He told me to rearrange his napkin on his lap and I did that too. Then he tore apart some of the sandwich bread and dropped the pieces on the carpet, like he was feeding pigeons. Kneel down and pick them up, he said, so I dropped to my knees and did as I was told. I know this sounds so pathetic on paper, so thoroughly humiliating, but it didn't cross my mind not to follow his orders, not to play along.

I was on all fours when he stood up behind me. You're terrible at what you do, he said. I paused. Was he talking about my temporary fake job, my temporary real job, or my real real job? And then it didn't matter. I felt his hand on the back of my head, removing my hairpins. Then he grabbed the whole tangled mess and pulled it back toward him. I closed my eyes. It didn't feel right.

I remember he poured water on the table and made me soak it up with my shirt. I remember he pushed me down and demanded I crawl, back arched and ass in the air, over to the stereo to turn the music louder. Again, I did as I was told, if only to escape his increasingly erratic orbit.

Something was off with him. With the whole situation. But I was more angry than fearful. Angry at myself for agreeing to the scenario, and at the client for being such an ill-humored asshole. Still, I told myself to see it through. I could deal with humiliation if that was his thing. I was foolishly proud. And then, of course, there was the money, which I suddenly realized then I'd forgotten to ask for up front.

I crawled back toward him. My shirt clung to my bra. My hair was a nightmare. I was about to stand up, to get off my aching knees, when he spilled more water on the table. It pooled in the narrow crevices of wood and began trickling toward the edge. Don't let any hit the floor, he said, and before I could protest he dragged me by my arm until I was positioned under the table side. He ordered me to tilt my head back and open my mouth, so I did. Drip, drip, drip, onto my tongue, and then he pulled me up by my hair and demanded I lick some off the table itself. I hesitated. I'd been prepared to have sex with him, but this felt far more invasive.

Now! he shouted, without warning. His anger snapped me back to reality. I told him I wanted to stop and started to push myself up, but he grabbed the back of my neck and forced me down again, hard. My head hit the table. My nose. My cheekbone. He kept me there. I remember the pooled water moistening my hair. I stopped struggling and tried to catch my breath.

Then he said, Lick it, bitch.

I pursed my lips, not about to lick anything. So he slapped me across my exposed cheek. I let out a yelp, or maybe something louder. He told me to shut up. With his free hand he forced my arms behind my back. I screamed for probably the first time since I was a child. But it didn't matter. He moved his hand from my head to my throat and squeezed me into vocal submission.

Then he kicked my legs apart. And I understood.

I thrashed and writhed and basically flipped the fuck out. Once or twice I shook my head free, but my protests were drowned out by the music, absorbed by the walls. I was fighting, wildly kicking my heels, looking around for anything I could use to fight back with. I tried to close my legs, but he kicked the inside of my right ankle so hard I was sure he'd broken it. Then the hand that had been holding my arms reached for my skirt. For several seconds we entered a kind of wrestlers' stalemate. He couldn't get leverage, and I couldn't move. He was trying to yank the skirt down, but it was too tight. So he switched tactics and simply unzipped it.

You should skip this part, Theo. I probably should too. But I can't. Not now. I'm in that room again. I realize now I never left.

Before that night, I'd never been sexually assaulted, and apart from the physical evidence, what stayed with me in the aftermath was the strange sensation of disconnection I felt during the attack itself. I half expected Eric to walk in, call a stop to things, and then tell me what areas I needed to improve upon. At the same time, I was struggling for what felt like my very life, and it was this battle, between mind and body, control and the lack of it, that was playing itself out when he pushed an elbow into my spine. A flash of pain shot through my torso and I stopped fighting long enough for him to grab my underwear and pull it down to my knees. I tried to turn over but he was too powerful. I tried to scream again, but he choked me silent.

Part of me still refused to believe it would happen, whatever it was, because he wasn't sexually aroused. But that didn't matter. It wasn't about pleasure. It was about rage. There was no prelude. My underwear came down and he pushed his fingers inside me. Two or three, I don't know, but he was rough, and he went as deep as he could. I kept fighting, but he was strong and determined. I felt everything and nothing. And then it was over. The penetration lasted thirty seconds. Maybe half that.

He took his elbow off my spine and backed away. I pulled my underwear up and closed my legs but otherwise didn't move, didn't turn around, didn't care what he was doing as long as his hands were no longer on my body. I was shaking involuntarily, my legs like a doll's legs, pliant and loose at the joints.

Eventually, I stood up. He was across the room by then, smoothing his hair in the mirror. The music was still loud, the room still dark. And then he was moving toward me again. I tensed up, but his demeanor was hurried now. Businesslike. He stopped a few feet away and opened his wallet. He counted out some hundreds and held them toward me. I didn't react, so he dropped the bills on the wet floor. I'm feeling generous, he said, but the words arrived garbled and distant, like a subway announcement. Then he pointed toward the bathroom and told me to fix myself up. I tried to think of something to say but couldn't. Anyway, it was too late. He was walking out the door.

I'm so sorry. I can't imagine what you're feeling, assuming you've even made it this far. How could I have kept all this a secret? Please believe me when I say I'd have told you long ago if the story had ended there. But it didn't, as you've surely guessed by now. So what, then, does a hellish sexual assault in 2005 have to do with some guy named Fender in 2011? The answer, I'm afraid, is everything.

As it happened, Fender was the first person I saw after the attack. (Attack. Assault. Rape. I've never been sure what to call it, which is not to say I don't know what it was. It was rape. I was raped. I understand this but still cringe at the term and the baggage it carries. Victim. Survivor. Member of the club. Or maybe it's simpler than that. Maybe I just don't want to be reminded at all. Of the specific event. Or that time in my life.) It was late the following afternoon, a Sunday in August, and Sarah and Iris were both away for the weekend, thank God, because I would have had trouble explaining why my nose was swollen, my right cheekbone contused, and my right eye turning purple. To say nothing of my throbbing head. I was basically helpless, and also had an overwhelming need for weed, so I called Fender. He was the closest we had to a fixer, and sure enough he arrived and administered a potent cocktail of aspirin, Xanax, bourbon, and pot. When he asked what happened, I launched into a lame saga about a kitchen calamity at Enid's, which he seemed to buy. Or maybe he just didn't care. Fender was a man of effect, not cause. He never needed a backstory. The present was exciting enough.

We were listening to music when Sarah and Chris came barreling in from Sag Harbor with sun hats and sunglasses and canvas beach bags hanging off every shoulder. When they saw me, the bags hit the floor. It wasn't just my face but my body too. My arms and legs were covered in bruises. Sarah came rushing over, and from the look on her face I knew I'd have to tell her the truth. And why not? Respecting Iris's privacy was the only reason to keep quiet, and I wasn't feeling particularly charitable toward her just then. Of course, telling Sarah meant telling Chris and Fender, but that was okay. They were both open-minded, and I knew they wouldn't judge me.

I never did this kind of thing, asked friends to gather around, and when I opened my mouth the room went silent. And stayed silent. It didn't take a genius to see where this was heading, but no one jumped to conclusions. Instead, my friends listened. At some point Sarah put her arms around me. She wiped away my tears, and then her own, as Chris sat shaking his head in disbelief. At the world I'd fallen into. And the pain it had meted out. Only Fender seemed to take my words in stride, shock not being a part of his general makeup.

As soon I finished, Sarah said we should go to the police. The same thought had crossed my mind earlier, but I'd dismissed it. It felt traitorous. Where I grew up, you didn't involve cops unless you had no choice. Besides, there could be real ramifications. Other girls would get in trouble, to say nothing of Eric and Gordon. Though why I still felt loyalty to their enterprise I have no clue.

I understand now, of course, that something else was going on. Already, part of me was feeling conflicted. Like I could have done something to change the outcome in that hotel room. Like I was somehow responsible. Maybe that sounds trite, but it's true. I'd always known that self-blame was a commonplace reaction to trauma, but I never understood why until I became a victim. I'd been independent for such a long time. I thought I was strong and smart, and that these qualities would protect me. To find out I was wrong, that everything could be stolen so brutally, so quickly, emptied me out, then slowly filled me with shame. All the freedom I'd worked for. The agency. That's the word they use these days. It wasn't the sensation of losing control so much as the realization that I'd never had control in the first place. Over my body. Over my life. It became hard to think clearly, difficult to project confidence. The questioning at the edges. The idea that anything could happen at any time. I didn't stop living, but I developed a different sense of being in the world. It became a darker place.

There was a period of silence after I shot down Sarah's suggestion. A kind of last-chance moment, in retrospect, because what happened next changed everything. Fender clapped his hands and told us he had an idea. We all turned his way.

Let's blackmail the bastard, he said.

That's how it started. Not that we took him seriously at first. We were tired and tense and stoned. We were also, all of us, steely veterans of late-night living room nonsense. But we ran with the idea, for the sake of distraction. Chris grabbed Sarah's laptop and attached the DSL cable. I had my attacker's cell number, and he entered it into one of those reverse phone websites. It came back registered to a New York investment firm called Longstream Capital. Chris was only vaguely familiar with Longstream, so he found their website and started clicking through management bios. Page after page of clean-shaven men with gray suits and tight smiles. Investment banking. Commercial lending. Asset management. Real estate. I saw a face and told him to stop scrolling.

Martin J. Cafferty. Managing Director, Debt & Equity Underwriting.

It was him.

Chris asked if I was sure. I said I was positive and pointed out the mole I'd mentioned. Everyone looked. Sarah put her arm around me again.

The evening found its rhythm. Fender ducked out for a while and returned with a case of beer and a fistful of Adderall. Soon we were whirring right along with the laptop, and as hours passed, his flippant idea gained momentum, and finally, a strange sense of inevitability. Fender threw out blackmailing suggestions, gleaned, no doubt, from a life of low-level con artistry, and Chris began streamlining them, providing a loose method to our friend's madness. And it was madness. All of it. But it was heart-warming too. That they were doing this for me.

Turns out planning a crime is like planning anything else. You begin with the extravagant and end up with what's possible. According to his bio, Cafferty lived on the Upper West Side, with his wife, Vanessa, and their two soccer-loving sons. But further googling turned up nothing. Remember, this was that weird time before Facebook and Twitter and LinkedIn, when the Internet was still organizing itself, and if you weren't young or famous there was a good chance you barely existed in the virtual realm. So Chris focused on the kids. He googled "Cafferty" and "Manhattan youth soccer," and lo and behold got a hit. "West Side Under 12s." He clicked on the link and up came the league website. The name Cafferty appeared highlighted in yellow on one of the team rosters. The Cosmos, I think. The kid's first name was Conor. Chris clicked on the Schedule tab. The team's next game was the following Saturday, in the North Meadow of Central Park.

That's our chance, Fender said, and rubbed his hands together.

And that's how we left it. Completely open-ended. We could wake up the next day, realize we'd been delirious, and call it all off. But I had a feeling we wouldn't. The collective will was already there, and late that night, as I lay in bed after our cabal had finally dispersed, I wondered why. Chris was attracted to the adventure of the whole thing, though I think he also saw it as a way to prove himself to Sarah in some perverse way. Or maybe it wasn't perverse at all. Maybe he did have something to prove. Because he came from Cafferty's world. He'd even played youth soccer on those same fields, he later told us. But I don't mean to psychoanalyze him. He was the same guy then that he is now. Exasperatingly superficial and surprisingly genuine. I think he was deeply upset by what had happened to me, and if he wasn't quite ready to roam the city playing private eye, he was more than willing to contribute behind the scenes. What you might call quarterbacking the thing.

And if Chris was in, Sarah was too, though more cautiously. She wasn't thrilled about the idea, but she wasn't about to bring a stop to things either. For one, she was furious at Iris, to the point of unleashing a verbal tirade in the direction of her still-empty room. But mostly, Sarah was horrified by the assault itself and, if nothing else, saw our plot as a much-needed distraction for me. A reprieve from the pain, both physical and otherwise.

As for Fender, his motives probably weren't so pure, but who knows. Occasionally in life, you look back and can't believe you were so taken by someone. But Fender had always been a projection of our desire to be surrounded by excitement, to live life beyond proper bounds. Because back then, Theo, that man shone. I know one thing for sure. None of this would have happened without him. He lived for the outlandish, and our developing plot fit the bill. So what if he saw dollar signs. It was his idea. Also, he'd be taking most of the risk.

The week leading up to the soccer game passed fitfully. On Tuesday, I worked my regular shift at Enid's, and aside from a stray glance or two at my discolored eye it went okay. On Wednesday, I read about a hurricane called Katrina threatening the east coast of Florida. I phoned Connie and made sure she was prepared, because the last thing she needed was the Banana River lapping up into her living room. On Thursday, Iris came home. I'd called her cell phone a few hours after the assault but hadn't left a message, and when we finally crossed paths, she pretended

I hadn't called at all. My eye was better by then, and unless she'd seen me naked it would have been difficult to tell I'd been attacked. Still, I think she sensed something was up. We spoke a few more times after that, but always just small talk, and she moved out a month later. As far as I know, she never learned what we did.

On Friday night, the four of us met in a back booth at the Abbey to finalize our plan for the next day. The bar was crowded and loud, and we huddled together conspiratorially, as a TV in the corner played interviews with relieved Florida residents. Katrina, it seemed, had fizzled over land and become a harmless tropical storm heading west.

Chris bought a pitcher of beer and we got down to business. Fender and I would go to Central Park together the following morning, the thinking being that if I could ID Cafferty, Fender could then hand-deliver the blackmail note. It was the only way to do it. Email and regular mail were too risky, too traceable.

What exactly did we want? Money, obviously, but how much? Chris explained the concept of pain thresholds, the amount Cafferty could comfortably part with before turning to some alternative course of action. Sarah's eyes went wide at that, but she didn't say anything.

We each wrote a number on a napkin. I showed mine first. $5,000. Everyone frowned. A dinner at Per Se would set Cafferty back more than that, Chris said. I shrugged. I'd never heard of the place, but I got the point.

Fender went next, turning over his napkin to reveal a smudged $49,000. I said that was absurd, no one would pay that much. Chris agreed. Plus, 49K seemed a bit arbitrary. Fender responded that at 50K it became second-degree larceny instead of third, and there was a huge difference sentencing-wise.

That silenced the table for about six different reasons. Finally, Chris turned to Sarah, but she said she wasn't playing. Her tone matched her words, but it didn't much matter. By now, it was obvious we'd go with whatever Chris had written down, and when he unfolded his napkin to reveal $25,000 everyone quickly agreed to it.

The size of the pie decided, we moved on to the size of the slices. Chris said the three of us should split the money because a) he didn't need it, and b) he wouldn't be the one running around the city assuming the risk. Then Sarah said she couldn't in good conscience take money either. Chris and I tried to change her mind. She was as broke as I was and still a few years away from the full protections of the Van Vleck financial umbrella, but she stood firm. Almost admirably so.

Fender, on the other hand, had become increasingly animated as the payout pool dwindled from four to three to two. I could see him doing math in his head. Chris could as well. To forestall any awkwardness, he took control and suggested 20K for me and 5K for Fender. Again, no one argued.

Next came the note, which we composed on the back of three Brooklyn Brewery promo cards.

> martin j. cafferty. bring a red zip-up duffel bag filled with $25,000 in twenty-dollar bills to your son conor's 10 a.m. soccer game next saturday morning, september 3. when the game ends, leave the bag under the cosmos team bench and walk with conor directly home. do not turn around or otherwise look behind you as you exit the north meadow.
>
> if you do not follow these instructions precisely, your wife (vanessa), the police, and your colleagues and clients at longstream capital will be told in graphic detail about the violent sexual assault you perpetrated on an unsuspecting woman at the crosby street hotel on saturday, august 20. we have evidence including photographs of your victim's injuries and time-stamped security video. do not attempt to visit or otherwise contact anyone involved in the escort service you utilized, or, again, the above parties will be notified.
>
> do as this letter states and we will not reveal your crime or contact you again. you have our word. asshole.

We were trying to make it sound like we knew a great deal about him and that a person other than me was doing the blackmailing. Eric or Gordon or someone connected with them. There was, of course, no video proof, and we never discussed how, or if, we'd actually contact anyone if Cafferty didn't pay up.

The following morning at eight a.m., I met Fender on the L platform and we hopped a train to Manhattan. I'd typed the note up by then, and I handed it to Fender in an envelope marked "M. Cafferty." We didn't talk much. I'd disguised myself in sunglasses, a long-sleeved shirt to hide the ink, and a softball cap I wore low. Fender was wearing a floppy fisher-man's hat, a bandana, and a khaki bird-watcher's vest to complement the binoculars hanging from his neck. Who knows where he got the outfit, to say nothing of the binoculars. He cleaned the lenses while we waited to transfer to the uptown 6.

We got off two stops early because we were so nervous, and entered the park farther south than we'd meant to. I'd only been there a handful of times, and I'm not sure Fender had ever left Brooklyn, so we traipsed, a bit lost, up past the Sheep Meadow to the bandshell, where a few dozen roller skaters were grooving along to seventies disco. A man in a T-shirt reading, DON'T THINK, was trying to dance with a full water bottle balanced on his head. It kept falling off, but he didn't care. I overheard a lady next to me say he taught philosophy at Columbia and showed up to skate every Saturday.

Don't Think. But how could I not? My brain was on fire. What we were about to do. And why. Were we righting a grave injustice or being self-indulgent fools? Kids playing cops and robbers? I looked around, as if the park itself might provide answers. All these people, alone together. I was one of them. The music I loved, the people I knew, the places I went: erase it all and the city wouldn't miss a beat. But this life was mine, and if it meant little in the open air of mass context, it meant everything to me. I needed to fight for it.

The water-bottle man stretched his arms wide, but gravity wasn't play-ing along. The bottle fell, but he caught it and placed it back on his head. And just like that, I was gripped, almost overcome, by the strongest wave of determination. To press forward. To see these misadventures, of the blackmail, of moving to New York, through to the end. Six years later, I still think about that roller-skating professor. I kept meaning to go back one Saturday morning to see if he was still there, skating in circles. Then, at some point, I realized I didn't want to know. It was better just to hope he was.

We pushed on, past Bethesda Fountain, the Boathouse, Belvedere Castle. On the far side of the Great Lawn we came upon the Reservoir, its water like a statue of water, dark and still. (Hah, Theo! Not bad, right?) We trekked single-file up the dirt path along the shoreline. Our dialogue dwindled. We were getting close now.

We'd studied a map and knew where we were going. Near the top of the reservoir, we veered up an incline and across the Ninety-Seventh Street Transverse. The North Meadow lay on the far side of a wooded rise, a giant, shapeless expanse dotted by a dozen softball diamonds with conjoined outfields like the ones in McCarren Park. But three chalk-lined soccer fields now overlay the diamonds. According to the league schedule, Conor Cafferty's team would be playing on the one farthest east.

I stopped to pull my cap down, adjust my sunglasses, and tuck away my hair. Fender told me I looked like a B-list actress coming home from her first face-lift, and we both laughed. How could we not? This situation ranked right up there, even for us. He looked at his watch. Eight minutes to game time. The field lay fifty yards ahead of us. We could see the teams warming up, doing passing drills, taking shots on goal.

Fender dug in against the trunk of a sprawling oak tree and started nervously cleaning the binoculars again. I grabbed them out of his hands and trained them on the field below. The lenses were out of focus, too much one way, then too much the other, then there it was, the world back in balance, little players milling around, refs meeting at midfield, a row of spectators on the sideline opposite the team benches. I zoomed in on their faces. Couples grouped together. Several unaccompanied fathers standing at carefully spaced intervals. And farther along, a cluster of older women. Nannies, maybe. Slowly, I backtracked through the fathers, one by one, then lowered the lenses.

Nothing, I said.

Fender shrugged and leaned his head back against the tree. Where had we gone wrong? Perhaps Conor wasn't Martin Cafferty's son after all. Or maybe the family had gone on vacation. It was August, after all.

I handed Fender the binoculars. What now? I wondered. If this lurid diversion had run its course, then it was time to face what I'd gone through head-on. To examine the psychological wounds. Figure out if I was okay. Or could I skip the self-assessment and just respect my family's long tradition of emotional repression?

I was so deep in my own head that I almost didn't hear Fender say my name. I turned to him. He had the binoculars trained on the blue team's bench. Look, he said, and handed them back to me. The game was about to start, and the players had encircled a man wearing khakis and a blue polo shirt, holding a clipboard. I squinted through the glass. The man's back was to me. And then it wasn't. And I saw his face.

It was him. Martin Cafferty was their coach!

We watched awhile longer in disbelief. That he held a position of power over children seemed to justify our actions, as if they needed further justification. But it was also confusing, because he looked so normal, a dad just helping out, and I'd be lying if I didn't admit to second-guessing myself, not about his identity, but about what exactly had occurred in that hotel suite. Maybe I'd missed a signal. Or he'd experienced an episode of some kind, a drug reaction or mental breakdown he didn't even remember. Because the situation was suddenly so hard to reconcile.

But I didn't say anything. Fender had the letter in his hand. The plan was to meet in McCarren Park in an hour. All four of us. I wished him luck and headed for the subway. If he noticed I was shaking, he didn't mention it.

Somehow, Fender almost beat me back. I'd been with Chris and Sarah for all of five minutes when he came loping toward us, birding vest, binoculars, and all.

He flopped down on the grass and stretched out to milk the moment until Chris looked like he was about to kill him. At which point Fender shrugged. It was easy, he said. He'd waited till the game started, then pulled the bandana over his face and approached the bench. When he got close, he said, Hey, Coach! and as Cafferty turned around he handed him the envelope and jogged off, nothing to it. Fender leaned back on his elbows. Chris and Sarah sat there openmouthed. I felt like throwing up.

All we could do now was wait. Cafferty would show up the following Saturday with a bag of cash, or he wouldn't. Fender was positive he'd gone unrecognized, so the only way we, or I, could be traced was through Eric or Gordon, and hopefully we'd headed that off in the letter. Chris spent much of the following week at our place, trying valiantly to exude calm. But one night we caught him reading the New York State criminal statutes on Sarah's laptop, and he admitted to being a complete wreck. Which made four of us.

Then the levees in New Orleans broke. It seemed like eons ago that Katrina had threatened Florida, then petered out. Now here she was, arisen from the grave to wreak havoc and worse. We watched the news in anguish. Tuesday. Wednesday. Thursday. By Friday, the storm had ripped America apart. A collective helplessness hung in the air, and while I'd like to say the four of us gained strength from defying that prevailing mood, by taking decisive action, righting a brutal wrong, I'd be employing artistic license if I did. We were too scared for self-admiration.

On Saturday morning, we saw Fender off, alone this time, and afterward retired to our rendezvous spot in the park. We talked awhile, then I put headphones on and tried to focus on some demo tracks I'd downloaded to my new iPod. Sarah and Chris bickered about something inane and finally got up to take a walk. They returned still looking perturbed. Sarah thought Fender had been gone too long. What if Cafferty had called the cops or somehow set up a sting of his own? I was starting to worry she might be right when Chris whistled at us, and we turned to see Fender loping toward us once again. This time, he was carrying a red bag.

He answered our questions as fast as we asked them. Yes, he was fine. Yes, it all went smoothly. Cafferty had left the bag under the bench, and after he'd walked off with his son, Fender had jogged down to the field and then grabbed it and hurried away. He hadn't opened it yet, but he could feel what was inside.

We rushed home, hoping Iris wouldn't be there. Sarah and I entered first, knocked on her bedroom door, and when there was no answer, signaled to the boys, who strode past us into Sarah's room. We locked the door and crowded onto her bed. Fender unzipped the bag. There they were, bills, stacks of them, bound with violet-colored currency straps. Sarah put her hand over her mouth as Fender dumped the cash onto her blanket. We stared at the pile in disbelief. Then something fell out among the stacks: an envelope, with "READ" typed across the front. I opened it and removed a single sheet of paper. I still remember it, word for word:

THIS ISN'T OVER. <u>I WILL FIND YOU</u> SOONER OR LATER. AND THEN IT WILL BE <u>YOUR TURN TO PAY</u>. <u>YOU</u> HAVE <u>MY</u> WORD. ASSHOLES.

A chill went through me, and I looked around at the others. Chris was still staring at the message. Sarah was staring at Chris. Fender reached for a stack of bills. It was impossible, he said. There was no way Cafferty could trace us.

It took the four of us fifteen minutes to count the money. It was all there. Sarah made us swear an oath of secrecy, then Fender packed his portion into the duffel bag and took off. Chris helped stash my share in small piles under my mattress. He told me to be smart and not buy a bunch of stuff or pay off a big chunk of student debt all at once. Same went for banks. Large deposits raised red flags.

I told him it was okay. I didn't have a bank account.

We never heard from Cafferty, and after a month of can-you-believe-it whispering, the four of us stopped talking about it. But thinking about it was a different story, mostly because the money itself, the endless stacks of newly minted bills, remained omnipresent. Dipping in carefully here and there, it took me three years to spend it.

So that's that, or was, before these latest events. I've discussed the Fender rumor with Chris and Sarah, and neither of them know what to think. Sarah's pretending otherwise, of course, but she's almost as rattled as I am. Chris will be too when he hears about the break-in and the list of names. You understand now, don't you? It's the four of us. Typed in all caps. With a check mark next to the guy who just happens to be missing. Has Cafferty found us? Or is there some other explanation? Maybe it's Fender, orchestrating all this for God knows what reason. I don't know. I feel like I'm going crazy. But I keep coming back to the fact that nothing was stolen, which certainly narrows down the possible explanations.

I've been working on this letter for days now, and I'm no longer sure what it is. An apology. A confession. An attempt at therapy. Revisiting this has made me understand how skillfully and thoroughly I've buried what happened to me in that hotel room. And while this isn't the place to parse my psyche, I hope this explains a few of my quirks and neuroses. Why I sometimes get distant, or, conversely, hyperaware. Why I have trouble sleeping. Why I scream myself out of dreams. How many times you've stayed up with me, asking what's wrong. How many times I've lied and said nothing. But none of it has been debilitating, and since I met you, the dark memories have faded, and my larger life, every part of it, has flourished.

Theo, I'm so sorry about everything. The lies and omissions. The hurt. I'm ready to talk, honestly, openly, about all of this, and I hope that after you've absorbed what I've written, you will be too. I'm scared, but we can figure this out. I know it. I want to feel safe in my home. And safe with you. Forever. I love you, baby. So fucking much.

XoXo
A.

PART THREE

Chapter Ten

H e walks. From the entrance of their building up Thames Street and left onto Knickerbocker. Past Guido's Auto Yard and Big Man Radiators and the wild-style tags on the concrete walls of All-American concrete mixing. The sun is out and he considers hustling back to trade his jacket for a sweater (he must be the only guy in Bushwick who doesn't own a hoodie), but today is about moving forward, pressing on. Besides, it'll get colder later, and who knows how long he'll be gone.

At the corner of Johnson he stops to wait out a procession of mud-caked dump trucks lumbering toward Queens. To his right stands a two-story building that someone, some night, had told him was once a brothel, and someone else, some other night, had told him might now be a brothel again. But on this Saturday morning, to his admittedly untrained eye, it looks completely abandoned. Not that he cares—about the subject matter or rumors in general. He's had it with hearsay. With lives lived in secret. He crosses Knickerbocker and starts west.

If the idea is to be alone with his thoughts, he's succeeding—at least geographically. Johnson Avenue is a curbless wasteland of corrugated doors and barbed-wire fencing, everything colorless and dust strewn and vaguely surreal. He imagines he's been dropped into some urban dystopia, the last one alive, or the last human, anyway, because a guard dog begins barking behind a wall as he passes. But Theo isn't spooked. He knows a thing or two about dogs—Lawrence didn't lack for them— and this one's just doing its job. Soon enough, the bark becomes a growl, then a whine, then a whimper, like a question:

What on earth are you doing here?

What *is* he doing? Walking to Manhattan, ostensibly—to Zuccotti Park to finally experience the month-old protest firsthand. Political activism isn't his thing, but the zeitgeist is—or was, when he was still employed—and he's amazed by Occupy's success, a movement with no real money or messenger, spreading across the world. He could get there far quicker by train, but he needs the fresh air and time away from the loft, where he feels claustrophobic and increasingly confused. In the week since reading Audrey's letter, his mind and body, his very *being*, have become so singularly attuned to her, to the two of them together, that he's stopped functioning in other realms. Work. Sleep. Life.

Up ahead, he spots a pair of sneakers dangling from a power line and is reminded of a walk he and Audrey took when they first moved to the neighborhood. Theo had pointed out a similar pair, above a similar street, and Audrey had smiled and told him it wasn't true that it signified a drug corner. Theo, until then unaware of the urban legend, took in this valuable information and, like everything else she told him, quickly accepted it as gospel.

Small signs on large doors. Orchard Sausages. Midland Meats. At the corner of White Street he considers altering his route to rejoin some semblance of civilization. But which way would he go? To his left are the infamous McKibbin Lofts, host to so many Audrey-organized band parties. To his right, past the old railroad tracks, sit the gutted carcasses of ancient breweries, the very buildings Audrey had offered up as archival evidence of Theo's Bushwick belonging. He gazes skyward and rubs his neck. Its blueness is deep and vast, and he wonders how closely it resembles the sky above Cape Canaveral. What did she call it? *The blue of daring.*

Alone at the edge of the city, and his every thought is still of her.

He finished reading and placed her letter on the coffee table. For a long time he sat very still, as the loft moved in and out of focus. And then he broke. Shame enveloped him, followed by rage. He wanted to find Martin Cafferty and hurt him. He wanted to torture him. Theo stood up and started pacing. His hands were shaking. He imagined stepping on the man's neck. Pushing down, letting up, pushing down harder. He had never hurt a person not wearing football pads, but he knew he was capable of it under the right circumstances. Which were these. His flights of violent fancy continued, one after another, so that for minutes at a time he could ignore the letter itself, its contents and consequences. And then those minutes passed, and he stared at the pages he'd just read and felt embarrassed to be a man. That this horrific, traumatic, life-changing *thing* had happened, and he'd never had the slightest idea. To be so close to her, for years now, and not be aware of her past—or her pain. That she'd been assaulted, abused, *raped*. The word sat uneasily with him. Its cultural power made it seem almost theoretical, when it was obviously anything but. Had there been signs he'd missed? She'd said it in the letter: she'd never been a good sleeper. She acted out her dreams, sometimes talking, even crying out. What was normal and what was not? The crying out wasn't normal, Theo knew that much, even as she'd always insisted, upon waking, that she was fine. Why had he never pressed her to explain what her dreams had been about? He could tell himself he'd been respecting her privacy, or that *she'd* tell *him* when something was wrong, but these were cop-outs, evidence of his ignorance, his inexperience. He'd spent his life fumbling his way through the language of feeling. Honesty and self-awareness weren't enough; you needed instinct, too. The ability to read others. How ironic.

He should have realized something was seriously wrong after the break-in. The way she'd acted. How weird she'd been about those names on the desk. She'd worked late every night for a week after that, arriving home and then heading quickly off to bed, barely able to meet his gaze, let alone sit down and talk. Theo had assumed she was shaken. He'd assumed she was scared. Someone had broken into their home. He'd changed the locks, of course, immediately, the morning after, replacing the latch with a keyed dead bolt. It had taken him a good part of the afternoon, but when Audrey got home and her old key didn't fit, she just knocked. ("Great, baby, I knew you'd fix it," she said when Theo pointed it out.) She looked exhausted. She told him someone had stolen her bike.

A week had passed. Seven days that had seemed like a lifetime. Theo had spent it feeling sorry for himself. She'd spent it, he now understood, writing a twenty-two-page letter. He looked again at the pages on the coffee table. Audrey would be home soon and he had no idea what to say or how to react. He tried to calm down, think sequentially, but his mind looped around three tectonic plates of thought. There was the immediate problem of their safety, and the apparently very real possibility of a vengeful psychopath out there bent on doing them harm. Then there were the chilling details of the letter itself—what had happened to Audrey, and how it had affected her, and what that meant in terms of their relationship moving forward. Finally, there was the nebulous issue of Theo's larger life in New York, of its fast-mounting failures and disappointments, of which this latest chapter seemed already like some definitive event. He had given everything to her. Everything he was and had wanted to be. He believed he'd come to truly know someone, one person in the whole world, and now he barely knew her at all.

Out in the hallway he heard the elevator gate slide open and the sound of Audrey's low heels on the concrete. Instinctively, he moved toward the door. What should he do? How should he react? He suddenly had no reference point for anything. Anger coursed through him. And sadness. And now, as Audrey searched for her keys, something else: dread.

Theo opened the door before Audrey could, and she dropped her bag and hugged him tightly, wordlessly, for a long time. When they disentwined, Theo reached up and felt the tears on his collar. His or hers; both. She retreated to the bedroom to change.

She emerged wearing an oversized T-shirt and black leggings, and they took up positions on either end of the couch. The letter still lay on the coffee table.

"I don't know what to say," Audrey said. The sun had set and through the thin panes of glass came the early sounds of Saturday night. Mufflerless motorcycles and Hot 97. "I wanted to tell you a long time ago. I just didn't do it and didn't do it and then it was too late."

She pulled her knees up under her shirt and rocked gently, back and forth.

"I should have figured it out," Theo said, searching for the right words in the correct sequence. "Or not *it*, per se, but something."

"You couldn't have known."

"The way you sleep," Theo said.

Audrey considered this, then let it go. "I lied to you."

"You didn't *lie*. You just didn't tell me."

"Yeah, for years." Audrey winced. "That's even worse."

The last thing he wanted was to veer into semantics, but no clear thread of conversation presented itself. He felt overwhelmed by the moment. He noticed, then, how far apart they were sitting: he leaning on one armrest, she pressed against the other. They had become, in their time together, an intensely physical couple—always touching, connecting, intersecting—and because of this, the space between them suddenly seemed as wide as a continent before air travel. Audrey must have been thinking something similar, because they both slid toward each other at the same time. They smiled at the inanity of the moment. Like it was reassuring. Audrey curled into his chest, the way she did when they were walking home from a night out. Roger padded across the floor, took a look at his empty bowl, and meowed loudly.

"I love you so much," Theo whispered, and Audrey burrowed in deeper. He placed his hand on her face, her cheek, and felt tears again.

They began kissing. The moment was languid and charged, like it could happen only once, but last forever. At the same time, Theo sensed an opportunity being missed. To talk, react, communicate. But maybe this was okay. Time was what was needed. To let things sink in. He didn't want to say the wrong thing.

Audrey moved her lips from his mouth to his ear. "I love you, too, baby." And then, like she was reading his mind: "I know it's a lot."

The city is so big. The city is so small. As he walks down Montrose the landscape fills in, block by block, with a century of jumbled history. Sharp-edged condos. Soot-brick towers. Plots of public housing laid out in X's, like prison wings. Twelve years spent exploring New York's streets, measuring eras by neighborhood. The Upper West Side. Hell's Kitchen. Bushwick. For most of this time Theo wandered alone, one among millions, each day's path determined by whim and fortune, traffic lights and scaffolding, the sunnier sidewalk. And then he met Audrey, and his walks became *their* walks, complete with the radical idea of destinations. He relished the companionship, his interior monologue now an outward dialogue, spoken, joined, and as he felt the city bend to their will, he'd forgotten his wide-eyed early excursions. Now, though, he remembers. Because they were like this. Contemplative. Restorative. The French have such good names for urban wanderers. Flaneurs. Boulevardiers. Roués. No, a roué is more of a degenerate, a broken man, fit for "the wheel." Okay, so maybe it's accurate after all.

Just past Union, he spies Shifty's Pizza. *And so endeth the idyll*. He was aware he would have to traverse a sliver of Williamsburg proper—that is, Audrey country—to get to the bridge, but he wasn't expecting such a definitive welcome. Not that Shifty's looks like anything special. On the outside it's just another pizza place, but Theo knows better. He knows, in fact, that Shifty's most popular item isn't pizza. "You can probably guess how it works," Audrey told him one night, a few months back, and when Theo said he couldn't, she sighed. "The drugs get delivered with the pies, taped to the inside of the box. You say the password and then order what you want: plain for coke, pepperoni for molly, and meat lovers for weed." Which made sense. Theo shakes his head. He could walk almost anywhere in Williamsburg and come upon another building like the one that housed Shifty's. The world behind the world: Audrey's secret Brooklyn.

He turns onto Broadway, a silhouette in the permanent shadow of the elevated train. He hurries past Trophy Bar (home base of the Westfield Brothers) and emerges into light at the foot of the Williamsburg Bridge. Bikers stream by as he begins his ascent, up and over the hollow husk of the Domino Sugar factory, and it is only now, as the borough falls away, that he gazes at the girders above him and realizes where he is.

Unable to face what needed facing, they ended up playing cards on the couch. Two hours of gin rummy, during which they spoke of everything but the letter. How easy it would be to let the whole thing go, Theo had begun thinking. It wasn't like he could change the past. And anyway, she had come clean and apologized. Why embarrass her further by asking questions, dwelling on details? Well, that one was easy: because they had no choice. They had to find a way forward. Audrey knew it, too. They would talk about everything—just not tonight.

But they *would* have sex. It was important, even imperative. Beyond its inherent pleasures, sex had always been a respite, something they could anticipate, and count on, no matter what else was going on. They had a lust for each other that was not episodic but enduring. They were passionate, if not quite performative, preferring to savor, to linger, to luxuriate in the familiar. And so it would be on this first night of their new reality.

They took it slow, button by button, zipper by zipper, followed by her bra, his boxers, her panties. And then they were standing beside the bed, naked and kissing, carefully, too carefully, and in the moment when they should have fallen together onto the sheets, they instead separated, to check locks and turn out lights, to brush teeth and wash faces, to refill Roger's water bowl. They did things that could have waited. When they reassembled, climbing from opposite sides into bed, they were tentative and self-conscious. They kissed again, partially entangled, not going through the motions as much as trying to get each motion right. Theo moved his hands across Audrey's body, her hip bones and hairless arms and cheeks like burial mounds. He touched the cluster of freckles on her back, the tattoo on her shoulder, and then the quote on her arm that had first brought them together. Audrey pressed his hand to it and started kissing him again, more deeply, and then she was running her other hand down his stomach and taking him in her long fingers. Theo closed his eyes. He let his mind go blank, or tried to, but found it difficult, found it, in fact, impossible, for he'd begun thinking, not of the specific contents of the letter, but of *not* thinking about them. Concentrating on not concentrating. Soon he entered a wormhole, made visceral by the knowledge that he wasn't getting hard, a rare enough occurrence that even Audrey seemed surprised, and started caressing him in places and ways she hadn't before, and then, from nowhere, the phrase "tricks of the trade" came into Theo's head, and with it, a deluge, his thoughts running every which way, the horror of what he'd read earlier, the choices made, men fucked for money, men touched in the way he was being touched just then, and he knew he was being unfair but he couldn't help it, couldn't get it out of his mind, to say nothing of his body, for he had gone completely limp, and after a time Audrey stopped and placed a hand on his cheek. She was staring at him, Theo knew, and when he opened his eyes, whatever she saw in them must have confirmed what she'd been thinking. She fell back onto the pillow, defeated.

Something isn't right. He is standing alone at the very apex of the Williamsburg Bridge, in a small cut-through joining the pedestrian walkway on one side with the bike lane on the other. It's breezy up here but hardly freezing, and he wonders where all the tourists are.

Traversing other bridges, he decides, and he can hardly blame them, for the views on this one are obscured by crossbeams and buttresses and metal fencing ten feet high. To say nothing of the racket rising through the grates beneath his feet: squealing trains and eight lanes of speeding traffic. He ventures across the bike lane to take in what he can of midtown. Is this where it happened? Where Fender jumped? He puts his fingers through the cage in front of his face. He would have had to scale this, and then . . . Theo looks down and immediately realizes what's been bothering him. There's no way Fender *could* have jumped from here, or anywhere else on the pedestrian level, because the roadway below juts out two more lanes on each side. He'd have been leaping onto cement. If his goal was the water—and why else choose a bridge?—he'd have had to jump from the side of the road itself, which meant he'd need a car, or at least a ride. Could he have leapt from somewhere higher? Theo stares up at the towering stanchions. The cables seem climbable, though it would be difficult, even in daylight, to say nothing of the cameras attached to the crossbeams. Surely they would have caught the act. As Theo peers up at them, what began as a mere notion becomes more manifest. There must be far better places to end one's life.

Not that Theo's any kind of expert on suicide. He's only known one person who killed himself, a former high school football teammate named Jamie Juarez. A senior team captain when Theo was a gangling freshman, Jamie had gone on to play at—yes—Central Connecticut State, but lost his scholarship after a bad concussion sidelined him his junior season. He returned to Lawrence the year Theo left for college and quickly commenced a decade-long bout with painkillers and heroin, during which time he fathered two children, overdosed several times, and did an eighteen-month bid for dealing. When he OD'd for the final time, seven months ago, the dose was too strong to be anything but purposeful.

Theo had learned much of this from Carl, who, from the sound of it, had grown surprisingly close with Jamie. The two were the same age, but Jamie was a jock who in his school days had hung out with other jocks, while Carl, lacking the drive to play a varsity sport, had thrown in with the stoner metal crowd.

"I had no idea you guys were friends," Theo said when his brother called him with the news back in March.

"Small town," Carl had answered defensively. "I was just letting you know. Don't come up. Doubt there'll even be a service, considering the circumstances."

But there had been, a small midweek affair at Farrah's Funeral Home, and Theo had rented a car and driven north. His plan, after paying his respects, had been to drop in on his parents, spend the night with Carl (who, since his breakup with Carly the previous year, had moved into the attached house where Theo had once found refuge), and then get back to the city the next day in time for lunch with an editor from Penguin. Occasion aside, Theo was looking forward to seeing his brother. It had been a long time since he'd been home (he and Audrey had spent their three Christmases together with Connie in Florida), and he wondered how Carl was doing. Since becoming single, his brother had made periodic plans to visit Theo in Brooklyn but had yet to follow through. More recently—and more worryingly—he'd all but stopped responding to Theo's calls and texts.

Farrah's was a bunkerlike building two blocks from Theo's childhood home. He arrived late, courtesy of traffic, and took a seat in the back row of the small chapel as a middle-aged woman addressed the two dozen attendees in Spanish. The scene was grim. The woman—Jamie's aunt, Theo surmised—stopped several times to choke back tears before finally, mercifully, returning to her seat. As a man stepped up to take her place, Theo peered around at a scraggly succession of childhood friends and former teammates, everyone jowly and tired looking. Carl was nowhere to be seen. When the speaker launched into a timeworn speech about addiction, there was movement across the room. Theo glanced over and spotted two brothers from the neighborhood, Abdiel and Diego. He remembered them as happy-go-lucky kids who used to deliver weed on dirt bikes, but they no longer looked particularly affable. He watched as they stood up, jostled past their pew-mates, and stalked out the back. People shook their heads. Theo pulled out his phone. *Carl, I just got to Farrah's, but I don't see you. Are you here? – T.* He pressed Send and waited. And waited.

When the service ended, Theo hurried outside. He tried calling Carl, but there was no answer and his voice mailbox was full. How could he not have shown up? Theo started toward his car, then noticed Abdiel and Diego sharing a blunt beside a telephone pole. They hid it as Theo approached. Then they recognized him.

"*Dude,*" Diego said, holding his arm up. Theo clinched it, and they half hugged. He repeated the greeting with Abdiel, who said, "Sorry, bro, you and J was teammates."

"You still in New York?" Diego asked, offering Theo a hit.

"I'm good," Theo said, "and yes. In Brooklyn."

The brothers nodded, impressed. "Brooklyn's the shit, right?" Abdiel offered.

Theo agreed that it was, then asked if they'd seen Carl.

"No, man, those guys all stayed away," Diego said.

"Which guys?"

The brothers glanced at each other. Theo thought he saw Abdiel nod.

"Jamie's, you know, crowd."

Theo didn't know. "Why did they stay away?"

"The cops, man," said Abdiel. "They come to funerals, all undercover and shit."

"They *infiltrate,*" Diego explained, "and then connect the dots. We wouldn't be here either, 'cept we're, like, known entities."

Theo had a vision of them, twenty years back, popping wheelies on Mongoose bikes. "Any idea where Carl is right now?"

"Naw," Abdiel said. "Don't really see him around. Same big circle, different small ones."

Diego motioned up the block at the crowd gathering around the addiction speaker. "Asshole's a 'drug counselor.' Does the same speech every time. Obviously ain't workin'."

"Let's bounce," Abdiel said. "Theo, man, we'll look you up in *Brooklyn.*"

The handshakes were repeated, and then the brothers loped off south toward town. Theo watched them go. How good was business if they didn't have a car?

"Theo Gorski!" Theo turned to see one of his former assistant coaches hurrying toward him. He remembered the guy's nickname—"Chatter"—and braced himself.

Over the course of the next ten minutes, Theo learned that Coach Raab (long retired) was battling lung cancer; Coach Raab Jr. had been fired from CCSU for recruiting improprieties; and Ms. Jansen had accepted a job at a boarding school near Boston. This last piece of news jolted him. He pressed for details. "I guess the market for college advisors isn't what it once was," Chatter said. "You were her big success story."

Theo's phone buzzed. He saw his brother's name and finally excused himself.

CARL: srry cdnt make it man, somethng came up. ill get dwn to nyc this summr promis

What could possibly have "come up"? During the ten months when there was no snow to plow, his brother was a part-time handyman—mostly light electrical, paid by the hour. Certainly, he could have manipulated his schedule to get to a friend's funeral.

THEO: But I drove all this way. Let's meet at your place. I'll run next door, say a quick hi to Mom and Dad, and then we can head down to Marco's for a beer. - T
CARL: dude u don't have to put a T after, I kno who it is! cant meet rgt now. also, woudnt drop by the house if I was u. dads fishingtrip and moms zonkd on Percocet 24/7

At least he spelled Percocet right, Theo noted ruefully. He tried one more time—*Why are you acting like this? Are you okay?*—and then climbed back into his rental car. The house was all of two minutes away, but Carl obviously wasn't home, and the thought of rousing his mother from pill land was less than appealing.

What should he do? Even if he spent the night—broke into his brother's place and waited—Theo would have to get up at dawn to make it back for his lunch meeting. And what if Carl didn't come home at all? Hell, what if he wasn't even living there anymore? Theo had never felt so disconnected from his brother, his family, his past. Carl could be reticent, but he'd never been untrustworthy. He also, as far as Theo knew, had never been addicted to anything more than poor decision making, which made this talk of cops and bad crowds that much more mystifying. One thing he did know: if his brother didn't want to be found, he wouldn't be. Carl was stubborn, a Lawrence man through and through, and any attempt by Theo to play the white knight would only exacerbate whatever was going on. He stared at his former teammates chain-smoking on the sidewalk outside Farrah's. Then he started the car and headed for the highway.

He was west of Waterbury when Carl texted him back. *Not realy*, the message read, and it took Theo a moment to remember the question his brother was answering. *Are you okay?*

He hasn't heard from Carl since. What kind of brother has Theo become? What kind of man? Seven months have passed since Jamie's funeral. He's called Carl periodically but to no avail, and as Theo's own troubles have mounted, his brother's—perceived or otherwise—have slowly faded from his mind. Until now. On this bridge. How did Theo land on this subject anyway? He looks out across the water. Right! Suicide. Jamie's. *Fender's.*

So if he didn't jump, what does that mean? That he's still out there walking the streets of Williamsburg? Surely that's the most likely answer. Or maybe he moved, or, more likely still, is in jail. Isn't that where junkies end up? And if he never did kill himself, if the rumor was just rumor all along, wouldn't that invalidate the rest of Audrey's fears? Or would it only prove the opposite? That something more sinister than suicide occurred. Theo groans. His whole life obsessed with answers, and now he can't even formulate the questions.

He shoves his hands in his pockets and starts toward Manhattan. It's downhill from here.

Which had been worse: the day Theo read the letter or the torturous week that followed? He'd woken the morning after to Audrey clattering around the kitchen, and emerged from their bedroom to find breakfast cooked and coffee made. Walking over to kiss her, he noticed the letter was no longer on the table and took the hint. They talked of other things. The ten-thousand-square-foot art gallery set to open around the corner. The Westfields' upcoming tour. Christ, even the weather, and what those Occupiers would do when it turned cold. Theo was embarrassed, not just by his lackluster performance in bed the previous night, but by his continuing inability to respond intelligently—or really at all—to what Audrey had written. The enormity of it overwhelmed him, and he found it easier, for the moment, to go along with her faux-normal routine. He'd seen it so many times with other couples: the oversensitization, the willful ignorance, the milquetoast niceties of lovers in extremis. And now it was happening to them, in real time, as they sat at the counter eating omelets. But what would he say if he did bring it up? He didn't know. Not yet.

The day passed, and so did Monday, then Tuesday, the week rounding into form like so many others. Audrey went off to work, texted him every few hours, and then came home to check in and change before heading back out to meet a band at Tandem or a publicist at Northeast Kingdom. Theo went through the motions of his life, too, only he wasn't sure what they should be. He hadn't heard from Win since being removed from Round Circle's payroll the previous week. Still, he kept working as if nothing were out of the ordinary—talking with editors, lunching with an agent. At the same time, he began researching job leads with film studios and production companies. He sent tentative emails into the void.

On Wednesday, he reactivated his Facebook account and signed up for LinkedIn. What choice did he have? Networking without social media was like reading without light. He even "friended" some friends, which felt ridiculous. He scrolled through their virtual lives, curated postings from some mythical realm.

On Thursday night he and Audrey found themselves at home together, and almost by accident—Theo was adjusting the screws on the new lock—they began talking, discursively, not about the assault itself, but the aftermath, the consequences, what might happen now. Theo said they needed to be careful, as a lock could only do so much. He suggested Audrey not stay alone in the apartment without him, at least until they knew more, and to his surprise—and then concern—she quickly agreed. (Left unsaid was the fact that Theo, now jobless, was usually home anyway.) Then he asked if they should file a police report. Audrey shrugged and told him, offhandedly, that she'd already stopped by their local precinct, the day after the break-in, and that they'd been no help. She said that's where her bike got stolen.

Theo managed not to ask why she didn't tell him this before. Instead, he absorbed the loose strands of their evolving melodrama and again sensed himself, sensed the two of them, purposely ignoring the deeper issues. How she felt. How he did. He understood the consequences of prolonged non-communication. He'd grown up suffering them. So why couldn't he say something? A simple *Babe, let's talk this through*. In many ways, he believed himself singularly equipped to deal with trauma. He was patient. He was present. And while he couldn't pretend to be anything other than a straight white male, he was attuned enough to issues of gender and patriarchy, to the politics of power and repression, that he knew he could offer more than sympathy. *Empathy*, maybe. True support. He could even shoulder some blame.

Except he wasn't to blame. He hadn't even been around back then. From the very beginning he'd been aware of their vastly different worlds of experience, and in the years since had done all he could to bring those worlds to light so that this—or not *this*, obviously, but something like it—would never happen. And he'd thought he'd succeeded. In the letter, which he'd located in a nightstand drawer and reread twice, Audrey had worried that her "sin of omission" would devastate him. Well, she'd been right. It had. But so had the sins themselves.

To think she'd had sex with strangers for money. To think she'd done it several times. Theo was not against sex work, but when the worker was your own girlfriend? The great love of your life? How had she not addressed *that* in the letter—the sexual aspect and its effect on them. On him. He hadn't been able to get it up all week—they'd finally had sex on Wednesday night, but it was a brief, lamentable act, and he'd almost apologized afterward—because every time they were naked his mind now went *there*, unconsciously, no matter what mental barricades he put in place.

He was so confused, his every thought twinned to its opposite. He'd step into the shower of one mind and get out, ten minutes later, firmly of another. He'd started the week dying to know what Audrey was thinking; by Saturday, he couldn't form a single thought of his own. Had he spent so much time in the fervent throes of cohabitation that he'd lost himself in the process? Or was it worse than that? Had there never been a self to begin with?

At which point, with Audrey off at work again, he'd grabbed his coat and started walking.

He steps off the bridge onto Delancey Street and immediately senses the shift. Manhattan is his domain, not Audrey's, and while pockets of her presence still exist, they are isolated and avoidable. He hangs a left onto Eldridge to skirt the Bowery Ballroom, and then a right onto Broome to miss Fontana's. At Bowery, he turns south and soon finds himself in a strange non-neighborhood where Chinatown meets the northern fringes of municipal New York. He opts for Worth Street, winding west, and makes it all of two blocks before stopping at the base of a small park. The corner looks familiar, but he can't figure out why. It's such a tucked-away place, with dumpling shops and mah-jongg parlors and . . . wait, he *has* been here before. This is Five Points! Theo was still new to the city when, having just read Luc Sante's book of the same name, he set off on a search for the once-nefarious neighborhood. Sure enough, despite the changed landscape—the "five points" had become three—he'd found it. The corner was on his list of places to take Audrey, but they'd never made it—a fact for which he now feels thankful. That he's found one spot on this journey that's still his. But why the urgent need to reclaim a past so marked by loneliness and struggle? He recalls the summer day, years ago, when his roommates filled his backpack with bricks. He'd heeded their message to "lighten up," to open up, and that had led him, finally, to Audrey. He never would have spoken to her at that concert if he'd still been so shy and self-serious. Indeed, he'd have never gone to a Westfield Brothers show in the first place; he'd have taken Carl to a Yankees game or Ground Zero, both of which his brother had wanted to do. Instead, Theo had followed his instinct, and taken a chance, and ended up happier and more fulfilled than he'd ever believed he could be.

So what's he doing? Why is he walking to Occupy? He could tell himself he needs time alone to regroup, and he'd be right. He could tell himself he's curious about the protests, and he'd also be right. But curious about what, exactly? Or whom?

Audrey's not the only one who can live in denial.

He's on Broadway, just above the Woolworth Building, when he hears, farther south, the faint chants of revolution. Soon the signs are all around him: police cruisers and paddy wagons and clusters of cops in riot gear, resting like soldiers swapped out from the front. Through the open door of an armored police truck, he spies dozens of black submachine guns arranged in vertical racks. My God, he thinks. What the hell is happening down here?

"ALL DAY ALL WEEK OCCUPY WALL STREET, ALL DAY ALL WEEK OCCUPY WALL STREET, ALL DAY ALL WEEK OCCUPY WALL . . ."

The sidewalk is swelling with curiosity seekers, cell phones and cameras at the ready. With a herd of others, Theo crosses Liberty Street and finds himself, finally, at the precipice of Zuccotti Park, though he can't see much through all the signs and bodies and barricades. What he can see, because she's directly in front of him, is a topless brunette, oblivious to the November cold, wearing platform heels and American flag leggings, holding a sign above her head. DEMAND TRANSPARENCY! it proclaims, and Theo slumps his shoulders. This is what he was dreading—that he'd trek all the way here only to find out Occupy was less a stage for societal change than a pop-up playground for neo-hippies and stunt performers. But then he catches sight of a middle-aged man in a wrinkled suit, standing beside a sandwich board: I WAS A WALL STREET TRADER FOR 22 YEARS. LET ME TELL YOU HOW THE SYSTEM IS RIGGED. Curious, Theo steps into his orbit and catches snippets of a discussion concerning credit default swaps. He should stick around and learn something, but he's already being swept up and away, past more protesters peddling causes—an Uncle Sam on wobbly stilts, a nurse diagnosing greed—all of them waving and cheering as double-decker tour buses rumble down Broadway. The passengers snap photos, shoot videos, wave back.

Theo squeezes past a fake reverend delivering a sermon on consumerism and steps down into the crowded park itself, a granite urban square with benches and tables attached to the ground. The scene is remarkable. The density and frenetic energy. A woman on a small platform is delivering an unamplified speech using a call-and-response style dubbed the "human mic," but she's being drowned out by police sirens and synchronized drums. The crowd is impossible to categorize, though more are young and white than not. Theo falls in behind two college kids discussing the need for more "safe spaces." Judging from the police presence, Theo can't imagine there's a safer space anywhere in the city, though he knows they mean something else and feels the yawn of the generational chasm.

Against a nearby wall he spies several tables piled high with books. THE PEOPLE'S LIBRARY, reads a cardboard sign atop one of the stacks. Theo can't believe it. Hundreds of titles lie in cataloged bins organized by subject, from *Art* to *War*. He looks around. The dedication. The palpable exuberance. How has he ignored Occupy for so long? He considers the question. It's not an issue of politics or the methods of protest being employed, but something more elemental—an inherent wariness of subversion, of flouting the system in place. He knows what it is: the old mill-town pull. Hard work, head down, don't cause trouble.

And if Theo has managed to defy that ethos—to make it all the way to New York—he's hardly been a rebel. He's done as he's been told. Taken only what he's been given. He recalls studying McCarthyism in a history class at Colgate and being struck not by the sordidness of Hollywood blacklists or congressional witch hunts but by the fact that there'd been American communists at all. It had never occurred to him that a person in this country might be something *other*. Twenty years later, and some of that ignorance still sticks to him, like a regional accent that comes out when you're drinking.

Theo wades in deeper, through a sea of animated faces, pretending he's not looking for one in particular. Luckily, the distractions are plenty, starting with the "media center," a cordoned-off area of frantic activity, activists working on laptops, speaking into video cameras, reporting the revolution in real time. This will be as close as he'll ever come to the true center of something, he realizes as he falls in behind a group of middle-aged women in overcoats, their heads swiveling like they're gallery hopping in Chelsea. He loses them in a bottleneck of bodies and, coming out the other side, finds himself near a row of compost bins on the outskirts of Occupy's "kitchen." He's read about the complex logistics of the undertaking—the feeding of thousands of people daily—but only now can he appreciate the enormity of the task and the brilliance of its execution. For spread out before him are dozens of buffet tables covered with containers of fresh meat and produce and an entire farmer's market of pies and salads and sides. Across the tables wait a long line of diners—vagrants and prepsters, punks and baby boomers, all of them talking, friend to friend, stranger to stranger—and it would make him uneasy, such utopian spirit alongside such visible need, were it not for the warmth in their voices, the pride in their eyes. Like this might be some kind of solution.

Past the line for food he comes upon small clusters of note-taking activists. The working groups. MEDICAL and EDUCATION. LEGAL AFFAIRS and COMMUNITY OUTREACH. SANITATION and SECURITY. Theo eavesdrops on the closest assemblage—DESIGN, reads the placard—where a discussion is under way concerning the extra expense of using nontoxic Magic Markers for sign making. A green-haired "facilitator" produces a price list and is about to go through it when a studious-looking teenager speaks up. "I think we should change the name of the group," he says, "because 'Design' could have religious connotations." The facilitator puts the price list down and asks for a show of hands. A vote on taking a vote. Theo decides to moves along.

He's reached the western side of the park, a crowded enclave of small tents and tarps. This is the realm of the diehards and runaways, the camp followers and late-model Deadheads. Theo wanders the gritty, troughlike paths of their patchouli-scented village trying not to look like a narc. Not that there's any weed in the air. Even the lost kids are too savvy to smoke on site, though other customs of the festival life are on conspicuous display—ukuleles and Hula-Hoops, button and jewelry making, the ubiquitous braiding of hair. The protest suddenly feels far away, its chants and orations giving way to a steady percussive pounding. Theo follows the noise through a jungle of obstacles to its source, the infamous drum circle, though it's more a collective, really, considering that several guitarists, a chorus of cowbellers, a spaced-out tambourine girl, and a man with a bassoon are peppered among the African drummers and kettle-drum drummers and bongo drummers and upside-down-bucket drummers, all of whom are nearing a kind of crescendo, an ecstatic fervor, and dancers are spinning and twisting and spectators are clapping and singing, and were it not for the "Occupy Donations" box, one could be excused for temporarily forgetting the reason for it all. Theo watches for several minutes, the beats bleeding one into the next, before remembering this isn't what he came for. He flips his phone open. It's 3:10 p.m. *Shit.*

He'd promised himself he wouldn't do this. But that was yesterday, at home on the computer, when journeying here had still seemed theoretical. He'd been on Facebook, and had noticed, by chance—oh, come on. He hadn't just "been on Facebook." He'd been on a specific page. Eleanor Thorpe's, to be exact. There. Just admit it. Though—and this seems important—he hadn't been seeking her out. She'd popped up unsolicited on a "People You May Know" list, and because he did indeed know her—or had, once—he'd decided to take a quick look at her profile to see what she'd been up to. Why, then, had the quick look turned into forty minutes spent combing through every post of the last five years of her life? And why—and here was the real question, the one he'd been semi-successfully avoiding all day—when he'd read that she wasn't just involved in Occupy but would in fact be facilitating a meeting of the Legal Affairs group today at three p.m., had he suddenly decided it was time to visit Zuccotti Park?

The word "rhetorical" enters his head, and he begins to ponder its etymology—how it emerged, then became estranged, from "rhetoric"—but now isn't the time. He's wandering through the working groups again, scanning signs and faces. Soon, he's covered the whole area, almost out to Liberty Street, and that's when he spots her, sitting on a low wall surrounded by a dozen activists in heavy coats covered with political buttons. He turns his collar up and moves off to the side. Eleanor is wearing fitted green cargo pants and a fashionable faux-fur-lined jean jacket. Her blond hair is shoulder length and stylishly streaked—or highlighted or whatever—with bits of darker blond. She's grown up so much, is Theo's first thought (though of course she has: it's been seven years since he saw her on the subway), but she doesn't look older as much as *seem* older, up there, out front, and he listens, almost proudly, as she leads the group point by point through some arcane law of state permitting. Theo could join them, wave a friendly hello and then take a seat and volunteer to help out with editing or proofing or some such (does he have no other skills?), and afterward, he and Eleanor would greet each other as the long-lost friends they are. He'd tell her he was just happening by, and, hey, why not grab a drink and catch up—

"WHOSE STREET, OUR STREET, WHOSE STREET, OUR STREET, WHOSE STREET, OUR STREET, WHOSE STREET, OUR STREET, WHOSE . . ."

The chant has erupted from the General Assembly, and peering back across the park, Theo spies a short man in a dark suit ascending the speaker's pulpit. He looks like Michael Dukakis, but that can't be right. Except he sure is someone, because an air of expectancy is falling over the protest. Theo decides to check him out. Eleanor's busy, and anyway, he'll look like a creep if she spies him staring at her. He'll come back when her meeting's wrapping up. In the meantime, he can figure out what, exactly, to say to her, this woman he'd once loved, or thought he loved, before he found a purer form of it. He thinks again of their encounter on the train, recalling the sense of melancholy he'd experienced in the aftermath. That the future world-saver had become a defender of its pillagers. Now here she is, reverting to her former idealism. Or maybe she never lost it. Maybe life isn't so inflexible, so devoid of nuance and positive compromise. A person can be a corporate lawyer and still care about the planet. A protest can harbor dreadlocked drummers and still awaken the world.

He's close enough now to see that the speaker, while not his father's mortal enemy, does indeed look familiar. Theo's been reading the news. He knows Occupy celebrity-spotting has become a daily event, though what began as a who's who of the nakedly political (Susan Sarandon and Cornel West, Noam Chomsky and Michael Moore) has turned into a who's who of the nakedly self-promoting (Don King and Roseanne Barr, Deepak Chopra and Kanye West). But this guy seems legitimate, and as he begins laying out the economic crimes of the 1 percent as thoroughly as the people's mic allows, the non-sound of finger-snapping approval spreads through the crowd. People are whispering to one another. Finally someone produces a name, and Theo shakes his head at his own ignorance. Of course. It's Jeffrey Sachs, director of the Earth Institute and America's leading—or anyway, most famous—economist. Theo's read his op-eds, seen him on *60 Minutes*. What a coup for the protests, getting a major intellectual's imprimatur, even if the poor man has no choice but to speak in generalities, sentence by echoed sentence. Ten minutes and then he's done, or almost done, because now he's holding up a book, and announcing . . . a giveaway? He's brought along a dozen copies of his "*New York Times* bestseller, *The Price of Civilization*," which he's "willing to donate for free" to the occupation, on the condition that whoever's not camping in the park buy one later on Amazon. Theo can't believe what he's hearing, and he's not alone, for pockets of boos can be heard as people absorb the inelegance of the moment. The sad irony of it. But Sachs is smiling broadly as he steps down and is surrounded by reporters. A camera light comes on and Theo suddenly remembers where he first saw him. It wasn't on *60 Minutes*; it was on MTV, with Angelina Jolie. Theo's Upper West Side roommates had been channel surfing one night and paused when they saw Lara Croft sweating in a tank top. But it turned out to be a documentary, not *Tomb Raider*, and when Sachs appeared, surrounded by African kids, the channel surfing resumed. Theo, bemused, had retired to his room, his mind pinwheeling between fiction and reality, image and intention.

The crowd has swelled; signs are everywhere. EAT THE RICH. OCCUPY BRAINS. I CAN'T AFFORD A LOBBYIST. Theo spies an elderly woman holding a banner reading I AM UPSET in shaky handwriting. And a man in a Reagan mask throwing torn-up dollar bills in the air. Everything is a performance. Everyone's onstage. And that's when it dawns on him, a truth so elemental he can't believe it hasn't occurred to him before. The reason he's so in love with Audrey, the qualities he finds so intoxicating, they all add up to this: she is completely and unabashedly *real*. And in that completeness lies the absolute world Theo seeks. The ideal life he still believes in.

He looks back across the park toward Legal Affairs. He should get in touch with Eleanor again, but not today, not like this. He's being reactionary, and shady, and he knows it. And so he retreats, past the library and up the steps, and that's when he spots—of all people!— Chris Van Vleck, walking right past him, his arm around a pretty, dark-haired girl. Chris glances back and their eyes meet. The girl has stocking-line tattoos running up her bare legs, and Theo's first thought, as he watches them disappear into the crowd, is not that he should have said hello (definitely not, the asshole), but that he—for some nonexistent record—abandoned his Eleanor jig before seeing Chris, before glimpsing betrayal in the flesh. He feels almost redeemed. And then he just feels tired. Exhausted. He yearns to get home to Audrey as soon as physically possible, so he heads for the subway. Walking takes too long.

Chapter Eleven

Where did Gatesy say the place was? Audrey tries to recall the drummer's exact words. "On one of those deserted streets out past the kill." Well, she's biked them all now, to no avail. It's the middle of the night, and she's drunk and shivering. Is this even Brooklyn anymore? It must be, since Newtown Creek is still east of her. Or is it?

What a forlorn backwater she's pedaled into, the cold air pungent with waste and chemicals. Since crossing the old rail tracks, she has yet to see another human being, and she's been riding around on Theo's crappy bike for twenty minutes now—up and down and over and across the same five blocks of warehouses and salvage yards, oil depots and body shops. She thought she'd find the club easily enough, spot a sign or a doorman, maybe a line outside. But there are no streetlights, and the curbs are lined with parked eighteen-wheelers she can't see past. Assuming there's even somewhere to see.

She pulls up in front of a beer distributor at the corner of Meadow and Gardner. Through the fencing lie hundreds of beer kegs, strewn haphazardly about like it's the last day of Lollapalooza. She checks the map on her phone, enlarging the screen with frozen fingers. Quality Foam. Alloco Recycling. Wing Sun Paper Supply. No nightclubs. No restaurants. No bars. Not out here. Why would there be? They require patrons.

To think she listened to a Westfield Brothers drummer. How desperate she must be. She puts her phone away. It's time to get home. She points the bike in the direction of civilization and is about to push off when two beams of light appear through the fog. A car, creeping up on her from behind. It hits her then—how defenseless she is. She's been in desolate places at desolate hours, but nowhere like this. She starts pedaling, but she's shaking and puts a foot down to catch herself. The headlights are almost on her. With a look of defiance—what other choice does she have?—she turns to face them, but as her eyes adjust, she sees a third light, blinking orange like, well, a blinker. She's been holding her breath, but now she exhales. The kind of person who would use a turn signal is not the kind of person who would do her harm, she tells herself as the car rolls up. Except it's not a car, it's a yellow cab, with three passengers crammed in the back. She watches it crawl past and turn, uncertainly, onto Gardner Avenue. The driver looks as lost as she is. Still, he must be headed somewhere. She waits a moment, then starts after him.

The Columbia Records–leased practice space contained a full GK backline, a PreSonus Studio mixing board, a QSC K-series 1000-watt PA system, two-channel Marshall tube half stacks, JBL speakers and floor monitors, a Lexicon multi-effects vocal processor, four vintage Shure mics, a Live HD audio/video recording system, wraparound wall mirrors, and several Persian rugs, but what Audrey couldn't get over were the plush mini-couches arrayed in artful little islands facing the platform stage. As the Westfield Brothers ran through their set list she found herself sinking deeper and deeper into a particularly welcoming set of cushions, prompting Arthur Westfield to change the lyrics of "What Now?" from "Amy, we're in deep," to "Audrey, you're asleep." Audrey opened her eyes and laughed.

It wasn't that they sounded bad. On the contrary, they sounded fantastic, and Audrey, happily stoned, wanted nothing more than to let their aural splendor wash over her like some ritual cleansing. She hadn't seen them since the ill-fated Terminal 5 after-party, and she'd been looking forward to hearing their new arrangements before they set out on tour. Also, she had to admit, she'd badly needed a night out. The mounting intensity of her life at home was taking a toll, the possibility of Cafferty's reemergence now an omnipresent reality (at least in *her* mind). At the same time, two weeks had passed since the break-in without any further incidents, a nominally positive sign all but obscured by the sudden fragility of her relationship with Theo. Still, what had she expected? That she could write a letter like that, a *confession*, without repercussions? No, but she hadn't imagined it would hit Theo so hard. She'd hoped he'd be relieved to finally have an explanation for her behavior (to say nothing of the break-in). Alas. She knew, on some level, that his reaction was a testament to the deepness of his love for her, but could it also signify a shift in that love? Some broken essence? Theo seemed stuck between two difficult conversations—about her past and their future—and the former was as painful to broach as the latter was impossible to predict. So the silence. The time. Let him process what he'd read, create an acceptable space for it. And then they'd talk. It would be good for both of them, she knew, even if she wasn't sure that delving even deeper into ancient history was a great idea. What had happened had happened, and she'd survived. She'd stayed strong. Or so she'd always told herself. But these timeworn mantras were showing cracks and wear, evidence of matter beneath. As for the future . . . Theo knew she adored him. Everything else was irrelevant.

But tonight was about forgetting all of that, at least for a few hours. When was the last time she'd just hung out—smoked weed and done shots and listened to her boys argue over chord changes and backing vocals and which guitar Easter should play on "Oneonta"? What she wasn't prepared for was the full-court press the band employed after the rehearsal as the five of them lay draped across the couches, Tecates in hand. She *had* to come with them on tour. They needed her, and to prove the point big Ben Westfield unsteadily lowered himself onto a knee and mock-begged. They would make sure she got everything she'd always wanted, but rarely received, on the road—the shotgun seat (when she wasn't driving), her own hotel room, Wendy's instead of Burger King (though out west they had In-N-Out, Easter reminded everyone, so that issue solved itself). Audrey asked if Lucas had put them up to this, and Ben said absolutely not. *They'd* convinced *him*, he told her, and she believed it. She was flattered, but she didn't play coy. She couldn't do it. Painful as it was, they had to cut the cord. She had other bands. And she had Theo. She couldn't just drop out of her life.

"Bring him along," Easter said. "He can be in charge of security."

Audrey laughed as she pictured Theo in a SECURITY shirt, protecting the band from nonexistent dangers. Then she shook her head. "Sorry," she said. "I really can't go."

"Well, that's not very rock and roll of you," Gatesy said.

She agreed that it wasn't.

Somewhat more rock and roll were the two hours of post-rehearsal partying she proceeded to partake in. Tequila and more beer. Ben grabbed his accordion and started playing a Clancy Brothers drinking song, and Arthur handed Audrey an acoustic and showed her the progression so she could strum along. She was getting drunk. She was having a good time. And for one or both of those reasons, she began to reconsider—or at least question why she was so definitely against—heading out on the road. Circumstances had changed since Lucas first raised the subject. If someone was really after her, going on tour would be safer than staying in Brooklyn. Hadn't Theo just asked her not to spend time at home alone? Surely, then, he could understand her leaving for a month while the situation with Cafferty or Fender (or whoever the hell it was who'd broken into their place) sorted itself out. Then there was the issue of money. Theo no longer had a job. Worse, he was refusing, for some antiquated reason, to collect unemployment. This meant they had half as much cash coming in, an untenable state considering their *combined* incomes had barely kept them afloat. For this, they could thank Audrey's student loans. The problem wasn't the size of the original amount (she'd gone to a state school, and for only a few semesters), but rather, her failure for several years to start to pay it back. Over time, the trickle of

warnings had become a deluge of letters and phone calls and accumulating debt that had all but fiscally drowned her. Even the blackmail
money hadn't helped that much. Only when Theo came along had she
managed, through her embarrassment and his attention to detail, to
begin sending in monthly checks that, while hardly making a dent in the
ominous "total owed" figure, had at least curtailed the threats associated
with her period of pointed disregard. Saying yes to Lucas and the band
would mean doubling, maybe even tripling, her salary while she was on
the road, as long as she could convince her boss, Cal, to count this as
paid vacation. (She could, she knew, since she'd never taken a real one.)
In sum, the tour could solve a lot of problems—or at least fend them off.

And yet.

She'd be leaving home with four boys in a band. Partying at rock clubs
every night. In bars every night. At hotels every night. She knew how it
would go. From the depths of the couch, she studied her friends. Ben had
started dusting the bellows of his accordion with a paintbrush; Arthur
was nodding to a beat through noise-canceling headphones; Easter was
destemming weed; and Gatesy was breaking down his drum set while
outlining, to anyone who might be listening, his plan to open an artisanal
beef jerky shop with the money he made from the tour. But there would
be no money from the tour. There hadn't been money when the band
was with Whale Creek, and there wouldn't be any with Columbia either.
Not yet. Maybe not ever. Audrey knew this, and guessed that Ben and
Arthur did as well. But why not live the fantasy? *That* was rock and roll.

A retro clock on the wall read 1:51 a.m. How had it gotten so late?
Audrey pulled out her phone to text Theo, tell him she'd be coming
home soon in case he was still up (he hadn't been sleeping well either),
but she couldn't get a signal. Had there ever been a practice space that
did get decent reception? Not that she could recall. She excused herself
and stepped outside.

November had arrived and settled in. She turned up the collar of her
leather jacket and stood behind the Westfields' van to block the wind
coursing down Maujer Street. Maybe Theo had texted *her*, she thought,
but when the signal bars appeared there were no new messages. Why

would there be? He knew where she was. He'd all but pushed her out the door when she'd wavered about going. Still, she chose her words carefully as she typed, knowing he'd study them for subtexts—and lies. No, she should give him more credit. He was doing the best he could.

She pressed Send and started heading back inside for one last whatever when the door flew open and Gatesy stepped out past her carrying two floor toms.

"What are you doing?" she asked.

"Loading out my kit," he said, stepping over to the van. He was wearing only a tank top. (And they wonder why they're always getting sick, Audrey thought.)

"Aren't you rehearsing here again tomorrow?"

"Yeah, but other groups use this space and I don't want anyone touching my shit."

Thanks to Arthur's leaping from it on an almost nightly basis, the Westfield Brothers' midseventies Ludwig drum set was in horrendous shape. As such, it was a tradition (and a test of temperament) that every new drummer who joined the band jettison his personal set for the janky Ludwig, with its deep creases, lifted seams, replaced inlays, and constantly unsticking black duct tape that spelled out "W.B." The few drummers (there'd been at least five) who'd embraced the change came to prize the kit above all else, which explained why Gatesy was schlepping it out here when it was surely the least valuable instrument in the studio. He had no free hands, so Audrey opened the back of the van and watched him climb in and place the drum boxes carefully on the filthy carpeting. Then he turned back around. "Hey, you know what's weird?"

"Not specifically," Audrey said.

"Remember that Fender dude you got all sideways about after the Terminal show? Well, I met his girlfriend—or his ex-girlfriend, I guess—at this club the other night. I meant to tell you. Actually, I didn't mean to tell you; I just remembered it now."

Audrey stared up at him. "What club? What are you talking about?"

"This after-hours place I ended up at with two dudes from the Antlers. I don't think it has a name. Or maybe it does, I don't know, I was pretty plastered. It was on one of those deserted streets out past the kill. There's a whole world of warehouses and shit out there. I had no idea."

"Tell me what happened."

He jumped down from the van and rubbed his thin, bare arms. "I don't remember much. The place was in a basement at the end of a hallway, a bunch of dark rooms with a sketchy vibe. I remember the main space had a disco floor and a small bar with a mirror behind it, because at some point I saw how shit-housed I looked and pushed the evac button."

"What about the girl?"

"The girl?"

"Fender's friend."

Gatesy frowned, trying to remember. "I was at the bar, about to leave, when this chick got back there and started making drinks—just pouring shit together. She was hot, but in a hard-core way, and she had that super-silver hair chicks are getting now, you know?"

Audrey nodded impatiently.

"Anyway, it was late, and crowded, and she was talking to someone on the next stool over. I wasn't paying attention, but then she said the name 'Fender' and I butted in and asked if she was talking about Fender the A & R rep, and she was like, 'Yeah, we used to fuck,' and then she turned back away from me."

"That was it?"

"I think so. Shit, it was almost six in the morning!"

"She didn't say anything about a suicide?"

"No, it wasn't like that. Anyway, was it even confirmed? That he killed himself?"

Audrey slammed the van doors. "Don't worry about it," she said.

"Okay, I won't," Gatesy replied, and shrugged. They walked back inside.

The cab crawls down Gardner and then—blinker again—makes a right onto Stagg Street. Audrey follows at a distance, and when it stops halfway down the block, so does she. Through the darkness she spots the roof light come on, and then a door opens and three bodies tumble out and disappear between parked trucks.

She waits for the cab to drive off and then pedals over and dismounts beside the eighteen-wheelers. Hearing nothing but the groan of a far-off trash compactor, she squeezes the bike through the trucks and finds herself standing under a sidewalk overhang attached to a brick building. It's like the old Meatpacking District, she starts to think, and then the odor hits her, a ruddy stink, and she notices bits of bone littering the gutter she's just stepped over. Looking up, she sees hooks, some with torn flesh still attached. She couldn't have missed the carcasses by much. All the people she knows—her boyfriend chief among them—who so love lamenting the lost city, the way it once was: she should bring them out here. If she can figure out where here is.

Where did those three people go? The entrances to the meat plant are covered by roll-down gates. All except one—a lone door just past the loading bay. She wouldn't have noticed it but for a hint of red light emanating through a small eye-level window. She locks the bike to a NO STANDING ANYTIME post and steps over to investigate. Maybe there's a bouncer inside, she thinks, though peeking through the dirty window, she sees only stairs, dimly lit, heading down. But the door opens when she pulls it, and such is her surprise that she quickly pushes it closed and stands there, wondering what the hell to do. A secret club below a meatpacking plant in the middle of industrial nowhere? It's not impossible. Those night owls must have gone *somewhere*. Feeling like a trespasser, she opens the door again, and this time, steps inside.

The stairs lead down to a cold, dingy hallway, lit red with a single bulb. She walks the length of it, maybe sixty feet, feeling unnerved by the eerie shadows on the water-stained walls. She tells herself she's being ridiculous. Besides, she can hear muffled music now, a reggae beat coming through a thick wooden door in front of her. It's locked, and there's no bell, so she pounds it with her fist. Nothing happens. Then she looks up and spots a tiny camera high in a corner. She's just about to wave when she hears a buzz, and like every good New Yorker she immediately pushes the door. This time it opens.

Again, no doorman. No promoter with a list. Just a dark basement room that remains that way even as her eyes adjust. What light there is comes from below her feet, where a grid of colorful squares blink on and off. *Gatesy's disco floor.* But the squares are dulled by grime and shrouded in a layer of hovering smoke. She moves deeper in, sensing people more than seeing them. The song she could barely hear in the hall now presses in around her. "Libertango" by Grace Jones. She should give a nod to the DJ if there is one, because the music sure fits the mood. Where *is* she? The outlines of tables and chairs emerge, cushioned benches along walls, and now bodies, here and there, spread out in languor or lust. She passes a woman in a short striped dress and knee-high boots, eyes closed, vaguely dancing. Like she's on something pretty strong.

Toward the back, she finds the bar. Five empty stools, a wooden countertop, a shelf of liquor, a mirror. She's thinking she'll never question Gatesy's memory again, when out of the smoke strides a heavily tattooed woman with bright silver hair—like she's hitting her entrance cue in some dungeon-themed play. She's wearing a black leather corset and ripped jeans, though the look isn't sexy, exactly. She's too tough, too cavalier. She tears open a large bag of ice and empties it into a beer-filled cooler.

"Drink?" she says, not looking up.

"A beer would be great," Audrey answers, though alcohol is the last thing she wants—or needs. "Whatever you've got."

The bartender pulls an opener from her back pocket and uncaps two Miller High Lifes. Then she grabs a handle of Maker's and pours out two shots. "Gotta get in the mood," she says, and Audrey wonders who she means. They clink glasses, down the whiskey.

Audrey thanks her, then reaches for her beer. "What do I owe you?"

"Five bucks."

"That's it?"

"You're welcome to pay more."

Audrey grins, though she can't quite read the bartender's tone, and digs into her jeans for some wadded-up cash. It's no easy task, and she ends up hopping up and down on one leg before miraculously producing a ten. She smooths the bill out and places it on the bar. She so rarely feels like this—out of her element, intimidated even—and the whiskey isn't helping. Not after the tequila earlier. And the beer and the weed and the cigarettes. (And, fine, the key bumps she did with Arthur.) The bartender returns to her prep work. Audrey watches her slip the opener back into her pocket and notices the familiar opener-shaped wear in the denim. For a decade every pair of jeans Audrey owned exhibited the same characteristic. Reaching for her beer, she feels a surge of camaraderie and is about to say something—compliment her outfit, maybe?—when the bartender turns back around.

"If you're looking for Johnny, he'll be here in a few," she says.

"I'm not looking for Johnny," Audrey says.

The bartender studies Audrey for the first time. "Do I know you? You look familiar."

"It's possible," Audrey says, and introduces herself. She mentions a few of the places she's worked.

The bartender—Nikki—nods knowingly. "Could be from Enid's, though my scene's a bit more derelict." She gives Audrey a brief rundown of her own employment history. Duff's, the Acheron, the newly opened Saint Vitus. "It's a great club, but metal every night gets old fast," she says. "All those weekend warriors carpooling in from the Island in Def Leppard T-shirts two sizes too small."

Audrey smiles and looks around. "So who's Johnny?" she asks.

Nikki's cleavage lights up and she pulls an iPhone from her corset. She taps an app and up comes a live video feed of the entranceway. There's a group waiting in the hall. The guy in front is making a peace sign with his fingers. Nikki enters a code, and a few seconds later, Audrey hears voices over near the door. "So now you know the password," Nikki says. "Inventive, I know, but it's all people can handle this time of night."

"So why'd you let *me* in?" Audrey asks.

"Cops don't usually pull up on vintage ten-speeds with drop handlebars."

There was a camera on the street as well? How did Audrey not see it? "So is this like a private club?" she asks.

Nikki stops what she's doing and looks Audrey over. "You sure have a lot of questions. Why don't you tell me what you're doing out here. It's a long way to come for a High Life."

Audrey explains that she heard about the place from one of the bands she manages.

"What band?"

"The Westfield Brothers."

Nikki nods, apparently satisfied, then takes a long pull from her beer. "Officially, this place is nothing," she says. "We're pretty much off the grid. Half the meatpackers don't even know we're down here, and they're our *landlords*. So, sure, I guess you could say we're private, in that you have to come with someone we know. Though 'club' is a bit of a stretch. Anyway, feel free to check the place out. I gotta get back to work."

Audrey needs to broach the subject but isn't sure how. Nikki's already wary. Still, she came all this way. And she has nothing to lose. "Before you go," she says, casually as she can, "one of the Westfield guys was in here the other night and overheard you talking about someone named Fender, and I was . . . I was wondering if it's the same Fender I know—A & R guy, life of the party, been in Williamsburg forever— because he's an old friend and . . ." Audrey tries to focus through the blear of intoxication. "I heard something might have happened to him."

Nikki leans on the bar top, directly in front of Audrey.

"Like what?" she says.

So it is the same Fender. Not that Audrey'd had much doubt. She hesitates before continuing. How much should she say? How much does Nikki know?

Audrey puts her hand around her beer like it's a blanket. "I don't want to upset you," she says, "but I heard a rumor a few weeks ago that Fender might have . . ."

"Jumped off the Williamsburg Bridge?" Nikki says.

"How do you—?"

"Because I saw him that night."

Audrey tries to hide her shock. "Is it true?" she manages to ask.

Nikki stands back and folds her arms. "You know, this isn't quite adding up," she says. "Why you're so interested. I dated that bastard for a whole year and he didn't mention you once."

"There's no reason he should have. We were never romantic or anything. But that doesn't mean I don't care about him. Hell, he was practically my tour guide when I first moved to Brooklyn."

Nikki considers this. "He was everyone's tour guide," she says, softening once more. "Until he wasn't. I met him two years ago and he was pretty screwed up by then—on drugs, booze, anything that might keep him safely oblivious. Of course, I lapped it right up, all that charm and danger. That need to be saved. Then one of his dealers got him into needles." She shakes her head, remembering. "It got bad fast, and pretty soon he stopped going out unless it was to score. I'd been staying with him at that musicians' crash pad on Keap Street, but I finally split. Moved in with a girlfriend in Sunnyside, which . . . at least the name is nice, right? I can't believe I stayed as long as I did, but what can I say. I'm the queen of codependency."

Nikki's breasts light up again. She checks the screen, enters the code. Audrey notices a guy at the far end of the bar, waiting to order.

"You said you saw him that night? At the bridge?"

"No, earlier, at the Levee."

"The old Kokie's," Audrey says.

"That's right!" Maybe it's the mention of the infamous Berry Street dive that sold stepped-on coke from a slot in a wall that has Nikki reaching for the Maker's again. She pours out two more shots. Audrey's too drunk to accept, but she does. They clink glasses and down the whiskey.

"I hadn't spoken to him in months," Nikki says, looking out past Audrey into the smoky darkness. "And then out of nowhere he called me, all hopped up on some riff, and sure, he was probably high, but he sounded like the old Fender, the boyish, playful one, not the moody, helpless piece of shit he'd become. And right away he was saying how much he missed me, and how he wanted to meet up that night, and of course I said yes, thinking it would be just the two of us, and a few hours later, I walk into the Levee all done up like a tart, and there he is, thin as a piano string, in a shredded leather jacket, painter's pants, and a conductor's hat, surrounded by a dozen old friends it turns out he'd also called. I'm sure he gave them the same melodramatic speech he gave me. I didn't talk to him for long, maybe five minutes, just superficial shit. Then he said he had to go, that he was meeting someone over at the bridge, which seemed weird, and drug related, and not something I cared to know more about. So I didn't ask. No one did. Ignorance is more than bliss in that crowd. It's a fucking necessity." Nikki takes a swallow of beer and wipes her mouth with her sleeve. "That's the last time anyone saw him."

"What do you mean?"

"I mean that he walked out of the bar, headed south down Berry, and vanished. Hasn't been home since. Hasn't been anywhere. And it's been weeks now. You're not the only person who's been looking for him."

Audrey feels numb. From the whiskey. From the story. "Do you think he killed himself?" she asks.

"Honestly, I don't know. But if he didn't, then where is he? He was a full-on junkie. They go to the same three places, if they go anywhere at all. My guess is he'd just reached the end of his rope, and getting everyone together was his way of saying goodbye. Christ, he basically spelled it out for us. I mean, 'business' on a bridge?"

"But you said he seemed excited."

Nikki's cleavage lights up a third time. "Look," she says, "I'm about to get slammed, but I've got a girl showing up to make drinks, so why don't you chill out in the back room and I'll come find you in a little while and we can talk some more. In the meantime, I'll send Johnny over to take care of you."

Audrey starts to protest, but Nikki's already moving down the bar. Okay, then. She takes a deep breath and tries to collect herself. The room isn't spinning, but it's not exactly still either. Couples are emerging from corners, more groups coming in. She's not sure if she should stay or go. She's exhausted, but revitalized, too. That she's found a like mind in the wilderness. Someone else seeking answers. If Nikki can find more time to talk, then so can she. Step by step, she wades through the smoke until she's found the room Nikki had pointed her toward. It's so dark she can't see the walls. Grace Jones is still playing—the full album straight through—which means the DJ is either a completist or doesn't exist. Audrey's bet is the latter, because this place isn't about music, or drinking, or dancing, or being seen. Which leaves one thing.

Her eyes are finally adjusting. She can make out couches against walls, a few small tables, threadbare rugs on the concrete floor. She nods at two intertwined bodies as she walks past, but they're oblivious. She and Nikki will need privacy, so she finds a velvet love seat in a far corner and sits down. She has to collect herself—figure out a strategy, an approach. What else does she need to know? Her mind is swimming again. Drowning.

She watches the form of a man enter the room and sit down with the couple she just walked past. *Johnny*, Audrey thinks, happy to focus outward again. She squints at the figures in the darkness, and when she sees the exchange she feels vindicated (though vindication would require a second party, when Audrey was only debating herself). The man puts something to his nose, and then the woman does. One of those little plastic bullets, it looks like—so no lines are laid out. Clever. There were places like this in Florida, shacks in swamps with in-house dealers, open a night or two a week to those in the know. Audrey used to tag along with Jasper Sash, but when she graduated to the permanent-invite list the parties lost their thrill. This place, though: How do they keep it on the down-low? And who, for that matter, is "they"? Nikki must have partners, investors, suppliers. Are the meatpackers in on it? The *cops*? Probably not, considering the cameras. Then again, Kokie's existed into the 2000s thanks to monthly payments to a captain at Audrey's favorite precinct house. And Kokie's was smack in the middle of Williamsburg—and named *Kokie's*! So why not a hidden basement way out here?

Through the gloaming, Audrey sees the-man-who-must-be-Johnny ambling toward her. She grabs her beer, takes a sip.

"Hey," he says, "Nikki asked me to make sure you have everything you need."

"That's nice of her," Audrey responds, flattered by the attention. Does Nikki see her as a kindred spirit? A fellow Northside survivor? Audrey's met so many girls like her—tough, cool, morally challenged queens of the night with enough ambition to keep the temptations somewhat in check. She'd been one, too. She misses those days.

Johnny introduces himself and takes a seat beside her. He's tall and scraggly, with a bass player's receding hairline and a con man's charisma. Audrey imagines he's good at his job.

"What's your flavor?" he says.

She's curious but manages not to ask what the flavors are. Coke, weed, molly, maybe some pills, is her guess. No smack or meth; nothing too far one way or the other. "I could smoke a bit," she says. She doesn't want to but also doesn't want to seem impolite or suspect. And coke at this hour would be crazy. It's as late as it can get before it gets early—or something like that. God, she really is out of it. She tries to remember how much cash she has. "Do you sell dimes or eighths or how does it work?"

"How it works is I give you a vape pen, you have at it and then give it back."

"Inventory control."

"Precisely."

Johnny removes two implements from his coat and holds them out, one in each hand. "Regular's fifteen, high-test's twenty."

"I'll try a little high-test," Audrey says, because who would choose "regular"?

"Cool. Just warning you, though, it can be a bit intense. It's wet."

It's also just weed, she doesn't say. She's not some high schooler. She stands up, does the jumping thing, fishes more bills from her pocket. A ten and two fives. She hands them over, and then sits back down and watches Johnny double-check the pen with the practiced attention of a chemist. When did everyone start vaping? One year it's mini water bongs, the next it's artisanal rolling papers. And now these electric things.

"Okay," Johnny says, and hands it to her. "It's smooth, but a little goes a long way."

She presses the button and sucks in slowly. And it *is* smooth. She can barely feel the smoke in her lungs, but when she exhales, it comes out in a long, steady plume.

"Nice," Johnny says.

"Want some?" Audrey asks, handing it back.

"Would, but I'm working," he says. "Stuff's not great for nocturnal mathematics."

Audrey nods, impressed by the dealer's restraint. "Are you ever worried about being busted?" she asks incautiously.

"Of course. But meat plants have an incinerator."

"Beats flushing," Audrey says. Then her eyes go wide. "Whew! Fuck."

Johnny smiles and stands up. "Hang with it until your friends get here."

"I'm by myself," Audrey says, feeling suddenly and intensely hot. "What's in that weed?"

"I told you—some dust."

"*PCP?* No, you didn't! Oh, God."

"That's what 'wet' means. What'd you think I was talking about? You'll be okay, just go with it. I need to make the rounds. Come find me if you're having issues."

Audrey watches him walk away, but the room is beginning to tilt, like that kids' game with the marble in the maze. She used to play it all the time but can't remember where. In Florida? In Michigan? *Florida.* Has she called her grandmother? There was the thing with Jasper Sash she was supposed to deal with. The weight Connie's been buying. But that was a while ago, right? Weeks or months. Her mouth tastes bitter, and she feels . . . not light-headed, exactly, but bleary, numb. *Heavy*-headed. She leans forward, nose between her knees, thinking it might help with equilibrium, but now the blood rush becomes its own thing. She can feel distinct veins in her brain, pulsing. A lighthouse light. A taxi blinker. She's looking for the floor in the blackness, but it's not there. Her feet are on it, her shoes, but she can't see it. Her stomach feels weird from the whiskey—like it's just sitting there, unabsorbed. She can hear people nearby, laughing. She wants to look at them, but the task of raising her torso seems monumental, and Grace Jones could help, but she's not helping, no one is, or no one was, because she hears a voice now, a woman seated nearby, talking at her through thick liquid, through golden smog, which was the name of a band, a supergroup, the greater sum of lesser parts, which could describe her relationship, her life, but the woman's voice, the words she's saying, they've reached her now: "Did . . . you . . . lose . . . something?" Audrey understands the question but not why it's being asked. Then she realizes she's still bent over, looking at where the floor should be. How should she respond? What do people lose? They lose their phones. "I . . . lost . . . my . . . phone," she hears herself say. "It's . . . in . . . your . . . pocket," says the voice, and of course it is, because that's where Audrey keeps it. She reaches for it now, takes it out. She tries again to sit up, but a wave of nausea hits her. She's in trouble. Voices on all sides. She achieves the feat of lifting her head and sees a room filling up—seats taken, people standing. To walk to the bar would be like walking to Mongolia. Why is she here? Her head keeps buzzing, the noise like mosquitoes flying into a zapper. She tries to circle back to a previous thought but can't recall one. The bar! The girl she was talking to. What was it about her? Oh! She knows Fender! *That's* why she's here. She's going to throw up. Are people staring at her? She tries to look around but sees only streaks of color against the black—like a highway in a movie at night, sped up, blurred. Johnny. He said to walk around. He said to come find him. But if she stands up, she'll fall. She's lost control. She never loses control. Has she done it on purpose? Grace Jones is talking to her and she tries to listen, but the buzzing. She puts her hand to her ear, except her phone is in her hand, so her phone is at her ear. She speaks into it. She says, "I need help," but no one talks back. She holds it out in front of her. She could call someone. She could call Theo. *Theo.* She needs him. He'll know what to do. But she can't call him—can't *dial*—and even if she could, she can't speak. It's too loud, and also, she really *can't* speak. She tries to say something. "I'm fucked up." No. "I fucked up." Which one? She can't hear herself. Then text. *Yes.* She enters her passcode, 1111 (because she kept forgetting everything else), then pushes the text icon. Up comes Pandora. She tries again. There he is, the last person she texted. When was that? What did she do before she was here? Today. Yesterday. How long has she been in the dark? Forever. She tries to type. *Come babyget mu me Help.* She presses Send. Okay. He'll come. She breathes. Two beats in, two beats out. Ed Beemis taught her that. It's how astronauts stay relaxed. How they don't get claustrophobic. She's in a small space now. Where is she? She doesn't know. Theo won't know either. She has to text again. The task feels impossible. To type more. 1111. The name of this place. She thinks but can't remember. Out past the kill. Someone said that. *Out passed the kill meetpacker*, she types. *Bike sinpost come pleease Im sic.* Send. Nothing. She looks in the upper corner. *No Service.* She looks at the message. *Not Delivered.* Then one bar. Then *No Service.* Then one bar. Then *No Service.* She holds the phone up, like that might help, but forgets to grip it, and it drops from her hand. She bends down to find it but bends too far and falls forward, out of the love seat. Her shoulder hits the floor—there is a floor!—and then her head. She hears the noise it makes. She hears the buzzing stop.

Chapter Twelve

CHRIS: dude I got the info you wanted

THEO: Are you serious? How? – T

CHRIS: 10 yrs of texting and ur still signing off w an initial?

THEO: Sorry, I can't help it.

CHRIS: yes u can, u can not do it

THEO: Okay, okay. So what did you find . . .

CHRIS: a guy I went to college w wrks at Longstream. diffrent
dept from Cafferty but still knows who he is.

THEO: That's amazing.

THEO: What did he tell you?

THEO: Chris? Are you there?

CHRIS: sorry, bit distractd. shits going down across at occupy.
looks like protesters r getting the boot. People in my
orifice right now.

CHRIS: *OFFICE!

CHRIS: Jesus. Call u in a few.

With a swell of affection for his Luddite friend, Chris pockets his
phone and stands up to join the three managing directors who've just
entered his office (without asking) and are now staring out his window.

He doesn't particularly like any of them, but what's he going to do? Tell them to leave? They work on the other side of the building, so this is their best view of the protest—or former protest is more like it, because the park they're staring down at is eerily empty now, its granite surfaces power-washed to a high shine. No people. No tents. No signs. No *drums*. Chris almost misses them.

"Finally," says one.

"Fucking Bloomberg," says another. "Letting this shit go on for months. Rudy would have fire-hosed 'em the first day."

Chris remains silent. He's wondering where they are now. The hundreds of human beings who'd been asleep in the park when the police moved in last night. How many were arrested? Beaten? From what Chris could gather online, dozens had refused to leave and were forcibly removed. Had Kinsey been among them? She'd been living in a tent Chris could see from his window. *Could* as in *had been able to, but no longer*. He doesn't know if she was there when the raid went down because they haven't been in touch since it happened. Chris was at home with Sarah all night and, as was now his practice, had blocked Kinsey's number until he left for work this morning. The risk of incoming missives was just too great. Sarah was already suspicious, and he could hardly blame her. His secretive cell phone behavior. His unexplained postwork absences. Obviously, he'd texted Kinsey—several times—as soon as he got to his office this morning and ascertained what had happened, but he hasn't heard back. Maybe her phone's dead. She was always complaining about how hard it was to keep it charged in the park.

The thought of her emboldens him, so he steps back over to his computer, clears his throat, and frowns at one of his monitors. The men at the window finally get the hint and shuffle into the hall without saying goodbye. Chris waits a minute, then closes his door and picks up the phone.

Theo answers on the first ring. "Sorry about that," Chris says.

"Why are you calling on your office line?"

"Because I get shitty cell reception in here. This building's a hundred years old."

"Yet somehow you guys run the world."

"Certainly our chances are better now that the resistance has fallen."

"What do you mean? What happened?"

"The police showed up in the middle of the night with huge lights and loudspeakers and ordered everyone to vacate or they'd be arrested," Chris says. "Then an army of sanitation guys threw everything—all the tents and signs and food—into huge dump trucks and started hosing the park down. It's crazy. The place is totally empty except for a handful of diehards over on Broadway chanting, 'We are unstoppable, another world is possible'—which, sadly for them, doesn't appear to be the case just now. I'm trying to figure out where the protesters went."

"Sounds like you're pretty invested," Theo says.

The comment catches Chris off guard, but he doesn't take the bait. "Let's talk in person. I'll tell you what I found out about . . . you know who."

"You can't say his name?"

"I work at a financial institution, Theo. Our calls get recorded and our emails get read. Let's meet at Union Square in two hours. It's halfway between us, subway-wise."

"Except you'll probably take a cab."

"More like a car service."

Chris spots Theo from a distance, seated on a bench in a peacoat. No hat or scarf, though it has to be close to freezing. He stands as Chris approaches and they clasp hands, half hug. Theo looks sallow, sunken, almost anonymous.

"The bench okay?" he asks.

"Sure," Chris says, and they sit down side by side. "Feels like we're in a Cold War thriller. You should have brought a briefcase you could hand off. I'm sure you have one."

"Funny," says Theo.

They sit in awkward silence, watching a flock of well-fed pigeons root around the path in front of them. Even with the cold, Union Square seems quiet for a weekday afternoon, but what does Chris know? He doesn't take his lunches on park benches. He takes them at Delmonico's.

"So," Theo says.

"So," Chris responds. He wants to acknowledge the absurdity of their anti-technology moment, texting to landline to meeting in person—the evolution of the species in reverse—but he knows Theo's not here for small talk. And who can blame him, after what he's just been through?

When Theo called him at the gym yesterday, Chris, mid-treadmill, almost hadn't answered. He didn't need to be reprimanded for being spotted at Occupy with a woman who wasn't Sarah. At the same time, he didn't want Theo telling Audrey about the encounter, so he reluctantly picked up. Then he heard Theo say the name Martin Cafferty. He quickly dismounted and listened, stunned, as Theo filled him in on recent events. The break-in. The list of names. Audrey's letter. And finally, the gruesome details of a meltdown she'd suffered in a basement drug den the night before. He was still digesting it all when Theo got to the point, asking if Chris could "find out" what he could about Cafferty's current life. Did the guy still work in finance? Did he still live in New York? That is, was there any chance he could actually be responsible for what was going on? Chris asked how Theo expected him to do this. It wasn't like he was a private investigator.

"I don't know. You found out who Cafferty was the first time, didn't you?"

Indeed, he had. But that was years ago. Did Chris really want to get involved with all of this again? Standing amid rows of runners going nowhere, he recalled the moment at Ulysses, a few weeks back, when Audrey first told him about Fender's rumored suicide, and once again felt a reflexive disinclination to connect the news with any larger plot. What possible reason would Martin Cafferty have for coming after Audrey all these years later? He didn't even know who she was. Or did he? Chris was wary of coincidence, and what were the odds of a break-in occurring less than twenty-four hours after Audrey learned of Fender's demise? To say nothing of that list of names left on the desk.

Their names. Which led to the next logical question: If someone was after Audrey, couldn't they be after him and Sarah as well? The more Chris considered it, the more he wanted some answers himself, so he told Theo he'd see what he could do. *Thank God I live in a doorman building*, he found himself thinking as he hung up and hopped back onto the machine.

"According to my guy," Chris says, still eyeing the pigeons, "Martin Cafferty was fired from Longstream Capital in August. But not because of anything nefarious. Turns out half his department was laid off. He worked in real estate lending, which, as you might imagine, has been decimated by all the loan defaults these last few years."

"So what does that mean?" Theo asks.

"It means he probably got a decent severance package but not a ton of cash, because he wasn't a top guy. As for another job, there's nothing new listed on his LinkedIn. In fact, it still says he's with Longstream, so he's either trying to hide the fact he was canned or . . ."

"What?"

"Or he doesn't give a fuck. Also"—Chris can't help but milk the moment—"his wife left him this past spring. Took the kids, the whole deal."

"Your buddy told you all this?"

"Yes, but it was hardly a secret. Everyone at Longstream knew, and no one was shocked. Seems Cafferty wasn't exactly loved."

"So basically everything in his life has gone wrong at once. Sounds like the perfect recipe for losing your shit."

Chris sighs. "The thought's crossed my mind, too. Still, you don't really think he broke into your place, right? You live in Bushwick. Breaking and entering is practically a pastime out there. As for the list of names, it's like you told me on the phone: there were papers strewn everywhere."

"But that page was the only thing on the desk. And it was right in the center."

"If you say so. But there're tons of reasons Audrey might have written—"

"Typed."

"—sorry, *typed* out our names at some point, what with everything that happened."

"I know," Theo says. "And I agree with you. But I need to *prove* Cafferty's not involved, if that's possible, because Audrey deserves some peace of mind." Theo looks skyward, and for a moment Chris thinks his friend might tear up. But Theo exhales, recovers. "It's been tough."

"I bet," Chris says. He waits for more, but nothing comes. For the first time, he wonders if Theo and Audrey might be in trouble relationship-wise—what Theo's just learned would be a lot for anyone to deal with—but he puts the thought out of his mind. For most of his life he'd thought "passion" a foolish word, until he witnessed the vibrating intensity of Audrey and Theo together. They were that rare couple that proved, inexplicably but irrefutably, that the whole cosmic order might just make sense. Monogamy. Happiness. To think New York might consume them, too: he would have never believed it.

He should say something, man to man. *Are you okay? Do you want to talk about what's going on?* Except he can't. They don't have that kind of rapport. Or maybe they're just not those types of people. *Communicators*. Besides, Theo didn't come here for therapy. He came for information.

Chris needs to get back downtown. He's got client calls this afternoon—assuming his office hasn't been subsumed by Occupy rubberneckers. Which reminds him. The comment Theo made on the phone earlier, about Chris being "invested" in the protest. He can't imagine Theo would have told Audrey what he saw last Saturday in Zuccotti—the two of them have enough going on—but then again, imagination isn't Chris's strong suit. Calculation is. And leverage. He's given Theo what he asked for. Now he needs something in return.

"Speaking of the protests," Chris says, even though they haven't been, "the girl you spotted me with is a friend from work, if that's what you were alluding to earlier."

"I wasn't 'alluding' to anything," Theo says a bit mischievously. "But now that you mention it, I do seem to remember you had your arm around her."

Chris's mind hits on reflexive denials, before settling on something slightly truer.

"She's involved in the Occupy scene, and I became interested."

"I'm sure."

"In the *protests*."

"Yeah, you're a regular Che Guevara."

Chris looks down at the ground between his feet. "Look, I just did you a favor. So tit for tat. I'll keep this little meeting we're having a secret if you keep—"

"You don't have to lay it out like that," Theo says. "Like a veiled threat. You're my friend, you can just ask me not to say anything. Which I haven't, if that's what you're wondering. Your private life is none of my business."

"You're right, sorry. Look, I obviously haven't been the perfect boyfriend, but I'm working on things, working on *myself*, and—"

"If it makes you feel better, I went to Occupy that day to see an old girlfriend of *mine*," Theo says. "I basically stalked her on Facebook and saw that she'd be there."

Chris stares at Theo, dumbfounded. "Does Audrey know?"

"She didn't at the time. I told her afterward."

It *does* make him feel better. Remarkably so. *The more you think you know someone.* Chris can't help himself. "Did anything happen? With you and your ex?"

"No, I never even spoke to her. But still."

"But still." *Here's to the girls of the revolution*, Chris almost says, but wisely doesn't. He knows it's not the same thing, their two situations. He'd followed through and Theo hadn't. Of course he hadn't.

Theo starts to stand, but Chris puts a hand on his shoulder. "There's something else." Chris roots around in his pocket and produces a slip of paper with an address written on it. "My buddy got this, too. From Longstream's employee directory. I probably shouldn't give it to you, but since we're sharing trade secrets . . . I'm guessing it's Cafferty's bachelor pad. Obviously I have no idea if he's still living there, or if you even want it."

"Sure, why not," Theo says, a bit too casually.

Chris hands it over as a bitter gust of wind whips past them. Through them. *The sense of an ending.* The phrase enters Chris's head and swirls around like one of Sarah's blended juice concoctions. Where'd it come from?

Theo stares at the address, then carefully refolds the paper and puts it in his wallet.

Ah, right! It's the title of a new book he saw in the window of the Barnes & Noble on Eighty-Sixth. Christ, is he becoming Theo? Hardly. From the sound of it, *Theo's* becoming more like *him*. Who'd have guessed.

"Just be careful," Chris says.

"Come on, I'm the most cautious person you know." Theo smiles for the first time, then stands up, startling the pigeons. One takes flight. Then they all do.

Chapter Thirteen

Through the weathered panes of the living room window, Theo watches the last of the police cruisers drive away. They'd been outside for hours, double-parked on Thames Street as the investigation unfolded upstairs. Theo had nosed around the building and found out what he could—which was enough. More than enough. It all makes sense now. He can finally breathe again, and so he does, deeply, in and then out. How close he'd been to accepting Audrey's sinister theory concerning Martin Cafferty, to the point of soliciting information from Chris. What had he been thinking? Vengeance and murder? It had always been too improbable. Not that he blames her. Sometimes the world closes in so tight. The intensity, the heaviness. It meddles with your mind, obscures basic truths. What was that slapdash notion Win's authors were always citing in their books, about the simplest explanation so often being the correct one? *Occam's razor*. The principle of parsimony. Never make more assumptions than needed. Yes, well. Easy for Occam to say. Whoever he was.

Theo looks around the loft, feeling strangely uneasy. He realizes he hasn't seen the cat in a while, so he starts searching for him, above the counters, in the closet, under the bed. He calls his name, to no avail. Great. Audrey's missing and now Roger is, too. Theo shakes his head, exasperated. Audrey should be home from work by now. He considers texting her to explain what just happened upstairs but then thinks better of it, thinks, indeed, of the reaction she'll have when he tells her in person. The elation. The relief. That she's safe now. That her past can recede, like some terrible rogue wave, and they can rebuild. Move on. Or can they? Is *he* ready? For the first time since all of this started, he's not so sure. He's still shaken by the scene he came upon in that meatpacking basement two nights ago. It's consuming him. She'd claimed it was a mistake, a misunderstanding, and Theo believes her. But still. In the aftermath of the letter, he's done his best to be understanding. He's given her time and space and what has she done with it? Overdosed on drugs in some four a.m. dungeon hellhole.

Not that he's been perfect. Far from. But at least he's been up front about his behavior, arriving home from Occupy last Saturday afternoon and immediately admitting to his (mental) dalliance with Eleanor. Admitting? More like *unburdening*, for he'd felt downright euphoric in the aftermath, his guilt all but gone. It had helped, of course, that Audrey had handled it so well, telling him she understood, that they'd both been unduly stressed. (She'd even suggested they invite Eleanor for dinner some night.) Still, Theo can't help wondering if some level of payback was involved in Audrey's drunken exploits—the all-night band party that led to that horrifying climax.

He wills his mind not to go there, revisit the moment he found her, crumpled in a dark corner, her head bleeding . . . but it's too late. On comes a rush of images, memories, the whole indelible nightmare, confusion turning rapidly to panic as he woke to her barely coherent texts and scrambled down the stairs, grabbed a random bike from the storage room, and then pedaled, all adrenaline, through a frozen predawn mist, up and down the streets of that godforsaken backwater until he spotted her bike (which was his bike), chained to a signpost outside that doorway to hell. And down he'd gone.

Day as night and night as day. Theo hadn't exhaled until he'd gotten her safely home (the manager woman had called them a car—as if she suddenly cared) and was cradling Audrey's ice-packed head in his arms. He'd wanted to take her to a hospital, but she vehemently—if groggily—refused, so he sat there with her as she fell asleep, listening to her breathe. He knew about concussions. Hers wasn't too bad.

He held her through the early morning, gazing down at her face, its beguiling width and wonder, recalling after a time the trepidation he'd felt in their first months together, anxieties born of sudden luck and overwhelming attraction, but also a faint yet persistent concern that they were fundamentally ill matched, for Audrey was as comfortable with chaos as he was with order. With answers and remedies. A world that made sense. Love, of course, had soon dissolved these worries into little more than amusing anecdotes—*the story of our beginning*—but dissolved is not the same as disappeared. The former still exists, in some secreted fashion.

She'd slept most of yesterday and finally woken after dark with a golf-ball-sized bump behind her ear where her skull had met the floor. At least that's what she thought had happened. Half lucid, she gave Theo a shaky account of events—from the Westfields' rehearsal debauchery, to Nikki's connection to Fender, to Johnny's laced weed—and then ate a light dinner and fell back asleep until eight thirty this morning, when, to Theo's great surprise, she got up, swallowed four Advil, cobbled together an outfit, and headed off to Whale Creek. An hour later, Chris texted him about Cafferty, and Theo had set out for Union Square.

Theo's on his knees, peering under the sofa, when the front door opens and Audrey strides in.

"I won't ask," she says, dropping her bag by the broken coatrack.

"I'm looking for Roger."

Audrey nods toward the bedroom doorway, and sure enough, there's the cat, stretching lazily, tail up and back arched, like he's modeling for some Ptolemaic tomb carver. Audrey snaps her fingers and Roger prances over and weaves through her legs. Theo stands up sheepishly, looking back at the bedroom. He thought he'd checked every inch of it.

"How are you feeling?" he asks.

"Like I need a cigarette," she says, exhaling. Then, to Theo's aston-ishment, she produces a pack from her jacket pocket. Parliaments. "I'm gonna run up to the roof while I've still got my coat on."

And before Theo can even say, *You won't believe what happened*, she's gone. In all their time together, Theo has never seen her smoke. She had when she was younger, he knows, because she'd told him once how proud she was to have quit, but he had no idea she'd started again. Also, why does she need one this second? Couldn't she have indulged on the way back from the office? Maybe it was the sight of him. He ponders that for a minute. What if it really was?

Enough. He'll tell her the news when she comes back down. But why string her along, have her pace and smoke and worry for no reason? He slips on some shoes and heads down the hallway to the stairwell. When he gets to the top he pushes open the fire door and steps out onto the roof. The wind whips through him and he shivers in the cold. He takes a few steps toward the western side of the building, with its Manhattan skyline backdrop, but Audrey's not there. He spins around, momentarily frantic, before—thank God—discerning her outline on the darker eastern side. As he sidles up beside her, he notices dozens of cigarette butts ringing her feet.

"Come here often?"

"You should put a coat on," she says without looking over.

Theo makes it a point not to rub his arms.

"So you're not going to believe what happened," he says.

"Try me."

"Remember that couple from Maine who lives on the floor above us—Cassie and Lyle? We've met them a few times. She's a chef and he's some kind of artist."

"An unemployed one."

"Yes, well, someone broke into their apartment today, around lunch-time. I was in the city, but when I got home a little after two there were cop cars out front and people milling around everywhere. Turns out the intruder used a key, but failed to plan the rest of the crime very well because Lyle was *home*. Napping in his bed. He woke up when he heard

noises in his living room, and out he went, in his boxers, to investigate."
Theo grins, warming to the story. "Of course, Lyle's a pretty big dude,
so the burglar immediately took off down the hall. But Lyle went *after
him*. Chased him barefoot into the stairwell and . . . you know that old
couch wedged into the landing just below our floor? Well, the guy tried
to vault it, but he clipped the top and ended up sprawled out with a
broken ankle and fractured wrist and Lyle pinning him down."

"Jesus."

"And guess who it was."

Audrey shakes her head.

"*Miguel*," Theo says triumphantly. "The weasel who collects our rent
every month in the back of the deli. Turns out our landlord's trying to
sell the building and he paid Miguel to break into their apartment so
they'll get scared and move out. That's what must have happened to us,
too. Which explains why nothing was stolen."

Audrey doesn't speak. She turns away, gazes out at the blackness.

"This is great news," Theo says. "We don't have to worry about
that asshole Cafferty anymore. You'll be able to sleep again. We both
will."

"Sure," she says, and fumbles for another cigarette.

"I don't understand."

"Look, can you just let me absorb this?"

"Of course," Theo says. "I just . . . I thought you'd be excited."

She lights her cigarette, takes a deep drag. "You said Miguel used
a key to get into their loft?"

Theo nods. "He probably has a master for the building. He must
have used it on our door, too."

"But a credit card could have worked as well."

"Theoretically."

"So *theoretically*, someone other than Miguel could have broken
into our place."

"Audrey, come on."

"*Come on?* That's your answer? Lyle and Cassie always have eviction
warnings on their door because they never pay their rent. If I were the

landlord, I'd have someone break in there, too. And what about the names on our desk? Did Miguel leave those as well?"

"That page must have already been there. You saw what our place looked like, there was crap everywhere. Drawers emptied out. Papers, letters, books, bills. Our entire file cabinet was turned over. You probably typed those names out years ago—for whatever reason—and the sheet got stuck in a folder, and then ended up on the desk when the place got ransacked."

"How? Levitation?"

"I don't know. Maybe Miguel was going to leave a note and picked up a random page from the floor."

"There's nothing random about those four names."

Theo takes a deep breath. "How can you still think Cafferty has something to do with this? Even if you're right about Miguel, didn't that bartender say Fender definitely committed suicide on the bridge?"

"She *thinks* that's what happened. No one actually saw him jump, or even walk up onto the bridge. Look, let's just forget that whole club thing, okay?"

If only it were so easy. Theo tries to collect his thoughts, but they've unspooled. A half hour ago he'd known exactly what he wanted to say, but his practiced eloquence has vanished, leaving in its place only basic vocabulary, tentative syntax. The rutted language of love.

"Audrey, I know you're dealing with a lot of . . ." He pauses. His voice in the air sounds thin and unfamiliar. He doesn't want to reprimand her, but almost two days have passed since he extracted her from that dungeon and he's owed an explanation. *She* created this crisis, with her epistolary detonation—to say nothing of the actions it detailed. And to carry on like this in the aftermath . . .

"I wish you would just talk to me," he says. "Tell me why you're acting like this. So distant and unpredictable. Is it me? Is it that thing with Eleanor? Because I already apologized for that. I was out of sorts, as you might imagine, after losing my job and then, barely a week later, receiving your letter. Frankly, I think I'm handling it pretty well, all things considered."

"Do you?"

"Yes."

"Because I think you're being a fucking asshole."

Such is Theo's astonishment that for a moment the words don't penetrate. They hang in the air like they might hitch a gust and blow away. But they don't. They rear and gather and bore into him instead. She has never so much as raised her voice in his direction.

"How can you say that?" he asks, suddenly feeling the cold through to his bones.

"Incredibly easily." She takes a long, toxic drag from her cigarette, then blows the smoke out and turns to face him. "What's happened to you? You used to be the most thoughtful, considerate man. Have you spent even one minute wondering what this has been like for me? Reopening these wounds? Reliving the worst moment of my life in exquisite detail? I need your support so badly and instead . . ." She shakes her head and turns away. "I can still smell that hotel room, Theo. I can still taste the wood on the floor. Feel the violation. The shame. Of being overpowered. Losing control. I know you can't imagine what that's like, and I'd never expect you to, but I thought, I *hoped*, you'd be able to imagine what that was like *for me*. In the moment. And in the years after. To live with the emptiness. To be incapable of trust. *Trust*, Theo. Your holy fucking grail. Well, I had none for years. No trust in men. No trust in relationships. Have you ever wondered why I never had long-term boyfriends before you? Sure, my mother's lovely disappearing act didn't help, but going through this on top of it? Theo, it almost destroyed me. And then you came along—*you*, of all people—and I suddenly realized how lucky I was, and I circled the wagons around you so tight the wheels couldn't turn any farther inward. And don't you dare tell me that's a cliché. Because that's the kind of bullshit that got us here in the first place. It's like your whole life is just one huge grammar problem, and all anyone needs is the right reference book. But that's not how it works, you idiot. Nothing's ever definitive. Nothing stays the same. You feel your way around and if you're fortunate, once or twice in your life, you happen upon something profound. Like I happened upon you. And, of course, because it always works this way, you were the complete opposite of everything I'd known and experienced. But I *adapted*. Because I never loved someone like I loved you. You were my person, from the very beginning. You made me more honest and more open. And now look."

She takes another deep drag. Burns the cigarette down to her fingers and tosses it over the side. Theo fights the urge to peer over, see where it lands. His ears are ringing. He wonders if he's in shock. The things she's saying. The tenses she's using. Mostly the past.

She shakes her head slowly. "I'm starting to think writing that letter was a big mistake. I should have listened to my grandmother."

"What do you mean?"

"She told me once that I should never be afraid to keep secrets."

"I don't agree," Theo says.

"Thanks, I got that."

"Why didn't you tell me all this in the beginning? One of those nights down on the docks."

Audrey doesn't respond, so he turns to her, and now he sees the tears. So rare are they on those high cheeks that he reaches for her arm, but she pulls away.

"Do you know why I didn't?" she says, her voice rising, cracking. "This. Us. Right now. I knew you wouldn't be able to handle it. That I'd be tainted in your eyes, damaged in some unfixable way."

She turns back to the edge and stares out across . . . what? Ridgewood? Maspeth? Forest Hills? The city keeps going, on and on and on. Is that why she chose this side of the roof? To search out someplace new? Someplace untainted? And what of him? Will she leave him behind as well? Is that what this is? It doesn't feel like a breakup, but how would he know? For the first time, he wonders if he's less the apogee of her life than a fragment, a phase, experimental, perhaps, but in the end no more notable than any other. He can't decide if he knows her too well or not at all. You can dig and dig and never get to the bottom of someone. You can only try to understand the layers.

Should he have asked her more about her history? The litany of loss that's defined so much of her existence? Father. Mother. Best friend. He'd never wanted to burden her. Better to leave it all behind. Only now does he begin to comprehend his mistake. The lines of the past course through us forever. Her fear of relationships was a direct result of desertion. Which made her willingness to commit to him all the more shocking—and sacred.

What has he done with all that faith?

She lights another cigarette, her third, and something about the action—still so foreign to him—ignites in Theo another voice. Angrier and more aggrieved. What he's done is give her all of himself, every ounce of who he is. Because that's what love is. Even now, her mere proximity stirs up an ache that leaves him short of breath. But has that yearning only camouflaged deeper signs of incompatibility? How much has he ignored? How much has he forgiven? He knows he should stay silent, but he can't help himself.

"Audrey, I feel like I've been fighting really hard to make this work. I know you've made sacrifices for me, but I've made—"

"Shut up! Seriously, Theo. For once. Just *stop talking*."

She lifts her hands to either side of her head and squeezes her temples. Then she rubs her face—that face—and turns to him.

"What you said before. About Miguel and the landlord. I'm sorry, but I just don't think that's what happened to us."

Theo sighs, too loudly. "But why, aside from the names on the desk?"

"It's just a feeling I have."

"Based on?"

"*Based on the fact that I have feelings.* Can't that be enough for you? Jesus, whose side are you on?"

"I'm on your side."

"Then why are you acting like none of this is real?"

"I'm not! I changed the lock on our door for Christ's sake."

"Great. How helpful."

"What else should I be—"

"*Something! Anything!*"

He should tell her about his meeting earlier with Chris. That would certainly count as "something." But he can't. What Chris told him would only bolster her argument—whatever her argument is.

"I've been looking out for you the whole time," he says instead. "I'm the one who suggested you not stay home alone."

"That was common sense."

"Well, you must have misheard the recommendation, since you suddenly don't stay home when I *am* there."

"Seriously? That's what you think? That I'm avoiding you? You know what? Maybe I should be, because I can't tend to your wounded psyche while you—"

"Audrey, calm down."

"*What did you say?*" She stares at him. Into him. She's only inches away, her eyes wild, tears and makeup, everything blurred. "Don't you dare tell me—fuck this, I can't. I'm leaving." She pushes past him, starts back across the roof.

"Wait, I didn't mean—"

But she's already halfway to the stairs. He calls her name, once, twice, but she doesn't turn around. This isn't happening. He needs to go after her, but his feet are rooted in place. He looks down, willing them to work, and sees the cigarette butts. Then the fire door slams and he looks back up. There's the city in the distance. He feels the cold again, that immobilizing chill, but even now he resists the urge to shiver. To show weakness.

Can you still call it stubbornness when you're all by yourself?

Chapter Fourteen

Sarah paces, checks her phone, paces some more. She can hear Audrey in the guest room shower, singing an old Westfield Brothers tune, the name of which escapes her. Or maybe she never knew it. She looks around, sees auction house catalogs everywhere, stacked on the coffee table, lining the bookshelves—like they're mocking her. *Sotheby's*. She suddenly can't get away from the place. She reaches into her pocket, feels the envelope, the evidence. Of what, she's not sure. A developing nightmare, or the opposite, her foolish paranoia. She takes a healthy sip from the wineglass in her hand. It's her second (glass, not gulp), and she's been home all of fifteen minutes. Whatever. She walks over to the kitchen, pours herself some more.

The shower stops, but Audrey doesn't. How many times Sarah's heard that husky voice, so carefree in its toneless splendor. She supposes it's a good sign, that Audrey can relax a bit in the midst of this insanity. She thinks back to that lunch at Balthazar—less than three weeks ago—and feels a sense of shame. To have been so uncaring. So quick to brush her old friend off, as dramatic, as hysterical. She understands, now, how Audrey must have felt. Helpless. Panicked. *Targeted*. Because she suddenly feels that way, too.

"Auds!" she calls out, the old nickname increasingly comfortable on her tongue. "Auds, I'm home!"

"Okay, be out in a sec!"

Perhaps it's their physical proximity, or the sound of her voice, that awakens in Sarah a once-familiar sensation: that Audrey will know what to do. It had so often been the case that it became a refrain, an inside joke, back when they shared such things. Sarah's never felt this anxious. This exposed. She takes another long sip of chardonnay, then puts the glass down on the new kitchen countertop. Italian-quarried Statuario marble with gray veining and a three-inch mitered straight edge. If she thought hard, she could probably remember the exact catalog page she first saw it on, too. How important it had been to find the perfect surface for a kitchen she barely cooked in. How vital to put her own stamp on Chris's family-bought classic six a block from Park Avenue. But why? What was wrong with the old counters? She can't remember now.

She checks her phone again. Seven thirty p.m., and Chris is still MIA. She'd texted him as she left Sotheby's, demanding he come home as soon as possible, but fifteen minutes had passed before Sarah's phone buzzed with his one-word response: *why?* Sarah had stabbed her thumbs at the little screen: *bc somethngs happened.* Another ten minutes: *like what?* Seriously? What was wrong with him? *JUST GET THE FUCK BACK HERE!* she'd replied.

She knows where he is. She'd gotten suspicious a week and a half ago, after he (almost jovially) went into the office for the second Saturday in a row, so she checked his phone later that night. It wasn't difficult. His passcode, like his ATM pin, was his birth year. Nor was it difficult to find his partner in treachery, since he stored her as an initial instead of a name. "K." Like that wasn't a red flag. It was probably one of those wearisome millennial deals—Kiley or Kari or Kiara. Which was perfect. As was the fact that she and Chris had been hanging out together at Occupy, of all places, until the protests were shut down two days ago. Indeed, "K" appeared to be some kind of activist, and if their texts were any indication, they had a real connection. (Chris had even promised, in a particularly nauseating exchange, to read a book called *Rules for Radicals*—like that was going to happen.) "K" must be beautiful, and in that inked-up, smoky-eyed way that fed Chris's contrarian fantasies. Which would make Sarah the dreaded straight woman. The ogre back home. How had she let that happen? Had she overplayed her hand by disavowing so completely her previous Brooklyn incarnation? She peers down at the all-important marble countertop. She's like a politician who hews to the center, only to be outflanked by the base, the diehards, the ones who got you there. But that makes her sound calculating when she isn't. None of this was gamed out or planned. She met a man and fell in love: therein lay the history of the world. But love, she now knows, comes with an asterisk. It comes with concessions. To keep it alive, passion and pragmatism have to exist in some kind of workable balance. She needs look no further than Audrey and Theo to see what happens when you close your eyes and go all in.

On cue, the guest bedroom door opens and Audrey emerges, hair wet and makeup free, in a cinched-at-the-waist blue jumpsuit. "Sorry," she says, "I didn't know you were home."

"No problem, I just walked in."

Audrey spies the mostly empty wine bottle and raises her eyebrows.

"Okay, fine, like fifteen minutes ago," Sarah adds. "And please, finish it."

Audrey pours herself what little is left and hops up onto one of the two kitchen island bar stools. Sarah can feel herself being assessed, so she turns around and opens the fridge.

"I think there's another bottle in here somewhere if you're—"

"Hey," Audrey says, "what's going on?"

"What do you mean?" Sarah asks, bending down to scour a lower shelf.

"You almost killed a bottle of wine in the time it took me to shower, and now you're hiding behind the refrigerator because you've got the worst poker face in the world."

Sarah's about to respond—is she really so transparent?—when she hears the front door open, followed by the familiar clomp of Chris's Ferragamos on the hardwood floor.

"This better be something important," he calls out from down the hall, annoyance dripping from his voice. He tosses his keys onto the side table and comes striding into view.

Sarah appears from the depths of the fridge with another bottle of wine. "Oh, hi," she says coolly. She's not sure if she wants to stab him or hug him.

"I just raced all the way back here," Chris says, "and that's all you have to say?"

She fights the urge to confront him. Not in front of Audrey.

"Something happened at work today," she says.

"For once," Chris replies, and shakes off his coat. Then he sees Sarah's expression, and his smirk disappears. "I'm sorry, I didn't mean—"

"*What* happened?" Audrey asks.

Sarah puts the bottle on the counter and runs a hand nervously through her hair. "I think he might have been there."

"*Who* might have been *where*?" Chris asks.

"Martin Cafferty. At Sotheby's. Looking for me."

When Audrey showed up on their doorstep two nights ago, Chris did all he could to make her feel at home. Sarah, meanwhile, kept a certain distance until Audrey sat them down and filled them in on the sordid news from Brooklyn—from the loft break-in and her visit to the precinct, to her club breakdown and her rooftop fight with Theo. Chris, surprisingly, took Audrey's report in stride. Sarah did not. Immediately—and who wouldn't have?—she zeroed in on the list of names on the desk. Did Audrey seriously believe Cafferty was responsible for it? Yes, Audrey answered without hesitation. But Sarah didn't stop there. What about the check mark beside Fender's name? What about it? Audrey said. Well, what did it imply? Apart from the obvious—that the check mark appeared beside the only one of them currently missing—Audrey had no idea, which was exactly as helpful as it sounded. Still, Sarah had pressed on. How about Theo? What did he think? Dutifully, Audrey posited Theo's crooked landlord theory, and then sat in silent frustration as

Chris and Sarah both warmed to it. Why not? Apart from its undeniable plausibility, it didn't feature a psychopath in the lead role. Not that Sarah meant to belittle or discount what Audrey was going through. It was just that the whole saga remained at a healthy distance from her own life, and she meant to keep it that way. At the same time, she wanted to support Audrey (especially now, with her relationship crumbling around her), so she implored her old friend to stay with them as long as she wanted. It felt good to say it, noble even, and in all that magnanimity Sarah almost missed it when Audrey politely declined.

"But you can't go back to Bushwick right now," Sarah said, "no matter what's going on."

"I'm not," Audrey told her. "I've agreed to go on tour with the Westfields. I told Lucas Duff yesterday. I need to get out of the city, and the timing's perfect. We leave in a couple of days and won't be back for a month."

"Only you would take off with a rock band to clear your head," Sarah said, a bit relieved.

"What about Theo?" Chris asked.

"What about him?" Audrey answered.

Which was all she had to say on the subject.

Sarah was shocked. That Audrey and Theo could be done, just like that. At the same time, the words "I told you so" crossed her mind. But of course it wasn't that simple. Lying in bed later that night, Sarah had found herself reminiscing for the first time in years. She recalled the day she and Audrey met, the very moment, that fortuitous collision at second base, followed by a torrent of other moments, each singular and electric, pulsing with life. But paradise has an expiration date—a fact only Sarah understood. She'd gotten out while Audrey had stayed. And that had been her friend's undoing. How strange to journey through life knowing where the road *not* taken leads as well. Because that's what Audrey and Theo were. Her counterbalance. Her could-have-been. How could she look at them and not see her own relationship reflected back? She used to wonder if she'd miscalculated. What if—and God, it sounded so cloying—but what if true love really *could* conquer all?

The possibility challenged the Theory of Rationality that lay at the very center of her life, and in that way, had been too much to bear. So Sarah had disengaged, cast her best friend adrift out of nothing more than spite. Worse, it had taken Audrey and Theo's implosion for Sarah to admit any of this to herself. How small she's been. How petty. For the first time, it occurs to her that she should apologize. "For what?" Audrey would say. Well, for abandoning her, for starters. And not just recently, but before, in the aftermath of the assault, when Audrey had truly needed her. Because that's when Sarah's hypocrisy had begun. She'd used Audrey's sordid actions—and yes, they were sordid—as a wedge to separate herself from her own past, even though it was exactly that past that Chris had been attracted to. The scuffling authenticity of her former Brooklyn self.

What is "K" if not proof?

"So what the hell happened this afternoon?" Chris says, loosening his tie. They've migrated to the living room, which feels odd, as they only ever use it to entertain. Still, it fits the mood. The gravity of leather, the secrecy of lamps. Somehow, Chris and Sarah have ended up in club chairs, with Audrey across the coffee table on the couch. It's a bit inquisition-like, but it's too late to switch. Anyway, Sarah's the one in the hot seat. She looks from Chris to Audrey and back again.

"I'm not completely sure," she says, choosing her words carefully. "I was at Atlantic Grill for lunch with a few coworkers, and there was some prosecco involved, and when I got back to the office it was close to three and I was a little tipsy." Sarah pauses, waiting for the inevitable comment from Chris, but nothing comes. He's just sitting there, lips pursed, frowning. "So I'm walking back to my desk when Elise, our completely hopeless receptionist, hands me a sealed envelope with my name on it. 'SARAH F' in all caps. I figured it was an invitation, or a thank-you note from a client, so I tossed it onto my desk and forgot about it. And then it was six thirty and I was getting ready to leave and there it was, still sitting there, so I ripped it open and, well . . ."

She digs into the front pocket of her pants and produces the envelope, from which she removes a single folded page. She smooths it out on the coffee table and Chris and Audrey edge forward to read it:

DEAR SARAH,
  YOU MUST BE OUT AT LUNCH. I'M SORRY WE MISSED EACH OTHER. I'LL TRACK YOU DOWN <u>SOON</u>.
YOURS,
M.

For a moment, no one speaks. Audrey picks up the note, her eyes going over the words again and again. Then she drops it on the table and falls back into the couch with her head in her hands. Sarah waits for her to say something, but she doesn't. Finally, Chris breaks the silence:

"Did anyone see who dropped it off?"

Sarah shakes her head. "I caught Elise just as she was leaving, and she said she barely remembered *giving* me the envelope, let alone receiving it. Which is about what I expected."

"What about cameras?" Chris says.

"What about them?"

"They must be everywhere with all that art around."

"Of course. But I wasn't about to go down to security and ask to watch footage because someone left me an innocuous note while I was out drinking at lunch."

"It doesn't sound like you think it's innocuous," Chris says.

"I don't know *what* the hell it is," Sarah responds. And she means it. In the hours since she opened the envelope, she's considered any number of possible explanations, including the most obvious: people with that initial who may have actually been looking for her. Melissa Saunders down in catalog production. Max Eastland in collectibles. Even the elusive "Mr. Gable." Could the object of her auction-night flirtation have swung by? Does his real name start with "M"? She has no idea.

"Anyway," she says, peering over at Audrey, "I wouldn't have thought twice about the note if you hadn't told us all that stuff two nights ago.

But Cafferty was still fresh on my mind, and I saw the 'M' and . . . I'm sorry, it's probably nothing."

Audrey's head is down. For a moment everyone is quiet, then Audrey slowly brushes her hair aside, like she's opening a curtain, and looks up. "It's not nothing," she says quietly. "It's him."

The change that's come over her face—her color drained, her eyes turned dull, glassy. Sarah moves deeper into her chair.

"Let's not jump to conclusions," Chris says. "It could be anyone. A friend. A client. Hon, you should go through your phone contacts, see if anyone pops out at you."

For a moment, Sarah thinks this is some oblique reference to "K," a private admission of guilt. But then she realizes it's not. He's just that oblivious. She almost admires him for it.

Chris leans forward, rereads the note on the table. "This is definitely odd, but it's not evidence of anything."

"It's not?" Audrey says. "Look again."

Chris picks up the page, makes a show of studying it.

"I don't—"

"It's typed!" Audrey cries. "Don't you get it? It wasn't written in the moment. It was written in *advance*. By someone who knew Sarah would be at lunch. Someone who . . ."

"What?" Sarah says.

"Who's been watching you."

Sarah puts her hands over her mouth, curls her legs up under herself.

"And it's in all caps," Audrey continues, "just like the list of names on the desk. And just like the note he put in the red bag with the money all those years ago."

Now it's Chris's turn to blanch. He pulls at his thick hair, leaves it standing in a messy clump. "How do you remember that?" he says.

"How do you *not*?" Audrey leans forward, points at the page on the table. "Look at the word 'soon,' how it's underlined. He underlined words in the other note, too. When he said he'd find us. That it'd be our turn to pay."

Sarah shivers involuntarily. She'd needed proof and here it was. Irrefutable, even to her. And just like that, the language she's been speaking with such fluent certainty, of condescension, non-belief, becomes a different thing entirely—stronger and more terrible. As the seconds pass and their new reality sets in, a sense of dread descends on the room—like someone's siphoning away the air. She's about to acknowledge as much, just say how scared she is, but finds herself suddenly overwhelmed by another emotion entirely, an intense warmth she recognizes as intimacy. Whatever's going on, at least the three of them are in it together. For the first time in years, she feels alive to the world. She wants to reach out and hold both of them, right now, in this moment of moments. But she chooses only one. Without a word, she stands and makes her way around the table to the couch. Audrey throws a pillow aside and Sarah sits, the two of them close, almost touching. Then Sarah puts an arm around her and they are.

Chris clears his throat. "So what do you think he wants?" he says.

The rationality of the question catches Sarah off guard. She hasn't thought past accepting the threat as real. But Audrey clearly has. Her eyes come alive, like she's found the battle she's been looking for, and maybe the army, too.

"I'm not sure," she says, "but it has something to do with Fender. I just know it."

"I need a drink," Chris says, eyeing the wine bottle they somehow left on the kitchen counter. But no one makes a move for it.

"What if it *is* Fender?" Sarah says. "Maybe he's trying to freak us out for some reason."

Chris shakes his head. "That doesn't make sense."

"Then, what does? Why, after all these years, would Martin Cafferty risk everything in his life to come after us? Knowing what we know about him? What he did? It's not like we shook him down for a million bucks. What's changed?"

Chris gets up, walks across the living room, then turns around and comes back. "There's something I need to tell you," he says tentatively.

He's standing behind the chair he was just sitting in, like it's a shield. "I know someone who works at Longstream Capital, so I asked him what he knew about Cafferty. Turns out his wife left him last spring. Took the kids, too."

Audrey groans painfully.

"It gets worse. He was fired in August. His entire department was laid off."

"I don't understand," Sarah says. "You just decided to play private investigator without telling us?"

"I didn't just decide." Chris pauses, then looks at Audrey. "Theo asked me to."

"*Theo?*" Audrey says, like she's never heard the name before. "When? He doesn't even believe any of this."

"This past Monday. He called and asked if I could look into it. So I found out what I could, then met up with him on Tuesday—before your fight on the roof, I guess. I'm sorry, I would have mentioned it, but he asked me to keep it a secret. He didn't want to upset you more than you already were."

"Where is he now?" Sarah asks. "Not still out in Bushwick, I hope."

"He texted yesterday to tell me he was driving up to visit his brother," Audrey says. "I didn't respond. I can't talk to him right now."

"Don't you think he should know what's going on?" Chris asks, retaking his seat.

"Why? It's not like Cafferty's after *him*. As far as I'm concerned, he can stay in Massachusetts for—hang on." Audrey's pocket is vibrating. She takes her phone out and checks the number.

"Who is it?" Sarah asks, leaning over.

Audrey frowns. "I'm not sure. Someone in Brooklyn."

"You should answer it," Chris says.

Audrey presses Talk, says, "Hello?"

"*I was hoping it was Theo,*" Sarah whispers to Chris, but Audrey puts a hand up.

"Yes, Officer Renzo. Of course I remember. How are you?"

Chapter Fifteen

"That's a bad beat!"

Carl slams the edge of the blackjack table and his chips, or what's left of them, go airborne. The dealer, a stone-faced Asian woman, rakes up his bet and Carl immediately places another—$15, the table minimum.

"Why was it a bad beat?" Theo asks from over his brother's right shoulder.

"Because I should have won! I split my nines against a seven, which is exactly what the book says to do. Then she deals me a face on each nine, and before I can even start celebrating, she turns an eight and a five for twenty. *Twenty!* Which even you can figure out beats a nineteen."

"*Two* nineteens."

"Fuck you."

Carl counts his meager stack, sliding the chips through his fingers the way the poker players do on ESPN. Behind him, Theo consults the laminated Blackjack Strategy card his brother had handed him earlier. A pair of nines against a dealer's seven. He scans the columns, across and then down, and arrives at a red "S"—for "stand," not "split." He shakes his head and slips the card back in his pocket. He knows better than to correct his brother just now. Just ever.

"Forty-five fucking dollars," Carl announces. He'd had ten times that amount when Theo arrived, two hours ago. The cards in that brief but heady period had been so compliant that even Theo joined in the fun, taking a seat beside his brother and changing in three wrinkled twenties. He'd lasted exactly six minutes, or four hands, depending on how one counted. Loss. Loss. Loss. Loss. Worse, he'd infected Carl, who commenced his own losing streak at exactly the same time. Other players would join the table, only to sense the vibe and quickly depart. But Carl had dug in, placing bet after ill-fated bet, until he was the last player left—a designation he still holds.

Carl unzips his blue Adidas tracksuit, takes a loud slurp of his empty Jack and Coke, and looks around the blackjack pit. "Fuckin' bait and switch," he announces. "You people promise free drinks at the tables, but there's never any waitresses."

The dealer doesn't respond. She tosses out cards. A nine and a four to Carl, a king to herself. Carl taps the table, but before she obliges, she checks her undercard in the electronic mirror. The light turns red. "Blackjack," she announces, and flips an ace.

"Look at that Chinese shit," Carl says, and Theo cringes.

She's the second dealer of the night. The first, a gregarious older black man, had been at the helm during Carl's winning streak, and Carl, not surprisingly, had sung his praises. "They're the best," he'd told Theo in a stage whisper (the "they" apparently referring to African Americans), and Theo, in a real whisper, had asked why. "You seriously don't know? Black dealers are always good luck, whites can go either way, and Asians, forget it, they're assassins. Especially the chicks. If they come in midgame, find another table." "What about Native Americans?" Theo had asked, horrified by the conversation, but also curious, since they were at an "Indian casino." "Dude, that's funny," Carl responded. "Let me know when you see one."

Why, then, had Carl not followed his own juvenile advice and cashed out when the "assassin" appeared? Theo does have to admit: the table had turned immediately upon her arrival. He looks around at other dealers, other games. From where he stands, the casino floor appears endless, the long rows of blackjack and pai gow and three-card poker tables surrounded by complicated digital slot machines he hasn't the slightest idea how to play. The ones he remembers had pull handles that produced a simple, if never quite winning, combination of red cherries or lucky sevens. When had they morphed into movie-themed HD screens with wailing sirens and multilevel windows promising "twenty-five ways to win"? Technology, he thinks: it's like a friend you increasingly grow apart from, until you realize you've been off his Christmas list for years.

"Screw it," Carl announces, and Theo turns back to see his brother pushing the entirety of his meager stack forward. "Can't get rich betting the minimum all night."

For the sake of expediency, Theo doesn't disagree. How this drama will resolve itself is no longer in question, so the faster, the better. He hasn't come all this way to stand around a blackjack table; he's come to talk, brother to brother. And so he watches, dispassionately, as the cards are dealt, a queen to Carl, a seven to the dealer, a jack to Carl . . . and before Theo can even calculate his brother's high odds of winning, the dealer turns over a second seven, and then a third, for twenty-one. Carl stares at the woman as she sweeps up his chips, and for the first time, she meets his gaze.

"Don't," Theo says.

"Don't what."

"Say whatever you're about to say."

But it's the dealer who speaks first: "No more play. You're too angry."

Theo had arrived at Foxwoods via Greyhound from the Port Authority, a two-and-a-half-hour car trip that by bus had taken five, courtesy of several stopovers in the poorer localities of coastal Connecticut. Each station had produced a handful of drifters and degenerates, but it wasn't until New London that Theo gained a seat partner—a mephitic octogenarian who whacked Theo with his cane as he slumped down beside him. Oblivious, the man began thumbing through a stack of rubber-banded coupons. "All from this week," he announced proudly, and Theo, supposing he was the intended audience, had asked what he meant. What followed was a detailed lecture on the shadowy world of casino bus freebies. With the purchase of a return ticket, each Greyhound passenger received an all-you-can-eat grand buffet coupon and a $15 credit for the slots. The freebies, the man explained, were the only reason most of the passengers were on the bus at all. "Ten hours round-trip for a free meal and a few pulls of the lever?" Theo asked, surprised. "Ten hours in a warm bus," came the wary response, and Theo's face reddened in shame.

He'd needed to get out of the loft. The neighborhood. The city. If Audrey was right, he was placing himself in real danger by remaining in Bushwick, but to Theo's mind the greater problem was the loft itself, that relentless reminder of their life together—and now apart. But where could he go? To whom could he talk? The leading candidates, flawed though they might be, were currently unavailable, courtesy of Audrey's beating Theo to their door. He'd tried to think of other New York friends or (former) coworkers, but in the throes of an all-consuming love he'd drifted too far from those few he'd once considered close. Besides, who could possibly understand the overwhelming nature of the crisis he now faced? Personal. Professional. Possibly criminal. It was this last component that had made Theo think of his brother. But Carl, while well acquainted with failure, was hardly known for his sympathetic ear. Anyway, he was impossible to get ahold of.

Including Carl's no-show at Jamie's funeral, it had now been three and a half years since Theo had last laid eyes on his brother, the night of that Westfield Brothers concert at Webster Hall. The night that changed his life. It was like some magic baton had been handed over—from his dreary past to his golden future—as Carl left and Audrey appeared, an inked-up apparition. Theo had tried his best to stay in touch since then, periodically inviting Carl down to Brooklyn, but it had all been in vain. His brother had never met Audrey face-to-face, a fact most people would associate with estrangement. Except Theo didn't feel particularly estranged from Carl, because distance, both physical and emotional, was baked into the Gorski psyche. Still, months, and then years, had rolled by. There was only so much reaching out a person could do—even a brother. But this time was different. Theo would come to Carl. The morning after Audrey's hasty departure, Theo started badgering his brother with texts and voice mails, but they all went unanswered. So Theo changed tactics and messaged Carl once more, saying he'd reserved a car and was driving up to Lawrence the next day no matter what. This, finally, elicited a response:

> CARL: hve fun I wontbe their
> THEO: When won't you be there?
> CARL: wenever your coming
> THEO: Have you gone somewhere? Boston?

Theo waited more than two hours for a reply.

> CARL: u just shoudnt come home, sucks up here
> CARL: if u realy wnt to meet ill be at Foxwoods tomrw nite
> THEO: The casino?
> CARL: no the wood with foxes in it dumbass

Theo thought about it. A casino was better than nothing. He hadn't been aware that his brother had started gambling, but in the upside-down logic of Gorski World, he hoped it might be a positive sign—that Carl's new habit had replaced a far more toxic one. If Theo had to speculate (and he did), his guess was that Carl had flirted with heroin, both using and dealing, but had managed to quit before he got in too deep. Maybe Jamie Juarez's overdose had opened his eyes. Maybe the Lawrence smack scene was too hard-core. Or maybe Carl just hadn't been desperate enough. So where was he getting the money to gamble? Dealing weed, probably. A safer felony, not that Theo approved. On the contrary, perhaps he could confront Carl—get him to come clean, then *go* clean. Some real good could come of this. Sure, Theo had issues, but so did Carl, and it was high time Theo stepped in to help. He'd been missing from his brother's life for too long.

They're walking through a pavilion of apparel shops and gaudy jewelry stores, ostensibly looking for food, though another casino floor looms up ahead. Theo knows Carl isn't done for the night. Being banned from one blackjack pit doesn't mean he's banned from them all. At the same time, even Carl seems to recognize he needs a break, and when they spot a Fuddruckers, he suggests they grab a table.

"You're kidding," Theo says.

"What, you only eat sushi now?"

"No, it's just—"

"You city fuck."

It's just that Fuddruckers was where they'd gone as kids, on the rare occasions when their father took them out to eat. Birthdays and . . . birthdays. The restaurant, located in a strip mall near the AT&T plant, was imprinted in Theo's memory—its root beer floats and kitschy décor, all checkered and vinyl. That Theo, aged eleven, understood Fuddruckers wasn't quite real, that it was trading on nostalgia, spoke to a budding discomfort with the inauthentic, even then. So why the sudden yearning as he eyes the loud and cheesy logo: FUDDRUCKERS: WORLD'S GREATEST HAMBURGERS. Does he actually miss those awful nights?

"Nostalgia." He knows its roots. "Nostos": homecoming. "Algos": pain.

The brothers order at the counter—the same thing: burgers and floats—and after paying are handed an electronic food pager and led to a booth by a hostess with a smile that suggests employee surveillance. They slide in on opposite sides, and Theo gives the wall photos a cursory glance. Elvis, James Dean, Marilyn Monroe: the three he would have guessed. He turns to assess the dining room—the busboys near the service stand, the cooks in the open kitchen. "It's not just the casino," he says. "There aren't any Native Americans anywhere."

"Seriously?" Carl says. "Didn't we already discuss this? The only Indians around here are the wax ones in the fucking diorama by the entrance."

"But I thought the whole point of casinos on tribal land was to spur job creation."

"'Tribal land'? Christ, you make it sound like Apache country in New Mexico."

"They're mostly in Arizona."

"You're a dipshit. The *Pee*-quots, or whatever this tribe calls itself, only have a few hundred members, so they quite wisely said fuck it and handed the reins to a gaming company in exchange for yearly payouts. Now they all drive BMWs and hire contractors to renovate their ten-room teepees. And I bet they still bitch about the white man stealing everything."

"Okay, Dad."

"I'm just saying."

When had Carl gone all in with this racist victimhood crap? Was this what unemployment did? Or was his ex-girlfriend Carly to blame? Certainly, Carl had been the victim there. Theo wants to ask about her. Is she still with the MMA fighter? Does Carl ever see her kids? Hell, is he even dating again? There's so much he doesn't know, and not just about his brother. How's their father's health? Their mother's sanity? What if something serious were to happen to one of them? He and Carl should discuss contingencies. Senior centers and elder care. All these questions, the reflexive guilt of the prodigal son. But Theo isn't a prodigal son. He hasn't wasted all these years away from home—has he?

"Here you go, sweeties! Two root beer floats." They look up in unison to find an impossibly chipper waitress grinning down at them. She's older, late sixties, maybe. Striped apron, name tag, the whole deal. She places the whipped-cream-covered floats on the table with practiced ceremony. "Straws are right there next to the ketchup." She turns to leave them be. The two brothers look over at the plastic container.

"Be my guest," Theo says.

Carl pulls up the top, and the straws fan out like umbrella spokes. He chooses one—*one*—and plunges it into his drink, like he's planting a flag on the moon.

Theo shakes his head and grabs his own.

"So tell me what we're doing here?" Carl says, looking around the restaurant.

"Hanging out."

"I mean, what *you're* doing here. Why do you suddenly need to see me so bad?"

"Because you're my brother and it's been way too long." Theo stretches his back and shifts uncomfortably in his seat. "And, fine, I've been worried about you. Since that whole thing at Jamie's funeral."

"Bullshit."

"What do you mean, 'bullshit'?"

"I mean I don't believe you. First of all, you look like you haven't slept in a week. Seriously, you're pale as fuck. And second, we've been together all night and you haven't pulled any of your usual crap, inviting me down to Brooklyn, telling me how much Audrey wants to meet me. In fact, you've barely said a word."

"We've been gambling."

"You can talk at the tables, if you haven't noticed."

Theo has. He puts a hand to his forehead, not sure what he's checking for—a fever or a chill. Does he really look that bad? It's true, he hasn't slept more than a few fitful hours since that scene on the roof two nights ago. But Foxwoods has worked its gaming magic, pumping in enough oxygen that he's started to feel human again. He takes a long sip of his float, then stirs it with the straw.

"Audrey and I have been having issues."

"Welcome to the world."

"Gee, thanks, Carl. You're just teeming with compassion. Ever thought of being a shrink?"

"A what?"

"A psych—"

"I'm *kidding*. Jesus Christ." Carl leans back in the booth. "How bad is it?"

Theo rotates his head in a circle, like it's become too heavy even for *his* body. He's envisioned this moment, almost hoped for it—that his brother might care so much—but that doesn't mean he feels comfortable. He's such a private person. Or is "proud" a better word? He remembers Audrey asking him once how he could be so stubborn and sensitive at the same time. At moments like this he burns with that tension. *Behold the stunted lives of men.* Another opening line to run past her. Except that game was over.

"Hey," Carl says, and kicks him under the table. "You okay?"

"I'm supposed to be asking you that question," Theo responds gamely. But he's close to tearing up. Is it possible to experience the tug of intimacy, of *evolution*, with only the most cursory of real-world connections to support it? But whose fault is that? How frustrated he'd always become when Carl canceled plans to visit him in New York. And yet, Theo's the one who did the abandoning—left his brother all alone on the front lines of dysfunction. He wants to acknowledge as much, but he doesn't know how. They speak different languages now. They barely speak at all.

Still, he needs to try. Explain what's happened. Open up and be vulnerable. Maybe Carl will return the favor. Theo clears his throat. "So there's this guy named Fender—"

The food pager erupts, blinking red, startling them both. Carl tries to turn it off, then flings it at Theo. "You deal with it, I'll get the burgers." Theo watches him stomp off, before catching the waitress's eye. She bustles over, tray on shoulder, and Theo hands her the pager.

"He was supposed to take this with him," she says jovially, "but it's okay, I'll take it. Does your brother know there're fixins at the Fixins Bar?"

"I think so," Theo says as the device goes silent in her hand. How'd she do that, he wants to ask, but it's a very different question that comes out. "How'd you know he was my brother? We look nothing alike."

"Oh, I can tell," she says with a wink.

Theo watches her move on to the next table, feeling like he's just been exposed. But for what? Being *related*? There it is: the word that never ends. What does he owe his brother? How much should he tell him? Carl will be the first person not named Audrey that he's opened up to since . . . Ms. Jansen? Is that possible? Certainly he's never been to a shrink, having decided long ago that the profession, in its nonclinical iterations, offered little more than a permissible forum for self-indulgence. Audrey's never been in therapy either, but her reasons, as usual, were simpler, and more sensible. "That's what you're for," she'd said the one time he inquired, and Theo, thrilled, had never brought it up again. Now, though, he understands the faulty logic of these buried-head approaches, how they'd fostered a kind of insular drift that—

"Don't tell me she's banging him," Carl says, returning with two burgers and, yes, a pile of "fixins." He slides the tray onto the table, then sits back down and rubs his hands together.

Theo frowns. "What are you talking about?"

"You said there was some dude."

"Fender? No, no, it's not like that. He was more of a *catalyst*, I guess you could say, an old friend of Audrey's who fell on hard times and killed himself a few weeks ago, jumped off a bridge apparently." He watches as Carl loads up his burger, and then, as if Theo never mentioned someone dying, takes an enormous first bite, smearing juice all over his face. Theo finds it strangely calming—that in all these years his brother has changed so little. As Carl looks around for napkins they don't have, Theo stares across the restaurant floor and hears himself begin to speak, self-consciously at first, and then, as he warms to the tragedy of his tale, more freely. He starts with the fateful after-party, when Lucas Duff first uttered Fender's name, then moves on to the Win Groom meeting that never was, followed by the termination of his employment. He describes the break-in, and how he rushed, adrenaline fueled, into his bedroom with the splintered arm of a coatrack at the ready, and then all that followed—the questions, the silences, the unspoken accusations, everything leading eventually, inevitably, to the Letter. At some point, as Theo pauses to take a sip of his melted float, he sees that Carl has not only stopped eating but is sitting dead still, as if in shock. But Theo's on a roll now, so he presses on, from the substance of the letter to its fallout—the drugs in the dungeon; the argument on the roof—and what strikes him, as his story unfolds, is the surprising speed with which his failures have multiplied, his life collapsed. To think it all grew from a single rumor, a distracted aside: a mysterious death in the night. How has it come to this?

When Theo finally goes quiet, Carl slowly shakes his head. "You used to be so boring. What the fuck happened?"

Theo laughs ruefully.

"To say nothing of Audrey," Carl continues. "I knew she wasn't puritanical like your sorry ass, but prostitution and blackmail? Damn."

"I'm not sure 'prostitution' is the right word."

"No, the right word is 'moron,' and the right person is *you*. Seriously. I don't understand. What's she done that's so wrong?"

"You just said it yourself."

"I wasn't judging. I was impressed."

Theo senses the uselessness of any argument he might make concerning immorality. How can he explain his innermost thoughts to a man with no inner life? Still, maybe Carl has a point. What *has* Audrey done that's so wrong? While it makes him physically ill to think about the sexual components of the saga—both willful and forced—enough time has passed that Theo can comprehend how they came to occur. Audrey was just trying to survive. How can he fault her for that? And yet he has. Again and again over the last two days, he's replayed that scene on the roof. What he said. And what she did. About empathy. About trust. Of course she'd been right: though he'd like to think otherwise, he couldn't have handled the truth of her past. Not before. But what about now? *Yes.* Without question. But does it matter anymore? Martin Cafferty has broken them.

"I don't understand," Carl says. "How could you just let her storm off like that?"

"It all happened so fast. Also, I was upset. And frustrated. There was a perfectly reasonable explanation for the break-in, but she wouldn't even listen to it. She was so convinced it was Cafferty. And I'm sorry, but I can't be a party to a conspiracy theory. That this guy, evil as he might be, is out there lurking in the urban weeds, waiting to strike. Or strike *again*. It strains credulity."

"It strains what?"

"It doesn't make sense. But there's no reasoning with her. It's like this whole experience has exposed differences that we've been glossing—"

"*Differences?* I'll tell you what the difference is: you're a bonehead and she's not. So she has an interesting past. So she's got an independent streak. I'd *die* for a chick like that. I may not know her, but I unfortunately know you, and let me just say that you were sleepwalking until she came along. You were buried so deep in your own thick skull I'm surprised you could lift it off the pillow in the morning. Seriously. She's smart, she's hot, she's wicked cool, and though I can't understand why, she appears to be in love with you. Who cares if she thinks someone's after her? Honestly, it doesn't seem far-fetched to me. The guy got taken real good. Why *wouldn't* an asshole like that want revenge?" Carl shakes his head, exasperated. "And what about those names on the desk? You think the wind blew them there? That they got caught in an updraft, then nailed a perfect landing?"

"That's not exactly what—"

"I've got some news for you. Shit like this happens all the time in the real world. People lose their fucking minds. Hell, I've come close to losing mine. And that's not an invitation to get all therapist-y on me, so don't even try. Why don't you focus on eating your burger. I've got to take a leak." With that he gets up, adjusts his crotch, and heads for the bathrooms.

Theo slumps against the vinyl, defeated. He's supposed to be helping Carl, not the other way around. But his thoughts are turning spongy, his arguments doubling back on themselves. He can't get the question out of his head: *What's she done that's so wrong?* What if Audrey *is* perfect for him precisely because she's so evidently *not*? For so long they'd championed their dissimilarities. Why, then, are they suddenly straining against them, to the point where living together has become impossible? Because Audrey *is* his New York. The two have become inseparable, and if he can't make his relationship work, he can't make the city work. If only he could think more like his brother, in monosyllabic certainties. Hot. Wicked. Cool. But he can't. His mind turns his thoughts, tangling them, until everything is linked: Fender's disappearance, the demise of his relationship, the loss of his job, the end of erudite culture. That's what this really comes down to, isn't it? The city he'd first sought out no longer exists. Knowledge has lost the war against populism. Community has surrendered to the individual. Theo can't stare up at buildings anymore because he'll run into someone staring down—texting or taking selfies. He can't stand screens. He hates advertising and self-promotion. He doesn't like the word "hero" or the appropriation of the military. He's averse to pill popping, artisanal chocolate, and *The Voice*. And he despises pension-swallowing "Indian" casinos. There was a time—he almost remembers it—when others railed against these things, too, the falseness of the American narrative. They said, "I can't believe Moby licensed that song to Volkswagen." They said, "Where are Paris Hilton's parents in all this?" Now such thinking is as old and out of touch as his own father. Leonard Gorski: that great totem of inflexibility. Theo hears echoes of the man every day, reminders of his misappropriated tantrums against everyone and everything—AT&T (though the company employed him for forty years), the Iraq War protesters (though he himself skipped Vietnam with "heel spurs"), or that nemesis of all nemeses, Michael Dukakis (though Leonard was a registered Democrat—at least back then). Theo had spent his youth steeped in his father's fury, only to grow up and find that the man was not behind the times but ahead of them, for millions had joined him, red faced and fists waving, their TVs tuned to the endless counternarratives of persuasive opportunists. It was inevitable that the country that invented branding would become a brand itself, a staged production, but what Theo doesn't understand is why he's the only one seemingly bothered or confused by this force-fed alternative reality. It's not a question of head-in-the-sand ignorance. People know what's happening. Hell, they're in on the joke: championing the Kardashians, letting their kids play football, questioning climate change. All that American ingenuity, that technological achievement, and what has it led to? The end of thought. Is it just him, or was this year—he hates the phrase but can't conjure a better one—the tipping point? 2011. The year cell phone screens became large enough to disappear into. The year idealism was stripped bare and proved lacking. He remembers Audrey's tears as they watched—online, because the networks didn't carry it—the final launch of the space shuttle, back in July ("It's *Atlantis*," she'd said, "you can tell from the markings"), and recalls, too, the sadness in the announcer's voice as he said everything except the most important thing: that America was done with men in space. With grand adventures. With dreams of something better. But that wasn't quite true. There'd been one more: Occupy. A last quixotic flame, extinguished by hoses in the night. Where, then, does this leave an unemployed and suddenly middle-aged man of letters? Right where he should be. At a Fuddruckers, just off the casino floor, telling his brother that he's tried and failed, in life and love, and now doesn't know what to do.

What the hell is Carl doing in the bathroom? If there's one truth Theo's learned from Audrey's crowd, it's that "taking a leak" rarely means taking a leak. He imagines his brother dumping a small mountain of powder onto a sink or the back of a toilet or wherever such mountains are dumped. Or maybe he's crushing up pills. Whatever keeps him awake for another session at the tables.

The restaurant's getting crowded. Theo looks toward the entrance and sees a line of people waiting to be seated—at one a.m. on a weeknight. Still, there's something freeing about the bustle, proof of a world outside New York, crowded and oblivious. Context changes everything, widens the lens of perspective. Only at a remove can he see the entirety of the city, the madness of the place, what it does to those who can't tame it. He was wrong. His life hadn't fallen apart all at once. It had been happening for years, a slow erosion, a rotting at the core. In Audrey's last text—a day and a half ago now—she'd told Theo she was heading out on tour, and he doesn't blame her. He'd take off, too, if he were her. But he's not, and anyway, he doesn't have a band, he has a brother. For whatever that's worth.

And here he finally is.

"You've barely touched your food," Carl says, assessing the table as he sits back down. "You want me to order you some tofu?"

He looks jumpy, but no more than usual. Maybe Theo can convince him to call it a night.

"Look, why don't we head up to your room? We can have a drink and catch the Bruins highlights. Please tell me you got two beds."

"I didn't get any beds," Carl says. "I didn't get a room."

"Why not?"

"Because they're three hundred bucks. And I don't need one. I play cards, and when I'm done, I drive home. If I'm too buzzed, I sleep in the truck awhile. Though they're cracking down on that. They've got rent-a-cops walking around looking through windows with flashlights."

"Well, *I'm* not sleeping in your truck."

"You're right. The only place you're sleeping is on the bus back to New York." Carl leans over the table, leveling his eyes on Theo with startling directness. "Listen to me. You need to fix this shit with Audrey."

"How? She's holed up with Chris and Sarah and won't answer my texts or calls. And I'm not going back to Bushwick."

"I thought you didn't believe in this Cafferty thing."

"I don't. I just can't be there without her. It's too hard."

Carl claps his hands together. "I've got an idea. Why don't you move back to Lawrence? I could use an assistant snow plower for all those storms that never come. Or maybe you could start a publishing house in one of the abandoned mills. Half the city reads the Help Wanteds every morning. You can turn them on to *literature* instead!"

"Carl—"

"Or how about coaching some football at the high school? Think of the headlines: *Golden Boy Returns*. Maybe you could do some college counseling on the side, work with that lady you were always going on about."

"She's not there anymore," Theo says.

"Of course not. There's no need for her. No one gets out of Lawrence—except you. Somehow, you fucking managed. Yet here you are, whining about life being so tough down there in the big city. You know where it's actually tough? *Where I live.* The wrong side of a dying town. But one thing gave me hope all these years, through all the bullshit with Dad and Carly and every other stupid thing. The fact that you weren't with me. That you'd escaped and made something of yourself. I never admitted it but I was so damn proud of you. Because you'd *earned* it. You were always so determined, so focused. I used to sit there at Marco's—back when I still went out—and blather on and on about the books you were publishing. Not that I'd read any of them because they all looked terrible, but the point was you were out there *doing it*, bringing things to life. And when was the last time a Gorski man could say that about anything except AT&T transmission equipment?"

Theo feels the tears. He tries to hide them with his shirtsleeve, but Carl's still staring straight at him, so he finally gives up and lets them flow.

"You never told me any of that," Theo says, grinning sadly.

"Like you're God's gift to communication," Carl says. But his eyes are going glassy, too. "What I'm saying is that you better not give up now. All that shit our family's made of, the mud and wires and poured concrete, the fucking factory floor, remember that side of you, where you came from, how tough you are. And I'm not talking about the football field. I'm talking about *life*. Your girl's in trouble? Then get your ass back down there and help her. I don't care if you believe this Cafferty asshole has reappeared. Audrey does, and that's all that matters. *Do something*, Theo. Fight for her while you still can."

The words take a moment to penetrate, so weighty are they, and unexpected, and true. Theo grasps at something coherent to say, a response worthy of the moment, but he's never been good at that. Anyway, Carl's grabbing his coat and squeezing out of the booth. *Wait*, Theo wants to say, but he doesn't. There's no reason. Carl stretches, then turns, puts an arm out. Theo grabs it and pulls himself up. "Thanks," he says.

They make their way out to the concourse, side by side, as that song "Pumped Up Kicks" wafts down from above. Theo smiles, remembering how much Audrey hates it.

"I'm heading back to the tables," Carl says.

"I figured."

"I think the buses run all night."

"Okay," Theo says. They slap hands and half hug.

"Listen to me," Carl continues. "I'm dead serious about Lawrence. Show your face up there and I'll have someone break your legs."

"What about Mom and Dad?"

"They're fine. I'm looking after them."

And who's looking after you? Theo knows the answer, just as he knows the futility of asking the question. Anyway, this is the old Carl standing before him now, the brother he grew up with, the one he followed everywhere, to the ballfields and corner stores, through the thousand secret doors of youth.

Carl takes a few steps toward the blackjack pits, then stops, turns around.

"One more thing. All this shit you told me tonight? *That's* the movie idea you've been looking for, you dumb fuck. Sitting right in front of your face. Sexy escorts, evil bankers, vigilante justice? I'd go see that shit in a heartbeat. If you and Audrey really are done, you should pitch it to that Win dude. He'll probably think it's great."

Chapter Sixteen

SARAH: only a police station would hve no seats in the waiting area

AUDREY: i know srry

SARAH: and nthing to read but WANTED posters, which lose there thrill after 30 mins

AUDREY: has it been tht long?

SARAH: almost 40

SARAH: also they hve framed photos of the police commish, the mayor and the governer, but Obama is mysteriously mssing. hes been president for almost 3 yrs. im gonna complain to the receptionist.

AUDREY: oh god dont she's an idiot. shes reading the same book as last time I was here

SARAH: maybe shes illitarate

SARAH: illiterate

SARAH: hah

SARAH: anyway I didn't mean to interrupt

AUDREY: yeah im super busy right now

SARAH: is it like the movies? a cinderblock room w a table in the middle?

AUDREY: yup. 2 chairs on one side, 1 on the other. btw im pretty
sure there fucking w me so this could take a while. u
totally dont have to stay

SARAH: thks but im totally going to

AUDREY: if u get bored, ask someone about my bike. it got stolen
from acrss the street

SARAH: hows that possible

AUDREY: hows any of this possible

Audrey hears footsteps in the hallway and puts down her phone, but whoever it is keeps walking. Has it really been forty minutes? She looks around the room. She's in Interview Two this time, which, unlike Interview One, has an ominous waist-high steel bar running the length of one wall and a rectangle of dark glass along another. She assumes people can watch her from behind it, but she has no idea. Nor does she care.

She rubs her eyes. She could nod off right here, in the world's most uncomfortable chair. She's been exhausted before—for most of her twenties—but what she's experiencing now goes deeper than a lack of sleep. It's more like a loss of hope, and her lifelong assumption that things would work out. Has there been any upside to these last weeks? Sarah, maybe. It had taken the sky falling in for her to rally to Audrey's side, but now that she has, she seems to truly mean it—to the point of insisting, over Audrey's objections, on accompanying her to the precinct this morning. "C'mon, the two of us back in the borough—it'll be fun," she'd said, and while Audrey doubted that, she appreciated the deeper sentiment and finally relented.

They'd arrived via the L, disembarking at Bedford Avenue as they had so many times in the past. But Audrey had been in no mood to reminisce. The previous evening had shaken her. The news that Cafferty had turned up at Sotheby's—and Audrey was certain he had—meant he could be anywhere. Several times on their journey from the Upper

East Side, Audrey had glanced furtively at men loitering on corners, leaning against subway poles. She'd even turned around once or twice, suddenly convinced he was following them. (Such was her distress that she was surprised when she *didn't* see him.) Anxiety was clouding her thoughts, constricting her lungs. That she was attempting to hide all of this from Sarah only made it worse, but what choice did she have? In the absence of Theo, she *needed* her best friend, and while their reconciliation was genuine, it was also tenuous and untested, and Audrey didn't want to drive her away.

This was her mind-set as they'd neared the top of the crowded station stairs. Audrey, having fallen behind amid a tangle of bodies exiting the turnstiles, was trying to catch up when she glimpsed Sarah several yards ahead, pulling at her collar, then digging her hands into the pockets of her Vuitton ruffle jacket. No one else would have noticed—it was such a small thing—but to Audrey it meant the world. That her old friend still remembered what was coming, after all these years. They emerged aboveground and the wind, funneling up from the river, hit them with a blast of cold air that might have knocked them backward had they not been ready. But they were ready. *This was their city, too.* The mantra materialized from nowhere, and as Audrey digested it, she experienced a surge of determination that felt a bit like courage. She stepped in front of Sarah and led her to the corner.

Bedford and North Seventh. They used to call it the center of the universe, back when their universe was only ten blocks long. The McCarren softball fields were just up the street, and Audrey had a fleeting urge to drag Sarah over there, despite the temperature. But the precinct was the other way, and this was no time for sightseeing—not that there was much to see these days. The neighborhood stalwarts were almost gone, replaced by eyewear shops and vegan pizzerias and angular glass condos, remarkable only in their ubiquity. But Audrey suddenly didn't care. As they started south down Bedford, she noticed a few old favorites, still hanging on against the odds—the Verb, Rosemary's, Spoonbill & Sugartown—and in a not-quite-unconscious nod to Theo, she started pointing them out. Soon the memories were washing over her, and entire blocks began to pass without her thinking about Cafferty. Sarah, too, appeared lost in reverie, and Audrey wondered if she might be experiencing some kind of closure. But that would suggest her years in Williamsburg were still an open and pending part of her, when in fact Audrey knew she'd moved on wholly and without regret. Moved on and moved up. Just two nights ago she'd referred to the monstrous new Gehry building near Chris's office as a *positive economic indicator*. Then again, two nights ago was like two years. So much was happening, yet somehow time had stopped.

They turned left at the municipal pool and were walking east on Metropolitan when Audrey spied the top of Fillmore Place off to her right. The curious block-long street with its century-old Italianate row houses and wrought iron balconies had long been Audrey's favorite, not least because it reminded her of the night she'd introduced Theo to Chris and Sarah. Audrey had planned the dinner—in the back garden of DuMont—so that her friends could get to know him, a rare enough event made downright bizarre when Chris and Sarah realized how different Theo was from Audrey's usual band-boy quarry. Afterward, as they ambled, like an album cover, four abreast up Fillmore, Theo had stopped, abruptly, and announced that he was quite sure the street they were on had been Henry Miller's favorite block, the one he'd described so beautifully in *Tropic of Capricorn*. Chris and Sarah glanced at each other, eyebrows raised. Audrey took Theo's arm, grinning like a lotto winner.

Now it was Sarah's arm she grabbed as she turned abruptly away from Fillmore Place. There were other ways to get where they were going. Soon, former haunts loomed in every direction. Trash Bar and Midway and Clem's. During particularly ambitious happy hours, Sarah and Audrey used to hit all three just to get warmed up, douse their lingering hangovers before facing the new night head-on. They crossed Grand, the onetime dividing line between Northside and South. Time to zip up your purse and pocket your phone—at least that used to be the rule. Now it was oyster bars and indie theaters and cocktail lounges with pint-sized patios. They stepped aside to let a posse of cackling girls in ripped tights and fake furs pass by. Where were the Puerto Rican corner dealers? The Italian toughs from Graham Avenue? Those girls wouldn't have made it three blocks back in the day.

"So what exactly did he say?" Sarah asked.

"Who?" Audrey said, momentarily confused.

"Detective What's-his-face. On the phone last night."

Audrey's shoulders sagged with the gravity of her pending reality. "He said he needed to speak to me, and could I come in ASAP."

"What do you think that means?"

"I don't know," Audrey said, more tersely than she meant to. "Probably some stupid administrative follow-up." The truth was she had no idea why Renzo wanted to see her again, though she could tell, from his manner on the phone, that something had happened. The detective had framed it as a request, a favor she'd be doing him, but it was obvious she had little choice but to comply. Which was worrying.

"You know you don't have to come all the way to the precinct," Audrey said. "You can find a coffee shop and I can meet you after."

"Don't be ridiculous," Sarah replied.

"But what if . . ." Audrey fought the temptation to glance back over her shoulder again. "What if this isn't just about Fender? What if Renzo somehow knows what we did?"

"Then we'll be saving him a trip to the city. He can have two for the price of one."

With that, Sarah reached over and interlaced her fingers with Audrey's like they used to years ago. Audrey, touched, squeezed her hand, and they walked wordlessly through the chilly Southside streets. Soon they came upon a familiar sight. There was no sign, just a neon red trophy glowing in a window.

Sarah stopped. "Do you know what we need?" she said.

"A shot?"

"Yup." She looked at her watch. "It's twelve fifteen. Doesn't Trophy open at noon?"

"How quickly we remember," Audrey said, and smiled for the first time all morning.

Sarah pulled open the door. "Come on, I'm buying. Officer Renzo can wait."

But it's Audrey who's been waiting, for nearly an hour now. What do they want with her? She still has no idea, so she's been trying to focus on other things. Like the Westfield Brothers tour. They fly out tomorrow night. First stop: Atlanta. Then rent a van and head to Florida, then Louisiana, then . . . she can't remember. Great. And she's the tour manager. Should she even go? After her argument with Theo on the roof three nights ago, she'd viewed the tour as a perfect escape, a chance to leave everything behind. The constant dread and looming danger. But after last night's Sotheby's revelation, followed by whatever this—

Her thoughts are interrupted by more footsteps in the hall. Two sets, paused now just outside the door. She hears the murmur of low voices, and then the door opens.

"Well, well," says Detective Renzo, striding into the room along with a second, younger officer, who closes the door behind them. "Let me introduce Detective Torres," Renzo says with faux grandiosity. "This is his case." Torres extends his hand and Audrey stands and shakes it. She recognizes him from her previous visit as the lone Hispanic detective in the squad room. He's dark skinned and square jawed, and were it not for his cop-fade haircut, he might be handsome. But Audrey's stuck on something else. She's wondering why this is a "case."

"Coffee?" Torres asks perfunctorily.

"No, thanks," Audrey says, and sits back down.

The detectives settle in across from her. Renzo glares at her phone on the table. "Those aren't allowed in here," he says. "You need to turn it off and put it away."

"Sorry." Audrey switches the phone to airplane mode and slips it in her jeans.

"We appreciate you coming in on such short notice," Torres says, more amiably. "I'm sure you're asking yourself what this is about."

"I can guess the general ballpark," Audrey replies.

Torres takes a small pad from his jacket pocket and frowns at it, like he's trying to figure out where to start, or how. Seconds pass. Maybe she should crack a joke to break the tension, but she can't think of anything even mildly amusing. Torres is still frowning, so she shifts her gaze to Renzo, who looks away. And that's when she figures it out.

Torres clears his throat. "I hate to be the one—"

"You found Fender," Audrey says flatly.

"Yes. Two days ago."

"Was he . . ."

"Deceased? I'm afraid he was. I'm sorry." Torres waits a practiced beat. "His body had washed up on the rocks near the Domino Sugar factory."

Audrey absorbs the news, unsure of what to say. She feels like everyone's been given a script except her. "Are you sure it was him?" she asks. "He never used to carry a wallet."

"And he still doesn't," Torres says.

"Didn't," Renzo says.

"Though it could have washed away," Torres continues. "Luckily, his prints were on file from a trafficking charge a couple years ago. Now, Detective Renzo here tells me you were friendly with the deceased, so if it's okay I'd—"

"Can you hold on a second?" Audrey says. She's feeling queasy. The shot of whiskey is sitting uneasily in her stomach. To think Lucas Duff had been right all along. Fender *was* dead. Here, finally, was the confirmation. She'd thought it would never come. She tries to consider the deeper ramifications but realizes she's missing the most pertinent information.

"How?" she says quietly.

"Excuse me?"

"How did he die?"

Torres leans forward, clasping his hands on the table. "Why don't you tell us."

"What does that mean?"

"It's a simple question," Renzo interjects.

Audrey frowns. "I have no idea. I assume he jumped off the bridge, if you found him along the shore. But I don't understand why you're asking me that."

"Because we think you know more about James than you're letting on," Torres says.

"Who's James?"

"The deceased."

"*Fender?*" Audrey says, confused.

"Yes. James Fender. You didn't know his first name?"

"No. He never . . . He was a mysterious guy. I told you that last time I was here. I told you everything last time I was here."

Torres looks at Renzo, who shrugs.

"Why don't you refresh our memories," Torres says.

Audrey sits up, trying to work out what's really going on. What is it they think she knows? What is it they *do* know? Torres is drumming his pen on his notepad, waiting. She needs to say something, so she clears her throat and starts talking, tells them the same barebones story as before: that an old friend had gone missing; that she heard a rumor he'd killed himself; and that, well, it looked like it was true.

"Did Mr. Fender have any enemies?" Torres asks, scribbling notes.

"Enemies? Not when I knew him. But then he got into dope, so who knows."

"Was he dealing?"

"Didn't you just say he got busted?"

"Yes, but was he a known guy on the street?"

"You're asking the wrong person," Audrey says, exasperated. "I hadn't seen him in years."

"Yet you were worried enough to stop by the precinct two weeks ago," Renzo says. "Mighty thoughtful."

"I already explained that," Audrey responds, shifting in her chair. She knows she's sounding defensive.

Torres looks at his pad. "Have you spoken with any other acquaintances of Mr. Fender's?"

"No. Like I said, we kind of grew apart, ended up in different circles."

"And the woman waiting out in reception. Who's she?"

"A friend. She was with me when you guys called last night, and wanted to come for support."

"Does she know the deceased?" Renzo asks.

"No."

Torres studies Audrey pensively. "So there's nothing else you can tell us? Nothing you might have heard since you were last here that might be pertinent to the case?"

"Why is it a *case* if he killed himself?" Audrey asks.

"Everybody's a case until they're not," says Renzo.

Everybody or every *body*? Are they screwing with her on purpose? She gazes past them, sees the steel bar on the wall and suddenly realizes what it's for. Restraints.

"Will one of you please tell me why I'm here?"

"Sure. Just as soon as you tell us why you're lying," Torres says calmly. He's staring directly at her. Audrey senses a shift in the room, everything slowing down. She tries to deaden her eyes to keep them from darting around.

"I'm not lying."

"You just stated that you haven't spoken with any of his acquaintances," Torres says.

"That's right."

He looks at his notes. "Does the name Nikki Verlaine mean anything to you?"

"No," Audrey says uncertainly.

"How about 'Nikki the manager of the underground club you purchased drugs at last Sunday night'? Maybe that rings a bell?"

"Not really."

"We know you went there, and we know why," Renzo interjects impatiently. "Ms. Verlaine sat in this very room yesterday and told us you approached her to ask about Mr. Fender."

Audrey starts to bite her lower lip but catches herself and stops.

"It's time to tell us the truth," Torres says.

"I went there for the same reason I first came here. I was trying to find out if he was still alive."

Torres sighs. "She said you were acting suspicious."

"It's an after-hours club. Who's *not* acting suspicious?"

"*Was* an after-hours club," Torres says.

"We shut it down," Renzo says smugly.

"Thanks, I got that."

"Okay, enough," Torres says brusquely. "Let me explain the situation how I see it, Ms. Benton. A body washes up. We ID it and start asking around, and just like you, we end up with the name of an ex-girlfriend. A familiar name, as it happens, since we'd been surveilling her little drug den for about a month. Seems she wasn't paying the meatpackers upstairs quite enough hush money, but that's a different story. What's pertinent here is that the moment we informed her she was facing more than a dozen narcotics charges, she was suddenly happy to talk about any subject that came to our minds. And your old pal was high on our list."

"But why?" Audrey says. "He killed himself. You said it earlier."

"No, *you* said it earlier." Torres stands up, walks slowly toward the dark glass mirror, then turns back around. "I know how he actually died, and so do you. I'm giving you one more chance—right now—to tell us what you know."

"I *am* telling you—"

"Who shot him?"

"*What?*"

"Who shot James Fender?"

"I don't—"

"Three times in the chest, once in the head."

Torres is back at the table, leaning over it, glaring at her. She can smell him. Cologne on top of something more permanently male. This is the only fact Audrey can process. That, and the mirror. She'd forgotten completely about it until Torres peered in that direction. Is someone on the other side? Watching all of this? Recording it? She understands, through some kind of American osmosis, that this is the moment she should ask for a lawyer. But of course she doesn't have one. She doesn't even know one. Anyway, wouldn't that be implying she's guilty? But of what? She's not a suspect, is she? The word stuns her. "Suspect." And so, too, its partner: "crime." There's only one explanation. Cafferty shot Fender. *Three times in the chest, once in the head.* Not just a murder: an assassination. Of course, it makes more sense than a suicide. She's known that all along. And yet, it still seems so unlikely. That kind of violence, so close. Connected to her. *Because* of her. She tries to imagine how it went down but can't. Did it even happen on the bridge? Hadn't Theo told her that was impossible? She can't remember now. Images. Faces. Fender and Cafferty. Theo and Sarah. Her life in black and white. And now this room, her physical reality, its own kind of cell. Renzo propped in his chair. Torres still in front of her, no longer leaning over, but standing, speaking again. Only a few seconds have passed, if she's counting time like that. It doesn't matter anymore.

". . . may be here awhile." This is what Torres just said. What came before it?

"I didn't hear you," she sputters.

"Which part?"

"All of it."

"Jesus Christ," Renzo barks. He pushes his chair out, too dramatically, and it grates against the floor with a piercing screech.

Torres shakes his head. "I said we'll give you some time alone to recollect your thoughts. We'll explain to your friend that you may be here awhile."

"She won't leave me."

"I don't know," Renzo says, stepping over to the door. "People get tired standing out there with nowhere to sit."

"But I don't have anything else to tell you!"

"Famous last words," Renzo says, and steps out into the hall.

Torres follows him but turns and lingers a moment in the doorway. "I really hope you're not mixed up in this," he says, his voice suddenly softer. "But if you are, we can help you. *I* can help you. I don't think you pulled the trigger, but I have a strong suspicion you know who did. So what I want you to do is think very hard about your next move, because this isn't a joke anymore. Do you understand?"

Like it was a joke before.

"We'll be back in a while," Torres continues. "I hope you've changed your tune by then."

Audrey looks away as the door closes. She hears his footsteps recede and then nothing, silence. Like they were never in the room. She slumps back in her chair. So much for defiance. It's like they can see through her—or Torres can, anyway. What's she doing? Why doesn't she just tell him everything? A fucking *murder*. He's right: it's real now. Beyond real. She can't believe it. Even as she'd intuitively suspected it, she presumed she'd be proven wrong. Yet here she is. Here they all are. She pictures their names sitting neatly on her desk, sees the check mark next to Fender. One down, three to go. Just like she told Theo. And what had he done? He'd laughed at her. No, he hadn't. He'd tried his best to believe her. It wasn't his fault; his mind just didn't work that way. He was too decent to process malevolence on such a scale. Too decent, and too naïve. She leans forward, puts her face in her hands. She can feel herself spiraling. She hasn't been alone in so long. All her life she's chafed against anything that might impede her freedom, and now what she misses most is dependence, companionship: him. Ah hell, she's crying. *Again.* She wipes her cheeks on her shirtsleeve and turns her chair away from the glass wall. She knows they're watching her. If there's one thing she still has, it's her instincts. She's been right about everything. Terribly so.

Where's Theo now? Still with his brother, probably. But when he comes back, he'll surely go to the loft. She needs to warn him. Warn them all. Cafferty knows who they are, where they live. So what's she waiting for? Just tell Torres. Give him the name. But she can't—not without giving him everything else. Chris and Sarah. Theo. He's part of this now, too. Which is to say, it's not just her story. It's not just her crime. Could Chris lose his job? Could Sarah? Could the three of them be prosecuted for extortion? If so, they need to decide as a group, as they had the first time. They'll be safe another night in Chris's doorman building. Right?

How long has she been in here? Is Sarah still waiting? She should check her phone. But what if they see her with it? No, she was texting Sarah earlier and no one said anything. And why would they? She hasn't been arrested or charged. Still, she's scared now, and vulnerable, all alone like this. Could they confiscate it? Everything's on there, her entire Brooklyn life. How, she wonders, has that life led her here? She looks around, but there's nothing to catch her eye, nothing not drab or colorless. She feels claustrophobic, helpless, like she's no longer in control. Is that the real problem? That she's lost the arc of her own narrative? Why does she equate confessing with conceding? She's not at war with Torres; in fact she almost admires him. Certainly, he's good at what he does. Maybe she can trust him. And yet, this isn't how it's supposed to go. She's always taken care of her own business. That's how she got this far. Eleven years in Brooklyn, mostly broke and struggling, but they've been *her* years, it's been *her* life. The thought buoys her, and she sits up straight. *This was their city, too.* She just needs a little time to think, figure out what she's doing. What *he's* doing. Cafferty. Try as she has to get inside his head, she still has no idea why he would come after them all these years later—even with his downturn in fortune. Maybe he's gone insane. Or . . . is it possible he *didn't* shoot Fender? Could the murder be unrelated to the break-in? To the Sotheby's note? Fender was desperate and dealing drugs; anyone might have killed him. Could the events of these past weeks each carry their own explanation? Certainly, the break-in could. Theo said it himself: it was the landlord. Oh, not right now. God, *this room*. Every minute she's in here is a minute Torres is winning. But what can she do? She could walk over and bang on the glass. Or she could . . . she turns and looks at the door. *Could she just walk out?* It's not locked. She didn't hear a click when they left. She goes back through what Torres said. That he doesn't believe she did it. So does he really think she knows who did, or are they questioning her because they have a murder on their hands and no other leads? If that's the case, why is she still sitting here? Just get up and leave, and if they stop you, demand to speak to a lawyer. Chris must know one.

She stands up, walks to the door, pulls it open. Nothing happens. No alarms go off. Reception is twenty feet away. She turns back to the glass mirror, stares straight at it, through it. And then she steps out into the hall. The door slams swiftly behind her, the noise briefly startling her, and she hurries the small distance to the lobby. One last door. She holds her breath and pulls it open, and just that easily—is it possible?—she's free.

She peers through the milling crowd of officers and citizens, everyone moving at bureaucratic half speed. Where's Sarah? Has she left? Or—why didn't she think of this earlier—are the cops questioning her now? Shit. Audrey pulls out her phone, turns off airplane mode, and starts typing before she even gets a signal. To Sarah: *Where are u!!??* And then Theo: *If ur back in BK be careful!! Cafferty SHOT Fender, the cops just fnd his body! Let me no ur safe please!* She presses Send.

Her phone vibrates, Sarah responding: *outside on the steps, couldnt handle it in there.* Thank God. Audrey weaves her way to the front doors and pushes them open, as her phone, still in her hand, begins buzzing with other calls and texts she's missed. Sarah is leaning against a wall near the sidewalk, and Audrey rushes over to her. They embrace, tightly, neither letting go.

"What the hell was going on in there?" Sarah asks. "Did you turn your phone off?" She cups Audrey's face in her hands. "You don't look good. Are you okay?"

"I'm fine, I'm fine," Audrey says. "I couldn't—something's happened. Let's get out of here, find a place to talk." They start walking. She glances at her screen. The texts are still coming: two from Chris; five from Sarah; one from Arthur Westfield. And now the calls: Lucas Duff; Ed Beemis; Sarah; Lucas again. Finally, her phone goes quiet and she slips it back in her pocket. She'll deal with everything later. She turns to tell Sarah they should grab a cab back to the city, but her phone starts up again. Another call. Probably Lucas—for the third time—with some tour-related emergency. *The tour.* The words are like a distant memory. Of course she can't go. Won't go. She'd be running away. Abandoning her friends. She needs to tell the band, but not now. She pulls her phone out to silence Lucas's call, but it's a different name she sees on the screen. She stops walking, presses Talk.

"Hello?"

"Audrey, it's Ed Beemis," says Ed Beemis.

The connection is terrible, as it usually is when one party is in Cape Canaveral.

"Hey," Audrey half shouts. "Everything okay? Do you mind if I call you back a bit later?"

"What was that? I can barely hear ya, honey."

"I said, can I call you back in a little while?"

"Audrey, you're breaking up. Is there somewhere . . . I've been trying to reach you . . ."

She hears a crack in his voice. "Ed, what is it?"

"I'm sorry, honey, but it's your grandmother." Ed coughs into the phone. "Hello? Are you still there?"

"Yes!"

"It's . . . well . . . I don't know how to say this, but I'm . . . I'm afraid she's passed. Audrey? Darlin'? Can ya hear me?"

Chapter Seventeen

Central Park West. It's the New York he'd imagined years ago, combing through the stacks in the Lawrence Public Library. He'd even resolved to live on the famed boulevard, surrounded by books and trees and tranquility. He didn't know; he'd been so young. He thought every New York apartment came with a doorman and terraced views of the park. He walks past them now, the great buildings with their uniformed sentries, standing guard under awnings the colors of royalty. Cobalt and cordovan. To his right, the barren trees shiver in the flat light of mid-November, as does Theo himself, not from the wind but the cold.

He's been walking awhile now, up through Hell's Kitchen and Columbus Circle, past the Time Warner Center, sleek and angular, someone's idea of the future. As usual, he could have taken the subway, but he'd been sitting in discomfort for hours and badly needed fresh air. Turned out his brother had been wrong about one thing at least: the buses hadn't run all night. And so Theo had slept fitfully on a plastic chair amid the stale smoke and decrepitude of the Foxwoods bus lobby until the first city-bound Greyhound rolled out at six fifteen a.m. Five hours later, he arrived at the Port Authority, more tired for all the catnaps he'd taken than if he'd just stayed up all night. The sun was high in the sky by the time he stepped out of the terminal, and like millions of arrivals before him, he looked up and down Eighth Avenue and realized he had nowhere to go. No one who needed him. Nothing to do. Truly: nothing. Unless you counted finding another job, another apartment, another life. Directly across the street stood the gleaming new headquarters of the *New York Times*. Theo had never had occasion to enter the building, but its mere proximity stirred life into his bus-weary body. That the larger world continued apace. It was a good thing to remember, when everything else had fallen apart.

Do something. Fight for her. The words have been ricocheting through his head for hours. He has to admit, they're a potent rallying cry—until you find yourself alone amid the mighty throng, facing the callous vagaries of reality. Audrey has communicated with him exactly once since their fight on the roof three nights ago, a terse text in response to a desperate string of his own, in which she'd asked—no, told—him to stop contacting her. She needed time, she said, and would be in touch when she was ready. Of course, he'd responded within seconds to ask when that might be, but his message, despite the temporary appearance of pulsing ellipses, went unanswered. How long he'd stared at those three dots! And how long he would have kept staring, had they not suddenly, cruelly, disappeared.

Which leaves him where, exactly? If she doesn't want him contacting her, she most definitely wouldn't want him showing up at Chris and Sarah's. So, fine. If she needs space, he'll give it to her, even if that means not seeing her before she leaves on tour—which really hurts. But what can he do? He has nothing new to offer, no answers or solutions to the predicament that has overwhelmed their lives. In a rare lucid moment on the bus ride back, he'd replayed all that had happened, hoping some small insight might present itself, a morsel that he, in turn, might offer up as a way forward. But he'd come up empty. He remained as confused about Martin Cafferty—and everything else in his life—as he'd ever been. Eventually, overcome with fatigue, he'd dozed off, or tried to, his head wedged awkwardly between his seat-back and the rattling window, and it was in this state of half delirium, as the bus trailed the sunrise west, that he suddenly remembered something. He sat up, pulled out his wallet, and groggily searched through a muddle of small bills and receipts and months-old dry-cleaning tickets. There it still was, the simple slip of paper. How had he forgotten about it? He unfolded it and stared at the scribbled-down address.

He'd consulted it again outside the Port Authority, and now, as he reaches the Museum of Natural History, he takes it out once more. Like it can't be real. Or worse, like it could. He started walking almost as a dare, a game to play with himself, but he hasn't yet stopped or veered off. He has no plan. The address is just a destination, a place to get to, if it even exists—demarks a real building. He can't think beyond that.

He can't think at all. The West Eighties are a blur. Doctors' offices and day schools and more doormen, watching him pass, a shoddy curiosity. What does he look like? He hasn't showered or changed clothes in two days, and his hair is a greasy mess. In the low Nineties, the marble-fronted co-ops give way to utilitarian towers and the scatter-shot tenements of the Upper *Upper* West Side. It's cold enough that he can see his breath, and his mind flashes back to high school, those late-season games played under the lights, his vigorous exhalations freezing to the face guard on his helmet, becoming actual ice, fogging his vision, but focusing it, too. He feels that way now, like the city has quieted for him, become almost deferential. He could be somewhere else entirely. Perhaps he is.

He stops at the corner of 103rd. It's a hilly street, more crowded than the others, and surprisingly inelegant considering its proximity to the park. Why, he wonders, and then spies the subway stairs on the opposite corner, and understands. It's one of those up-all-night blocks, an artery to the underground and the city beyond. What a perfect place to lie low, become anonymous. Theo recalls what Chris had told him in Union Square. How desperate the man must be. And how broke. He'd need a place that's cheap but within walking distance of his old apartment, where his kids still live, twenty-something blocks to the south (assuming his ex hasn't moved them somewhere else). Theo takes a few steps up the block and, one last time, checks the address. *7 West 103rd, #6.* There it is, directly across the street, a derelict-looking five-story building fronted by rusted-iron fire escapes. So the address *is* real. Well, that doesn't mean it's right. It doesn't mean Martin Cafferty actually lives here.

Now what? He has no idea. Finding some less visible place to loiter would be a good start. It's not just Cafferty he's worried about. It's early afternoon and 103rd Street is alive with activity, interest, *eyes*. Sitting on Cafferty's stoop is a heavyset Hispanic man reading a newspaper. He's dressed for the weather in an ear-flapped hat and winter coat, like he's not going anywhere for a while. The door behind him is propped slightly open, but the narrow hallway is too dim to see down. Assuming two apartments per floor, number 6 would be on the third, unless there are back units, in which case—oh, fuck it. What does it matter? He can't see inside the windows from where he is anyway. He could go ring the buzzer (if there is one); maybe Cafferty would answer. But then what? It's not like he'd invite a stranger up. Or is Theo no longer a stranger? The thought unnerves him. *Does Cafferty know what he looks like?* It's possible, if he's the one who broke into their loft; there are framed photos of Audrey and Theo all over the walls. There'd been one on their desk. Of the two of them embracing. The two of them happy.

He suddenly has the sense of being watched. Like Cafferty's peering down from somewhere, awaiting Theo's next move, or his first. But that's ridiculous. He's being paranoid. Still, he can't just stand here. How did he not think this through? Develop a plan of attack? No, that's a bad turn of phrase. He doesn't want to confront Cafferty; he just wants proof the man exists in some other realm than tear-stained paper. It's not Theo's place to make unilateral decisions. So why doesn't he text someone to say he's here? Chris, who hates missing anything, would surely drop whatever he's doing to join him uptown. But join him to do what? Stand here looking confused? Then how about Audrey? She must be reading his texts, even if she isn't answering them—right? Theo looks over at the man on the stoop, wrestling in the breeze with an unruly fold of newspaper. No, he can't tell Audrey, for the same reason he couldn't tell her he had this address in the first place. The less she has to think about Martin Cafferty's presence in the world, the better. Which brings him back to the problem at hand: proof of that presence. Maybe he can walk over and see if Cafferty's name is on a mailbox in the vestibule. Except he'd have to get past the stoop-sitter, and anyway, Cafferty doesn't strike him as someone who'd announce himself like that. Or he could just *ask* the stoop-sitter. *Do you know a man in your building who* . . . what? Has a mole? Theo realizes it then: he has no idea what Cafferty looks like. He'd never wanted to know—he didn't think he could bear it—so had made a point of not looking him up online. He sighs heavily. What's he even doing here? A stakeout? Really? At least it beats Carl's great idea: selling Audrey's life story to Win Groom. The thought of that brief insanity is too mortifying to revisit for even a moment.

But enough. He's getting colder. He should go home, even if that word, once so comforting, no longer fits the place he lives. In the weeks since the break-in, the loft has become a haunted cage of memories. How that night still consumes him. His mind, always so jumbled, had turned clear and elemental as he spied their open door and tiptoed inside. Safety and protection. Courage and resolve. What's happened to him since? How has he grown so spongy and tentative? Whoever said that awareness is the key to life is full of shit, because Theo is overwhelmingly aware, and what good has it done him? He shouldn't be here. This isn't his story. He's never quite believed it anyway.

He cuts across the street, hunched into his coat, and makes his way down the subway stairs. The C to the L: he'll be in Bushwick in forty minutes. He remembers he needs to pick up cat food. God knows what Roger's been up to all alone for two days. Through the turnstiles and down another flight to an almost empty platform. In other circumstances he might laugh, recalling those arduous Upper West Side commutes with that stupid backpack full of manuscripts. But that was years ago, another lifetime. He's all but forgotten that ache of youthful ambition. Now he waits as the platform slowly fills, everyone staring at their phones. He can't help it, he takes his out. Thank God he charged it in the Foxwoods bus lobby. Not that he has many apps. He can't even access the *Times*, since they put up their paywall. Maybe he should stop being stubborn and just subscribe to the damn—

Audrey. He sees the letters of her name on his home screen and for a moment doesn't react. He's so used to them. They fit there. And then he snaps back to reality and comprehends the simple fact that, after two days, she finally texted him back. Seven minutes ago. He must have been too distracted to feel the phone in his pocket. He enters his passcode, apprehensive but hopeful, as the station fills with the rumble of an approaching train. Her message appears on the screen. He starts to read it, then puts his hand over his mouth.

If ur back in BK be careful!! Cafferty SHOT Fender, the cops just fnd his body! Let me no ur safe please!

He scans it again, wishing it were a terrible mistake, knowing it isn't. *Cafferty SHOT Fender.* Audrey must be okay, is his first thought, because she's been in contact with the cops. The message itself takes longer to absorb. What it means, beyond the words. *That she's been right the whole time.* He suddenly feels light-headed, like he might faint. Noises. Screeching. He has to text her back. No, not text. Call, like a real person. He needs to hear her voice. The train is in front of him, just sitting there, doors open, but he doesn't even look up. He's staring at the bars on his phone, or the blank space where the bars would be if he were getting a signal. Which he's not. Of course he's not, these stations don't have cell service. He starts walking, then running, back through the turnstile and up the stairs, gripping the phone in his hand like it's an armrest in bad turbulence. Let her know you're safe. Let her know you love her. Let her know everything she is, which is the world. That a man could hurt her and come back for more. And what had he done? Stood aside and watched it happen, a spectator in the only moments that mattered. This despite everyone urging him on, Audrey and Chris and his brother, act, act, act, earn this life of yours, save her as she saved you.

He's on the street again, staring urgently at his screen, the bars that won't come.

She wants to know he's safe.

He needs to know that *she* is. That's what's important.

He's not waiting for a signal. He's moving again. Number Three. Number Five. Number Seven. He doesn't hesitate. He pockets his phone and steps past the man on the stoop, nodding slightly as he pushes through the door. He doesn't stop at the mailboxes. Doesn't even look over. He takes the stairs two at a time, like he always has, the light from the entrance hall giving way to a single exposed bulb on the second-floor landing. He pauses under it, looks around. Paint-chipped walls covering old moldings, discolored laminate hiding the floorboards. He hears a muffled radio inside one of the apartments. 1010 WINS. "The unemployment rate has fallen to eight point six percent," the newsreader says, "the lowest it's been since 2009." Theo would be part of that minority, but he hasn't filed for unemployment. He's untethered, unaccounted for. Not even a statistic.

He was right: two apartments per floor, so number 6 must be on the third. He keeps climbing, his thoughts jumbled, disarranged. He sees Ms. Jansen, hears her words of praise. How proud he'd been of that essay, his exposing of long-held family secrets, age-old family lies. It didn't matter that it didn't matter, that what he'd written wouldn't alter perceptions or change history. It was about the search for truth and its ultimate discovery. Manic snapshots. Random sensations. The bitter winds of Lawrence winters. The smell of the Colgate locker room. The crack of the coatrack as he broke off an arm. Tunnels and stairs. Darkness. The scene in that basement, Audrey bleeding and alone. And then, like he's stepped through a trapdoor, the moment he dares not fathom, visualize, make real—Audrey fighting and fighting in that hotel room. He sees it now, all of it, and he understands. The singular horror. And the residual damage.

To Audrey.

To all of them.

There's a 6 on the door in front of him. No peephole, no bell. He listens, holding his breath, but hears only silence. What are the chances Cafferty's here? Theo has no idea. And he doesn't care. He's done with percentages. Ifs and mights and probably-nots. Where have they ever gotten him? He tries to lengthen his breathing, slow it down to a—*wait.* He hears noise behind the door. A kind of shoeless shuffling.

He doesn't pause long enough to change his mind. He knocks—normally, not hard—and then rolls his shoulders back and straightens to his full height.

"Who is it?"

The voice is gruff but not aggressive. Still, the question catches Theo off guard.

I'm your neighbor from downstairs.

I'm a volunteer with the Census Bureau.

I'm the estranged boyfriend of the woman you raped.

Come on. Focus. He's waited outside apartment doors like this dozens of times before, courtesy of his days as Win's errand boy at Prosaic. All those manuscripts he hand-delivered to authors, sallow shut-ins in T-shirts or tights or even pajamas, who quickly brightened at the sight of him. That their publisher deemed them worth the expense. Maybe it works the same way in business.

"I have a package from Longstream Capital for"—he swallows—"a Mr. Martin Cafferty."

More shuffling, but closer now. "Aw, Christ. Okay, hold on."

Theo freezes. The organs in his body, that push and pump, exude and absorb, all cease their activities at once. Numbness passes through him like it's been injected. He hears a chain undone, a bolt unbolted, and now the door is opening and a man is standing there, dark haired and modest in stature, but Theo can't home in on features, can't process the moment at all. He tries to make eye contact, but Cafferty is looking for the messenger bag that should be holding severance papers or insurance forms, but there is no bag, only Theo's empty hands, which are closing, becoming fists, and just as he did back outside, he senses his body react before his mind can, feels his arm moving, his right hand—unballed again—grabbing Cafferty's collar and lifting him off the ground. Then, like it's nothing, no strain at all, Theo launches the man, shotput-like, across the narrow hallway.

Cafferty hits the wall—his body, then his head. The sound it makes is deep and cranial, but Theo doesn't hesitate. He's already on him, lifting him upright, pinning him back with a forearm to his throat. There's no question of what he'll do next, and he wastes no time, driving his right knee into Cafferty's groin with such force that Theo feels a compression, a gruesome displacement, against his leg. Cafferty emits a high-pitched bleat, a bungled opera note, and then falls, leaden, to the filthy floor. Theo hovers over him, watching as Cafferty tucks himself into a fetal position, the pain overwhelming him. He's wearing a T-shirt and sweatpants with an elastic band, and for a moment Theo almost feels pity for the man, until his eyes lock onto Cafferty's face, his forehead, and he sees it, the dark mole he's read so much about, staring up at him like a brazen declaration.

Cafferty puts an arm out to block what's coming next.

"My wallet," he whimpers, nodding toward the open door. "Whatever you want—"

"Look at me!" Theo shouts, and kicks him in the ribs. "Do you know who I am?'"

Cafferty groans and glances up, his hands cupping his balls. "No," he gasps.

"Bullshit."

"Swear to God. Never seen you before."

Theo kneels down, a foot from his face. Stale breath and gray whiskers. "The loft in Bushwick, the one you broke into. What were you after?"

"I don't know what you're . . . I haven't been to Brooklyn in—"

Cafferty winces, then moans again—longer, louder—tears clouding his eyes.

"Don't lie to me," Theo says, "or I'll kick you harder."

"I'm not ly—"

"You're Martin Cafferty."

"Yes."

"Who worked at Longstream Capital."

"Yeah . . . but I don't—"

"Who rapes women."

"No—"

"Escorts in hotels."

Cafferty's eyes widen, for just an instant, before he recovers, turns away, masks himself again. But it's enough, the flicker of recognition, of confirmation, and Theo shudders, his body tightening around a central point, behind his heart. He feels sick. The coursing of his blood, the spark of his nerves, his brain settling on a specific image, Audrey facedown on a table, legs splayed, panties at her knees, helpless but still struggling, crying out above the music. And then his mind goes blank, it goes *black*, and he lifts Martin Cafferty off the floor again until he's almost standing under his own power. Theo wants to give him a fighting chance, he really does, but some other person is in control now, someone base and impulsive, and as Cafferty opens his mouth to speak, it is this second person who turns sideways, pulls his right arm back, and like he's done it a thousand times, though he's never done it once, throws a hard, flat punch—a *haymaker*, his father, so fluent in the language, would have called it—that lands squarely on the underside of Martin Cafferty's left cheekbone. Something dislodges, a bone, shifting upward, breaking, and Cafferty crumples back to the ground. Theo, following through, almost falls on top of him but steadies himself, rearranges himself, pulls his coat sleeve down. Cafferty is lying still, dazed, maybe unconscious, his blood streaming, pooling, and Theo should leave things there, part of him understands that, but instead of stepping away, he bends back down and hits the man again, and again, in the nose, above his eye, the punches landing unimpeded, the damage becoming severe. Theo hovers above the moment, wondering at small things—where skin stops and flesh begins. The blows—four? five?—are cathartic, purifying, almost spiritual. He feels close to some essence, a hidden truth, like maybe this, too, is love, the other half of it. *If Audrey could see me*, he thinks, not wanting to stop. Then he hears a voice, outside himself, abstract and foreign, and pauses in his drudgework long enough to comprehend the sound as coming from down the hall, the stairs. He matches the words, accented, Spanish, to a likely face, the man on the stoop, and all at once he understands what's happening. He straightens, steps back, and sees—as if he's just come upon him— Martin Cafferty damaged, destroyed, barely there. What's he done? The question could be asked of either man. Theo wipes his hands on his pants, the blood smearing into the denim; he can smell it, a molecular stench. From Cafferty comes a deep guttural noise. The man from the stoop has heard them and is coming up. How brave, Theo thinks. And then: how cowardly of himself. He looks back down. Blood is running from Cafferty's nose, his mouth, his left ear. Had Theo hit him there? He has no idea.

He steps over and looks down the stairwell, sees the top of the man's head as he labors up the first flight, a strenuous step at a time. Cafferty is still sprawled across the hallway, conscious, but not by much. There's too much blood—on the floor, the wall, Theo's clothes, Cafferty's. He needs to move him, get him inside, so he bends down, puts Cafferty's limp arm around his shoulder, and then pulls him up and drags him through the open apartment door. He tries to close it, but Cafferty's weight is shifting away. He must be collapsing again. Theo turns toward him just in time to glimpse, to *feel*, Cafferty lunge toward a side table by the door. He tries to restrain him, pull him back, but Cafferty is grasping at something. A black outline against the dark wood. Theo sees the gun just as Cafferty's hand is gripping it, but he's ready, alert from Audrey's text, and he hits Cafferty's arm at the elbow, dislodging the weapon, both men twisting, falling, hitting the wall, the floor. There's a bang. Theo squeezes his eyes shut. Waits. Hears silence. The door. It was the door slamming shut. They'd fallen against it.

Cafferty's not moving. Theo looks around for the gun, spots it a few feet away, skittered under a bureau. He reaches over, picks it up. In all his life, he's never held one. He read somewhere that guns feel cold to the touch, but that's not true. He glances at the body on the floor, then back at the weapon in his hand. *Made in Austria*, it says above the grip. Like it could be anything. A Christmas toy. And then the words underneath: *Glock Inc.* He doesn't know if it's loaded or where the safety is. He doesn't know why it was on the entry table, but he can take a guess: for visitors like him. Visitors who *are* him. Or Chris or Sarah. Or Audrey. He turns and points it at the body on the floor.

"Open your eyes."

Cafferty opens the only one he can, and Theo watches it go wide. So it *is* loaded.

"Why do you have this?"

Cafferty lies still, doesn't speak. Theo puts his finger on the trigger.

"Tell me!"

"Protection."

"Bullshit."

"Please," Cafferty whimpers. "Put it down."

"Answer me."

Theo hears heavy footsteps in the hallway, and then: "*Que está occuriendo?*"

"I'll tell him to call the cops," Theo hisses.

"*No,*" Cafferty moans. "Please, no."

"Then talk."

"I—I was being blackmailed," Cafferty stammers, a bubble of blood inflating, then popping on his lips.

"By whom?"

Cafferty doesn't answer.

"*Hola?*"

"*Espera un segundo,*" Theo shouts through the door. He points the gun between Cafferty's legs. "Why did you kill Fender?"

"I didn't kill anyone."

"The cops found his body."

"No."

"Shot with this gun would be my guess."

"*Estoy llamando a la policía.*"

"He's calling the police," Theo says.

"*No. Wait.* Tell him not to. Just you and me. I'll tell you everything."

Theo looks down at Cafferty's battered, haunted face, then turns to the door. "*Adelante, llamalos.*"

"What are you saying?" Cafferty rasps.

"That I'll call them myself." Theo lowers the gun, takes his phone out. Up comes Audrey's text from before. He looks at her name and winces. The old feeling again. That he couldn't help her. That he'd failed. Maybe that's what love is: an unending string of failure. No, that's only part of it. Analogous to that failure, superior to it, is forgiveness.

What had taken him so long?

He aims the gun again. What does he have to lose?

"*Please,*" Cafferty moans. "Don't do this."

Theo stares down at him. His finger tickles the trigger.

Her. He could lose her.

He closes his eyes. Opens them.

"Then start talking," he says.

Chapter Eighteen

"Van Vleck? You're kidding," says Ed Beemis. "Did you know there's a Van Vleck crater on the moon?"

"No," Chris responds, trying to sound surprised. Of course he knows. He even knows where it's located: the northeast rim of the walled plain Gilbert. He had a framed photograph of the crater in his childhood bedroom.

"Well, it's there," Ed says, "I promise you. I was a member of the International Astronomical Union when they named the damn thing. This was back in the seventies when every country with a launchpad was claiming a corner of space. The Russians were the worst, of course, always coming up with crap that didn't exist. Fake planets and stars, all named for Gagarin."

They're scrubbing a grill. Or Chris is scrubbing and Ed is watching. Overseeing. Why not just tell him the truth—that the crater is named after his great-grandfather John Van Vleck, one of the original physicists on the Manhattan Project? Is it the family connection to the atom bomb? No. Chris has never worried over history, matters beyond his control. What he's struggling with is a more immediate problem: he doesn't want to come across as a rich kid. Not to someone like Ed Beemis. Why he's suddenly embarrassed by his own last name he's not sure. Maybe it's a result of his recent, if tentative, foray into self-examination. He's working on awareness. Isolating faults, correcting them. He has, for instance, decided he's done with lies and sneaking around. And he can supply proof, in the form of an engagement ring currently locked away in his hotel room safe. He purchased it several days ago and was planning on proposing in Mattoon, over Christmas (his first holiday with Sarah's family). Then Audrey got the news about Connie, Theo went rogue on Martin Cafferty, and the most insane week of all of their lives had commenced. When Audrey asked if Chris and Sarah would come to Florida for the memorial, they'd immediately said yes (of course). Almost as quickly, Chris sensed an opportunity and had his travel agent tack on two nights in the Bahamas. His new plan is to propose on a Harbour Island beach at sunset, which definitely beats taking a knee in the bedroom of a bungalow house in central Illinois.

"You haven't even touched the bottom." Ed sighs, peering into the grill. "There's still grime below the grates."

"Ah, Chris, don't listen to him," Sid Stevens says, striding toward them across the lawn.

Ed looks up. "What happened, Sid, you get tired of drinkin' rosé with the girls?"

"No, just wanted to come watch you speechify. Don't worry, Chris, you'll get the hang of things soon enough. Most of us carry earplugs."

Chris laughs. He's been laughing all afternoon. He and Sarah had arrived the previous evening, and after checking into the La Quinta Inn at Cocoa Beach, they took a cab to River Palms. Chris had never been to a trailer park, and while he was curious about the experience from an epistemological standpoint, he was planning to spend most of his non-memorial-attending time shuffling between the La Quinta pool and the pristine white beach beyond it. Then he settled into a patio chair behind Connie's trailer, and Audrey made drinks, and one by one the neighbors arrived, the Beemises and Stevenses and a half-dozen others, all of them pleased, amid the general sadness, to meet Audrey's friends, these faces from her distant life, and as old stories of Connie were traded back and forth, Chris found himself falling under their tractor-beam pull—Ed's and Sid's especially. He'd never met anyone like them, these rough-hewn men of high science and low humor, who seemed to enjoy his company in the provisional way that wise men have always suffered fools. At some point, well into the evening, a telescope appeared, and Ed and Sid gave their Yankee guests a guided tour of the Milky Way. That an astronaut and a mission control man were showing him the stars: it was a thrill beyond words.

According to Audrey, the festivities had been Connie's idea. She'd never been religious and couldn't stand the somber ceremonies surrounding death (she'd asked to be cremated). Only a party would do, as it carried on certain traditions, years of cookouts and community gatherings on this very lawn. Well, the grill will certainly be ready. Chris stands back to give his new mentor a look at his handiwork, but Ed's busy helping Sid lift a beer keg into a plastic garbage can.

"Can I help?" Chris asks.

"We need a hammer to attach the hose," Ed says. "I think there's an electric one under Connie's sink."

"I'll grab it," Chris offers, happy to be of more use. He hurries over to the trailer and steps inside, expecting to find Sarah and Audrey moving frantically about the kitchen. Instead, he spots them out on the patio, sipping wine. A joint is teetering on an ashtray between them. Audrey's in the same comely vintage T-shirt—"BOWIE: A Space Oddity"—she was wearing last night, but it's Sarah's simple ribbed tank top that draws his attention. It's the kind she'd worn so often when Chris first knew her, and so seldom in the years since, for it failed to cover the bright flowers and tangled thorns crawling across her upper arm. Chris has always loved Sarah's half sleeve, and now, admiring it anew, he can only hope it's a sign of things to come.

Tattoos. His great weakness—or one of them. He's decided, reluctantly, not to let Audrey in on his plan to propose. She has enough going on. Also, she knows a bit too much (she may even know about Kinsey). He wishes he could explain himself, tell her how he's changed. It was Kinsey who scared him straight. Chris had never met a true radical before: a woman who lived for brief moments of sheer clarity. Kinsey knew about cam girls because she'd been one. She'd also waitressed at a strip club, skydived from a biplane, traveled solo through Venezuela, studied immersive yoga in some place called Rishikesh, chained herself to the entrance of an immigrant detention center in Miami, and faced off against cops at Occupy. It was like everything she did was a test of will, and Chris had begun to wonder, as he got to know her, if Kinsey's actions were not an end in themselves but a means, an attempt to beat back pain through some ecstatic opposite. He was curious, coming from the clench-jawed world of WASPs, why she lived as she did, and one night had made the mistake of asking her. He'd been expecting a brief, pithy answer, but had received instead a long, roller-coaster account of various anxieties and depressions buffeted by pills and support groups and psychiatrists who specialized in rare manias and multipolarities. "Having the feels," Kinsey called it, which was like calling a tsunami a good surfing wave. It had become clear that Kinsey was an all-or-nothing proposition, and Chris was not in the "all" market. He didn't have the heart to explain that people like himself—the unafflicted, for lack of a better word—could live their entire lives skimming the surface of sensation, emotion, *innerness*, without facing a reckoning of the soul. The day after Kinsey's revelations, he ended things, such as they were, and returned with a newfound determination to the suddenly splendid consistency of Sarah Foster. Like him, Sarah believed in sensible limits to the search for self. He'd purchased the ring soon thereafter.

And for the first time in his life, he truly believes he's ready. The irony, as his gaze travels from Sarah to Audrey, is that the relationship he most believed in—far more than his own—is the one that's imploded. Audrey and Theo had always been purer of motive and more deeply in love. And, like Kinsey, they'd been unafraid to delve below surfaces. Maybe, then, it wasn't ironic at all. Maybe their troubles just proved his half-baked theory.

"Hey!" Sarah shouts through the screen. "Stop staring at us like a perv!"

Chris is about to protest, then realizes that's exactly what he's been doing.

"Are the boys out front picking on you?" Audrey asks, grinning.

"No, Ed needs the electric hammer to attach a beer hose to the keg."

Audrey bites her lip. "And you need a *hammer* for that?"

"Well, I—"

"An *electric* hammer?"

The girls erupt in laughter at the same time. "Oh, Chris," Sarah says.

He glares out at them, then shakes his head and slowly trudges back to the front door. He pauses a moment, steeling himself for what's to come.

"He's having the time of his life," Sarah says. She picks at her bra strap and repositions her chair in line with the sun. "I must say that, circumstances aside, I am, too. It's really nice to be here."

"The place has its charms," Audrey says.

"With you, is what I meant."

"I know. Me too."

They start laughing again, this time at their own awkwardness. Audrey reaches for the joint and takes a hit. Sarah watches in hazy affection, glad to see her friend finally relaxing. She's heard so much about River Palms through the years, from the launch parties to the starlit nights spent right here on this patio. Still, she never got the chance to meet Connie in person. She wishes she had. She leans forward and takes Audrey's hand.

"I'm really sorry," she says, meaning the words as an apology as much as a condolence.

Audrey smiles sadly and stares off into the middle distance. Sarah follows her gaze, but there's nothing there. Shrubs and low sky. A flock of shorebirds she could never name. A familiar buzzing brings her back—Audrey's phone on the table. Audrey checks the screen and frowns.

"Is it Theo?" Sarah asks, too eagerly.

"No, it's Ben and Arthur," Audrey says. She stands up, puts the phone to her ear, and wanders several paces into the yard.

Well, it could have been Theo, Sarah decides, feeling bad for bringing him up. It *should* have been. There's been a massive elephant in the room—or the air—since the moment she and Chris arrived, and it starts with a T, ends with an O, and has an appropriately masculine HE in the middle. Why isn't he here? According to what Detective Torres told Audrey, Theo broke several laws in his turn to vigilantism, and while he isn't in real trouble—not anymore—he's also not allowed to leave the state of New York. There are more witnesses to interview and stories to corroborate, and Theo has become the unlikely lynchpin to the entire case. It makes sense—there'd been a murder, after all—but it also doesn't, because Sarah can't imagine his *not* being here, no matter the circumstances. Three days have passed since Theo knocked on Martin Cafferty's door, and it's still all Chris and Sarah can talk about, at least when they're alone. The enormity of what he'd done. The courage it had taken. He probably saved their lives.

Yet Audrey's barely mentioned him. How's that possible?

Sarah sighs. What can she do? She's not here to cause more problems. She's here to support her best friend. Anyway, she has her own private drama unfolding. She knows Chris is planning to propose because she—accidentally!—read the beginning of an email he received from a salesperson at Harry Winston. She'd been surreptitiously scanning his inbox for any sign of the mysterious "K" when she came across the famed jeweler's name, followed by the subject *RE: Ring size*, and the first line of a message: *Dear Chris, The engagement ring has arrived and it looks absolutely* . . . Sarah had stared at the words. What came next? Her mind reeled with superlatives, but she couldn't click on the full email because Chris would notice it had been opened. No matter; what she'd read was enough. She tracked the words again and again—"Chris" and "engagement" (and, fine, "Harry" and "Winston")—as her eyes moistened. They'd been together a long time now, more than six years, and while she'd outwardly shrugged off the idea of marriage—and the time her boyfriend was taking to come around to it—she'd inwardly begun to wonder if it would happen with Chris at all. How far was he willing to take his phony war on convention? Far enough to lose her? Or was it more elemental? Did he simply not love her like that? Her girlfriends and close coworkers, most of them married themselves, had stopped teasing her about the situation some time ago. And then there was the problem of Chris's extracurricular activities. The problem: as if it were something fixable. Yet she continued to believe it was, and that, despite all evidence to the contrary, marriage might be the solution. Institutional commitment. She understood this was wishful thinking but didn't care. She was who she was, and she felt how she felt. Add to that the simple fact that she was in love, and deeply so, and a person—not Audrey, perhaps, but most of her Sotheby's cohorts—might begin to understand why she's stayed. Despite what she knows about Chris's behavior, she has never confronted him. That sounds ridiculous, and surely is, but his trysts—and she knows there's been more than one—have always been brief and discreet. Only this latest had truly worried her. But then, as with the others, it abruptly ended. Two days ago, Sarah logged into his computer, thinking he and "K" might have switched to email, and found instead the ring correspondence. From agony to ecstasy, at least theoretically. In truth, it was such a shock that she's still processing the discovery. Not that she won't say yes. Of course she will. Sarah Foster can rationalize with the best of them.

She gazes out at Audrey, still pacing the lawn. Sarah's dying to tell her, but she knows this isn't the time or place. They're out of wine, so Sarah ducks inside and grabs another bottle from the fridge. She's refilling their glasses when Audrey pockets her phone and returns to the table.

"How's the tour going?" Sarah asks.

"You're not going to believe this, but the Westfields are on their way here. All four of them. They played Gainesville last night, some club near the university, and have a day off before their next gig, so they're coming down to pay their respects. Which is insane. It's like a three-hour drive. And they didn't even *know* Connie."

"Yes, but they love you."

Audrey shakes her head disbelievingly. "On the plus side, they offered to play a few songs at the party, which means we won't have to listen to Ed's scratchy Sinatra CDs. Do you want to walk over to the community center with me? There should be an amp and some mics in there. I don't want them unloading half their van, the poor guys."

"Always looking after the musicians," Sarah says.

"Bring the bottle."

They set out across the yards, the river on one side, rows of trailers on the other. Audrey points out license plates and explains the concept of impermanence. That anyone could just up and leave for no reason. "Speaking of which, we may be getting another surprise visitor. My mother."

"Seriously?" Sarah says, caught off guard. She tries to recall what little she knows of Sharon McAllister. None of it's good. "When's the last time you saw her?"

"When I was a teenager. But I know she's come by here looking for money over the years. It was Connie's one great flaw: she could never say no. Though I guess I can't either, because I found her number in Connie's address book yesterday—or her *latest* number, since there were five or six crossed out—and called it. I figured she had a right to know her own mother was no longer with us. Anyway, you can probably guess what happened."

Sarah has no idea. It seems anything is possible.

"It went to voice mail," Audrey continues. "Which, to be honest, was a major relief. So I left a message explaining that Connie had passed away and that we'd all be getting together to celebrate her life this afternoon if she cared to make an appearance."

"Jesus, Auds. And you think she'll come?"

Audrey shrugs. "Maybe, if she still lives in Florida. But it won't be out of some great sense of loss. She'll be focused on the assets to be divvied up. The trailer and whatnot."

"I could think of worse places to live," Sarah says, looking out at the river.

"Well, unfortunately for her, I met with Connie's lawyer yesterday, who informed me I was the sole beneficiary of her will. The property, the car, a little money in the bank. Connie always said I would be, but it was still a shock. To suddenly be a homeowner after a decade of roommates and rentals. Not even rentals. *Sublets.*"

"You think Connie told your mother she was leaving you everything?"

"Probably not. She hated confrontation, especially when it concerned family. But it doesn't matter. I'm going to give my mother the trailer. I doubt she'll want to live here, but she can sell it and take the proceeds. Why not, right? What would I ever do with it?"

"Sell it and take the proceeds," Sarah says.

"No, she needs the cash more than I do. But there's one thing she'll have to do to get it. She'll have to show up today. If she can't even do that, well . . ."

Sarah shakes her head in admiration. How far her old friend has come from the softball fields of McCarren Park. She wonders what will happen now. How Audrey will deal with all this loss. Sarah has no idea, but she'll do everything she can to help her get through it.

"This is it," Audrey says as they approach a cinder-block building in a clearing between trailers. She leads Sarah past the washing machines and dryers—her nemeses—and into the main room, where three rows of folding chairs sit facing a rudimentary nativity scene.

"Aww, that's sweet," Sarah says.

"It's for the children's annual Christmas play. I used to help direct it—being a major actress and all. It's the least I could do."

"Like J.Lo going back to the block."

Audrey laughs and flips on the lights to reveal walls covered with River Palms mementos—fishing photos and framed newspaper clippings and vintage NASA signs. Sarah peruses them slowly, like she's at a museum, as Audrey wades into a pile of clutter behind the manger. She emerges with two mics and a dented Peavey amp. She plugs it in and the power light comes on. "I can't believe it still works! I used to lug this thing to parties fifteen years ago."

"Check out this photo," Sarah says, squinting at a faded eight-by-ten hanging above a card table. "It looks like a cookout in your front yard."

"I'm sure it is," Audrey says, walking over. She leans in to inspect the image. "See that man in the shorts? That's my grandfather. This must be from the late eighties—one of the first launch parties. There's Sid and

Ed. And the scrawny kid with the sullen expression? That's Sid's son, Kurt, who, despite his parents, became the neighborhood shithead."

"Is he still around?"

Audrey relates the story she heard two nights ago. According to Rose Beemis, Kurt had received four years in Avon Park for breaking into an ex-girlfriend's trailer in Bithlo while under a restraining order for breaking into the same trailer the previous month. She wasn't home the second time, Audrey explains, but Kurt was carrying a gun in the waistband of his sweatpants and managed to shoot himself in the leg while he was snooping around. He had to call 911 on himself because he was bleeding and couldn't move.

"I have no idea what to say to that," Sarah says.

"That's only medium-weird for Florida."

"Where the hell is *Bithlo*?"

"It's a swamp town halfway between here and Orlando. The locals call it 'the Nightmare Before Christmas,' Christmas being the next town over."

"I'm so glad you got out of here," Sarah says.

Audrey doesn't disagree. She bends down and picks up the amp. "Will you grab the mics? We should get back."

They take the main road this time—the grass along the side of it—and pass the wine back and forth with their free hands. The air feels heavier, though the sky is still a deep-toned blue. Audrey takes off her sandals and puts them on top of the amp. She has a million things to do, but she can't think of one specifically. She's exhausted, hollowed out. It's been three days of meetings and memories. Long dinners with old friends. Sober appointments with lawyers. She's hardly had a moment to stop and gather herself, let alone grieve, or even begin to deal with all the problems waiting back in her own life—the one she once shared with Theo. Maybe that's a good thing, to just function and not think. The totality of her recent losses would overwhelm her.

Sarah asks about Jasper Sash, if he'll be coming to the memorial.

"Probably," Audrey says. "Everyone else is."

"Are you angry at him for selling Connie all that pot?"

"He's a drug dealer. That's his job description. Also, when did I tell you about that?"

"Last night on the patio, around three a.m. You said she'd been ordering more and more."

"Oh God, I don't remember anything past midnight. Anyway, it wasn't Jasper's fault. He left me a message about Connie a few weeks ago, but I was so consumed with Fender that I never called him back. I figured she was buying extra for friends. But now I wonder if she was actually in a lot of pain, and that if I'd just paid closer attention . . ."

She doesn't finish the thought. There's no good place it could go. Connie had died of heart failure in her sleep. If she'd been feeling bad in the weeks beforehand, she hadn't let on to her friends. The weed buying remained a mystery Audrey realized she wouldn't solve. *You should never be afraid to keep a few secrets.* Maybe it was best that way.

She tries to collect herself. She can see the yard up ahead, the growing crowd. It's 3:50 p.m. The invitations Sid delivered door-to-door read 4:30, but what else is there to do? They spot Chris at the food table, arranging Kraft Singles in neat rows, and Sarah heads over to make fun of him. Audrey falls into conversation with Rose Beemis but keeps glancing over at the entrance road. She can't help it. She recalls the last time this happened, at a launch party years ago, and that sense of helplessness born of evolutionary hope—that a parent might emerge from the dusty American mirage. It was almost as bad as the realization that no one would come at all. Abruptly, she turns her back to the entrance. She won't allow herself to revert like this, become a pawn again, a vassal: a child.

When Ed calls Rose away, Audrey slips back over to Sarah. "I need to clear my head," she says quietly, and Sarah nods. "If the Westfields roll in, will you introduce them around? Ed can help them set up, he knows where all the cords and outlets are. I'll be back soon."

"Take your time," Sarah tells her. "We've got everything under control."

Audrey doubts that—just wait—but thanks her nonetheless and sneaks around the side of the trailer. She wants to relax on the patio, maybe come up with a few anecdotes she can sprinkle into her remarks later on, but something pulls her past the table, a kind of unsettled longing. She traverses the length of the yard to the thigh-high brush leading down to the river. She hasn't been to the dock in years, has no idea if it's still there. The old path certainly isn't, so she picks her way carefully down the slippery bank, her feet sinking in places as she nears the water. Then she sees it, warped and rotted, poking out like a frayed nerve. She takes a half leap onto the planks, steadying herself against one of the supports her grandfather long ago drove into the riverbed. It's loose now, like it might come up if she pulls. She steps to the far end and looks east toward the ocean. She can smell it, almost taste it. In the years since she moved north she's dreamed about this moment, and in every one of them she sits and dangles her legs off the edge of the dock, as her grandfather had on that fateful day fourteen years ago. He'd been fishing alone that afternoon, but on most others he'd taken Audrey along, the two of them listening to ball games on a transistor radio as they cast worms across the shallows. They never thought about alligators—not in that way. Sure, they were around, and sometimes even visible, but so were snakes and snapping turtles and poisonous toads. Worrying over one thing meant worrying over all. Besides, gators kept to themselves unless provoked, or so everyone said.

The last support on the right seems stable enough, so Audrey sits against it and pulls her knees to her chest. Bill had loved the quiet down here—the birds and the breeze, the lapping water. They'd been spared the roar of powerboats because the area was a manatee refuge, though most old-timers believed that was just NASA's way of keeping boats from getting too close to the space center. Now she closes her eyes and listens. What she hears is what her grandfather heard: nothing and everything. These are the first moments she's had to herself since she arrived, and immediately her mind starts drifting. She doesn't want it to. She can't go there—not yet. She wants to focus on the memorial, but it's too late. The tragic names of these last weeks envelop her. Lucas. Fender. Cafferty. *Theo.* She opens her eyes, momentarily dizzy, and grabs the dock to steady herself.

Deep breaths. She peers up at the sky, its boundless blue flecked now with clouds. It's becoming the type of afternoon that gets weathermen fired. She's facing north, toward the launchpads. Even now she wishes Theo could have seen just one—experienced the resplendence, felt it reverberate inside him. Because it felt a lot like love. Of course she wishes he were here. She'd even lobbied Detective Torres to let him come down. But cops don't care about heartstrings. They care about cases. And Torres has a career-maker on his hands. It's been all over the papers the last two days—EX-FINANCIER MURDERS HIPSTER DRUG DEALER IN BOTCHED BLACKMAIL ATTEMPT—the facts leaked, no doubt, by the police themselves. She can't blame them. It's good copy. The *Post*, the *Daily News*, even the *Wall Street Journal*, have all been running with it (according to Chris, who'd been providing updates until she asked him to stop). So far, the reports have focused on the details of Fender's murder, which Theo extracted at gunpoint in the six minutes between when the police were called and when they charged, weapons drawn, into his apartment. What happened years before has not been made public, though the police know about it now. Audrey assumes it will all come out at some point, but she doesn't really care. Theo was the only person she'd ever worried about telling.

She's been hearing the whispers—from Sid, from Ed, from everyone. *Why isn't Theo here?* None of them know what's unfolded up north, not yet, so Chris and Sarah have come up with a cover story—that he's in LA for work—which Audrey appreciates, even if it's hard to believe. No reason makes sense, unless they've broken up.

It's strange, but they haven't, at least officially. They remain in an ill-defined limbo. After their argument on the roof, she'd thought it might be a question of time and space. Of cooler heads prevailing. She'd go on tour. He'd find a new job. Then they'd face the Cafferty threat together. But fights grow lives of their own. Absence breeds insecurity. The news of Cafferty's visit to Sotheby's solidified something in Audrey's mind, not just about her intuition, but more gravely, about Theo's inability to believe her. After that night in Chris and Sarah's living room, Audrey had accepted, for the first time, that she and Theo were truly over. They existed in different realms, and merging them had proved impossible. There was no one to blame. Theo was what he'd always been: earnest and unbendable. Once, she'd believed these were qualities to fall in love with. But the world had grown too malleable for such stringency. And it moved too fast. What else was there to say? Maybe big things ended like small things—in whimpers. She hadn't been in enough relationships to know.

Then he'd knocked on Martin Cafferty's door.

The voices in the yard reach her as a pleasant murmur. She closes her eyes again. To think: as she was sitting across from Torres and Renzo, Theo was walking uptown, a scribbled address in his pocket. She shouldn't have been surprised. There'd always been something heroic about him. Perhaps no one else saw it. Perhaps it was a pedestal she alone had placed him on. It didn't matter. He'd done what no one else would have. And he'd done it for her.

For three days she's kept it inside, but now she finally lets herself go—back to Brooklyn, the precinct, fleeing the interrogation room and hurriedly sending Theo that text. Then came the call from Ed Beemis. After that it was all a blur. She wouldn't learn what Theo had done until the next day, so everything in those first hours centered around her grandmother. She was on a plane to Florida that night. Chris bought her the ticket and arranged the ground transportation. Audrey didn't argue. She was numb. Connie's death. Fender's murder. She was in too much shock to be scared for her life, though she knew she should be. She tried to call Theo from LaGuardia, and again from Orlando, but his phone was off. She left messages. Two, three, four. And then his mailbox stopped accepting them. She couldn't believe he wasn't calling her back.

Even now, she's not clear on all the details. The police had arrived to find Theo standing over a savagely beaten man, a gun within arm's reach. Cafferty was taken to Mount Sinai, where he was listed in serious condition. Theo was arrested for breaking and entering and assault with a deadly weapon, and led off in handcuffs to an Upper West Side police station three blocks south. For the next fifteen hours an ever-expanding team of detectives listened and relistened to his story of blackmail and sexual abuse, a tawdry, years-long tale that ultimately came to explain James Fender's murder. The cops believed him. The charges were dropped. It was Detective Torres, newly arrived from the Ninetieth Precinct, who officially released Theo at dawn the next day. He was given his phone, wallet, and keys and told not to leave the tristate area. Right away he called Audrey. They hadn't let him use a phone while he was in custody.

It was just after six a.m. when her screen lit up. Still dark in Cape Canaveral. She was lying awake in her old bed, staring listlessly at the glowing stars she'd long ago stuck to the ceiling. She'd arrived from the airport at midnight but hadn't slept. She either couldn't stand being in the trailer or never wanted to leave again, she couldn't decide. When she saw Theo's name she almost didn't react. She was too drained to be furious. Too exhausted to be hurt. She wanted to lie still and pretend her life in Brooklyn had never happened. That the man she'd loved had never existed. It was surprisingly easy to do. Theo didn't even know Connie was dead yet, because he hadn't responded to her calls or texts. Not until now. She willed herself not to answer, but she wasn't that strong, or petty, so she swiped the screen. He was talking before it even reached her ear, a rush of words so drenched in emotion she sat up in the darkness, confused, and then astounded, by what he was saying, the things that had happened. She took in what she could, and then she was speaking, they both were, over each other, past each other, and it took two or three frenzied minutes of cross-talk for either to take a breath. Finally, they settled into a comprehensible dialogue. He hadn't asked where she was, so she didn't tell him. One crisis at a time. The news about Connie could wait.

How was it possible? He'd not only found Martin Cafferty but he'd gotten him to talk, and then gotten him arrested. She couldn't believe it. Still, she knew it must be true—this was Theo, after all—and right away, before she even felt relief, came a wave of intense guilt. That he'd almost been killed because of her. As he spoke, she began sobbing quietly in the darkness. She tried to squelch the sound but couldn't, and when Theo heard her through the phone he stopped speaking and, after a moment, said her name, softly, firmly. He told her it was okay now. But nothing felt okay. The world as she knew it, a confusing but ultimately definable place, seemed no longer to exist. She had so many questions. Like: Why?

Why did Martin Cafferty kill him?

To her surprise, Theo had an answer. Cafferty wasn't targeting Fender. It was the other way around, at least in the beginning. Fender was desperate for money, and at some point he decided to try to blackmail Cafferty again since it had worked so well the first time. Audrey shuddered as Theo told her it worked the second time, too. Cafferty paid Fender twice—ten grand in cash each time. Then Fender got greedier and tried to double the amount, and Cafferty balked. So Fender contacted his wife, and whatever he told her wasn't good because she kicked her husband out of their apartment. A few months later, Cafferty lost his job. Fender was responsible for that, too.

"And Cafferty *told* you all of this?" Audrey asked breathlessly.

"Yes, though I was pointing a gun at him so he didn't have too many options. He was also hoping I wouldn't call the cops, which, unbeknownst to him, his neighbor had already done."

"Did he admit to the murder?"

"Not exactly. But he did tell me how their meetings went down. They'd rendezvous at this desolate spot under the Brooklyn side of the bridge. *Under.* Not *on.* That's where Fender must have been going after he met Nikki that day at the Levee. She said he was in such a good mood, remember? Which would make sense if he thought he was about to collect twenty grand."

They went on like this awhile longer, speculating, absorbing, fitting the last disparate pieces together. Soon, the conversation stalled, became a series of tentative silences, as each of them tiptoed toward another subject. But they couldn't get there. They were both too overwhelmed. Instead, Theo spoke of logistics. Audrey would have to fly home from the tour. She wasn't in trouble, he insisted. None of them were. It turned out Fender had been right: because the original blackmail amount was under $50,000 it wasn't considered a serious crime and the police were letting it go. Still, she was a key witness, and Torres needed her to come by the precinct in the next day or two. Audrey sighed through the phone. She wasn't on tour, she said finally. She was in Cape Canaveral. And then she told him why.

In the silence that followed, she heard Theo's heart break.

It was too much. Neither could continue. They hung up, five minutes later, agreeing to talk again soon, but in the two days since, they've only managed to text. Encouragements and pleasantries. *Hang in there. How's Roger? Hope you're okay.* Messages so banal as to be embarrassing. Still, it was nice to be connected again.

Yesterday, Audrey had given Torres a statement over the phone. He was pleasant, almost friendly. She told him everything, and he was appreciative. Then she asked if he could let Theo fly down to Florida for her grandmother's memorial. It would just be a day or two. Torres said he wished he could, but that wasn't how it worked. Audrey thanked him anyway.

She should get back to the party. Everything else is too much to contemplate. A future without him. It's not that she doesn't love him. It's that she does. What she can't handle is the weight of the burden. But she's a survivor. She's spent a lifetime adapting. A small apartment in a new neighborhood. Bed-Stuy, maybe. Or somewhere off the G so she can get to Whale Creek by train. It's not all bad; she still has her job. And from the sound of it, she's about to have the Westfield Brothers again, too. Predictably, the tour has started badly and Columbia Records is already canceling dates. Soon they'll drop the band or the band will drop them—it doesn't matter which. She'd known it wouldn't work out. They're too talented for a major label. Too precious for the larger world. But she'll never say I told you so. She believes in making mistakes. What matters is how you respond to them.

A decade of antic noise. It won't go on forever, but right now, she can't imagine another life. Brooklyn is her home. She can learn to be single again. Maybe it'll even be good for her. She should never have allowed herself to grow so deep—

"Audrey."

She stops breathing—just stops taking in air. Then she turns around and there he is, picking his way down the hill. He raises his hand in greeting, but before she can speak, even process what's happening, he stumbles on the embankment, pitches forward, and disappears amid the high weeds. She attempts to call out, to say his name, but she can't. Her voice isn't working. Instead, she watches, helpless, as his head pops up, like a puppet's, and he slowly rises back to his full height. He's covered in mud.

"This is embarrassing," he says. "What an entrance."

She is overwhelmed by a sense of déjà vu, not of an identical moment but of an identical thought: seated on the VIP platform in that awful club the night it all started, watching him emerge from the crowd as if she'd conjured him forth. That eerie coincidence, which then, as now, was no coincidence at all because she was always wishing he was with her, always hoping he'd appear.

"*Theo.*" The mere utterance of his name feels like an Olympic victory.

"Can I join you?" he asks. He's arrived at the dock, looking like he just lost a tractor pull.

She nods, and he steps tentatively onto the planks. Audrey tries to stand.

"Don't," he says, so she stops. She doesn't trust her legs. Instead, he comes toward her, the dock swaying under him. He bends down and pecks her on the cheek. It's the clumsiest of kisses, and she wants to acknowledge as much, but to do so would involve too many syllables. She tries something simpler.

"What are you doing here?"

"Torres gave me permission," Theo says warily. "I think he changed his mind after you told him about your grandmother. I'm sorry, I shouldn't have surprised you like this, but I thought that if I asked, you might say no, and I just . . . I really wanted to be here. Audrey, I don't know what to say. She was such a wonderful person."

He's standing a few feet away from her. On top of being filthy, he's managed to cut his arm, but he doesn't want her to notice so he tries to keep it hidden.

"Ben and Arthur are setting up microphones in your front yard," he says. "Aren't they supposed to be on tour?"

"I guess they added a stop," Audrey responds, squinting up at him. "Why are you standing like that? Are you . . . are you bleeding?"

"It's nothing." He starts to—

"Don't wipe it on your pants!"

Theo looks around nervously. "Do you mind if I sit down?"

"Please."

He arranges himself awkwardly on the planks. He can sense Audrey staring at him but he can't meet her gaze.

"You shouldn't have done it," she says.

"I know. I can leave."

"Attack that asshole, I mean. It wasn't your problem."

Theo frowns. "Of course it was my problem. He was coming after you. After all of us." He blinks, a bit dazed. "We were the only people who could connect him to Fender, and he needed to cover his tracks. He must have forced Fender to give up our names. Probably right before he shot him."

Audrey shivers. "Do you really think he would have tried to kill us?"

"He swore he was only trying to scare us into silence, but I don't believe him. The guy's a psychopath. Audrey, you were right about everything. He admitted to breaking into our place. And to showing up at Sotheby's—which I didn't even know about. I'm sure Chris was next."

She raises her arm to block the sun from her eyes. "I still can't get over what you did," she says. "Marched right up to his front door."

"I didn't think he'd be there, and then suddenly he was and I . . . I lost my mind. Audrey, I almost killed him."

"*He* almost killed *you*, you big idiot."

"And he would have if . . ." It's too much to say. And she won't believe it anyway. Still, it's true. Those seconds have played out over and over in his head, a sequential blur. And yet he's never been more sure of anything in his life. "He would have shot me if you hadn't sent that text," Theo says solemnly. "It's hard to describe, but when he reached for the gun, I was ready. I could react. Because you'd warned me. You saved my life." He can sense Audrey watching him, studying him. He feels too small for the moment, the company. "They matched the ballistics, by the way. Torres messaged me an hour ago, said he thought we'd like to know."

He sees tears running down Audrey's cheeks and stops talking.

"What is it?" Theo asks.

"Nothing. Just this. You. Here."

They sit in silence, the noise from the party a dim reminder of another world.

"You probably need to get back up there," Theo says after a while.

"Not yet. Tell me more. Anything. How was Lawrence? Did you see your brother?"

He explains that they met at Foxwoods instead. That Carl had traded vices, or perhaps just acquired a new one. "I'm still glad I went," Theo says. "After that night on the roof I was so lost, and I thought if anyone could understand, it was my brother. He's the king of things falling apart. Though I must say, he had some good advice. He told me to stop feeling sorry for myself and to fix things with you."

"Smart man."

"Well, he's not *that* smart because he also thought this whole Cafferty affair would make a great movie—that it was the story I'd always been looking for. And in my derangement I actually considered calling Win to pitch it. I'm so sorry. I'm such a—"

"Theo."

"No. Let me just . . ." He searches for better words, a deeper meaning. "I feel like I'm losing my mind. Like the time we're living in is making us crazy. What's real and what's not. What matters and doesn't. I remember when Win first told me about *Source It!*. The idea sounded absurd—that people needed to be told how to root out the truth. And now it's, what, five years later, and the book's already an anachronism. That people would even care about truth in the first place has become laughable. But what am I even talking about?" He picks at a splinter of wood like a nervous teenager. "What amazed me, right from the beginning, was how authentic you were, even as you abided all the bullshit going on around you. The posturing, the noise. Like that was part of it, too. Art and emotion. Creativity. It was all just a world." His eye catches the gleam of a spiderweb waving in the breeze, just above the water, the spider itself resting dead center, between dock and pole, like it's showcasing the thing. The web is magnificent. And the first real wave will wash it away.

"Audrey, I didn't have enough experience when we first met—not with failure, but success. Things turning out okay. I was so used to struggling that when I read your letter, I didn't know how to react. How to process what I was feeling. I was consumed by this awful sense of inevitability, like everything had been too good to be true, and instead of supporting you, believing you, *trusting* you, I collapsed inward." His voice is dry and he clears his throat. "James Salter has this great line—in *Light Years*, I think—where he describes a character as being 'stunned by love.' Well, that's what I was, and still am. But no one tells you how paralyzing it can be."

She lowers her arm and he can see her green eyes staring at him. She looks sun-kissed, almost golden, and he experiences the familiar sensation of wanting to touch her, not lustfully, but lightly, just to prove she's a person. And so he does.

"I love you," he says.

She's still seated with her back against the dock support, so he arranges himself beside her, his feet dangling off the edge.

"How much?" she asks.

"A massive amount."

"No, how much do stories like mine get optioned for?"

He feels his face redden. "Oh. A lot. God, I really am sorry. I never should have—"

"So let's do it."

"What?"

"Come on, it's not like we don't need the money. Last time I checked we were about to be homeless. Besides, Carl's right. It is a great story."

A shock of electronic noise interrupts them—the sound of a circuit surge as a cable is plugged into an amp.

Audrey shakes her head. "I should have turned the volume down."

"Not a bad opening line," Theo says, and watches a smile alight across her face. He places his hand on top of hers, and she doesn't move it away. His legs are hovering just above the water. It feels good to tempt fate. He's getting used to it. They squeeze their hands together.

"I love you, too," she says softly.

They look at each other. All the things he wants to tell her. That he'll stop fighting the spin of the world. That she's so incredibly brave. That if she'll take him back, he'd love to stay in Brooklyn. Because Kings County has always been theirs.

"Testing . . . testing . . . one, two, three."

It's Arthur Westfield.

"Audrey Benton and Theo Gorski, please report to the stage."

Theo has never heard their names spoken into a microphone, let alone by the lead singer of his favorite band. They hear the amplified crunch of the mic being passed and then the deep clearing of a throat. Audrey shakes her head.

"This is Ed," says Ed Beemis. *"You two lovebirds get your asses up here right now."*

Audrey stands, then turns and helps Theo up. They pause, inches from each other, the tension like a living thing, almost visible. Then Audrey burrows her face into his shoulder. A minute passes. Two.

"I have a little surprise of my own," she says, her voice raspy against him. "It's my mother. She might be—oh, who am I kidding, she's not coming."

They hear the first chords of a guitar, but neither moves. He glances down, sees the tattoo on her shoulder blade. Two cowboys riding off into the distance. He remembers the first time he saw it, at that Westfield Brothers concert years ago. It had nothing to do with her life, she'd said when he asked about it. She just thought it was cool.

Acknowledgments

I worked on *Kings County* for years and years, and so many people helped me along the way. First, thank you to my friends who read early drafts, and whose smart suggestions improved the book in innumerable ways: Aryn Kyle, Teddy Wayne, Kate Garrick, Vanessa Vitale, Carrie Neill, A. J. Springer, and Stuart Evers. Thanks to Stephanie Danler, Joseph O'Neill, Melissa Febos, Joshua Ferris, and Matthew Thomas. For early encouragement and shelter, thank you Jonathan Franzen.

Thanks to everyone at Avid Reader Press/Simon & Schuster who brought *Kings County* to life: Jonathan Karp, Carolyn Reidy, Marysue Rucci, Ben Loehnen, Meredith Vilarello, Wendy Sheanin, Alison Forner, Laura Wise, Amanda Mulholland, Brigid Black, Megan Manning, Tyler Comrie, Kyle Kabel, Carolyn Kelly, Morgan Hoit (aka @nycbookgirl), Aja Pollock, Kayley Hoffman, Elizabeth Hubbard, and Allie Lawrence. Thanks to the best publicist in the world of books: Jordan Rodman.

To my friends and family, thank you for your wisdom and your company: Michael Balser, Katerina Barry, Stefan Block, Kieran and Jennifer Brew, Ryan Chapman, Ricky Festa, Ana Mena-Gonçalves, Kevin Goodspeed, Janie Goodwillie, Doug and Sophie (and Isabelle and Violet) Goodwillie, Steve and Jill Goodwillie, Sabine Heller, Amy Herrick, Bradfield Hughes, Cristal Jones, Kick Kennedy, Zoe Kontes, the Laundon family, Liese Mayer, Dennis McFarland (who taught me the root of the word "nostalgia"), Josh Morgan, Lisa Meyers, Kevin

ACKNOWLEDGMENTS

Raidy, Jamyle Rkain, Scott Sherman, Ira Silverberg, Summer Smith, Doreen Stedner, Eliza Swann, and Billy Ventura.

I'm indebted to Alex Marvar and Deenie Hartzog-Mislock, the stylish real life wearers of Audrey's ink; to Luzena Adams, for making me smile in my author photos; and to the Felice Brothers, one of the great bands of the last two decades, whose music permeated enough of my psyche that I (loosely) modeled the Westfield Brothers on them.

Though this is a novel, I did a great deal of research to try to capture the essence of the characters and their worlds. Thanks to everyone I spoke with or interviewed, including Jason Dobson; Chris Goldberg; Ken Hamm; Alex Shelton; the staff of the Immigrant City Archives in Lawrence, Massachusetts; and the tour guides at NASA.

Two books brought me closer to the Brooklyn I was seeking. Robert Anasi's *The Last Bohemia: Scenes from the Life of Williamsburg, Brooklyn* is a rollicking history of the neighborhood in all its pregentrified grit and glory (and it's also where I first read the joke about TV on the Radio going on tour). And Lizzy Goodman's *Meet Me in the Bathroom: Rebirth and Rock and Roll in New York City 2001–2011* is an oral history masterpiece chronicling indie music's decade of ascendance.

And finally . . .

To Marin Ireland, the best reader of writers I've ever met. You unmasked all the weak spots and somehow turned them into strengths. Thanks for speaking my language.

And to my parents, Gene Goodwillie and Marcia Harrison. I'm so grateful for your love and support.

Two people are responsible for *Kings County*'s existence. My agent, Melissa Flashman, at Janklow & Nesbit, read my unwieldy manuscript and then took me to lunch at the Oyster Bar and told me it had potential. Thanks for your unerring literary instincts and your preternatural cool. And to my friend and editor, Jofie Ferrari-Adler, who pushed me harder than I've ever been pushed and, in the process, helped me find the book I've been trying to write my whole life. Thank you for your patience, your dedication, and your belief. We finally got there.

Kings County

David Goodwillie

This reading group guide for Kings County includes an introduction, discussion questions, and ideas for enhancing your book club. The suggested questions are intended to help your reading group find new and interesting angles and topics for your discussion. We hope that these ideas will enrich your conversation and increase your enjoyment of the book.

Introduction

A deeply resonant story about love, consequences, bravery, and forgiveness, *Kings County* follows a young couple as they come of age in an ever-changing city. Audrey Benton, a minor celebrity in Brooklyn indie rock circles, meets her unlikely match in Theo Gorski, a shy but idealistic mill-town kid who's struggling to establish himself in Manhattan's still-patrician world of books. Their friends all believe that Audrey and Theo have the perfect relationship, until an old acquaintance of Audrey's disappears under mysterious circumstances, sparking a series of escalating crises that forces the couple to confront a dangerous secret from her past. From the raucous heights of Occupy Wall Street to the comical lows of the publishing industry, from million-dollar art auctions to Bushwick drug dens, *Kings County* captures New York City at a moment of cultural reckoning.

Topics and Questions for Discussion

1. Audrey and Theo play a running game as a couple where they suggest potential opening lines for a memoir. *Kings County* opens with the line: "They came in hot, the band and Audrey Benton, a raucous cocoon of color and sweat." Discuss this opening line. How does it set the tone for the story to come? What are some of your favorite opening lines from literature?

2. The title of the novel *Kings County* comes from the official yet little known county name for the borough of Brooklyn. What does Brooklyn mean to the characters in the novel? What does Manhattan mean to them?

3. In *Kings County*, readers meet Audrey and Theo many years before they first meet each other. How does Audrey change after meeting Theo? How does Theo change after meeting Audrey?

4. Why do you think Audrey and her best friend, Sarah, grow apart over the years? What do we learn about Sarah from chapters 7 and 14, the two chapters in the novel that take readers inside Sarah's perspective?

5. Chris is the one character in *Kings County* who comes from a background of wealth and privilege. How do you think this influences his actions in the novel? How does he conform to the stereotype of a Wall Street financier, and how does he defy the role?

6. The 2011 Occupy Wall Street Movement is active in the background of the novel. How does this movement speak to the novel's themes of power inequalities and vigilante justice?

7. As a teenager, Theo writes a college application essay about uncovering lies in his family history. How is his family's invented mythology, hiding a shameful truth, reflected in the later events of the story?

8. When Audrey falls for Theo, she has to decide whether or not to disclose her most painful secret to him: "We promised to share everything, from our hopes to our histories." Why do you think she can't bring herself to tell Theo about Cafferty? Are her reasons different when she continues to keep the truth from him after Fender's death?

9. In the aftermath of Cafferty's attack, Audrey writes, "I thought I was strong and smart, and that these qualities would protect me. To find out I was wrong, that everything could be stolen so brutally, so quickly, emptied me out, then slowly filled me with shame. . . . It wasn't the sensation of losing control so much as the realization that I'd never had control in the first place. Over my body. Over my life." How does her sudden loss of control influence her decision to blackmail Cafferty?

10. Audrey's letter to Theo rocks their relationship. How does Audrey's disclosure upset Theo? How does Theo's reaction upset Audrey? How do you think you would react if you were in Theo or Audrey's situation?

11. Audrey spends much of her adolescence in Cape Canaveral, Florida, and the last chapter of the story also takes place there. Why do you think the final scene in a novel called *Kings County* is set in Florida's Space Coast? How do we view the events of the story differently from such a different place?

12. If Audrey and Theo had the seemingly ideal relationship at the start of the book, thought by Chris to be "that rare couple that proved, inexplicably but irrefutably, that the whole cosmic order might just make sense," where does their relationship stand at the end of the book? What about Chris and Sarah's relationship?

Enhance Your Book Club

1. Theo loves to walk around New York City and immerse himself in the colorful history of the streets, buildings, and neighborhoods. Research your local landmarks and take a trip to visit them.

2. Theo and Audrey have a special connection to a tiny Cuban restaurant that nobody else knew about for years. What "secret" restaurants do you know? Eat a meal together at a favorite hidden spot or discover a new one.

3. Theo's job as a literary scout requires him to choose books that could be adapted for film. If you could choose a book to be made into a movie, which one would you choose and why? Discuss and choose a book that has a film adaptation for your next book club read.

Conversation with David Goodwillie

Q: *What was your favorite part about writing* **Kings County?**

A: Developing the two main characters, Audrey Benton and Theo Gorski, was absolutely my favorite part of the process. I didn't start with a plot; I started with a loose idea of who my protagonists were, and then trusted that as I fleshed them out they'd find their way into trouble and conflict—and they certainly do. It's the enduring novelist's question: Do you start with a well-defined plot or strong characters who will lead you into the story? With *Kings County* it was always the latter. I worked on this book for several years, and because I had such a vivid idea of who Audrey and Theo were, and how they might react to a given situation, it was a pleasure to come back to them day after day (after day).

Q: *What was the hardest part?*

A: The hardest part was also the most interesting: writing difficult subject matter from a woman's perspective. Luckily, I have some very smart female novelist and actor friends who read early drafts and challenged me as a writer (and a male) to broaden my perspective and dig far deeper emotionally than I previously had. It was a fascinating lesson, and certainly changed the way I approach writing (and reading) female characters.

Q: *What is the most interesting research you did for the book?*

A: I'm a detail-obsessed novelist on the page, and research is an integral part of my writing process. I always eat at the restaurants, visit the clubs, and walk the streets that appear in my books, but I also travel much farther afield. For *Kings County*, I toured Cape Canaveral and the Kennedy Space Center; explored the abandoned textile mills of Lawrence, Massachusetts; and interviewed all kinds of people, from film scouts to sex workers, hedge fund managers to music engineers. It's a part of being an author that never gets old.

Q: *How long did you spend writing this book?*

A: It took four years to write and three to edit and publish. I just shuddered when I wrote that.

Q: *The two main characters, Audrey and Theo, move to New York City in the great tradition of young people pursuing dreams in the Big Apple. What was your experience like during your first few years living in the city?*

A: All three of my books have touched on the subject of moving to New York. What makes someone pick up and leave their small town or leafy suburb to try their luck in the big city? What inner drive or ambition? What desperation? It's an age-old story, and one I know well, having arrived in New York in my early twenties as clueless as I was determined (after a failed baseball career) to somehow make it as a writer. I lived downtown, in a series of apartments I won't even attempt to describe, and quickly proceeded to do everything but write. I worked as a food runner at a theme restaurant, became a private investigator at the world's largest investigative agency, was (somehow) hired as an expert at Sotheby's auction house, and then rode the first dot-com wave up and up and up, until the inevitable crash left me scraped and bruised enough to finally give writing a chance. Or maybe it was the other way around.

Q: *What novels does* Kings County *build upon in the literary tradition? Which authors inspired you most?*

A: I've always had a fondness for big, sprawling novels that capture a whole world. Novels of time and place, background and foreground, teeming with life. I'm thinking, contemporarily, of Zadie Smith's *White Teeth*, Jonathan Lethem's *The Fortress of Solitude*, Rachel Kushner's *The Flamethrowers*, Edward St. Aubyn's Patrick Melrose novels, Emily St. John Mandel's *Station Eleven*, Philip Roth's *American Pastoral*, and of course, Jonathan Franzen's *The Corrections*. As a reader, I want to be wholly transported—it doesn't really matter where. (Alternatively, as a writer, it's my job to create a time machine that works.)

Q: *What do you think is the most important thing that Audrey and Theo learn or realize about their relationship in the book?*

A: That it's the rarest thing either of them will ever possess.

Q: *New York City itself is essentially a character in this story. If the city could speak to Audrey and Theo, what do you think it would say to them?*

A: Audrey and Theo each have their own deeply personal relationship with the city, but the one thing they share is an overarching desire to make their New York lives work—to not take that bus home defeated. I suppose, if the city were to pipe up, it would remind them that "success" is a life's work and that they're not in it alone. There are nine million other dreamers out there too.

Q: *One of Theo's jobs in the literary scene is to scout books for movies. If your book were made into a film, who would you cast as your dream actors for Audrey and Theo?*

A: Dakota Johnson and Ryan Gosling.

Q: *Do you have a favorite spot in Manhattan or Brooklyn that didn't make it into the book?*

A: The East Village played a formidable role in both the early indie music scene and my own twentysomething New York life, but *Kings County* is a Brooklyn story, and as I started writing it, downtown Manhattan quickly took a back seat to the more delinquent (in the early 2000s) neighborhoods across the river—Williamsburg, Bushwick, and Greenpoint. That said, I did manage to throw in a few East Village cameos, and the neighborhood certainly remains fertile ground in my mind.

Q: *If you don't mind sharing, what are you working on next?*

A: I'm writing a novelistic account of one of Europe's largest (and mostly unknown) twentieth-century bank robberies and tracing what happened to the money—and the people who came into contact with it—in the years afterward. It's my first foray into historical fiction after three quite contemporary books, and I'm enjoying it immensely.